FACE
TO
FACE

FACE
TO
FACE

Edward A. Rogers

William Morrow and Company • New York • 1962

AUTHOR'S NOTE

The events and characters in this novel are entirely fictitious. The character relationships are also fictitious. The author has not utilized the 1960 campaign except as a general background for a work of fiction. The story that is told here sets forth what could happen—not what did happen—under the influence of the pressures and circumstances governing any Presidential campaign in this age of the jet plane and television.

CONTENTS

Consider . . . which is more fundamental to man, the name of man, or his image?

Inscribe in any place the name of God and set opposite to it His image, you will see which will be held in greater reverence!

LEONARDO DA VINCI

FACE
TO
FACE

1

April in Denver

It was two o'clock in the morning, but Charles Dale was wide awake, and worried. He was still thinking about Andrew Conger, the man who had first introduced him to politics and Denver. And now it was Andrew Conger and politics which were threatening to take him away.

Dale rolled over quietly on his side of the outsized double bed and groped for a cigarette from the night table. Finally, in irritation, he snapped on the bed lamp.

Janet, his wife, was lying quietly beside him. But he saw immediately that she was no longer asleep. She was looking at him.

"I'm sorry, Jan. I'm sorry I woke you."

"Something on your mind, Charlie?" she said softly.

Dale was silent for a moment, then he said, "I got a wire today at the office. . . . Andy Conger's telephoning me here tomorrow." Dale saw Janet's face stiffen, then relax.

"Do you know what he's calling about?" Janet asked.

"It's probably about my going back on the campaign."

"You're still going to tell him no, aren't you?"

"Yes. But, goddammit, I'd sure give my right you-know-what to go back with him." Janet raised her head and turned on her side to get a better look at her husband.

At forty-two, Charles Dale had the appearance of a man several years younger. He was tall, six feet three. His nose was crooked, broken first at twelve in touch football, later at twenty in soccer. He had a ruddy complexion that tanned easily. He looked strong and ambitious, and he was. He had fought his way up from the first "severance pay" days after World War II to a new television production company—all his own—in Denver.

"We've been through all this, Charles. You simply can't do it. My God, I've only been here two months. You've just barely started out here. You can't go away now."

"I know, I know," Dale said softly, and ever so gently pressed her head down into the pillow. "Relax." He stroked her head, holding it still.

"It isn't fair," Janet continued, her words going into the palm of Dale's hand. "It would be awfully selfish of you to leave us here. Too selfish."

"Just because I want to go doesn't mean I'm going. There isn't any harm in wanting to go, is there? So I'm being truthful with you. I want to go. But I know it isn't possible. I want my life in Denver, too. I couldn't face myself if I left now, and left you in the lurch. But a presidential campaign! The Big One, in this day and age of TV. It sure would be a gas!"

"Charles, do me a favor. Drop that word 'gas.' You promise me you're not going?"

"I promise."

"How are you going to put it to Andy?"

"I don't know. That's what's keeping me awake. I guess I'll just have to level with him. You need me here."

"*And* your business, *and* the children," Janet added. "Charlie—I know it's a tremendous sacrifice for you. I love you for it."

"I love you too, Jan. Everything's going to be all right. Don't worry. I'll handle it." But even after Dale had switched off the lamp and tried to compose his mind for sleep, he couldn't stop thinking about the past and how it had led him to this impending crisis.

When the war was over, Dale was in Hollywood, living on his Captain's severance pay—earned as fighter pilot in the Pacific. His first job was as a backstage doorman in a Republic radio theater; twenty-eight dollars a week take-home. He had gone on the road within a year as company manager for a traveling comedy unit built by one of the large talent agencies. The unit played a theater on Broadway for four months.

During those weeks Charlie Dale met Janet Dalton. After the year of loneliness, scraping and digging to make his way up the ladder on the Coast, struggling to make ends meet, she was the perfect tonic. Here was prewar life and fun again: the familiar haunts, Janet's easy entertaining of friends in her apartment near Gracie Mansion on the Upper East Side, and week-ends at her family's home at Mead Point in Greenwich. One fall Saturday Dale had asked Janet to marry him. He had already made up his mind to leave the road show and get a job in New York at one of the networks.

Three months later they were married, and Dale threw himself into his work as a staff radio director at Global Communications. Then suddenly he found himself accepting a job back in Hollywood. It was an opportunity to make the transition to television. Janet was thrilled with the prospect of moving to the Coast. "I have more friends in San Francisco and Los Angeles than I have in New York," she had said. And so it went. New York to Hollywood, Hollywood to New York. The polarity of life in television. Their oldest daughter Betsy had lived in six houses by her eleventh birthday. Finally it caught up with Dale. He saw life, values, his relationship with Janet, slipping away in the rat race. It was then he had selected Denver as a base for a small film production business of his own.

It had taken a lot of talking to convince Janet that their move to Denver was practical. Dale wasn't sure he ever had. But he believed that Janet and the family would thrive in the new surroundings and make a new life among new people.

With the children, Janet and Dale were having a late lunch on the outside patio. The mountains behind the house glistened, their icy peaks reflecting the unseasonably warm sun. Only a wisp of white plume over one peak marred the otherwise startling clear, deep blue sky.

"Incidentally, Jan," Dale said, "the statement on your securities which the bank is holding came yesterday. I meant to bring it home —it's a photostat for your files. Thanks again."

"Anything for The Dale Organization," said Janet. "Thank God I had the stocks to put up to cover your loans. By the way, I forgot to tell you, The Friendship Lady's coming today. Pass the pepper please, Lisa."

"Who's the Friendship Lady?" asked Charlie Junior.

"She's a woman who comes around and tells you everything you're supposed to know about where you live when you first move there, and you don't know anything," said Betsy.

"Like the Welcome Wagon?" asked Dale. Janet nodded. "She's a little late," he added. "If she's here when Conger calls from Washington, I'll take it upstairs."

"Is Mr. Andrew Conger calling *you?*" asked Betsy, her eyes wide.

"Betsy, don't be so dramatic. You know Daddy and Mr. Conger are very good friends," said Janet. "Your father has worked with him many times."

"How long have you known him?" asked Betsy.

"Let me see," said Dale. "It was either 1948 or '49. I was producing a panel show on radio in New York. He was a guest."

"It was 1948," said Janet. "Right after our honeymoon."

"That's right. I can't even remember the name of the show," said Dale, "but when the show was over, he asked me to have dinner with him. That was before he was Secretary of State—he was then a United States Senator."

"Then what, Daddy?" Lisa asked.

"I got a call from Mr. Conger, like I may be getting today, only then he said he was probably going to run for *Vice* President in the fall, and would I help. He was nominated, but we lost," Dale said. The children laughed as he flamboyantly wiped away nonexistent tears. "But, by golly, four years later I got another call. He was practicing law then, right here in Denver."

"He was?" asked Betsy.

"Yup," said Dale, "and that's the first time I spent any real time out here in Colorado. He called me when I was producing a television show in Los Angeles. We lived out there then. Conger told me he was going to run again for the U. S. Senate in Colorado. And he asked me to join him."

"And before I knew it," said Janet, "your father was horseback-riding over the thousands of acres of Andrew Conger's ranch every week-end," Janet smiled. "I think all your father did that campaign was hunt and ride and fish."

"But hear this!" said Dale overdramatically. "We won. In a land-slide."

"Yippee, my Daddy won," said Charlie Junior. "Yippee!"

"Down, boy, down," said Dale. "So it was all over. And your mother and I talked 'way back then about maybe moving to Colorado some day. What we planned to do was start taking vacations out here. I wonder whatever happened to that idea?" Dale said.

"The same thing that happens to every plan we've ever made," replied Janet. "Nothing."

"Hmmm . . . ," Dale murmured. "No fair."

"What happened with the next President, Daddy?" asked Lisa.

"Don't you know, silly?" Betsy said impatiently. "It's the same one we have now. He has been President eight years. Everybody knows that."

Dale smiled. "You get an 'A' in history, Betts. She's right, Lisa.

The President was re-elected in 1956. And I went out with Mr. Conger again. He did a lot of campaigning for the ticket as a Senator. I did some television shows for the President that year, too."

"You did? The President?" Lisa asked.

"Yes indeed," said Dale. "He and Senator Conger were good friends by that time, very good friends. And sure enough, along came the call. I talked to your . . ."

"I remember that time," Betsy cut in. "We were living in Rye then, weren't we, Daddy?" she asked.

"You have kept track of our moves better than I have," said Janet. "I think you're right. We moved back East in 1956."

"Sure, she's right," said Dale. "Don't you remember? Right after the election, the President made Conger Ambassador to the UN, and I was working in New York. That, Betsy, is when Andy and I really became very good friends. The two years Andy was at the UN, we worked together a lot. Andy Conger was on television almost every week. I never knew when I'd get a call from him. I'd be in rehearsal, meeting with writers, out in Rye for the week-end, and boom—the phone would ring. 'Come on in right away,' he'd say. 'I need a map.' Or, 'How can I show best on television the such-and-such problem in West Berlin?'

"And, the next thing you know, in 1958 old Hudson Somerton ups and dies—he was Secretary of State before Andy Conger. And, because so much of what the United States was doing about problems in the world was all mixed up and tied into the United Nations, the President asked Mr. Conger to become the new Secretary of State. And now he may be running for the Presidency himself. Class dismissed."

"You explained all that famously, dear," said Janet.

In Washington it was indeed common gossip Conger would lead his party's ticket in the Presidential election. It was also common gossip over at Foggy Bottom in Conger's office at State that Charlie Dale would be at Conger's side every mile and day of the campaign.

The letters Dale received from his friends on Conger's permanent staff at State bore this out. He had been waiting several weeks for

the other shoe to fall. But he had made up his mind to stay away.
Neither he personally nor his marriage could stand another pro-
longed period of strain or separation. The same was true of his
business. With every campaign he had participated in had come the
sudden halt to his career. To Dale, it invariably meant picking up
the pieces and starting all over again from scratch after the pro-
longed period of campaigning. In past years the excitement, the
thrill, the travel, people, and change had been worth the setback.
Dale knew full well that the magic, the spotlight, the aura of a
presidential campaign this year—with a friend such as Conger as the
candidate—could be the greatest experience of his life. He wanted
very much to be a part of it. The risks, however, of ruining the new
business, disappointing the children, losing Janet, were great enough
to keep him where he was—where he belonged. Dale's conscience
told him it was wrong to want to hit the trail with Andrew Conger.
Just the same, he wanted to. The Run for the Roses, he thought.
With Andy Conger. Jesus, what a thing to blow. What a game to
sit out!

"Are you going to work for Mr. Conger again?" Betsy asked.

"Who put you up to that?" Dale asked.

"Go ahead, answer her question," Janet said.

Dale rose, walked a few paces away from his chair, then turned
and faced his family. "Under no circumstances am I going to work
for Mr. Andrew Conger, leave my wife, leave my children, or leave
Denver in 1960," he said grandly.

"Hooray!" said Betsy. "You promised!"

"Yes," shouted Lisa, clapping her hands, while Charlie Junior
with a mouth full of food jumped up and down.

"Amen," said Janet. "C'mon girls," she continued, "help me take
the dishes in. Charlie Junior—bring your glass in after you finish
your milk." The girls rose to help their mother.

"Jan, aren't you going to help me in the garage on those barrels?"
Dale asked.

"Give me one more week, will you, dear?" Janet pleaded. "I just
remembered I want you to take the samples for the girls' rug and

curtains to the decorator on your way to work tomorrow morning, and I have to take those measurements this afternoon. Can't you get started on your workshop around the barrels?"

"No, and I am going to start unpacking the power tools today after I move the bags of feed," said Dale. "Don't blame me if I break something."

Betsy appeared at the kitchen window. "Mother, there's a lady at the front door. She says she has an appointment."

"I'll bet it's the Friendship Lady," shouted Lisa.

"Shhh, not so loud," said Janet. "Everybody quiet down. You children help your father. I want to do this quickly and get it over with. I'll be in the living room with Mrs. Mosby."

"I'm going to ride Bubbles," announced Betsy.

"No, it's my turn," shouted Lisa, running toward the box stall.

"Lisa, come back here," Dale called. "All right, Betsy, whose turn is it?"

"Mine," Betsy said.

"Whose turn do you think it is, Lisa?" Dale asked.

Lisa hung her head and kicked a clod of dry dirt. "Betsy's," she said. "But then me."

"It's all settled, then," said Dale. "C'mon, Lisa. And, Charlie, you too. I could stand some help in the garage." He paused on the low wall bordering the patio and, lighting a cigarette in the warm penetrating sun, watched as Betsy saddled Bubbles. She had learned quickly from Janet, who was an excellent rider. Betsy walked the mare to her father, and Dale took a hitch in the saddle's cinch.

For years Dale had watched Janet in her Eastern habit riding and jumping around and around in the confinement of an indoor ring at Round Hill. The horse had become the big symbol of the move to Colorado long before they had left Rye.

He watched until Betsy had mounted the gentle golden mare and trotted around the corner of the patio toward a trail leading back into the foothills. Then, with Lisa and Charlie bounding ahead of him, he walked in the garage into a maze of bicycles, barrels, shipping cartons, and stacks of books.

A good hour later Janet put her head in the door from the breezeway. "A long-distance call, dear. Washington. Mr. Andrew Conger."

"I'll take it upstairs," Charlie said.

"The Friendship Lady's just leaving," said Janet.

"I'll take it upstairs anyway," he answered.

"Charlie," said Janet, as he turned to walk out of the garage, "Charlie . . . You're not going to—"

Dale stopped. He gave her a long look. "You have nothing to worry about, Jan," he said. "I promise." He stooped down and kissed her. Then he bolted out to the terrace and into the house.

A voice said, "Is this Mr. Charles Dale?"

"Yes, it is."

"Go ahead, please," the voice continued. "The party is on the line."

"Hi, Charlie. Andy Conger. How are you?"

"I'm fine, Andy. Good to hear your voice on this beautiful day in Denver."

"It's raining and lousy back here. What've you been doing? How's the company going? What do you call it, The Dale Organization?"

"That's right, Andy. It's going fine. Been busy as hell. Picked up a new client in Dallas, and we're in the middle of producing a beautiful color film for the National Parks right now. I've got a crew in Yellowstone and one in the Everglades this week-end."

"Why aren't you with them? Ought to be pretty nice this time of year."

"It's nice right here in Denver, Andy. What can I do for you?"

There was a slight pause.

"Well, I've been thinking it's about time we rounded up some of the key people for the campaign. I've stayed out of most of the primaries, you know."

"Yes, I've been following you in the papers."

"Most people think I did it for political reasons. That's not the whole story. This damn international situation has kept me either tied to my desk or flying to some place such as Bangkok or Paris on almost no notice at all. I simply felt either politics or the country would suffer if I tried to campaign too early—I wouldn't be able to do justice to either one."

"I see."

"But now Rufe Little tells me there's plenty to do back here for you. And there certainly are things you and I can talk about if you would come back by May first. Do you think you could do that?"

"May one? I'm not sure, Andy. I'd have to look at our schedules at the office. This National Parks film is a big one. And, you know, this time there's no one to ask for a leave of absence except myself. The guy you have to ask is me this time."

"Yes, I guess that's true, with your own company. How're Janet and the children? Is it two now, or three? I've forgotten."

"Three, Andy, and growing like weeds. They're all fine."

"Good. When do you think you could get back, Charlie?"

"Well, this is a little sudden, Andy. It's quite a surprise. I didn't expect to hear from you this early, if at all. It's been a big drain on me financially to make this move out here, and I guess time just went by without my realizing how close you were getting to a campaign again. Do you think you'll get the nod at the convention?"

"Nobody can be sure, but with Rufe Little in charge of such things I think it will go about as planned. I imagine we'll go into a campaign after Chicago with no real worries."

"When would you like an answer on this, Andy?"

"Well, I'd like to hear you say today that you'll be with us."

Typical, thought Charlie. Haven't heard from the guy in over a year, and now he's got to have an answer today. "I don't think I can do that. I have an awful lot of things to straighten out here in order to come back, if I can spring myself at all."

"There's no danger of your not being with us, is there, Charlie? I mean for the campaign?"

"No—I mean, yes, there is." Jesus, what was I thinking? Charlie thought. Steady, old buddy, steady. Charlie took a breath and then said, "What I mean is, I am not certain I can keep the Dale Organization going if I leave it for eight months. Or six, or four. We're in a very critical period right now. Maybe if the Committee could throw a little business our way on documentaries, or short films, or spots, or something, we could see . . ."

"I wouldn't want to do that, Charlie. No, I wouldn't want that."

"It was just a thought. Lookin' out for Number One, you know."

"Yes. Well, we certainly want you back here. And what we should do now is figure out the best way for you to unencumber yourself and join us. The sooner the better. There are some things I'd like to go over with you personally."

"Let's do it this way, Andy. Give me a few days to think it over, and I'll send you a wire."

"Fine. You call, or wire me. I'll be waiting to hear from you. Good to talk to you, Charlie."

"I appreciate the call, Andy. And I'm very honored by it. I'll be getting in touch with you this week. I hope we can work something out. After all, I've been with you all those other times. It'd sure be great to be with you when you run for the Roses. Believe me, I want to come back very badly—but . . ."

"It's where you belong. Good-by, Charlie." And Conger rang off.

You bet your ass it's where I belong, thought Dale. He walked downstairs, and joined Janet in the living room. She was sorting out the samples left by Mrs. Mosby.

"Well, according to what I heard, you gave the old boy every encouragement, that's all I can say," Janet threw at him. "Now, what will he think? You sure have his hopes up."

"A man in Conger's position doesn't have hopes. Where's the Friendship Lady? Gone?"

"Yes."

"Look, Jan, it's this way. Conger wants me badly. If he decides I'm needed, maybe nothing I do or say can stop it."

"You *can* stop it. Very simply. By saying 'No!' You should have given him chapter and verse on the phone why you can't come back. That's all he needed."

"Don't panic," said Dale. "That's exactly what I intended to do, but I didn't want to get into a wrangle on the phone. I'll write him. I'll handle it," he insisted, pacing in front of the coffee table. "I told you I wasn't going back. I intend to keep that promise." He stopped and looked at Janet.

"What was that talk about May first?" Janet asked.

"That's when he wanted me back there."

"Charles, dear one, add it up. We have just pulled up roots in the East, and . . ."

"I know, I know," Dale interrupted. "You don't have to . . ."

"No, hear me out," Janet said. "We had a wonderful home in Rye, loads of friends, and the children were well adjusted in school and with their own friends. You were the one who decided the rat race, the commuting, New York wasn't for you. I didn't make that decision. I went along with you. Mother and Dad still think you're crazy, but we'll work that . . ."

"Jan," said Dale, "I said I realize all this."

"So now I'm in a new town. I don't know anybody yet, you're working night and day to get started in a new business, which now I'm tied into because of the loan. You've been here a very short time, the children and me even less. How can you walk out on this for eight months? What the hell has happened to your sense of responsibility?"

"Nothing, for God's sake," Dale shouted. "Nothing! I told you."

Janet paused, lit a cigarette, and looked at her husband with deep love and sympathy. "Look, Charles, I understand. I know how badly you'd like to go back. I know what it means to you. I admire your strength of decision. I know how difficult it must be. And I thank you for giving me and the children this kind of consideration."

"It's not that difficult, Jan," said Dale, smiling. "I belong here. Even though I'd like to be somewhere else, temporarily. So here I stay."

"If we could all go back to Washington with you, I'd love it. But we can't. Lord, I've got dozens of friends from school and Greenwich in and around Washington. A little time in the Capitol wouldn't hurt the kids, either." She paused, exhaled, and tamped her cigarette on a heavy crystal monogrammed ash tray which had been a wedding present from her brother. "So we do that, and what happens to the bank loan? What happens to the budding Dale Organization?"

Dale looked at her steadily. "You're right; it won't work. But you're not mad at me for wanting to go, are you? You don't begrudge me that, do you? It's only natural."

"Of course not, silly. I'd think it was damn strange if you didn't want to go. As I said, I'd love to have us all go back, get out of this dust bowl for the summer . . ."

"It's not that bad. It's beautiful here in summer."

"Okay, so it's beautiful, but I haven't seen it. So stay here, and we'll learn together."

"Yeah," Dale said, "I'm afraid I have to agree with you." He yawned, rocking on his heels as he stretched his hands high over his head and arched his back. "Wow, I'm pooped. Too much excitement for one day. I think I'll take a nap. I'm really beat."

"Mind if I join you, for an hour or so?" Janet asked, snuffing out her cigarette.

"Be my guest. You can give me a back rub."

"You know what that leads to. . . ."

Monday morning Dale drove on a new system of parkways and highways to Mountainview Road and the office. He found it was two miles shorter than a route he habitually used, but it took the same length of time. As he swung behind the building into the parking space marked "President," Dale was mentally composing various approaches to his answer to Conger. None of them satisfied him. He decided to give it another try later in the day.

Victor Hanson was sitting at Dale's desk when he strode into his office.

"Hi, Vic," Dale said. "Have a good week-end?"

"Yeah, but an expensive one, Charlie," Hanson replied. "You forgot to warn me about the poker players in these parts," he added, smiling.

"You've worked on enough Westerns in Hollywood to realize these boys out on the range know how to shuffle cards, Vic," answered Dale. "They clean you?"

"They sure did. But I'll get back at 'em next week. I'll be even by the end of the month." Hanson rose and slid a letter in front of Dale as he came around the desk. "Those beer guys in Dallas are screaming for story boards on their thirty-second and one-minute spots. I'll see if I can't speed up the artists. Also, we need production boards for the last three weeks of shooting on the National Parks film. We should get those done today."

Victor Hanson was the only employee Dale had not hired locally. Dale and Hanson had worked together for several years in Hollywood. Dale had seen him develop into one of the best Production Managers in the television film business. He knew that men such as Hanson received little or no credit on the screen. Their worth to a series, however, was inestimable if they were good. They were the ones who knew how far to go with the Teamsters' Union on a transportation problem. They knew when the best "action" cameraman would be available, and which construction chief gold-bricked to satisfy a payoff between the crew and himself for phoney overtime. Production Managers were like a bar checker in a huge cocktail lounge—and more. The dollars which were at stake, however, were even greater than the daily bar receipts at the Twenty One. Dale had flown to Los Angeles and convinced Hanson it was time for him to make a change. The clincher was a small percentage of ownership offered him in The Dale Organization, plus the opportunity to organize a production office exactly as he wished.

"Victor," said Dale, leaning back in his chair in the modest but comfortable office, "what if you had to run the show out here for eight months or so? Do you think you could do it? The whole schmier?"

"Why not? I've been running it by myself since I came here," said Hanson jokingly. Dale chuckled with him. "Sure, I guess so. What's up?" said Victor.

"I'm trying not to go back to Washington for the campaign with Andrew Conger. Although, boy, how I'd like to do it."

"I've been waiting for that, Charlie. I figured it would come. Okay. I'll try to mind the store. I hope you won't expect any sales when you're gone. That's something I couldn't deliver and also find time to finish the stuff we have on the boards now. I'm not that good a manager."

"Yes, you are. But I'm not going to go back, Vic. I've got to pass on this one, dammit! I just wondered how you felt about it. If you'd be comfortable here, alone, if I'd get drafted?"

"Sure, I guess so. I'd miss you. I can't read a profit and loss sheet, so there'd be things I'd have to bother you with as I went along." Hanson twisted a paper clip into several strange shapes, twirling it as he talked. "You know the one thing I can't figure about you?" He paused.

"What's that?"

"How can you work for a guy like Conger?"

Dale was aware of the difference in their political allegiances, but it had never mattered. It wouldn't matter now.

"You know it goes way back, Vic," said Dale. "It's probably a lot more personal loyalty to Conger than it is political ideals."

"I'd like to think that."

"Well, think it, if it makes you feel better. I almost pulled a coup talking long distance to Conger yesterday. But I got caught."

"Oh?"

"Yeah. I told Conger I'd come back if he'd get the National Committee to throw a little film biz our way. It didn't work. He said no dice."

"On my honor, I will do my . . . Crap!"

"Amen. Well, you can be damn sure I'm going to write the Committee this week and tell them we want to bid on the production. You don't have any ideological qualms about that, do you?"

"Just show me the money. No qualms."

"Good. Well, I'm going to hold firm and turn Conger down. I'll keep you posted." Dale looked at this man who had given up a comfortable, safe career in Hollywood to join him. Full of respect and warmth for him, he tapped Vic's arm lightly, for emphasis, and said, "Don't worry. I'm here to stay."

Dale asked the girl who handled at least four other jobs in addition to his dictation, to come into his office.

"Here's a Night Letter, Mary. 'To The Honorable Andrew H. Conger, Secretary of State, State Department, Washington, D.C. After serious consideration of your flattering offer to join you as soon as possible in Washington for the duration, I must decline. My decision is based on deeply personal reasons, as well as considerations for the future of the business I have so recently started here in Denver. My thanks again for thinking of me. I deeply regret I shall not be with you. Letter follows. Best regards.'" Dale twirled a gold paperknife on his desk that had been given to him by Conger in an earlier campaign.

"Read that back, Mary."

Mary started at the top. When she came to the word "duration," she stopped.

"Do you mean to say 'duration' here, Charlie? That doesn't make sense."

"It will to Andy Conger, Mary. It might be the only thing in the wire he'll understand."

2

New York

THAT SAME April week-end the Dales spent under the clear skies of Denver was raw and rainy in the East. In midtown Manhattan Friday evening, after most of the employees of North American Broadcasting Company had left, a group of top-echelon executives were still hard at it with no end in sight.

The conference room on the thirtieth floor of North American was strewn with cardboard coffee containers and cigarette wrappings. Mingled cigarette and cigar smoke hung in an evil-smelling cloud over the tired men around the table. As the voice of North American Broadcasting's President, Fred Morgan, droned on, each of them was wondering how much longer this meeting would last. It was already 10:30. They'd been closeted with Morgan in this same room since noon. All eight of them, without exception, wished they were somewhere else, anywhere else but in this room with a man whose survival instinct was more animal than human. When was he going to let them up for air?

The "payola" scandals, the quiz show riggings, followed by streams of incriminating witnesses, had given television and broadcasting the blackest days of their history. Something had to be done quickly to restore public confidence. Who had the magic idea that would turn the viewing public to their television sets again? Who would instill in them once more trust and affection for North American Broadcasting?

And now, whether they deserved to be thrown off or not, Morgan was in the midst of his discussion as to which programs would be sacrificed on the altar of ethics and public opinion.

"Farley," said Morgan, turning to his Director of Programs, "if we take off these three shows can we retain the billing? Do we have any shows in inventory or at Talentco which the advertisers can be pitched and sold?"

That was a typical Morgan comment. It described the man beautifully. If he presented something to a client, it was sold to that client. He wasn't familiar with defeat. Whatever Morgan turned his attention to at North American was successful. He had been known literally to lock a prospective advertiser in his office, stay with him throughout the night until he agreed to buy on North American. In a sales presentation at the highest level Morgan was disrespectful, informal, sometimes mercilessly profane (for effect), but always the shrewd businessman. Some said he had dollar antennae longer than NA's transmitter on the Empire State Building. In a sales meeting involving from ten to fifteen million dollars on a major nighttime sale to a prime advertiser—more than one show—Morgan was as attuned to the situation as a cat. His casual mannerisms belied this incredible sense of his to know exactly the dollar on which the prospect would sit tight. Morgan would lean back in his chair, eyes half-closed, busy himself with any one of a dozen standard preoccupations he had developed for the tense moments, dollar figure at which NA would stand. And, nine times out of and then, in a voice barely audible to the others, would quote the ten, it was the figure which brought the business to NA over his competition at the other two television networks—Telenet and Global. Morgan balanced an intense mental concentration with an outward show of disinterest and confidence. There was something very personal in his attachment and love of the deal. It was as if he were putting out his own final and rock-bottom bid for a piece of land on which he expected to live for the rest of his life. It was his company, his dollars, his network, he was committing. The buyers almost always sensed this. For his word was as good as his bond. What Morgan promised, he delivered. He was asking Farley Burke now to come up with the product: programs which he could not only pitch to agencies as a stopgap against wholesale defection but sell to those agencies at increased prices.

Farley Burke, a rather harassed and addled man at this moment, once more consulted his program schedules. In charge of filling in NA's daily hours of broadcasting as Vice President of Programs, he was now thoroughly confused. He had been shuffling and re-shuffling program hours, half-hours, series, one-shots, and specials of all kinds to try to accommodate the lightning changes in Morgan's thinking.

"Shows in inventory, at Talentco—I don't know right now . . . Gimme a minute," Burke said, as he fanned through the schedules.

"Dammit," said Morgan. "Just give me an answer, do we have them, yes or no."

"I can't," said Farley. "Not until I check some production schedules in Hollywood. It's a matter of who's got shows in the can tonight." He consulted his notes, files, program sheets once more, while there was silence around the table. Just the heavy breathing of Morgan and a soul-wracking cigarette cough from the other end of the room. That would be Alfie, thought Farley. Alfie Hill. Why isn't he sweating this thing out with me? "Fred," said Farley to Morgan, "I'd like to hear what Alfie has to say about agency co-operation before I get into the program side of what we might use to replace this stuff we're throwing off."

Alfie Hill, Executive Vice President of Sales, had been expecting this moment for some time now. So far, the panic and the crisis hadn't touched him. It was too early for the notices to the agencies and advertisers. He'd weathered the initial storm when the quiz and game shows had been exposed as rigged; the advertisers had quickly dumped film product in the time slots, and all had gone rather smoothly. It went the way the agencies wanted it: a minimum of fuss and feathers. You know—maybe if they looked the other way it would blow away. But blow away it didn't. And now the newspapers had stirred things up so much that the public was screaming for blood, and Morgan was going to give it to them. And this could mean a big hunk of Alfie's income right down the drain, plus the dreaded con job of the resell of an inferior show at an inferior time period. Jesus, what a mess! thought Alfie.

"Well, Farley, a lot depends on how fast we can move once we notify cancellation of the shows. And if, and this is a big if, we have some product from you to throw in which they'll swallow," said Alfie. That, he thought, put the ball back in Programming's court.

"I see no other way out, Fred," said Farley. "I'm going to take the midnight balloon to the Coast. Tonight. I'll call you tomorrow afternoon from the Bel-Air Hotel. I'll cover the producers and packagers tomorrow and Sunday, then fly back here late Sunday night. Can we put off a decision on this until Monday morning?" Farley looked at his watch, hoping perhaps even this small gesture might break the rhythm of Morgan's relentless demands on his staff.

"Okay, let's do it Monday," said Morgan. "But I must have all the facts first thing. We're going to work on the public statement Monday afternoon, and I may have to run down to Washington Tuesday on those goddam free time hearings. I want to have the press conference no later than Wednesday morning. Any later, and the agencies and clients are going to scream—loud and hard. We may not be able to hold them in check."

"I assure you, Fred, I'll have the dope for you Monday morning. But I have several 'musts' on the Coast before I commit myself," said Farley.

"You do just *that*, Burke," said Morgan. "And tell those gang-sters at Talentco we want complete co-operation from them. We've bailed them out many a time and obtained healthy renewals on their lousy shows. Now it's their turn to bail us out." Morgan paused, shifted forward in his chair, and went on: "North American Broad-casting has been hit, and hit hard. But we are not going under. To this I pledge the last drop of blood that's in me."

Too bad he didn't say booze, thought Lou Wells, President of North American's News and Public Affairs Division. Wells had been quiet, trying desperately to keep up with Morgan's darting probes, knowing that the brunt of the burden to pull NA out would fall ultimately in the Public Affairs area. When the scandals had origi-nally broken, the first programs to be shoved in their place on a temporary basis were non-fiction film shows, in order to give the network a breather. The programs had been put together in Wells's division, on a "crash" basis. The reviews and ratings were not good. Everything had been done too quickly, Wells explained. But he knew his stock had declined in the interim, and it had happened at a time when he wanted it to be on the rise. Perhaps I've become careless, thought Wells. He'd been on the throne of his profession so long, perhaps he hadn't been able to see the insurgents surround-ing the palace gates.

"Wells!" snapped Morgan.

"Yes, Fred," said Wells. He wished he'd said "sir" instead of Fred.

"What have you got?" Morgan asked.

I've got something right here in my pocket, thought Wells to himself. But dammit, I haven't had time to think it through. It's too quick to spring it now. What's more, I'm a veteran of your jungle, Morgan. I'm not about to spill what I have in front of the jackals sitting around this table. You'll hear about it alone, just you and me—at the right time. "What do you mean, Fred?" he asked, lean-ing forward.

"We've had a good reading from Legal," continued Morgan. "We know where Burke stands; we know Alfie can keep the big ones in

line if he has the proper product in his hands. But we don't
know where *you* stand."

That was a good question, Lou Wells thought. Where did he
stand? With North American, with the other guys around the
table, and with Fred Morgan.

Lou Wells was a newsman through and through. He was forty-
three, married, and the father of two children. He had been
enormously successful as a broadcasting newsman and now, recently, had turned administrator. Wells was in excellent physical
condition and prided himself on the fact he weighed eight pounds
less than the day he came home to North American from Europe,
after his hitch as chief European Correspondent for Armed Forces
Radio. Wells had been enormously popular with the staff of correspondents reporting to him. Many had come to NA after the War,
and were the backbone of his world-wide reporting team. During his
war years Wells had won a prize for a series of radio programs entitled "Journal of Valor."

Wells, as a senior executive at NA, did well financially. He had
smelled the power of television and news the first time he saw an
experimental broadcast. At that time Wells had gone to Morgan
and asked to supervise television as well as radio. He simply absorbed
what had grown to be, outside of one's daily newspaper, the largest
news power in the history of communication. Wells had become
possessive about his new baby. It was a combination of his tenacity
toward a story and his personal involvement with his department,
newsmen, and cameramen that had given him the reputation of a
difficult man to work for, a man who assumed that every level of
production and editorial development was his own personal prov-
ince, his rightful domain. Because he had grown with television
from its infancy, there were few who were more expert when it came
to news production, the editorial strength in a documentary, or
balancing the fine edge of controversy with impartiality. Riding
above this tenacious approach to the news presented on NA was
Wells's own possessiveness toward a big story. Every top story

was his own baby. Everyone at NA knew it and kept hands off.

That was the way things had been for fourteen years at NA—until this year, thought Lou. What had happened? Why, all of a sudden, were the guns trained on his department and him? Was it the old saw about "time for a change?" Hadn't he kept pace with audience taste, production techniques? Lou Wells didn't know. He couldn't come to any conclusions. He was rather hopeful, at this late hour, that he would get through this session without any questions coming up. They hadn't in the two previous Program Plans board meetings. Because his department hadn't been involved in the malpractices of rigging shows or "coached" contestants, Wells felt like saying to Morgan, "We stand where we always have, Fred. For the story, wherever it takes us, and for the truth." But Wells didn't think such a reference to ethics would go over too well at that moment. What came out was rather meaningless.

"News and Public Affairs stands ready to help, Fred, in any way we can. What do you need from me?" Wells asked.

Morgan started to say something, paused, and then addressed the entire room:

"I happen to feel the answer to our basic problem lies somewhere in Wells's area. I don't think the public is going to forgive us if we simply put on more Westerns or shoot-'em-ups. Somewhere there's a master program idea which is going to turn the tide. I'm not going to sit around for Telenet or Global to come up with it. They always look to us anyway, and why do they? It's because we care, I care, about North American. I've been sitting on this powder keg for twenty years, and two or three dishonest schlock producers and money-happy contestants aren't going to kill off North American." Morgan paused, tamped out a cigarette. He breathed in and out heavily. "I admit things are black. But the agencies haven't indicated serious revolt. I have heard rumors along the street. So has Alfie. If we don't propose something startling to grab the public right where the hair is short and yank 'em back to television, we may lose 'em. Not for good, but for a good long time. So think—this week-end—all of you. But especially your gang, Wells. It should come from you. That's it for tonight, men, and thank you. Very much."

Chairs were pushed back. Alfie Hill asked Farley if he wanted to share a cab to the East Side. Morgan nodded to Wells, "I'd like to see you a minute before you go, Lou."

"Fine, Fred," said Wells, wondering what was coming.

Morgan turned to talk to Burke about a production contract which involved Hollywood. Wells busied himself with his notes until the others had left. Then he walked up to the end of the table near Morgan, where Burke had been sitting. The remains of food and cigarette butts mixed together started to make him feel queasy. Lou shifted his chair and looked at Morgan. Morgan's eyes were on the ceiling. He rubbed his temples with the palms of both hands. Jesus, he looks horrible! thought Wells. Older than God and twice as tormented. The pale gray scar, which ran diagonally across Morgan's forehead from the top left down to just above his right eyebrow, was almost scarlet tonight. It made him appear more ugly than usual. His face sagged; his temples pulsed with fatigue. But even now with this weariness, the eyes were alert, darting, glistening with intensity.

"It's about time you did some serious thinking, Lou," Morgan said. "I don't have to tell you you're showing a horrible loss in news and public affairs—not so much news but definitely public affairs— and that's to be expected. But there's a situation now, Lou, where you're heading into some tough sledding. The inferior quality of the crash stuff on the air from your department is hurting you. The short notice is no excuse for bad shows. You're supposed to have creative technicians who can deliver on severe deadlines. That's the function of a news operation."

"True," said Wells. "I must admit it hit us during vacation double-ups, and the crisis in Algeria threw us way off base. But the shows were not—"

Morgan cut him off. "I don't want to know why. I've said I

think the answer to our mess lies somewhere in your area. If you can come up with something that makes sense against the torment of the goddam public and the dailies *and* Congress, it would augur well for you and your operation. There are wolves snapping at your heels, Lou. Find a club to beat them off!" Morgan looked at him hard, eyes flashing.

Don't kid me, thought Wells. The only threat around here is the Big Bad Wolf named Fred Morgan who runs this jungle. Haven't you got the guts to come out and tell me you're the one who's dissatisfied?

"I think I know what you mean, and what you're trying to say, Fred. I appreciate the tipoff." Wells fished inside his coat and pulled out his wallet. It's now or never, he thought. Here goes.

Morgan went on as if he hadn't heard Wells. "Somewhere, by Jesus, there's an idea for television big enough to bring the herd back to us. Big enough to throttle Washington, shut up the dailies, and get the public thinking once again television is their answer to the good life. We've got to find it, Lou."

Wells opened the billfold and removed an envelope.

"I've got something here I'd like you to read, Fred," he said, carefully unfolding a long clipping from the *Herald*. "If things are as bad as you say they are, I can't think of a better time to show you something. I was going to work on it a while, but I think you should read it now."

"What is it?" asked Morgan. "It's late."

"I know, but this is right to your point." Wells held the clipping in his hand as Morgan sat disinterested. "It's a letter to the *Herald*," said Wells, "written a couple of Sundays ago. It's by Ed Banion. That name ring a bell?"

"Vaguely. Who is he?"

"He was a National Chairman in politics back in the forties. I've had a habit of reading letters printed in papers for years. It's a good way to keep a finger on what's bothering people."

"Get to the point."

"The gist is to find a way to cut down on the physical de-

mands on presidential candidates and to remove the enormous cost
of campaigns from the National Committees. He says campaigns are
getting too costly and too much of a physical and geographical
nightmare. He also talks about the Madison Avenue razzle-dazzle,
politics by sloganry. He has an idea to take the gimmickry, the
showmanship out of presidential elections, and he thinks television
could be the Great Deliverer."

"How?" said Morgan, yawning.

"With a series of nationally televised presidential debates. A confrontation of the candidates on TV. He doesn't actually say it, but
that's what I get out of it." Morgan looked at Wells, who had
straightened in his chair.

"Let me read it." Wells handed him the clipping. God, thought
Wells, of all times to try to sell this to Morgan.

As Morgan read the column, Wells thought of how carefully he
had wanted to present this to management. He had already ini-
tiated research into debates and their historical precedent in
politics, who might be the current candidates, and how a debate
idea might be affected by the hearings in Washington. He had
wanted to be so careful. He felt he had an important idea by the
tail. A big idea, and Wells didn't want to expose it to a quick turndown. But now, in the light of Morgan's threats, literally fighting
for his survival, he felt he had to show the column to Morgan.

Morgan gave no hint of his thoughts until he had completed his
reading. He flipped the sheet of paper onto the table, took off his
glasses, and chewed the earpiece as he said, "This hasn't got a damn
thing to do with our problem, Lou. It's more of the same goddam
thing—grabbing time."

It took Lou a moment to recover. "As far as Banion goes here,
yes. But I think there are in this thing, Fred, two great potentials. A
Lincoln-Douglas type debate between the two presidential candidates, and two, a great club to swing down in Washington *against*
the free time bill."

"I don't get either point."

"If we take Banion's proposal to its extreme, we come up with the idea of a Lincoln-Douglas confrontation. A face-to-face debate between the two presidential candidates. Now he skirts that, and I don't know if it's possible. But, if it were, you'd have the damnedest field day of favorable public relations that broadcasting has ever seen. Over night all this hue and cry about the scandals, the violence, rigged shows—all of it—would disappear instantly—*if* a presidential debate could be delivered."

"It never has happened yet. In 1952 and 1956 stuff like this was proposed by Telenet, the others too."

"I remember. But look what you have in Congress now. The 'equal time' provision will be knocked out if that resolution goes through. But the free time is involuntary—it's a grab, as you say. What if you could kill the involuntary aspect of it? What if, instead of giving the time to the candidates to do with what they please, we propose a face-to-face debate between the two presidential candidates? A format and program the *networks* control, not the candidates?"

"You mean kill the free time bill with a counterproposal for a series of presidential debates?"

"Right. And at the same time have everyone in the country praising you."

"Who's going to deliver the candidates?"

"I don't know, but I want to explore it."

"You'll never get 'em. It's impractical."

"There must be a way to do it, Fred. Lord, the public would grab onto this like a drowning man grabs a floating log. We'd be away and running. And with a program and idea that is television's own, no one else's. The print guys would scream bloody murder. But you'd have a bombshell to drop at the hearings when you testify against the free time bill. You could knock out that lack of control over programming in a second. I've looked up the sponsorship of the bill. Most of them, all but two, are in Governor Green's and Senator Pender's party. It looks as if Conger will be the standard-bearer of the other party. Now, strictly off the cuff, with no deep study—although I've got all my research people and the news bureaus around the country looking into it right now—it appears the senators who have put up this bill which calls for uncontrolled use of free time are in the same party which would gain most from a series of debates. So, if we could get to some of them, tell them of television's proposal for debates which broadcasting then announces in the hearings, I'll bet they'll cave instantly on their demand to turn the time over scot-free to the candidates with no hold on program. This only works because we're already halfway home on the equal time position. All they care about is the free time. We know that. But let's counter-propose the debate idea, when and after we know one of the parties will endorse it."

Morgan had listened intently, fascinated. "And the party to endorse is the one most anxious to grab the free time with no strings attached? So we put the restriction on them, but we offer something through which they'll benefit even more. So it's us on a voluntary basis then, not Congress?"

"That's it, Fred." Wells looked directly at Morgan, who, after a moment, started to look around the room at the line where the top of the wall met the ceiling.

"So how do we get the other party, the party which stands to lose most by debate, to go along with us? Even if we win our point?"

"I don't know, but I'm going to find the answer to that. And even if the debate never comes off, what has North American, what has television got to lose? It'll be a blockbuster in the hearings, Fred. It's bound to start a hue and cry immediately. I'll bet any dough I've got the time-grab bill will be withdrawn. The senators supporting it will leap with joy at the idea of a series of debates."

"And who's going to deliver the other party?" Morgan repeated.

There was a beat before Wells replied. "I don't know. But I don't see where it makes any difference. We will have come up with an idea that kills the give-away on the time. And we will be presenting something which removes instantly the spotlight of guilt *re* the quiz shows. If we're lucky enough to get both of the candidates to agree, then we're really sailing."

"That's a big 'if.' Too big. But it's the only way to approach it.

Our reprieve will be short-lived *if* we don't deliver this fall what we propose this spring. Christ, we can crank up a publicity offensive which would last six long months—if we have something to publicize. Otherwise, it's a fast flurry for a couple of weeks, a few pats on the back, and then back to the mess. No, Lou, I wouldn't want to go too far unless we've got a pretty good idea we can pull this off. I grant you, it could do the trick on the time grab. But we will be talking to politicians. They'll know, better than we, the slim possibility of bringing off a debate. If they become certain it is unfeasible, we may even lose the round on the give-away of time."

Wells was silent a moment. Morgan's point made a lot of sense. He'd carried his thinking farther than Lou. Even if it were proposed at the hearings, and the sponsors felt it would do their party good, the debate would die right there if they weren't convinced it could feasibly take place. They'd rather get the time with no strings attached than lose the whole project because they'd gambled with something impractical. "I'm afraid you're right, Fred," said Wells softly. "And I don't know the answer to prevent this. But I'd like you to give me a go-ahead to explore it. On the pretense of gathering background material for the campaign, I've got a dummy project going in News and Public Affairs called 'The Presidential Possibles.' Both departments are working overtime to give me an exact reading—as of this week—as to who might be our targets, who might be the two men we'd have to deliver to a debate series. Furthermore, I plan to take a trip out to see Governor Joseph Green in Fairlee at the end of this week. I've got to see our affiliate there about coverage plans leading up to the Chicago Conventions anyway. While I'm there, I could present Green with your position on the time-grab bill, try and quiet him down. Then, I thought I might approach the idea of the debates with him. Sound him out. Off the record. His name shows up strong, no matter how you measure it, for the nomination of his party. Do I have an okay on that?"

Morgan thought a moment, then picked up the Ed Banion piece. He read it again from top to bottom without saying a word. Then he looked up across the top of it at Lou and said, "It could be risky, the whole thing could backfire. I want to mull it over for a while." And that was the last Morgan said to Louis Wells that evening.

Morgan abruptly left the conference room and headed down the long hall to his office. The soft orange glow from a floor lamp in the outer foyer of his office was his homing beacon. It had been a strange parting—silent, hopeless in a way.

As Lou Wells pushed the "Down" button on the elevator to return to his office for his coat and brief case, he watched the figure of Morgan blot out the light and then disappear inside. Once alone, Wells felt total exhaustion engulf him. He sneezed and walked into the waiting elevator.

It was a long way home that night for Wells. He couldn't remember when he'd been so completely spent, physically and emotionally. The anonymous faces which bobbed and lunged back and forth at him on the train to New Jersey were as so many judges, waiting for Morgan to say yes or no to Wells's request. Wells wished he'd spent more time putting together those film shows after the scandals broke. Maybe the knives wouldn't be out so far if he had.

Suddenly the thought of the knives out for him hit Wells hard. He had to do something—and quickly. It was then he decided to act on his own, to see Governor Joseph Green whether or not he ever got his go-ahead from Fred Morgan.

It was a big gamble, could mean his job. But if Green wouldn't go along with the debate idea in place of the free-time grab, who would have to know of the meeting? And if Green did go along with his proposition, there would be some very big game in Wells's bag on the return flight to New York.

The stakes were worth it, thought Wells. He slouched down in his seat, leaned his head against the soot-covered window, and slept.

3

A Trip to the Midwest

THE JET FLIGHT to Fairlee by way of Chicago was smooth and un-
eventful. Lou Wells was impressed, as always, with the new-found
quiet of the jets. In his News position, Wells flew over 50,000 air
miles a year. There were times when he blessed the jets and times
when he cursed them. When you were in a hurry they were great
—especially on overseas flights to the foreign bureaus of North
American News. But the airlines' ads were for the birds. They
played on the theme that in the Jet Age Daddy got home earlier, or
he actually got home for the night or the week-end, when in the
days of the slower piston engines Daddy wouldn't have been home
for a week. For Lou, or anyone like him, it didn't work out that
way. Jets meant that a man's company tried to cram twice as much
into every twenty-four hours—order a guy out to the Coast and
back in one day if necessary. Nobody Wells knew spent more time

at home because this was the Jet Age. In reality, they spent less. And, Wells thought, no more sleeper flights to the Coast. How he missed them. The midnight flight out of New York had been like a private club. Everybody was in show business, news, or merchandising. Poker, good drinks, great hostesses, and good conversation. Then the sack. A bump, and Los Angeles.

The change to the feeder line at O'Hare was the usual frantic run from one end of the airport to the other. He made the plane to Fairlee as the ground attendants were shutting the gate. As Wells walked off the plane at Fairlee airport around six, Amos Whiting, Director of News at KZVI, was waving at him from the gate.

"Welcome to the ugliest town in America, Lou," said Amos. They shook hands warmly.

"Good to see you, Amos. Had no idea it'd be this soon," said Wells.

Amos Whiting had made his own choice years ago to stay out of New York. He was one of the best newsmen on Wells's staff. He had decided to come back to his home town, Fairlee, when television and KZVI went on the air.

In a state capitol you couldn't ask for a better man. Whiting's ability went far beyond the news or creative demands of Fairlee, but he was very happy. He looked even younger than the last time Wells had seen him, almost three years previously. They drove to the hotel. Amos said the bar was the best in town and that after Wells checked in and they'd had a drink, they'd hit a steak house on the outskirts of Fairlee that had a fine blues pianist who started at ten.

Lou Wells wanted to know more about Governor Joseph Green. Amos obliged by giving Wells clues as to what made Green tick.

"Don't let this guy fool you, Lou," said Amos. "He's a shrewd man, has a mind like a beaver trap. He's a man of infinite patience. You have to be, to tie the kind of trout flies he does. He also cleans everyone at poker. He's a brilliant strategist. Whatever bad anyone says about him, stack it up against what he's done for this state. And what he's done for his pet hate, drug addiction. His penal system is a model for the whole world. Why, the guys from the Federal

Bureau have been out here to study his state system, which is quite a switch. He may be totally disarming, tell one joke after another, look as relaxed as he can be. But behind it all, that man's thinking, planning, and filing away. He'll read you like an X ray."

"Can he be convinced he's wrong? Will he change a stand he's taken?" asked Wells.

"Sure. Providing two things are in it. One, you've convinced him it's the better position, and two, that there's something in it for Joseph Green." Whiting got up, made a call to the station, and confirmed Wells's appointment for nine the following morning.

Wells was waiting in the lobby for Whiting at eight-thirty. It was a short drive to the State House. Wells suggested that after Whiting introduced him to Green, Whiting manufacture an excuse and leave them alone.

"It will be better that way, Amos, because I've got to do some infighting that may get a little sticky. No use your suffering. You've got to stay on good terms with this boy. You live here, but I'll be back in New York tonight. If it goes poorly in there with him, it better be all on me." With that, the two men were ushered into Governor Joseph Green's working office.

There was nothing unusual about Green's appearance that day, except perhaps the flower in the buttonhole of his suit coat. Wells couldn't ever remember seeing him wear one before. He better knock that off when he campaigns, thought Wells. They all shook hands affably, and Governor Joseph Green led the way over to a magnificent conference table, complete with pads, pencils, and cigarette boxes.

Amos Whiting said he had to cover a committee hearing, and that Wells, as News President of North American, was the important man to talk to that morning anyway—and left.

Wells looked at Green, composed, self-assured as he sat with his hands resting quietly before him on the polished surface of the table. This was his man, thought Wells. This was the man he had to have—or no debates. And, so far, no flak from Green about the quiz scandals. He thought of something his grandfather used to say to him about times such as this: "The best way to begin is to commence."

"Governor, we at North American naturally are aware of your sentiments on the bill before Congress which would give the presidential candidates free time this fall. We also believe, after studying your latest statement on it, that your feelings about the unrestricted use of that time by the candidates is a paramount condition of your interest and endorsement of the bill. Have I correctly stated your position, sir?"

"Exactly," said Green pleasantly. "I assume your management has sent you out here to tell me how wrong I am, how I'm destroying the conservative approach to free enterprise?"

"Not at all, Governor. North American does feel there are two damaging things to television in the bill. The infringement on corporate enterprise and the idea of an actual law, an involuntary bill, taking over and, in effect, deciding what type of programs we will present on the air. But I'm not out here to convince you our position is right, or yours is wrong. I am a news executive, a program man. In my own field I have a proposition to present to you, which I feel may be of more than passing interest and could result in a change of your attitude toward the current bill."

"I'd be interested to hear it." Green picked up one of the silver cigarette boxes, which was clasped shut, and slid a legal tablet over in front of him. He placed one of the sharp corners of the box on the tablet while holding, on the long bias, the corner directly above it in his fingers. He then spun the box slowly around and around as Wells talked.

It didn't take Lou long to get to the point. "What television proposes, Governor, is that instead of the government ordering the networks to give the candidates the time free, to do with what they please, the television industry, as a unit, offer to the two presidential candidates the use of its networks and stations for a face-to-face encounter—a series of Lincoln-Douglas type debates presented in a rotating fashion among the networks."

Green chewed on it for a moment. "A bold idea, Mr. Wells. But impractical. Actually, if I were the standard-bearer of my party, I would probably enjoy an advantage by such a presentation. It's the type of political tactic a candidate such as myself would probably employ during a campaign, whether or not the television networks had the slightest idea of presenting it. But no, Mr. Wells. Unfortunately, like the tango, it takes two to debate." Green chuckled and went on:

"If you're talking about a literal face-to-face encounter, you haven't got a chance. I know. I've challenged many an opponent when it was politically sound for me to do so, and I have been challenged more than once. Not one debate ever took place."

Green pushed back his chair, crossing his legs neatly. "Mr. Wells, you are fooling with one of the oldest truisms known to politics," he said. "It goes like this: If you are better known than your opponent, do not accept a debate challenge from him. If you are ahead of your opponent but not so well known, do not accept a debate challenge. If you are not so well known and are behind in the running, challenge your opponent, and pray he will accept. If you are better known than your opponent, but the polls show you behind, challenge your opponent, and pray it is the correct thing to do politically. There is no political situation, to my knowledge, where it is politically correct for both candidates to debate each other. It would be a purely theoretical situation. No two candidates are ever that evenly matched. Therefore, if a debate takes place during a major political campaign, one candidate or the other is quite possibly committing political suicide. In the case where it is politically sound for a candidate to challenge his opponent to a debate or accept a challenge from his opponent, the purpose is not to win the actual debate."

Wells frowned. He had lost Green's train of thought. "I don't quite follow you, sir."

"It's very simple," said Green. "If a candidate ascertains his strength at the voting booth is less than his opponent's, then he must use every device to win. He must pull out all the stops. He must use every means available to him to reach the voter. One means, in that situation, is the debate form. The candidate's purpose is to increase his exposure, to enhance his stature. His purpose is not to win the actual debate. Today issues in campaigns are a matter of degree in most instances, not black or white. It makes little or no difference who wins or loses. I have heard it said there could be a situation here it would be correct politically to lose a debate, but I don't see how. I merely know it is not important to win. A draw is the best any candidate should hope for."

"To carry this a step further, then, in a national presidential campaign it is highly unlikely that *both* candidates would accept an invitation from television to a series of debates."

"You are correct. One or the other would assume it is politically unwise for him to do so. One or the other would hold the position the other had more visibility to gain or more votes. Therefore, one candidate would decline."

"It seems almost cut and dried."

"It is. There is another element in national politics, Mr. Wells, even in congressional and senatorial races. The political press corps are a very sophisticated and intelligent group of fellows. Through the years a label of weakness has been slapped on the candidate who *accepts* a debate, not the one who challenges. For all the reasons we've covered. The political press corps know these sophistications as well as I. They would be quick to report it. The press would scream to high heaven so-and-so had admitted weakness by accepting the debate, had said, for everyone to hear, he was trailing his opponent, was losing out with the voter. There's no way to combat that type of hostile press coverage. No, the press interpretation of a candidate who accepts a debate challenge is one of weakness. This adverse publicity and coverage is usually much more damaging to the candidate than whether or not he wins or loses the debate. That is why the debate outcome, unless there is an unusual circumstance, is unimportant. What is important is: which side will benefit more by the publicity; how will the other side combat the 'weakness' stories, and the increased exposure to its candidate. Of course, the public does not think of a debate in these terms at all. The general public feels it is the sporting thing to do, in the best American tradition of freedom of expression, free competition. As I have said, I would obtain the benefit of the publicity over such a better-known candidate as, shall we say, the Secretary of State, Mr. Conger."

So this is what politics is all about, thought Wells.

"In the case where one or the other of the participants is an incumbent," Green continued, "where the debate is between someone 'in' and someone 'out,' it is suicide for the incumbent to accept debate. Oh, there's the argument the incumbent must be willing to publicly defend his actions in office, but that has very little to do with the hard facts of politics."

"Why is the man in office so vulnerable?" asked Wells.

"Because he cannot make false, wild, irresponsible claims, as can the opponent seeking office," answered Green. "Also, he automatically must assume a posture of defense, of defending his record, his administration; whereas the other man can take the attack, the offense throughout the entire debate. And the candidate seeking to unseat the incumbent can make promises of future action, what he will do if elected. Promises, I might add, which are not always kept. But the incumbent cannot use promises. He can debate only on his record which, incidentally, may well bring up how well he did or did not keep his own campaign promises." Green chuckled. "So there are many negatives and pitifully few positives for a candidate to accept debate."

Wells waited until Green was silent, obviously finished with his train of thought, before he leaned forward and looked at Green intently. Now, he decided, was the time to bring out his most potent argument. "What about the Lincoln-Douglas Debates, sir? I have seen few or no writings which argue Lincoln made a serious mistake in challenging, or Douglas in accepting, these encounters."

"Ah, there are several important differences. First, and most fundamental, it was a senatorial race, not a presidential campaign. The stakes weren't nearly as high. Second, the issue of union or secession was monumental—and clear-cut. It was a single topic. The debates were limited to that one subject, a subject immensely more important than either candidate's victory. The two men became symbols for something far more meaningful than themselves. Do we have an issue today as awesome as 'Shall there be a union of states, a United States, or shall there be two sovereign bodies instead of one?' I think not. The issue of peace in our time is large and pervasive, but, I daresay, at the time, the Lincoln-Douglas Debates foreshadowed that issue in sharp focus and then went on to debate over the future of the very corpus of our sovereignty."

"That certainly explains why we have never had a debate in a presidential campaign."

Green nodded. "Even considering the great part debate has played in our process of free speech, law, and the history of American politics, this is the situation today. And shall be so forever, I presume. The public simply doesn't have as its frame of reference the delicate balance which dictates the challenge or acceptance of debate, the nuance of advantage over disadvantage, the dangerous courtship with political defeat."

Wells smiled and said, "As you mentioned a moment ago, Governor, I am aware it takes two to debate. I am here to advise you the television industry is prepared to deliver the other candidate. Whether he wants it or not." Wells, who was now very serious, had lowered his voice and was leaning across the corner of the table, his face close to Green's.

"I don't follow you, Mr. Wells. You've made a very strong statement."

"And I am prepared to deliver what I have just said, providing you will reverse your position on the time-grab bill, give the networks control over the time and programs on a voluntary instead of involuntary basis, and endorse one hundred per cent the notion of presidential television debates."

Green was looking directly into Wells's eyes. The full impact of this stranger's incredible statement was sinking in: deep, clear, and powerful. He leaned back in his chair, ever so slightly, never taking his steady gaze off Wells.

"I said, Mr. Wells, I would in all probability be the candidate to benefit most by such a debate procedure. Why don't you first go after the other candidate when he's selected? Then you'll have the debate, because you already have me."

"Because, Governor, the television industry is not going to propose the use of its facilities for presidential debates unless the time-grab bill is killed. And the committee of senators proposing this bill is made up of ninety per cent of your political persuasion. They will act according to what is best politically for their party. If you refrain from further public endorsement until after our proposal and then come out in favor of the debates, the bill will die right there. Right now your party is ahead with the time-grab bill."

"Possibly. But this still doesn't deliver the reluctant candidate to the debate—the man who would be hurt by it. Undoubtedly Andrew Conger." Green snapped the cigarette box open and shut for emphasis. He continued:

"What makes you chaps in New York television think you can make Secretary of State Andrew Conger do something he does not wish to do?"

Wells was ready for Green. It was his big gamble. He had turned it over in his mind for a week. He was totally convinced he could sell his argument. If he won, he could then worry about selling it to Fred Morgan.

"It won't be the New York television people who do it, Governor," said Wells. "It will be the American public."

Green raised an eyebrow, nothing more. "Please explain, Mr. Wells," he said.

"I think with the public's awareness of the power of television, Governor, and the simplicity and purity of the idea of a television presidential debate, the reluctant candidate—the candidate inclined to refuse a debate—will be forced by public clamor to accept an invitation tendered by the television industry. This would not be either candidate challenging the other. It would be television, inviting both candidates to debate the issues. The candidate most likely to suffer from debate would have no say in the matter. And that candidate may very well be your opponent in the presidential campaign."

"Who arouses the public, Mr. Wells?" Green looked at Wells with new respect and interest.

"We do with television, the greatest means of communicating with the masses ever known to man. It is an instantaneous pipeline to almost every living room in America. Enormous forward strides have been made in all types of mass persuasion and publicity in the past few years. Television sets have increased by the millions, ever since 1956. We are living in an age very different from 1952, or 1956 for that matter. I believe television alone, to say nothing of the press when they realize the importance of the idea, can put a reluctant candidate in a position from which there is no retreat, no way to survive the public pressures and insistence for a debate. Any consistent attitude of refusal will be construed as a weakness on his part, or, shall we say, Andrew Conger's part. He will be depicted and editorialized as not acting in the best American tradition, and he will be condemned for repudiating fair play. Mind you, a debate couldn't have happened in 1956, couldn't have happened before this year. Congress has made it possible by suspending the equal time provisions of the Communications Act. We don't have to give exposure to the sixteen other nuisance candidates now."

Wells then proceeded to give the entire propaganda plan, a picture of the effort which would be expended to arouse the public to clamor for the debates. Radio and television would be employed by all networks. All newscasts would demand and editorialize in favor of the debates. Special documentary programs would trace the history of debates, their historical importance. He swiftly ticked off the thousands of daily impressions this would have on a national scale, the announcement at the end of each program which would be made telling television-viewers to write the candidate of their choice, the National Committee of each party, demanding the debates. He hoped Morgan could deliver the other networks, as he had said he could.

"It is our belief, Governor, and I have checked this out with reasonable thoroughness, no candidate today will be able to withstand the propaganda and pressure brought to bear by the broadcasting media and resulting public demand."

"Such a series of programs this fall would certainly help you clear the air of your scandals and rigging practices, would it not, Mr. Wells?"

Wells had wondered if Green would be smart enough to realize that point, and had been waiting for this ever since he started the conversation.

"Yes, it would, sir. It would help us a great deal. That's the main reason I'm sitting here today."

"The debates help us both. But I have already come out for the free time bill. Furthermore, I have always been under the impression that North American was politically inclined toward the other party."

Wells concurred. He gave Green a quick run-down on just how bad things were back in New York and Washington because of the scandals. Merely the announcement made in the hearings of a proposal for face-to-face debates would augur well for the networks.

"The proposal is hollow, Mr. Wells, unless it culminates in a series of debates this fall. For whoever the candidates turn out to be, it is a waste of my time and energy unless they can be delivered. In addition, it embraces a change of position on my part, publicly."

Wells was losing the game. He could feel it. Green was not warming to the idea. "Governor, I guarantee you the broadcasting industry can force your opponent into accepting a debate. If you are the candidate."

"That's a very foolish statement, Mr. Wells. Television can't be that desperate."

But I am, thought Wells. Jesus, I'm out on a limb.

"Governor, I will pledge the full facilities of North American News behind your candidacy at the convention and from this day forward, for that matter, if you will endorse the debates and repudiate your support of the free time bill."

He'd said it. Lou Wells had said it. Something he never thought he'd say as long as he lived. He'd had it in the back of his mind that, if the going really got rough, he'd offer it. Morgan would never have to know. No one except himself, and possibly Sandy Jones, his Convention Television Director. They'd favor Green at Chicago over all other candidates, cover him like glue, run his interviews and spots in the most favorable time periods at peak audience times. It was really quite simple, so delicate was the balance of impartiality and favoritism in news coverage.

"I'm sure you know as well as I, Governor, millions of Americans will cast their votes in November according to what they see at the conventions in July. It is seldom that the man ahead in popularity on August first does not walk into the White House. And television with its enormous 'image' power can project you, Governor Joseph Green, over and over, time and again, into America's homes as they watch your convention. In addition, we all know the power of the constituents represented by certain elected delegations. Manipulated imagery on television from a convention has swayed more than one delegation which reads the wires and listens to the phone calls from the people it represents back home." Wells paused for emphasis, watching his missiles one by one find their mark at ground zero.

When Wells concluded, Green jutted his chin out slightly and turned in his chair to face him. The game is going well, thought Green. This man is easier to play than I had imagined. I wonder if he'll take my last card. I've really got nothing to lose.

Green had done his homework well. He was perfectly aware what North American stood to lose by his current position endorsing the time-grab. And now Green was down to the final stages of his standard approach to such matters, a double barb which kept a wriggling fish on a hook, come hell or high water.

"Mr. Wells, a few months back your network presented a program dealing with the Post Office Department. Do you remember it?"

"Very well. It was a pet project of Fred Morgan's. Our president."

"I have met him. On that program you as much as came out for a new Cabinet chair, that of a Secretary of Communications."

"That is correct, sir. We feel the Postmaster General in the Cabinet is an anachronism of our time. He was originally placed in the Cabinet either because he had a friend in the White House back in those days, or more probably because at that time the only means of confidential military communications in this country were the U. S. mails. There was no wireless, no telegraph, no radio, no television. The sole way the Secretary of the Army or of War, for that matter, could communicate with his forces in the field was by Pony Express. Many of the Pony Express riders saw duty, at one time or another, as military couriers back in the earliest days of the postal department."

"And your program said the Postmaster General should be replaced in the Cabinet by a Secretary of Communications. That such a man would run the postal service along with USIA, the FCC, and other departments of information and communication."

"That is correct, Governor. Fred Morgan feels this very strongly. He has said—"

"How would your Fred Morgan like to be America's first Secretary of Communications?"

"I don't know, sir." My God, what is this man saying! thought Wells. Why, Christ, if he could take this back to North American with him, he might be safely able to let Morgan know about his deal with Green by balancing it with this incredible offer.

"Why don't you find out? And then have Fred Morgan call me," suggested Green. "I was extremely impressed with him last year at White Sulphur. And then this argument your program put forth bears merit. It was well thought out. It made a deep impact on me. If I am elected, I propose to initiate a Secretary of Communications in my Cabinet. And I cannot think of a better man than Fred Morgan to fill it. I'd be grateful if you'd pass this on to him. And have him call me at his earliest opportunity. Now, as to your proposal—" Green cleared his throat and shifted his weight in his chair—"I have decided to go along with you. I have nothing to lose—except mild wrath descending on me at the National Committee for reversing my position on the time-grab bill. You have a great deal to lose. All of television does. Therefore, you must pledge me you will use every means at your disposal to deliver the debates, just as you have outlined. It may bring television back from the dead. At least, it will keep me very much alive, eh?" Green chuckled, and Wells joined him half-heartedly. He could feel the change in attitude in Green.

"You are a sick and evil industry today," Green continued. "You are without morality, a house of cards, held in check by Washington. You are ethically unprincipled as a group of competitive men. And enormously successful, I might add. And now North American Broadcasting, the television industry, and I have made an agreement. Not unlike, I presume, one made by your people most any day in New York, eh?"

Lou Wells suddenly became frightened. But the moment passed quickly. He had sold his dream plan all the way. And a hell of a lot more. He had the biggest plum in the industry to offer his boss, Fred Morgan.

"Very few deals are made, Governor, which could be as meaningful for all parties concerned as this one," said Wells quietly.

The two men worked on a statement Green would release after the networks proposed the debates in the hearings. Green, at that time, would deliver a statement to the National Committee immediately. Wells assured Green that Morgan would call him within the week.

Green rose and escorted Wells to the massive, ceiling-high door.

"And at the convention, Mr. Wells, everywhere that Governor Joe Green went, North American's cameras were sure to go, eh?" He laughed. "I suppose I ought to enroll in a charm school with all this unexpected coverage I'll be getting on your television."

That's right, thought Wells. Drive it home, you bastard. You don't need any charm school. It's all in that stiletto you carry sheathed in sugar and honey.

"Just be sure the red light is on the camera, Governor. You know, we've fooled a lot of people that way," Wells said lightly.

"But you wouldn't fool Joe Green now, would you, Mr. Wells?"

Wells said nothing, withdrew his hand from Green's, and walked through the door.

Amos Whiting was waiting in the reception room for him. "How'd it go, Lou?" he asked.

"Perfect, Amos. You'll be hearing about it soon, I hope. But everything I said about covering Green goes double."

"He really gave it to television in there, huh?"

"No. Television gave it to him."

When Wells arrived at his office the following morning, there was a message prominently posted on his desk by his secretary that he was leaving at noon with Morgan for Washington. Wells rushed through a mound of detail on News Department administration and made it up to Morgan's office, just as he appeared with his coat, hat, and brief case. This was a break, thought Wells. The ride out to the airport and the flight down would give him plenty of time to spill the whole Green deal to Morgan. As the limousine swung into the East Side Drive above the U.N., Wells said to Morgan, "Mind if I put up the partition glass, Fred?" Morgan ran it up with the power button on his side. "Thanks," said Wells. "I have quite a story to tell you."

Suddenly Wells had cold feet. He was petrified. "I don't quite know how to begin."

Lou Wells had not foreseen what it would do to him personally to embrace dishonesty. He wasn't prepared in any way for what he was about to go through. The first part wouldn't be bad, he thought. It was all to his credit. But should he, or should he not, mention the deal on Green's news coverage? His palms were wet. What would happen if Morgan didn't call Green on the Cabinet possibility? It suddenly dawned on him that what he was about to say to

Morgan could either boot him out or put him on the inside with
Morgan for life. Did Morgan want the debates as badly as Wells
wanted them? Did Morgan want to get off the scandal hook as
much as Wells thought he did? Had he gone too far? Wells was
scared, and he knew it. He wondered if Morgan did.

"I—ahh . . . went to Fairlee to check on primary and convention arrangements for Governor Green," Wells started. "I didn't get
a chance to fill you in on the trip before I left."

"That's right, you didn't," said Morgan. "I wanted to get back to
you on the ideas you had on the debates—and how to proceed. I
missed you the day you left."

"I saw Governor Green, Fred. Ran into him with our stringer out
there in the State House." It was all Wells could think to say. He
blurted it out in the fear Morgan's next words might have been that
he had decided against making any approach to Green. Wells
couldn't take the chance.

"Oh?" Morgan's tone was noncommittal. "How did it go? Did
you make any nickels?"

"I got everything we wanted, Fred, and more," Wells stated.
"Green will publicly retract his endorsement of the free-time grab
as soon as we counter-propose the debates. He will endorse the
networks' control of the programs in a debate format, and also the
voluntary, instead of compulsory, contribution of the time. When
we drop the debate bomb in the hearings, Green will back it and
also try to deliver the National Committee. He sees no reason why
they shouldn't go all out."

"You asked for the National Committee support?"

"I don't remember. No, I think he volunteered it, inasmuch as
his party would benefit by debate. Green implied Conger would be
better known than any candidate his party could offer, including
himself."

"Sounds great. You're in, Lou."

Wells relaxed slightly. So far so good. "I wasn't in all the time.
Green was about to back out of the whole thing. Didn't think we

could deliver the debates in the fall. Wasn't interested in my deal at all unless we could guarantee it."

Wells then described the "propaganda blitz" idea he had sprung on Green. Wells outlined it beautifully, telling Morgan he had worked on it day and night the week prior to the Green meeting. Morgan frowned when Wells mentioned all three networks had to co-operate, for that meant meetings with the other two; but he didn't seem upset. He would accept, Wells hoped, his personal involvement so far.

"I agree with you on the propaganda approach," Morgan began slowly. "Furthermore, I believe it will work if Global and Telenet get behind the blitz with us. I may have a sticky moment or two, but they'll go along."

"The only way I got Green to sit still and listen to me, Fred, was in a *very* sticky moment," said Wells. He swallowed hard a couple of times, leaned over, cleared his throat as he looked at the tips of his shoes on the carpeted flooring. He touched the convenience strap hanging by the door and absently batted it forward with his fingers.

"What was so sticky?" Morgan asked.

"I had to go farther than I wanted to." He had started. It was out. Now he could say the rest, thought Wells. "I had to promise Green North American would favor him at the convention." There was a moment of silence.

"Did you carry it past the convention in any way?"

"No, not that I remember. No, I'm positive I didn't. It came out. It was something I'd had in the back of my mind. If things got tough, if I saw I was losing the debate thing for NA, I made up—"

"Losing it for NA or for yourself?" There was a long pause. Only the hiss of the circulating air was audible above the low hum of the tires on the road.

"For myself, I guess." Christ, Morgan's giving me the business, thought Wells. Can't he shut up and let me get to the Cabinet idea? "And then Green came out," Wells rushed on, "and offered you a new post in his Cabinet if he's elected. He's going to initiate a Secretary of Communications."

"Hmmm," muttered Morgan. He stared at his fingernails, which were not clean, and then unconsciously rubbed his palms together.

"Governor Green has played you for a pigeon." It's all over, thought Wells. "But a rare pigeon. I might even say a championship pigeon." Wells still didn't know which way it was going to fall. "Lou, when a man is in business he must expect that, once in his life, he will have to compromise his ideals. Or perish. You did what we all do to survive. You let a business crisis chip away at your integrity. Unless you come to grips with yourself on that, you will be a very unhappy tiger in the jungle. I think you picked an excellent moment in your life for your compromise."

"It was all I could do," said Wells lamely.

"No, it wasn't. There were many other things you could have done. But you did what you did; you sold North American News to Green for something he wanted. I'll buy it. You made a good deal."

Wells could hardly believe it—the total power at North American, Fred H. Morgan, had approved his breach of ethics. "Thank you, Fred. I wanted you to say that—badly." And this, thought Wells, is how a scrupulously honest executive embraces his first distortion of moral values. I have pleased my boss.

Wells then explained that Green wanted Fred to call him as soon as possible. He had seen the documentary on the Postal Department, and thought Morgan was the best man in the country for the new secretariat.

"It doesn't make a damn bit of difference what Green thinks. We've made one guy jump through the hoop, and we'll get Conger when we want him," said Morgan. "I don't care who gets the nomination. We've got Green to back us publicly against the free time and for the debates. Of course, it would be nice if he gets the nomination. It would sort of round out the whole thing, wouldn't it? But goddammit, Lou, be careful with Green at the convention.

He's got you, me, and North American on the hook. One jerk, and that barb's going to go right through to bone."

Morgan then briefed Wells on his approach for bringing Telenet and Global into the scheme. "I'll work between Washington and New York, Lou," he said. "I'll want to get together with the chief officers of Telenet and Global as soon as possible. You call Finnegan and Paul Fenton. Tell them I want to discuss plans for the hearings. Get me some immediate appointments."

"Theres no use wiring them in on the Green deal or the Cabinet possibility, is there, Fred?"

"My God, no!" Morgan shouted. "But they must be briefed immediately on the plan to propose the debates in the hearings."

"It seems to me that, almost as important, is their pledge to pull out all the stops on the publicity, programming, and propaganda blitz," added Wells.

Morgan nodded his agreement. "When I get to the Carlton, I'll place a call to Governor Green and tell him I'll seriously consider the Cabinet offer. Anything I should be aware of when I'm talking to him?"

"Just this. He knows as much about our business as we do. He's a very sharp cookie."

Morgan grunted, fishing in his pocket for a nail file. He cleaned his nails as he continued. "You don't know this, but Alfie Hill called me at breakfast this morning to tell me H-and-F Advertising is going to yank their billings off TV and put the dollars in other media. That ought to make my job with Finnegan and Fenton a pushover. We plan to lose twenty million in sales. Telenet and Global will also have big revenue losses." Morgan paused as he brushed his trousers of fingernail filings. "We're in this too deep to be the spokesman for the industry at the hearings—about the debates, I mean. I'm going to talk Fenton into doing it. Global's a little cleaner than we. Fenton's a big ham at hearings anyway. His ego will eat it up."

"Good idea," said Wells. "The more we can implicate the other two in the whole plan and integrate them into every phase of it, the more solid our joint stand will be if anything happens."

"I wish the man we were going to sandbag wasn't as tough and experienced a monkey as Andrew Conger," said Morgan. "Does it still look like he'll get the nod hands down?" he asked, turning to Wells.

"No question about it. He'll be the reluctant dragon."

"We better give him a wide berth between now and when we hit the hearings with the debate proposal," said Morgan. "I'll want you to expedite the shirtsleeve stuff with the news heads of the other departments. I'll advise you when I've got it set. Well, here we are. Grab that brief case."

"Right. I want to get the p.m. dailies. I'll meet you at the gate. It's Flight Forty-six."

"This is going to be some adventure you've come up with, Lou—some adventure!"

4

The Decision

"Daddy," said Betsy to Charles Dale, "will you play a game of cribbage with me? Now?"

"There isn't time, Betts," answered Dale, looking at his watch. "Throw me a couple of pretzels. And pass your mother the Fritos."

"My, what I couldn't do to improve this recreation room!" said Janet. "When do you think I should start on it, dear?" she asked, turning to Dale.

"Maybe in the fall," he said. "We won't be down here much this summer." Raising his voice, he said, "Lisa, honey, do me a favor. Turn the TV on Channel Five." To Janet, he said, "Now the kids can stay down here, but dammit, I want them quiet. I have a feeling old Fred Morgan's going to blow the lid off this debate build-up tonight."

"How long is the speech?" asked Janet, alert to the excitement in his voice.

"Half-hour," Dale replied. "We can eat at seven-thirty."

"Why can't we watch 'Monster Movie' at seven, Daddy?" asked Betsy. "Can't you and Mommy watch that silly old speech up in your bedroom?"

"Don't speak to your father that way," Janet scolded. "He's had a hard week. It's Saturday night, and we want to use this room. So either be quiet, or go upstairs."

"Okay," said Betsy, pouting. "I'll be quiet."

"I tell you, Jan," said Dale, "this thing is building up all out of proportion back in Washington and in New York. I've been watching it like a hawk. They're going to sandbag Andy Conger surer'n hell. You watch them use this telecast from the Broadcasters Confederation Convention to hammer home the debate theme."

"What debate theme?" asked Janet. "Lisa, turn down that volume. Down . . . more. We'll tell you when to turn it up."

"When?" asked Lisa.

"I said we'll tell you. It will be when the program changes at seven o'clock. Thank you, that's fine. Don't sit so close."

"If I don't sit close, I can't hear it," said Lisa.

"Okay, so sit close," said Dale. "Well, the networks have been working up on the Hill, in committee, to get a free time bill for political television killed," Dale explained to Janet. "The greedy bastards. They won't even give up twelve hours every four years to the two parties. Anyway, some happy idiot came up with the idea of having the two presidential candidates debate face to face on TV. So, Paul Fenton, President of Global TV, makes the announcement in a hearing. The joint explodes. The networks crank up a hell of a propaganda campaign for the public. That's why all these public affairs shows on the meaning behind the Lincoln-Douglas debates and all that crap have been on the air. They've also been loading their newscasts night after night with every nit-picking item they can get by with about the debates."

"Why not?" asked Janet. "They sound like a great idea."

"They are," said Dale. "For TV, and for one of the candidates. The one least known, the one who will be behind, who will need the exposure if and when the debates are held. I do not think the man helped by them will be Andy Conger, because the other guys don't have a candidate even on the horizon as nationally famous, as well known as Andy Conger. So, Conger gets hurt by the debates, right?" Janet nodded. "So this Governor Joe Green, he's got everything to win by debate, right?" Janet nodded again, a little less vigorously. "So Green has come out strong for them. He started about ten days ago. Day after day statements are coming out of his headquarters and his National Committee, even though he isn't the candidate yet. But who the hell else do they have—Homer Pender?" Dale chuckled. "Even Pender's bellowing around in that stupid Tennessee gibberish of his, saying how great the debates will be for the country. And what has Andy Conger said, pray tell?"

"What?" asked Janet.

"Not a goddam thing," said Dale, smiling. "In almost two weeks. Not one damn word."

"What should he be saying?" Janet asked.

"Not a goddam thing," Dale repeated. "There's nothing to say. They're trapping him, japping him into a box, a corner, so that he'll have to accept the debates even though he knows it'll help the other guy, no matter who he is, and hurt him. Boy, I feel sorry for old Trapper Conger tonight. You watch this speech. The networks will use this half-hour to do everything short of daring Conger to accept their challenge. Their current propaganda line is almost one of shaming Conger into it."

"The program changed," shouted Lisa. "Can I turn it up now?"

"Yes. Thanks, hon," said Dale.

"What happened to the free time bill, Charles?" asked Janet, wanting to be fair, trying to be interested.

"Oh, they killed it the minute they smelled the number of free hours and the enormous audience they'd get with the debates. Both parties will benefit, although Conger's National Committee, outside of a few platitudinous squeaks, has been almost as silent as Conger."

Dale rose and walked to the set. He adjusted it for contrast and brightness and walked toward the small bar to mix another old-fashioned. "Want another martini, Jan? We may have a wild half-hour ahead of us. You might need it with these characters speaking on the tube tonight, representing the grand and glorious leadership of the money-mad, hypocritical television industry!"

"Yes, I think I will need it," said Janet. "Make it on the rocks this time. Who's that?" she asked, pointing at the tube. "I know him."

"My God," said Dale, "that's Lou Wells, President of the News Division of North American. What the hell is he doing sitting up on the dais so close to the lectern?"

"Didn't we go out with him one night in Nassau a few years ago?" Janet asked.

"We sure did. He was in the party. I didn't spend much time with him though," said Dale. "If I've got this figured out correctly, they'll let Morgan welcome the idiots to Washington because NA is under the most fire on the quiz scandals. You know why the Broadcasters' Convention is meeting there this year, don't you?" Dale asked, stirring the bitters in his bourbon.

"Probably because it's an election year," said Betsy. "For President."

"You're absolutely right, Betts," said her father. "They go to Washington every presidential election year because there are so many congressmen and senators who own TV stations. These holier-than-thou guys get up on the floor of both houses, yell and scream about how terrible television is, and then turn around and tell their station managers to buy all the violence, blood, and guts they can get their hands on. They make me sick! I know a network president in New York who has an assistant in Washington who does nothing but keep a confidential list up to date—right to the week, mind you—of every congressman and senator who owns any part of a television or radio station. He can predict within one or two votes how the House or Senate will vote on any legislation involving broadcasting or regulation of the air waves. Don't get me started on that!" Dale walked to Janet and placed the martini in her out-stretched hand, then shifted his chair squarely in front of the TV. "Yup, by God, there goes Honest Fred Morgan . . . up to the lectern. The other reason they hold so many of their conventions in Washington is that it turns every broadcaster attending into a lobby-ist. And they all go around hugging and kissing the congressmen and senators who own stations. Oh, it's a great love feast down there."

Morgan made a brief introduction to Wells, which was followed by reasonable reaction from the audience in attendance.

"Lou Wells! I can't believe it," said Dale. "There he goes up to the lectern. My God, what a build-up they're giving him. He must be the real fair-haired boy at NA, in the whole industry, these days. As a matter of fact, Jan, I bet it was Wells who dreamed up the de-bate idea." Dale raised his voice, talking to Wells's image on the tube. "Hi, Lou, you old bastard. Let's meet at the Junkanoo in an hour. Okay? We'll listen to a little Peanuts Taylor."

"My," said Janet, "would I love to be there right now. I need it after this move."

"Where, Mom?" asked Lisa.

"Nassau, lovie," said Janet. "Bahama Mahn—that's for me."

"Down, girl, down," said Dale. "Louis Wells, the pride of NA, is about to speak. We mustn't miss a word!"

Wells barely mentioned the recent scandals, what broadcasting had done, or was doing, to combat them. In a matter of minutes he was into the debates and the great opportunity this presented to broadcasters to use to their utmost television's great powers of communication and understanding. Wells went on to articulate the purity of the debate idea. He said, "The debates will remove, once and for all, showmanship and sloganry from the sober process of selecting a national leader. The debates will place the presidential campaign on a plane higher than that ever achieved before. They will elevate the dignity and purpose of a national presidential elec-tion to new heights." At a point later in his remarks, Wells stated, "The television camera has powers which permit it to see beyond the professional façade of the political charlatan of the past. Such a person cannot survive the piercing, probing close-up inspection of the modern television camera."

Wells wound up his speech with all the drama he could muster, which, Dale thought, wasn't too much visually—but would make good reading next morning in the Sunday papers across the country. Wells said, "The American voter will see by face-to-face debate for the first time, will be able to compare instantly, the faces, thoughts, concerns, and leadership qualities of the two presidential candidates. The whistle-stop railroad yard, the airport and town square have been replaced for the purposes of political speech-making by every living room in America equipped with this greatest of all inventions since the printing press—television. Television has returned politics to the front porch. In closing, may I say that one hundred years ago Abraham Lincoln and Stephen Douglas were forced to travel to seven different Congressional districts in order to draw even their largest crowds—fifteen thousand people. But if these presidential debates become a reality, fifty-five million television-set owners in the land will have a front-row seat in the largest audience ever gathered at one time in the history of mankind. The debates will be presented by the broadcasting industry so that the American voter may know better the man behind the candidate and, in exercising his most precious privileges under the Constitution, may more wisely cast his vote by free choice in the privacy of his neighborhood voting booth. A God-given and constitutionally protected right, enhanced in its meaning and individual judgment by the leadership of America's broadcasting industry!

"And so, tonight, your great radio and television industry announces to both political parties and to their presidential candidates who will be selected in a few short weeks that the stage is set. The time has been cleared, the great production studios of television have been reserved in readiness, the cameras are hot and manned." Wells then paused. He removed his glasses slowly and folded the earpieces, his hands low, dead center at his waist.

"I'll bet Gertie Gordon, the NA Dramatic Coach, told him to do that," said Dale. "Right at that point. For emphasis."

"Shhh," said Janet. "I want to hear it."

"We in television—and Americans everywhere—await the only elements missing. The two presidential candidates."

There was a roaring ovation as Wells waved and sat down.

"Wow!" shouted Dale. "What a campaign this is going to be! And it's going to be television's all the way. Oh my, what I'd give to be in on this one!"

"You promised, Daddy," said Betsy. "You promised you wouldn't leave us."

Janet was looking at Dale wordlessly.

"I know, people, I know," he said. "I'll be here—dammit." Janet believed him; and he believed himself.

"Can I switch to Channel Four now?" asked Lisa.

"All right," said Dale. "I guess that's about it, Jan. Keep the volume down, Lisa, *down*," he ordered.

"Sorry, Daddy," answered Lisa, turning the sound lower.

"Well, that was quite a speech," said Janet. "I suppose these debates might be the biggest thing ever to hit television—or politics."

"You're absolutely right—if they come off," said Dale. "What if Conger's the candidate, and what if he refuses to debate his opponent? Then what?"

"After a few more speeches like this one tonight," Janet replied, "how can he refuse?"

"We could take the cut here, Charlie," said Victor Hanson in the screening room, "and then blend with a dissolve into that footage of Bryce Canyon at sunset."

"Could do, could do," said Dale. He was nervous, irritable, but trying to keep his mind on the cutting session in the small viewing theater of The Dale Organization. Word had come through from Washington several days ago that the Department of Interior was cutting back on their film budgets. Initially, feelers had been made as to how far along Dale was in production of the picture, that it might be cheaper to cancel the project. Dale, however, had saved the project and had agreed to pull back considerably on cost. The two men were now viewing "rushes" of footage to see if a large cut could be taken smoothly near the closing sequence.

"Where's the footage on the ranger?" asked Dale. It was a shame, Dale thought, to lose this exquisite color photography. Never had he seen inanimate nature captured so beautifully. His film crew had outdone themselves, and the park ranger they had used to tell a portion of the "Children and Parks" story was a real find. Dale resisted the typical sunset ending and wanted to review a sequence with the ranger to see if it could be re-edited to make a poetic closing—on people and their national parks.

"Isn't there some way we can save that ranger footing, Vic?" asked Dale. "God, against that skyline of mountains, that stuff is sensational. We ought to be able to do an optical there that will give us a gorgeous close."

The light bell blinked under its shield at the mixing console. Dale turned around in his seat and reached for the instrument. "Yeah, Dale here."

"On one, Charlie," said the voice. "Long distance, from Washington."

"Okay," said Dale. Jesus, who was calling now? He thought for a moment he should transfer the call to his office, then said the hell with it. "Put 'em on." He turned to Vic and asked him to kill the audio. "Hello, this is Charles Dale."

"Mr. Dale of The Dale Organization? I can't believe it. You're supposed to be in Washington. Or so Andrew Conger tells me. Hi, Charlie, this is Rufe Little."

Rufus Little was the top man in the Conger candidacy for president, the campaign manager, and head of the staff. "Hi, Rufe, nice to talk to you," said Dale.

"Will you be in Denver tomorrow morning?" asked Little.

"Yeah, sure. What's up?"

"Me. Meet you at nine at my suite at the Brown. Call from the lobby."

"Wait a minute, Rufe. What're you coming out for?"

"Did you see that broadcasters speech on the television Saturday night? The one about the debates during the campaign?"

"Yes, I did," said Dale. "Boy, what a snow job the networks are pulling!"

"That's what we're going to talk about when I get to Denver," said Little. "In the meantime, I'd like you . . ." The line went dead.

"Hello, hello," said Dale. "That damn Rufe Little, he's up to his old tricks."

"What do you mean?" asked Vic as Dale replaced the receiver.

"He cuts himself off on phone conversations. That way, people think he's actually been cut off. It's the way he gets himself out of phone calls. The bastard! I'll kill him for pulling that. Goddammit. I don't want him out here."

Dale picked up the phone again and told the operator where to reach Little in Washington. Little's secretary said he had left his office and was on his way to the airport for Denver. Dale hung up disgustedly.

"I've seen Little do this a hundred times. But never to me. So he knows he'll get a turndown, so he cuts himself off before you get a chance to say a damn thing. Balls." Dale swung his legs down and asked Vic to roll the rest of the footage. His mind, however, was a long way from the family camping facilities at Sequoia National Park.

Dale had convinced himself Washington would blow over. He had received a letter from Conger saying he was sorry Dale couldn't arrange his affairs to come back, and would he reconsider? Dale had written it was impossible. He had then heard from one of the Under Secretaries, a political appointee who was a mutual friend. The latter mentioned that Conger had spoken twice of his desire to have Dale back in Washington for the campaign. Two days after receiving the note Dale heard by phone from the Under Secretary. And again he turned down the idea of coming back. Conger's executive secretary, Ruth Platt, then called Charlie. They were the best of friends. The conversation was cordial, the purpose to let Dale know how much they were going to miss him if he weren't along with The Man this year, and could he reconsider? Once more, Charlie held his ground and said "no." He'd been steadfast through it all. He had predicted the pressure and was prepared when it came.

Rufus Little flying to Denver, however, was something else indeed. Why was he really coming out? Charlie wondered. Must be a money run, he decided.

Dale and Hanson stayed with the screening session until late that evening. They finally found a place to take a huge cut in the script pictorially. It would not be the picture they had started out to produce, but they'd be proud of it, and they hoped Parks would be also. Vic and Dale stopped for a quick drink, and Dale told him he'd be in late the following morning. If he was needed, he'd be with Rufus Little at the Brown Palace.

Janet was sitting in the living room when Dale arrived home. He went to her and kissed her lightly on the cheek.

"I got a call this afternoon, Jan, from Rufus Little in Washington. He's Conger's campaign manager. He's on his way to Denver, may be here now, for all I know. He wants me to have breakfast with him tomorrow at the Brown."

Janet leaned forward to accept the cigarette Dale offered her. Both their hands trembled a little.

"Just passing through?" she asked.

"I don't know. We got cut off. We didn't talk more than thirty seconds. If he's coming out here to con me into coming back, it won't work. I promise you that. I tried to call him back before he left Washington, but couldn't catch him."

Janet was lost in her thoughts. She wondered just how well her husband would be able to withstand the persuasive tactics of such a master politician as Rufus Little. As they went upstairs together a few minutes later, Charles Dale was thinking the same thing.

Dale arrived at the door of Suite 949 at the Brown Palace on time. He rang the buzzer and waited. After a long silence, his hand was halfway to the small knocker at the center of the door when he heard the bolt thrown from the inside. The door opened and there stood Rufus Little in his shirtsleeves, a smile on his face, the morning paper in one hand, a large white napkin in the other.

"Mr. Charles Dale, I presume, of The Dale Organization of Denver?" he said, pulling Dale in by the elbow. "How are you, Charlie? Good to see you."

"Welcome to Denver, Rufe. Been about two years, hasn't it?"

"Has it been that long?" Rufe asked, as he continued to hold Dale's elbow and guide him toward the room service table which was set up in a bay at the far end of the living room of the suite. "Come on, sit right down. I've got eggs for you in the warmer. Sunny-side-up, basted. Is that okay?"

"Fine, Rufe," said Dale. "Anything's okay." Dale sat, and was silent as Little poured coffee in both cups. He drank the orange juice ordered for him and lifted the ice container and put it to one side as Little brought the plate of eggs up from the warmer.

"Watch this plate, Charlie, it's hot," said Rufe, using a napkin as he handled the hot china. "There, my good man, eat and be hearty."

"I tried to reach you after your call Rufe. Dammit, you used that trick of yours—the cut-off. I wanted to tell you, if you were coming out here to talk me into going back, you were wasting your time. So, I hope you have some other reason for being here." Dale dug into his breakfast.

"I do. To get some of your wonderful Denver air after the miserable winter in Washington. And I want to look at your beautiful mountains. They are something, aren't they?" Little said, looking out the large window to the superb unbroken view behind the city. The morning sun, still low in the Eastern sky, lit the foothills dramatically, catching every highlight of the rich rusts and reds of the rock formations here and there among the lush spring-green cover of the earth. Higher up there was haze, reflecting every hue of the rainbow as sunlight struck it from the low angle. Here and there a patch of snow could be seen through a wispy opening.

Dale gazed contentedly, as he did every morning from his own breakfast nook. "That's my view, Rufe. It's one of the reasons we came out here. We love it." Dale looked at Little, who was still facing the mountains. "Come on, Rufe, what's the real reason for the trip?"

"You, young man." Little turned from the window.

"Who else you seeing here? You out here for some McGooney?" Dale asked. It was a private term for Little's political-financing activities.

Little reached behind him to a sideboard and waved a plane ticket at Dale.

"I've got space on the three-o'clock plane back to Washington. I figured you and me'd be all talked out by that time. But I can change that flight to later."

"You won't have to. I'm not going back, Rufe. You can catch an earlier plane if you want to." Little sipped his coffee, eyes averted from Dale. As Little bent over his cup, Dale noticed his hair seemed thinner than two years ago. And more lifeless—a soft, mousy gray.

Dale loved Rufus Little—though he didn't always condone his tactics—with an affection that bridged hundreds of crises and moments of tension and fatigue in many past campaigns. He hated to be blunt with Little, but for once he was being honest to Janet and the children. He would hold the line.

Rufus Little was a controversial figure in national politics and loved every minute of every battle. It wasn't true that Dale hadn't seen him for two years. Dale had watched the panel news programs of the Sunday afternoon intellectual ghetto on TV. Originally, Little had lived in Detroit, where he had been a prominent corporation lawyer to the automobile industry. For the past ten years, however, he had lived in Bethesda outside of Washington. His law firm was well represented with its own offices in Washington, and Little had merely moved into the Washington premises. Dale had no firsthand knowledge of the close bond between Andrew Conger and his campaign manager but knew it was deep and strong. In national politics Rufus Little was the number one target of the press corps.

There was a reason for this. Little never said anything; therefore, the press reveled in "fish" stories and went wild with their "think pieces" on what was behind the enigmatic face, the silence. Many nationally syndicated cartoons caricatured Little as a Sphinx. All this made an event of Little's appearances on television or as a featured speaker at a banquet. Rufe Little knew the pitfalls of overexposure. What he did say was noted.

Dale occasionally wondered if Rufe's physical appearance had anything to do with his retiring attitude toward the public and his fascination for the behind-the-scenes power and manipulation manifestations of a campaign manager's role. Little was that: little. He was lean and hard but not more than five-feet-six. This meager frame supported a head the size of a small watermelon. Usually the face was about as green, for Little, as a matter of fact, hated fresh air, hated exercise. Dale realized Little was merely being kind when he admired the view. It's probably the first clean air he's seen in a year, thought Dale. Rufus Little thrived on all the accoutrements of a campaign manager: no sleep, crises, stale air, closed overcrowded rooms. He was really happy when the air in a hotel suite was thick enough to cut with a broken pledge to a delegation. Little's general outward appearance could be compared to a loosely coiled heap of heavy-duty frayed rope, the type used to moor ocean liners. Whatever physical attitude Little happened to land in upon depositing his sparse body on a sofa, in a plane, or automobile, that was the way Rufus sat until he was ready to change his location. What endeared Little to all who worked with him was his unshakable loyalty to his staff and the humanity of his cardinal premise: always to stand behind his people, backing them up even if they were wrong. To those who did not know him, Little appeared as an enigma, never moving in his chair, sitting over meetings like a statue with only his eyes darting and flickering here and there as he surveyed the scene. And right now, those eyes were looking directly at Dale over the rim of a coffee cup.

"What's the matter, Charlie, can't you keep the working press in line out here? *The Independent* this morning has come out for those damn television debates."

"Yes," said Dale. "I know all about it. I've been following developments closely. I must say they'd be good for television. God knows TV's in one hell of a mess right now."

"How do you think they'd be for Conger?" asked Little.

"Lousy," said Dale. "He'd kill whoever was up against him, but who needs them? Conger certainly doesn't, according to the popularity polls we see out here."

"You're right. Who needs them? Talking to yourself is not a debate, and that's what it'll be for anyone in the other party who accepts this goddam peepshow. Because I won't permit Conger to dignify the proposal with a comment." Little threw the paper to the floor, pushed back his chair, and lit an enormous cigar. Dale remained silent. This was Rufus Little's party, he thought. Let him carry the ball. I'll only put my foot in it if I try and second guess him.

"Want some more coffee, Charlie? Just help yourself."

"Thanks, I'm fine," Dale answered, inhaling deeply on his breakfast cigarette. He looked at his watch; the morning was going.

"What kind of a spell do you have on Conger, Charlie? He doesn't think he can run a campaign without you. I don't know why he thinks you're so important. I honestly don't know why he wants you back there so badly. He wants you, boy. What do you need?"

"Nothing, Rufe," said Dale. "Just a little understanding. I'd love to go back, but it's a terrible time for me to leave Denver. My family has just begun to phase in out here. I've worked myself silly trying to get this little company of mine going, and I just may make it."

"There's such a thing as duty, as obligation."

"I know, but you don't want me back there unless I can come back with a clear conscience. Lord knows, I want to."

"True, but I'm sitting here asking you to join us because Conger has told me not to come back without you." He smiled wryly. "So, how do we work it?"

"Well, you could guarantee me X thousand dollars in film production out of the National Committee. That would give me a backlog during the months I'm away."

"You know I can't do that."

"Yes, I do. That's why I said it." Dale paused and looked at the floor. "I can't leave Denver, Rufe. Not now. There are deep personal reasons behind it as well as my new company—this is the first time in my life I've been able to build equity in something. I can't turn my back on it."

"Can you turn your back on Andy Conger?" Little said the words slowly and softly. "This is the Big One," he continued, thoughtfully tapping ash off his cigar. "If our man wins, you will have been one of the inner circle of people who will have elected the next President of the United States. You sit down then, anywhere in New York, Los Angeles—you name it—in the nicest suite you can find. I'll pay for it. And I'll hire the secretary to take the job offers that will come in from all over the country for you. I'll rent a whole suite at the Huntington in Pasadena if you want me to."

Dale laughed, throwing his head back.

"Rufe, guys in TV don't go to the Huntington. Make it the Beverly Hills Hotel, Cottage Number Three."

"Don't make jokes. I'm serious. How can you sit there and say your career or company will suffer by doing this?"

"I'll go even further, Rufe. I will tell you my career will suffer whether Andy Conger wins or loses. And that's the truth. Perhaps it should work out the way you describe, but it doesn't. The PR guys, the lawyers, all the other people in a campaign, can carry back to their business direct benefits. The television guy carries back nothing but his unmarketable loyalty to the candidate. Which automatically makes him partisan and suspect in our business. Even precludes his obtaining certain jobs."

Little was silent, momentarily. "You know," he said after a pause, "your telegram to Conger—you shouldn't have sent it. It upset him."

"Well, I'm sorry if it did. But I felt why beat around the bush? I said I couldn't join him and gave him the reasons. I wanted to make certain he understood he'd have to get along without me this time."

"Do I have to get along without you too, Charlie?" asked Little. It was a puzzlement to him why Conger had put so much emphasis on Dale. He knew Dale had advised and guided Conger every step of the way through his years in public life. Dale was a master of the craft, but there were others. Perhaps Conger felt he could weather the debates with Dale at his side, someone who was a friend. But if Dale, too, were against them, it would be Little's best defense against Conger's making the wrong decision.

Absently, Dale glanced at a used-car ad on the back page of *The Independent,* lying at his feet on the floor where Little had thrown it. Dale had expected that Little would eventually trap him with the personal side of their long friendship. It was Little's last weapon. For a moment Dale thought he might be able to get Little so angry he'd say the hell with it. But he knew better: in a crisis, iced black coffee ran through Little's veins. Dale was still organizing his thoughts when Little broke the spell.

"Will you come back for me, Charlie, even if you won't come back for Conger?"

"I like Andy Conger very much," said Dale. "I like you, as you know. But this is the wrong year, the wrong time, for me to leave Denver."

There was a knock on the door. Little rose and admitted the waiter who had come for the table. The only sound in the room was the tinkling of ice in the water glasses as he rolled the table out.

Dale moved to the sofa, lit a cigarette, and stared at a garish piece of Conger literature on the coffee table entitled "The Cause for Conger."

Slowly, Dale began his last line of defense. "Look, Rufe, leaving my wife and family at this time has become a big issue in the Dale household. I have promised Janet—and the kids, for that matter— I will not go back on the campaign. There's such a thing as conscience, you know. Or do you?" Dale asked, smiling. "Janet and the kids have been kicked around all over the country because of my career. New York, Hollywood, back to New York. And then the interruptions of the times I've been out with Andy and the President. I tell you with all my heart and soul I'd like to say yes, Rufe. I want to be out with Conger this year. But my responsibility to the family, to myself—my own conscience won't let me say yes. It's become very personal with Janet, and I don't blame her. I can't leave her in the lurch after just moving her out here, away from everything she knew and liked in the East. It's too rough. I sometimes wonder if she wouldn't just tell me to keep right on going if I went away for a long hitch with Andy."

"Would it do any good for me to talk to her?" Little asked quietly.

"God, no!" said Dale. "If she saw you coming in the house, she'd meet you at the door with a meat cleaver!"

Little said nothing, continued leaning against the middle post in the bay window, legs crossed, as he stood watching Dale. To a muscular politician who had forced the deciding vote out of more delegations at more conventions than Dale would ever attend in his life, this was routine. The squeeze, the silent persuader, the point of no return. Charles Dale, television producer of Denver, was getting the treatment, the same pressure many a neophyte convention delegation chairman had felt from Little when the votes or pledges began to waver. And now Dale was under the same strain. He was tempted to bow to Little's pressures, rejoin the "big deal" rat race, the razzle-dazzle, glamour and excitement. But he wasn't going to.

Little, watching Dale, sensed his final conclusion. Charlie Dale, he decided, had made up his mind to stay in Denver, to turn him down. Little dropped his arms to his side, placed his cigar in an ash tray, and sank into the cushion beside Dale. He put his white, transparent hand on Dale's left knee, looking at Dale intently. After a long moment, he slowly shook his head.

"For a boy who's come as far as you have, with the honesty and integrity you have, what's happened to your sense of duty?" Little asked softly.

"Nothing. That's precisely what's keeping me here. My sense of duty."

"No, boy, I mean to the United States of America. I mean to the people of this country who want to live out their lives in peace. What's happened to your sense of duty, of obligation to a principle that is bigger than you, me, your wife Janet, or The Dale Organization?"

"For Christ's sake, Rufe, knock it off," Dale said disgustedly, turning his head toward the window.

Little's hand closed hard on Dale's knee. "No boy, hear me out. Our man Andy Conger puts this country first, above all other considerations. He's truly a dedicated public servant. You know that." Dale nodded. "For that reason," Little continued, "I have a small gnawing fear he may accept these goddam television debates some day when we least expect it. Because he may get around to thinking they're good for the people, for the country. If he does, it could cost him the election. I'm not saying it will, but I'm saying it could." Little removed his hand now that he had Dale's attention. "I am a professional politician, boy. And a professional manager never permits his candidate to place himself in any position of danger, of vulnerability. I don't give a good goddam how fine these debates may be for the country. If they present a danger to my man's chances of walking into the White House in January, I'm against them. Do you hear? Against them. Now . . . I've come out here. I've asked you cold what you think of the debates. You say you think they are bad for Conger. I didn't prompt that out of you: you said it all by yourself. And that's why I want you to come back to Washington. To help me hold the line with Conger against the debates. He listens to you, boy. You know that. If you're agin 'em, he'll think a long hard time before jumping in that cold water. And by keeping my man off those debates, you will be performing a service to the country. For we *do* need Andy in the White House; the country needs him there. The safety of the country is bigger than all of us, Charlie. And you can help guarantee it by prohibiting Conger from exposing himself to a needless danger, a politically unsound encounter with the other man." Little rose, turned halfway toward Dale, and looked down at him. "I don't see where your conscience comes into this at all. Your conscience should be clear as that sky out there. Come back for me, boy. Come back. You know you want to. I'm telling you it's vital—bigger than all of us. Come back."

Dale sat motionless, drumming the fingers of his right hand nervously on his thigh, his left hand in repose in his lap. He looked neither up nor down, neither right nor left. He was in a peculiar emotional daze, experiencing a strange, overwhelming mixture of feelings. He had heard every word Little said. They had found their ready mark. And it wasn't only talk. There was truth in it. Little *was* worried about Conger's sense of public responsibility to the people, and he sincerely wanted and needed Dale in Washington to help him hold the line with his candidate.

Standing quietly, Rufus Little now observed the fruits of his labor. It had been Dale's own admission of the weight of his conscience which had given Little the notion to use the argument of "duty to your country."

The room was silent except for the raspy, asthmatic rattle from deep in Little's throat. Neither man moved. Finally, Dale looked up, a half-smile on his lips.

"I'll go, Rufe," he said. "Goddam it, I'll go." In Dale's mind, at that moment, his conscience was clear.

"Good boy!" exclaimed Little. "Do you want to call your wife from here?"

"No, right now I don't want to talk to anybody," Dale said.

"This is going to make our man very happy. You made the right decision." Little shook Dale's hand firmly.

"Balls," said Dale. "I'm doing it for you. And, I guess, for myself." God, thought Dale, how would he tell Janet? How could he explain it? What was loyalty, responsibility, obligation? Loyalty to whom? Janet or Conger? Or Rufus Little, or himself?

"If you're doing it for me, you have my deep thanks, Charlie," said Rufe. "I'm going to rely on you heavily—with Conger and his television programs and with the advertising fellows in New York. Josh Holden will be running that show again."

"Good," said Dale. "He's the best. What about the convention? It's in Chicago, isn't it?"

"They're both there. At the stockyards. We did it to accommodate the networks. They came down and made a strong pitch to hold them in the same city. We go two weeks after the other man has been selected." Dale smiled to himself. "The other man" was Little's standard description of a political opponent. He couldn't bring himself, even in informal conversation, to mention the name of an opponent or his party at any time during a campaign. Dale made notes regarding Little's comments on a small piece of folded paper he habitually carried with him. "And when we start that first day," added Little, "one of your jobs is to see that the Hall is fumigated—visually—for television. We don't want one damn thing on TV to look like the sideshow those carpetbaggers are going to put on ahead of us."

"What have I got to do with that?" asked Charlie.

"Everything," said Rufus. "The Committee doesn't want to ask you to assume the supervision of it because you're a Conger man. Otherwise, you would have heard from the Chairman directly. He needs you, and wants you. But he's afraid to place you too close to the Committee before Conger is the man. Don't worry. We'll get him nominated. But in the meantime Conger's going to loan you to the Committee whenever there's need to help them with the convention."

"What's been done so far?" asked Dale.

"It's an unholy mess," said Little. "Nothing is co-ordinated, no one is really in charge. A couple of greeting card manufacturers from New Hampshire are running it in Washington now. Nice boys, but no experience. And no one at the Committee, not one single person, can tell you where they stand today on any of their arrangements."

"Perfectly normal. Who's going to produce it?" asked Dale.

"You," said Little.

"Now wait a minute," said Dale, his voice rising. "That would be very bad."

"I know," said Little. "Not you, literally. But I want you in on everything. You might even help them select the man to produce it. They've got one of those closed-circuit television companies under contract now—for something."

"What a mess that's going to be. One political party on a carry-out and us on a carry-in, all at the same time. But you know something, Rufe? Somehow our convention will get on, on time, and get off."

"It always does. Or did, I should say, until you TV fellows came along to mess it up." Little referred to a timetable in his pocket and announced there was a through plane in an hour for Washington. He asked Dale to drive him to the airport.

Dale had a final cup of coffee with Little at the airport. They agreed that Dale would report to Washington as soon as possible. And then Rufus Little was gone, as suddenly as he had arrived.

5

To Washington

THE INDECISION was over. Dale felt relieved. Then, the realization of his more immediate concerns momentarily pushed back the thoughts of the challenge, the new experience of the convention, and of a presidential campaign with Conger. He was overcome with apprehension about his personal life: his home, his Janet. Why had he done it to her, to himself? He knew, basically, it was because all along he had wanted to go—even knowing that it was wrong and selfish—and Rufus Little had magically cleared and cleansed his conscience. Dale was so preoccupied as he drove home that he barely made the turn into his street from the main road. The house was brightly lit and inviting as he eased the car into the garage. Betsy came running out of the kitchen in her bathrobe and switched on the breezeway light as her father walked toward her. They kissed and ambled into the house arm in arm.

The children were fed. Janet was stacking the dishes. She had changed into black velvet slacks and a shimmering blue Japanese banker's coat with heavy ornamental frogs and delicate gold embroidery on the shoulders. She moved nervously as she cleared away the last of the knives and forks and spoons. Her actions seemed too quick, too studied. Poor worried Janet, thought Dale. The sooner we get this over, the better.

Dale went upstairs and changed into slacks and a sport shirt. When he came down, Janet had mixed him a bourbon and bitters. She handed it to him as he approached her on the couch in the living room. He sat down and kissed her lightly on the left temple.

"Well," said Janet cheerfully, "how was Rufe Little? All alive and full of beans?"

"He was fine. Are the kids upstairs for good?"

"Yes. Did he come bearing burnt offerings or candy?"

"Both," said Dale.

"How did he talk you into going back?"

"What do you mean?"

"You're going, aren't you?"

Dale avoided her gaze. "Yes."

"Goddammit," Janet said with fury, "I knew it the minute you walked in the house."

"How?"

"For Christ's sake, I've been married to you for twelve years, haven't I? Why, Charlie, *why* did you do it?" Janet turned from him. Dale rose and paced in front of her.

He made an effort to trace through the conversation with Little. It didn't go well. Having difficulty with his memory, he said at one point, "I don't know. I can't quite remember what happened then. But, anyway, at about that time I told him I just couldn't go back because my conscience wouldn't permit it. That's when he started talking about how could I have a troubled conscience when Andy needed me so badly, when Rufe needed me, and how important it was to the country to have Andy in the White House, and how I had to protect Conger from the debates . . . and how much Conger trusts me."

"You! Protect somebody from something? Somebody trust you? That's a laugh! You can't even protect yourself from yourself!"

"Jan, please don't get so worked up," Dale said quietly. "We're in this thing. Now let's work it out. I'm sorry."

"I'm glad you are. And I'm sorry too, Charles. Sorry you fell for that junk Rufe Little threw your way. What a sucker! Jesus, I never thought you were this easy a pushover. You were snowed, conned, by an expert. And you fell for it—hook, line, and sinker."

"You don't know what you're saying or what he said. You weren't there."

"But I've heard enough from you, if what you say is true, to know Rufus Little played you for easy sucker bait. When he couldn't figure any other way to get you, he told you it was bigger than all of us. Old Glory waving from the highest mountain and all that crap— right? Didn't he?"

"If it makes you feel any better to think so, fine."

"Of *course* that's what he did. Jesus! What a sap you were." Janet spat out the words. She was fuming with anger. Nervously, she lit a cigarette. Neither spoke. It was Janet who broke the silence. "So here I am, two thousand miles from home and anything I know. Dumped in this goddam cowtown, and once more my wayward husband is leaving me. You know what you're like, Charles? A twelve-year-old boy who runs away to follow the circus. The spangles, the lights. Life is just too dull for him at home. So he follows the rainbow."

"A twelve-year-old boy." Dale laughed ruefully. "There's some truth in what you're saying."

"Well, at least you're honest enough to admit it. I've got half a mind to say to hell with the whole thing, grab the kids, and take the next plane back to New York."

Dale's head came up with a snap. "Now wait a minute," he said. "Let's not get silly around here."

"Who's being silly?" Janet replied. "How can I count on you, ever? Ever? Being where I need you, where we need you? You can't be trusted any more. I can't make plans which include you. I might as well start having a good time myself, and learn to plan a life without you."

"Don't say that, Jan. I love you." Dale looked at her, suddenly consumed with emotion.

"I'm not sure I do you. Goddammit, you make me mad. Well, I should have been prepared for this. You ran true to form. Christ, I guess Dad is right. You're nothing but an immature kid who likes to have me around when he needs me—which is not often. When it's convenient and fits his plans."

"Now look, dammit. There's a lot to do out here. You're not going anywhere!" shouted Dale. "You're going to stay here, be a good mother to our kids, and enjoy a damn good summer in Denver."

"The hell I am!" Janet shouted indignantly. Then she smiled. "You know? Maybe I will. Maybe this is as good a place as any to learn not to count on you, learn to live a life by myself. Actually, I think I could get to like it out here. If I weren't always faced with the fear you'd be leaving again, for indefinite lengths of time and undisclosed places. If I could learn to plan just for myself." Janet looked impersonally at her husband. "What happens to that bank loan and my collateral? How are you going to keep the company going?"

"I've had several talks with Vic, starting a few weeks ago. We had a long session this afternoon. He'll mind the store while I'm gone. I think he'll do a good job."

"I wouldn't be so sure of that," Janet snapped. "I told you, when you made the decision to bring him on, I had my doubts about him, and I still do. I wonder if he really left Hollywood because of the chance you gave him, or because he had played out almost every string he had in his bow out there?"

"He's a damn good man, Janet. I had a hell of a time convincing him to come with me."

"That's what you think. You're not the judge of personal character you think you are. I can tell you this: I don't like the idea of leaving my money in Victor Hanson's hands."

"Well, you're going to, sort of," said Dale. "My God, Jan, I'll be on the phone with him all the time. We've got enough production orders in the shop right now to tide us over until I get back. We may have to pull back on overhead to ride it through, that's all. The one thing which will suffer is new business. Sales."

"Who's going to keep the bank happy about your leaving?"

"I will," said Dale, irritated. "If you're so damn worried about Vic and your collateral, why don't you spend a day or so at the office? I've asked you to do this before. I could show you a couple of very simple records we keep, and with Mary helping you, you could be a great help to me while I'm gone."

"Oh no you don't," said Janet. "This is your cookie, kiddo. I didn't marry you to work as an accountant, and don't think I'm going to bail you out of this one. This is your tea party all the way, little boy. Your business is your business—not mine."

"Goddammit, you make me mad when you talk like that," said Dale, his jaw tight.

"I can't say I'm undulating with happiness myself right now." Janet crushed out her cigarette in the crystal ash tray. "No sir-ee, if I stay here, I'm going to get a bridge club going. And you, dear fellow, are going to get me a ninety-day guest card to the Lakeside Country Club, by hook or by crook—but mostly by Andy Conger. Tell him to call Don Corning and some of his other buddies. They all belong. And I'll tell you something else. You might as well reserve my suite in Chicago for the convention right now. It may just tide me over. I've got a lot of friends from Finch on the North Shore, and I just may come up there and have a real ball—at your expense. So there."

"That'll be fine, Jan." Inwardly, he was relieved. At least she wasn't going to walk out on him that night! "We can talk about it later, but you know I won't have much time free to be with you. I'll be awfully busy about then. And I'll be out at the stockyards night and day, in the Hall."

"Who cares?" Janet laughed. "I'm not planning to see *you* up there. I'm not planning to see you ever again. I can't. Haven't you been listening to me? I'm learning how to live alone—and like it!" She laughed. "What's more I'd rather have a dull time in Chicago than in Denver. But, kiddo, it won't be dull. I've got friends up there who appreciate me."

Dale was silent. Then he said, "Look, I'm sorry this thing has happened. I'm sorry you've become so worked up about it. It might do us both good if we had a nightcap. Sort of calm us down. I had to do this thing, Jan, and I'm sorry you've taken it this way. What do you want—scotch or bourbon?"

"You have whatever you want, dear boy. I'm going to bed." Janet rose and swiftly left the room.

"Jan," Dale called after her, "Jan, don't be silly. C'mon, let's be civilized about this thing." He raised his voice. "Jan!" he called.

He heard the door to their bedroom slam shut. He winced at the sound and set his jaw, lips compressed. Then he faced the foot of the stairs.

"Shit!" he yelled. "Shit, do you hear? Goddammit! The hell with you!"

No sound came from the second floor. All was silence. Thank God, he thought, the kids were asleep. I forgot. I lost my temper. "Shit," he said again, almost as a whisper, to no one.

Rising from the couch, Dale walked into the kitchen. He went to the liquor closet, removed a scotch bottle, and poured himself a long straight tumblerful.

All the way down it felt good. "Shit!" he said. "What a goddam mess!"

On the evening Charles Dale left for Washington, he was able to talk Janet into having dinner with him alone. It wasn't easy. Their relationship had become more distant, if anything, as his departure drew nearer. Dale spent long hours at the office in preparation for the seven months he would be absent. When at home, he devoted as much time as possible to the children.

The family gathered around the car as Dale threw in the last few personal things he would carry outside his bags. He drew each child aside and had his own private good-by. Betsy would baby-sit, since the plane left early, and Janet would be home by nine. All three children stood in the driveway and waved. Charlie Junior ran after the car, tripped, and fell. In the rearview mirror, Dale saw Lisa pick him up and brush him off. Charlie Junior struggled to get out of her arms and follow the car.

Once inside the steak house, it was a silent meal. Everything had already been said days before. Their emotions were exhausted, spent from the tension. Dale wondered how many men joining Andrew Conger were leaving their wives under similar circumstances. Damn few, he thought. Janet seemed outwardly gay. She was careful to restrict her few comments to impersonal things.

Dale, fishing for conversation, said, "Don't forget. You can use Mary at the office whenever you need to." He knew, however, if merely to prove her point, Janet would never avail herself of Mary's help.

There was nothing intimate or tender in their farewell at the departure gate at the airport. He held Janet loosely for a moment and felt a slight tremor go through her body.

"What's the matter? Cold?" he asked.

"Yes. Well, no. I'm fine." Janet kissed his chin, then looked into his eyes searchingly. "You're a bastard, Charles Dale. Will you write?"

"Of course I will, silly. You're my wife."

"Don't be so sure. You've disappointed me terribly. The hurt goes deep."

"Good-by, Janet." His lips delicately swept her hair.

And then he was gone—out onto the apron and walking toward the plane. Janet watched his back, stiff and erect as he mounted the steps.

Charlie Dale did not turn around to wave as he ducked at the plane's entrance hatch and disappeared inside.

That damn fool, Janet said to herself. Or am I the damn fool?

She turned and walked through the waiting room.

6

Welcome to Panic City

WALKING INTO Suite 800 at the Honeyworth Hotel in Washington that mid-May morning, Charlie Dale felt both sad and lonely. A bit apprehensive, too. The suite was Rufus Little's nerve center for the operation of the Conger bid for the nomination. In the main room were four girls, each one handling four phones, all light buttons across the bottom lit and blinking. Several "Fat Cats"—heavy financial contributors to the Conger Cause—were in a huddle at the far end. Dale went over to the nearest desk, which seemed to be a reception area, and introduced himself to the girl seated behind it. She was writing a phone message on a pad, her typewriter had a half-completed memo in it, and huge stacks of mail towered around her desk. In a soft, husky voice, overly theatrical, she said, "Well, we've been waiting for you a long time. My name is Barbara Beatty. Rufus Little has asked me to take care of you until you find your own girl. Welcome to Panic City." She smiled and rose from her chair to escort Dale to an office which had been prepared for him. Once in the small room, Barbara excused herself to retrieve notes of commitments which required Dale's immediate attention.

Dale walked down the hall to Little's office. It looked like a "boiler room" operation, the stock manipulator's home base. Side by side, twelve phones lined the edges of his desk. His secretary Maude Olson was talking to a visiting politician from Iowa, and Dale was introduced. Two Rufe Little contact men for convention delegations were seated on the couch, and as usual, Little himself was talking softly into the phone. Maude kept feeding him calls, none lasting more than thirty seconds. Dale smiled as he watched Rufe cut off one caller after another when he had received the information he wanted. In between the calls, Little welcomed him to Washington and advised him of certain meetings he must attend. Dale had that odd feeling of being out of rhythm with the tempo of the group. That sickening stab in the stomach, which comes when everyone else knows what's going on, but you don't, hit him as he listened to the counterpoint of political dialogue. The new man, dumped in the middle of a madhouse. Barbara stuck her head in the doorway. Dale followed her back to his office.

"First of all," said Dale, "I need an apartment. I can't stand this hotel. You know Washington, don't you?" he asked Barbara.

"Very well," she said. "May I call you Charles?"

"Charlie's fine. Could you help me find an apartment? For six months minimum?"

"I'd be happy to. I have a lot of ideas. Do you want to be off by yourself but centrally located in the city?"

"That's right, and just large enough for my needs. No room for visiting firemen. I don't want to use a car. Try and find something that's close enough to walk to our office, wherever that'll be. Do they have any plans in that respect?"

"Yes, but we won't move until after Conger has the nomination —if he gets it." Dale detected a hard political awareness. Barbara had made the comment flatly, without emotion, a pure tipoff that she wasn't a volunteer. There was no zeal here. She had the job because she was registered with the correct party.

"I do hope he makes it," said Barbara. "I love politics, like a lot of people around—the excitement you know—and I need the job. If he doesn't make it in Chicago, I'll be looking again." Dale watched her as she picked up a calendar from his desk and began writing in his commitments, referring constantly to her own notes.

Barbara Beatty was a member of a faceless battalion of similar girls in Washington. Not a division, just a battalion. They had college degrees, as did Barbara. They had a semblance of breeding somewhere in their families, as did Barbara. Somehow, they were working in the Capitol, and they were hooked.

"All right, here goes," said Barbara, looking up from her notes and replacing the calendar on Dale's desk. "You've got lunch with Mr. Louis Wells, a nice man from North American Broadcasting. Mr. Hugh Bole of Transnet has called, must see you. Jack Small, a good tennis player—he works for Global TV in charge of their News—has called. Wants to have breakfast with you tomorrow. *Variety* wants a story on the debates from Conger's point of view. You've a meeting at eleven this morning at the National Committee on convention plans in Chicago. This afternoon, you're supposed to meet with the Women's Division at the National Committee on special television for them in Chicago." Barbara stopped momentarily to hand a packet of phone messages to Dale. "All these messages are about the debates. You'll find stuff in there from twelve newspapers, three magazines, and fifty TV stations. I don't understand it, but the calls started to pour in here middle of last week when it was announced you were coming back. All three networks have called this morning, and insist they see you immediately. Some have complaints about stuff for Conger which Wilbur Jenkins isn't handling correctly, they say. They don't get answers."

"Has Jenkins moved, or is he handling Press from his office at State?"

"Oh, he couldn't do that. Hatch Act, you know. He's down one flight right here. Only handling political stuff now. What am I to tell all these network people?"

"Put them all off. I'll have lunch with Wells. Get me the time and place. You better leave me alone for a while if I have to go to the Committee at eleven. And start looking for a pad for me." Barbara smiled languidly and departed.

Dale looked at his watch and left his office for the National Committee. He wanted to duck debate sessions until he could talk with Little. Christ, thought Dale, Conger isn't even the candidate yet. But he had to start somewhere, and Wells at lunch would be the beginning. The debate concentration had hit him like a tidal wave.

The meeting room at the National Committee was hot, crowded, and musty. Introductions were brief. Dale was advised the entire seating plan for the main floor of the Convention Hall at the stockyards was being held in abeyance because of the impractical and inflexible demands of the television networks. It developed the networks were holding firm on the positioning of their huge central tower in the hall, the giant camera platform directly in front of the speaker's podium.

The intrusion of television on all gatherings involving a live audience was a constant and violent source of abrasion between the television people and the group conducting the meeting. It made little difference whether the affair was an annual stockholders' meeting, a beauty contest, or a political rally. The problem was always the same. Several hundred seats would have to be struck to accommodate the tower or platform, and an additional several hundred persons who were seated in chairs would find this monster in their line of vision to the rostrum—between them and the speaker. Until telephoto lenses for use under artificial light were improved in their characteristics, there was an optimum distance between the speaker and the tower for good television pictures, pictures which would afford TV acceptable closeups of the speaker. Conger's National

Committee, still living in the dark ages of the crystal radio set, had placed this monstrous tower, which also serviced and physically accommodated the news reels and the still photographers, exactly 125 feet out from the speaker's rostrum. Several thousand dollars' worth of construction, ten thousand dollars in addition, for decorating the area to be seen by television, had already been let out in contracts with the tower at this position. All three networks had been yelling for months it was too far away, that this convention would suffer by comparison with the earlier one if the tower were left in that location, but still nothing had been done to improve the situation. Lucas Farmer, Public Relations Director, who also doubled as TV Supervisor, mentioned to Dale in the meeting that the networks were anxious to discuss it with him.

"I have no official position, Luke," said Dale. "I think it would be improper for me to do so. What's there to talk about? The tower must be moved up—closer."

"It can't be," said Congressman Frank Love, Chairman of the National Committee, "unless someone can convince Lincoln Spofford."

"Who is *that?*" asked Dale.

"He's head of the permanent Convention Arrangements Committee. Has been for forty-eight years," said Farmer. "As far as Spofford is concerned, this convention is being held for the people in the hall only, the delegates—not for TV. Three months ago, he had those front cameras in the second balcony, two hundred and eighty feet from the rostrum."

"Good God, I don't believe it," said Dale. "Is this guy a throwback?"

"No, he's a State Chairman in a state we've lost for twenty-four solid years," said Love.

"Heaven help that state," said Dale. "Well, it's got to be changed. How do I reach him?"

"He's home. In Hamilton. Hasn't been to Chicago. Why should he? He's only the Arrangements Chairman," said Farmer.

Love's secretary placed the call to Spofford. From what Dale could gather, everyone had trembled at the thought of approaching Spofford directly. He was still formidable and powerful at eighty-five. He did not own a television set, according to Farmer. Spofford's weak and palsied voice came through the phone to Dale. "Yes, yes, this is Congressman Lincoln Spofford. Speak a little louder."

Dale spoke up, identified himself, and presented the problem. He covered the projected audience figures for television and explained the increase since the 1956 convention.

"Where would you like this tower, young man?" asked Spofford.

"Well, sir, you'd lose two hundred seats, and affect the line of vision of perhaps eight hundred delegates, but we'd like it thirty-five feet in front of the rostrum."

"And where is it now?" Spofford asked weakly.

"It's one hundred and twenty-five feet away from the rostrum, sir," said Dale.

"Move it to thirty-five," said the voice. "First time anyone ever explained it to me."

"Thank you, sir, very much," said Dale.

"I just bought some Global Television stock. Is it a good company, young fellow?" asked Spofford.

"Very good, sir," said Dale.

"Well, it's dropped way down with this scandalous mess I read about in the *Monitor*. So I bought some. It'll go up again. Good-by," said Spofford.

"Thank you again, sir. Good-by."

Chairman Love's secretary, who had monitored the call, couldn't believe her notes. Charlie laughed and rejoined the meeting. "Crisis over," he announced. "Spofford has capitulated. It's moved up—to thirty-five feet." The others applauded.

Dale rushed across town to the restaurant where Lou Wells had reserved a table. Dale was eager to obtain firsthand information from Wells on the debate panic, but was seriously worried as to his own ignorance of the situation. Lou rose quickly when Dale approached the table.

"Charlie Dale? I was sure I knew you. Nassau," he said, smiling warmly. "Nice to see you again."

"How are you, Lou? Sorry I'm late," said Dale. "Janet and I were talking about you and the Bahamas a couple of Saturdays ago." Dale passed up a drink and noticed Wells ordered his second martini.

"Were you?" Wells asked. "Well, they finally got you, eh, Charlie? You may not know it, but you were the most notorious hold-out on the East Coast besides Mickey Mantle." Wells chuckled and went on: "I think you got back here just in time. Any later, and Andrew Conger might have been in a mess so deep he'd never pull out."

"Andrew Conger doesn't get in messes that deep," said Dale, getting back into the swing of the political "sell." "But I agree with you. This place is a madhouse. Nightmare Corners. My phone's been ringing all morning, meetings all over town, the primaries, and on into the night with planning sessions. I haven't time to find a place to live."

"Could we help you, Charlie? Maybe NA has some ideas."

"Anybody can help me. I'll never have time to do it myself at the rate I'll be going this week."

"I don't suppose you've had much chance to talk to Conger about the debates yet, have you?" asked Wells.

"No, I haven't seen him. Won't until tomorrow when he's back from New York." This wasn't true, but was one of the oldest forms of staffsmanship in Washington. It implied he had easy access to the candidate.

"Well, as a TV man, you must be stunned by his lack of co-operation or interest in the debates."

"I'm not stunned by anything Conger does." Dale threw it back at him softly. "I've been with him a long time."

"It's going to get a little sticky if Conger doesn't get out a statement soon. The whole country's screaming for these debates. You can't buck the public's demands forever, you know."

"I haven't heard much screaming in Denver. Oh, one of the A.M. dailies slotted a front-page editorial on how good they'd be for the voters, but I think they did it more because the publisher owns four television stations. There isn't much talk about the debates, or the campaign, or even the conventions out where I've been. Sort of dull, as a matter of fact." Dale wondered if Wells would swallow the line.

"You better open your eyes to what's going on, then, Charlie. These TV debates are the biggest thing to hit New York, Washington, politics, and the country in a hundred years."

"You left out the candidates, Lou. How does it hit them?"

"Well, naturally, we don't know who they'll be, but the invitations are all set to go out. Only the name at the top is missing. If I had to send them today, I'd say Governor Joseph Green and Secretary of State Andrew Conger would be receiving the most exciting invitations in political history."

"You seem to have the feeling these things are actually going to take place," said Dale.

"I certainly do," said Wells. "We've taken the aspect of the historical debate challenge out of them—that I will admit. But everything else is there, every other value, every other element of excitement, conflict, and battle. The public's eating it up. It's a great idea, Charlie. Too big for someone to ignore, too big for someone to decline. It would be political ruin."

"Did it ever occur to you, Lou, that for one of the two men who may debate, it is absolute political ruin? That only one man can win?"

Wells, puzzled, frowned and leaned forward, his elbows at either side of his plate. "I don't understand that reasoning, coming from you. Why, your man is a master of the debate form. He'll kill anyone up against him. Why would he shun debate?"

"I hadn't heard he is."

"Well, we've hit him over and over for a statement, ditto the National Committee. The other guys have come out all the way in favor of them. I simply do not understand why your man can't even say whether or not he likes the idea. Christ, we're out on a hell of a limb. We've got to deliver these things, or the public will tear us to pieces."

"Don't you mean you've got to deliver the candidates?" asked Dale with a bite.

"Well, of course, we've got to have a couple of presidential candidates standing up there, or we won't have a debate."

"You're goddam right you won't," snapped Dale. "Which is just about what I figured you guys were doing. Not knowing anything about it until recently, I've been cautious. But you guys have got everything except a couple of very important stage props, haven't you? The candidates. And, as you say, you aren't leaving this up to either candidate. You don't care whether or not it fits into anyone's campaign plans. All you care about is that it fits into your network plans. Isn't that it, Lou?" Dale had become emotional, angered, in spite of promises to himself it wouldn't happen. He had permitted himself to become involved. He took a deep breath, smiled. "Well, who cares?" he said, backing off from his intense approach. "If there are supposed to be TV debates this year, there will be TV debates."

But Dale hadn't fooled Wells. Lou Wells had engineered the lunch on Dale's first day on the job, assuming TV would be acquiring a friend, an ally in the Conger camp. He foresaw trouble ahead during the entire campaign if some better common ground couldn't be found on which to do business with Charles Dale.

"I'm glad to hear you say that, Charlie. God knows, your and my television industry needs the debates desperately. It's the big chance to bring the public back to television."

"I'll agree with you there, and your own department at North American has been doing wonderful things. It's a shame Madison Avenue doesn't stop worshipping ratings, and think about what people really expect of their television set, what they hope TV will send into their homes."

Wells nodded and decided a quick switch might be revealing. "What would be your recommendation to Conger if he asked you today whether or not these debates were a good idea?"

"That's something between myself and Andrew Conger. You know that, Lou. Right now, today, I may not be up on all the panic and noise about these debates. But don't try to suck me into answering stuff like that." Dale tamped out his cigarette, saying he had to make an afternoon meeting.

Wells called for the check and once again offered to aid in Dale's search for an apartment. He advised Dale he'd send around a brochure which would bring him up to date on the political broadcast hearings and debate reaction thus far in all areas. In a pleasant, offhand manner, he asked, "What's going to happen to your little company in Denver while you're gone, Charlie?"

"Oh, we'll manage somehow. Things may get rough. It is going to be a constant worry. But I've got some good men back there and a reasonable backlog of business. Not enough, but it will keep the doors open, I hope."

"It's called The Dale Organization, isn't it?" Dale nodded. "A couple of my Midwest men know your cameraman. He's supposed to be very good."

"He's the best. Keep your hands off him," Dale replied, smiling. "I don't think he'd move, anyway."

"I promise you. No raiding. I was thinking of something else," said Wells. "Let's go. I've paid up."

And the luncheon was over. Wells had gained nothing, except the knowledge that Charles Dale was not a pushover and couldn't be played for a patsy. He'd hardly expected that to be the case. He was damned, however, if he'd let this newcomer from Denver jeopardize his debates.

The days and weeks in June were a blur to Charlie Dale.

Barbara did her best to screen, sift, and sort the heavy mail and phone traffic regarding the debates. It mounted daily. Dale insisted someone find him a girl as his personal secretary. Again, Barbara volunteered to find the correct person. It was quite a day when she announced an excellent secretary would be in to see him the following morning.

When Dale arrived at his office, it was the usual madhouse. Two networks were simultaneously filming a story about Conger's headquarters and activity before the convention. Cables, lights, technicians, and portable video equipment were strewn everywhere. Little stalked into Dale's office, asking who the hell's idea the filming was anyway, and Dale reminded him he had approved it himself. He was roughing a memo to Conger on network requests for "guest shots" when someone opened his office door.

"This your slave quarters?" a woman asked in a thick Southern drawl.

"Yes, it is. Can I help you?" Dale asked.

"You're goddam right you can. By hiring me," said the woman. "That is, if you're Charles Dale of television." She said the word "television" as if she were describing a crooked bingo parlor.

"I'm Charles Dale. Are you here at Miss Beatty's suggestion? About the secretary's job?"

"That's right, sir. Beauteous Barbara told me you needed a fireball. That's me."

"Come on in," said Dale, unable to believe what he saw.

"Why the goddam hell don't you people put some chairs out so's a body can set whilst they're waitin'?" she asked, hobbling toward Dale's desk, literally dragging an enormously heavy, thick, and filthy leg cast with her. The plaster went from her foot up beyond the hem of her dress.

"What happened to your leg?" asked Dale.

"None of your goddam business. You gimme the job—I might tell you. I might not either."

"When you first meet someone, do you always swear like this?" Dale asked.

"Nope. Just people who look like they've heard it before. Hope I haven't offended you."

"Well," Dale said, and then he stopped. The woman was incredible. "Forget it. What's your name? Here, let me get this chair more comfortable for you."

"I can take care of myself, big boy. I'll do all right. My name's Zella Ferguson. Fergie, they call me. You can call me that too."

"What are you," asked Dale, "some kind of a nut?"

Dale didn't know whether to throw her out right then and there or call a doctor, or perhaps a psychiatrist. Never had he met a woman who came on with such drive, such confidence, such total domination. She was as sure of herself as General Charles De Gaulle. As a matter of fact, she rather looked like the General: thin, lantern-jawed, and just as tall.

Miss Ferguson was from Arkadelphia, Arkansas. She'd been in and out of Washington for twenty years. Evidently, she came to the Capitol immediately after graduation from college. Looking at her over the top of her application form, Dale could hardly believe he was interviewing a college graduate. He decided to test her. "What year did you graduate from Poughkeepsie?" he asked.

"Read the application, stupid—sir, I mean," she said. "It says Smith, not Vassar."

"Oh," said Dale in mock surprise. "Thanks."

"I stayed up there in that cold, miserable Northampton for four years. I'da like to froze to death. Somehow, Smith and most things I do worth while don't rub off on me. Don't stick with me very long."

"How many years have you been a registered member of Conger's party?" Dale questioned.

"Ever since the day back in 1949 when I applied for a job in his office," Fergie replied, smiling. "I guess my Daddy woulda been the only white man in Arkadelphia for Mr. Conger, if he was still alive and kickin'," she added.

Fergie's list of business and character references read like a *Who's Who* of the Senate. She'd been married five times, but allowed as how she was currently between husbands. Fergie thought that was a good reference, as she wouldn't worry about irregular hours. Dale agreed.

Fergie had lived all over the world, and launched into her combat overseas experience as a WAC in the transportation corps. Dale advised her this background had little or nothing to do with politics. Fergie disagreed and continued with an outline of her duty, driving personnel cars on Saipan, half-tracks on Zamboanga, and six-by-six trucks in Japan.

"I scared the hell outta them itty-bitty slant-eyes, sir," she said. "They'd see me blastin' down on 'em like the Wabash Cannonball, dust flyin' everywhere, me yellin' and cursin' the no-goods to get outta my way with their goddam pushcarts, they like to think I was a she-devil from Outer Mongolia." Fergie leaned back in her chair, laughing her head off at the memory. In the middle of an unusually loud "Haw haw," her face twisted in pain. She clutched her cast below the knee with both hands and said, "Jee-suss Kee-rist! That's painful! What the hell you got me laughin' so hard for?" Dale fought back a smile as Fergie's face distorted in anguish. Her next story involved stowing away on a submarine between Pearl Harbor and Guam. The "Flag" at Guam was so stunned they acquitted her of any charges, she said. Dale doubted it.

There wasn't a body buried anywhere in Washington Fergie didn't know about. Every phoney lobbyist in the city was listed and tagged in her book. Across the width of the desk, Fergie tossed a sheaf of further references into Dale's lap.

"Well, buster, you gonna hire me or not? From now on, anything I tell you's a lie. I've run out of the truth." With that, Fergie settled back, fished in her purse for a battered and stained pack of crushed cigarettes, and said nothing. Dale smiled and continued to study the resumé in front of him. Something told him to take a chance on this girl. She was totally incredible, so much so there had to be a fiercely independent, self-starting, self-confident personality and drive behind it all. These were exactly the qualities Dale needed.

"There's one problem here, Fergie. You have little or no background in broadcasting, advertising, or television. You know anything about networks or theatrical production?" he asked.

"I know 'nough 'bout advertisin' to know they sugar-talk you into buyin' stuff you don't want or need. Theater folk are all drunks and queers. So I figure television must be a combination of the two, probably the worst of both. That ain't your regular business, is it?" she asked.

"It is," said Dale seriously, "and I make a good living at it."

"Ooops! Sorry. You're the first person I ever met in television who doesn't look like a queer."

Dale laughed. "Okay, you're hired. Now, take that damn coat off, go into the women's washroom and clean that filthy cast, get back in here, and get crackin'."

And so began a relationship between employer and employee which defied analysis. After three days of hobbling around on her weighty cast, Fergie announced it was slowing her down. She bought a pint of whiskey, drank it during her lunch hour, and smashed the cast to bits with a hammer. The whiskey, Fergie said, deadened the pain of the hammer. She told Dale she never felt a thing. In short order, she organized the office chaos and ran Dale like a fifty-jeweled watch. She screened every human within twenty feet of Dale, every phone call, and editorialized on all strangers before she knew their business, power, or position. It was refreshing, the confidence and what-the-hell attitude Fergie gave the office and everyone around her in an otherwise politically oriented atmosphere. Strong as an ox, expert at all things, Fergie plowed ahead through the political battlefield—carrying on her back an increasingly exhausted and red-eyed Charlie Dale.

The first serious meeting between Dale and Conger set the pattern for all that were to follow.

Dale was late when he was ushered into Andrew Conger's office by Ruth Platt, his executive secretary. It had been over two years since the two men had seen each other outside of a television studio. Dale inspected his man expertly and carefully as he walked briskly to the desk. He decided Conger had changed very little physically: slightly heavier, but that was all. Conger looked up and smiled.

"Nice to have the most important man in the campaign back here with us, Charlie," he said.

"Thanks, sir," said Dale. "I bet you say that to all the guys."

The three laughed.

"I thought for a moment we'd lost him," said Ruth Platt.

"Yes," said Conger, "I had a doubtful moment or two myself. Well, glad it worked out. Thanks, Ruth." It was Ruth's cue to leave the room. "Charlie, I'll be with you in one minute. Make youself comfortable." Conger turned to a memo on his desk.

"I think I'll just look," said Dale, walking toward an enormous pair of African drums resting in a far corner of the cavernous office.

It was true Conger's appearance had changed little since Dale had seen him last. But everything else had changed considerably, and Dale wondered if it were true in Conger's case that a man grew into a job, became the position. For even Conger's clothes were different. His suit was expertly tailored in rich, conservative material, cut with an international, diplomatic flair and feel. He stooped to read the presentation plaque on the drums, indicating they were a gift from a new leader of a neophyte sovereign state in Central Africa. High on the wall above was a magnificent tiger skin, in the middle of which had been woven a brightly colored map of Kenya. In the Jet Age, thought Dale, a Secretary of State covered as much ground in a week as he did twenty years ago in a month. Silver bowls from Austria and Spain, carved ivory masterpieces from Nigeria and Pakistan, magnificent silver-handled scimitars from Turkey, beautiful primitives from the Pacific, Japanese Samurai swords nestling in a red-lacquered tiered rack—all these and more filled the shelves. Autographed pictures of Nehru, MacMillan, Adenauer, De Gaulle, Ben Gurion, and a half-dozen leaders of Latin America looked out at Dale from a portrait gallery section on the wall opposite Conger's desk. In the middle was a plastic-enclosed section of barbed wire from the boundary separating Hungary from Austria, a memento of the Freedom Fighter riots. A superb collection of brilliantly polished historical brass horses, mounted on purple velvet and encased in a shadow box enclosed in glass, commanded a prominent position on the far wall. The inscription on the plaque said it had been presented by the children of Coventry, England. The date indicated the time of Conger's memorable speech there on an anniversary of the first Luftwaffe blitz of the city during World War II. Below the brass horses a beautiful replica of the UN building and auditorium stood under glass on its own brushed, stainless steel pedestal.

It was impossible to stand inside Conger's office without becoming strikingly aware of the shrinking size of the globe and the mandatory travels made necessary by the world's ultimate struggle for survival. Conger's walls, tables, and desks represented but two years as Secretary of State. Yet one got the feeling he had been on intimate terms with every dark, unknown corner of the world. It was as if the globe had become Conger's office, his "sales territory," his backyard. Conger's office gave the impression he knew the peoples of the world and their countries as well as his own "south forty" out in Colorado. I suppose, Dale thought, in pre-UN days, pre-jet days, pre-Cold War days, some pundit, perhaps Will Rogers, would have said Andrew Conger knew the world well enough to pitch horseshoes with the leaders of twenty nations and beat them. Today, however, it was a deadly game of Russian Roulette, played with not twenty but one hundred of the world's leaders. One wrong spin of the cylinder and—annihilation.

As Dale took a chair beside Conger's desk, he noticed a group of plaques indicating the number of miles Conger had flown each year in office. Underneath it, standing up along the baseboard, were three courier dispatch cases with the chains for the courier's wrist and the locks hanging open. Wow, thought Dale, just like the movies.

"Well, that's about got it, Charlie. Quite a room, eh?" said Conger.

"Yes, sir," said Dale. "I'm curious as to where all those phones go." Dale nodded his head toward a bank of differently colored phones on the table behind Conger.

"Well, I don't think it's a security breach to tell you. The red phone goes to the boss, the White House. The blue one to CIA, the green one to the Pentagon. I can't tell you who's at the other end, or where he is in the Pentagon." Conger picked up a small dagger which he used as a letter opener. The handle was minutely scrolled silver, with tiny jewels of every color forming a superb crown at the butt end. The blade was etched in heavy, dark and swirling patterns.

"What's the white phone for?" asked Dale.

"Susan," said Conger, smiling. "Sometimes my trips come unexpectedly, and I use that direct line to my wifely valet. She can pack me in five minutes for a five-month trip. Now about television. And film. I like the idea of this new film approach you wrote me about. Is there anything too complicated about it?"

"No, sir, it's just we've never done it before. It's common practice on TV these days, but you and I have never employed the technique. I thought it would be good to try it out in some of these primaries, and I'm pleased you approve."

Dale lit a cigarette after asking Conger if he objected.

"Charlie, things are going to be a lot different this time. Even from 1956," said Conger. "Of course, I wasn't a candidate then, but we did a lot of traveling and did a lot of TV. We were on three times with the top man, weren't we?"

"Yes, sir. A lot of people still think he would have lost without your appearances with him. I'm not in total agreement with that." Conger frowned slightly. Jesus, thought Dale, can't you talk honestly with this guy any more? "To knock the opposition out of the White House takes a pretty powerful man. I think you two complemented each other beautifully. But I do feel it was the team, rather than either one individually."

"Yes. Well, later we found who liked us and who didn't at the UN didn't we?" Conger chuckled as he remembered the battles of the East River. "Now, as to this campaign, I am told you are already on top of the convention."

"Yes, sir. Well, almost. I've been out to Chicago and suggested several important changes."

"Of course, this is all unofficial. It's merely that the Committee wants you personally to aid them, and you are working in my behalf here. So we must be a little careful with the press on that one."

"I don't think we'll have any trouble, Andy. They're good friends of mine." Dale threw it out, the "Andy." It's what he had always called him, up to and through the years at the UN. Conger's move to Washington, the stature of Secretary of State, the aura of presidential possibility, all had contributed to inhibit Dale considerably. He knew he had to break through the formality, the chill, of Conger's status and impressive office if he were to have a relationship with Conger worth two cents during the campaign. Nothing could come between the two if Dale were to perform his function properly. It wasn't as if Dale had never called him Andy. He had, for years. But the "sir" had slipped out in the atmosphere of Foggy Bottom, and now it was time to retrieve the easy rapport between them.

Conger smiled, realizing what Dale had done. "Remember Boulder City in 1952, Charlie?"

Dale laughed. It was a private joke between the two of them. Conger himself had brought back the old relationship. "I sure do, Andy. I've thought about it a hundred times."

"So have I." Conger's mood changed abruptly. "We haven't much time, and I want to go over this list with you." The two bent to the task, Conger filling Dale in on several new developments, which he felt Dale should be aware of, concerning Washington, the convention and the party, to say nothing of the White House. Conger also gave Dale a list of twenty names of men in and out of government.

"That is the manpower I plan to draw on most heavily if it is my administration after Election Day," said Conger. "I want you to memorize that list as soon as possible. Then I want that copy back—by hand—to Ruth Platt. What I want you to do, without these gentlemen realizing it, is to help them with their TV appearances whenever the opportunity presents itself. For instance, at the convention perhaps they can be suggested for suitable interview and panel shows. At any rate, I will use television heavily during the campaign, and if I am President. It is a marvelous tool, and I am comfortable with it. Therefore, I want these men who will have key positions in my administration also to be schooled in the best way to present themselves on television, so that they can be effective in the medium. I won't need any reports from you on it. I may ask you from time to time whom you've been able to cover. Just do it when the right time presents itself."

Dale placed the paper in his pocket, not in his brief case. He was surprised at several of the names he recognized as Conger explained the assignment.

"When we are ready, we'll make the regular long-range proposal to you on the use of television," said Dale. "I'd want to get Rufe Little's okay on anything before discussing it with you."

"Fine. When you're ready, we'll discuss it. Not before. I'd like you to make the convention as good a show for TV as you possibly can. I've seen some projected audience figures which are amazing. The hell with the delegates! Make it right for TV."

"I plan to do just that, Andy."

"I want Rufe Little to include you in several important 'Fat Cat' dinners. These fellows are not very knowledgeable when it comes to the cost of television. The campaign dollars will primarily come from them. I want Little to use you as Exhibit A. You might work up some remarks, say, about five minutes' worth, to use if asked. We've got to spring loose those purse strings, Charlie, or there'll be damn little television."

What a beautiful opener to go into the debates, thought Dale. But he kept quiet, as per Rufe Little's advice.

"As far as the convention is concerned," Conger continued, "have you made damn sure we're not going to look like the other side of the aisle?"

"Yes. It's going to cost a lot of money. The main expense, however, is not the necessary visual re-dressing, but correcting the mistakes already made by the Committee people in Chicago. It was pretty bad when I got into it. It's under control now."

"Good. By the way, you haven't forgotten I don't like drapes, have you?"

"You mean the upstage backing behind you? The velours?"

Conger nodded.

"Do you still feel drapes are bad for you?"

"I'm not as concerned about it as Susan. But, yes, we still feel they're not good for me. So let's not use them this year."

"Fine. There's no problem in Chicago, as we haven't frozen the final dressing of the speakers' area. We wanted to see first what the other guys were going to do. I'll see you have no folds, pleats, or curtains of any kind behind you. Incidentally, Andy, how does the National Committee select the people assigned to these conventions?"

"What do you mean?"

"Well, they have four guys, all brothers, out in Chicago in charge of visual arrangements in the hall. They work with the networks and the closed-circuit boys. I want to go into that with you at a later date, the closed-circuit thing. Well, these brothers in charge of your convention are nice guys. I've met three of them. The other one has never been to Chicago. The guy who is there is president of a mail-order maple sugar company in Vermont. The other day when I was in Chicago, he said he and his family didn't watch TV much. That's not a very difficult trick—he doesn't own a TV."

Conger laughed. "Well, I suppose it's more honorary than anything. If he's into things he shouldn't be, backstop him. Now, my family. I plan to have a small group of the staff out week after next, Saturday night. I'd like you to come, so mark it down. And while you're there, I'd like you to spend some time with Susan. She's changed a bit in the past four years. Perhaps you'll have some suggestions on make-up. I'm also going to see that the boys are there. Jack is eighteen now, and Frank is fourteen. Try and spend some time with them, too. Susan has very definite feelings about their participation in the campaign and at the convention. I will defer completely to her. She'll tell you about it when she feels it's time. She might not say anything to you until after the convention. If I am the candidate—and it's Rufe Little's job to see that I am—we may include the boys in on the night I make my acceptance speech. Perhaps they can go one other night. But you work that out with Susan. What she says goes."

Dale knew this wasn't true. Andy Conger would use the boys as much as he felt they would help the campaign. But it sounded nice. "Very good," he said, "I look forward to seeing Susan again."

"Susan has changed since we did our little campaign in 1956, Charlie. Take a good look at her. All right. Now, you know I plan to use Wilbur Jenkins, my Information Officer here at State, as my Press Secretary all the way through?"

"Yes. Rufe Little advised me of that."

"Fine. Everything you do in TV must be brought to the attention of Jenkins. Keep him advised as to all your activities."

"What about requests for your appearance on existing shows, panel shows, the Sunday Q and A programs?" asked Dale.

"Send me your recommendation, with a carbon to Jenkins. I will buck requests which come in here to Jenkins and have him get in touch with you."

"Couldn't we simplify that by your sending them directly to me? I'll then make a photostat immediately for Jenkins."

"Fine. We'll do it that way." Round One: Winner, Charlie Dale. Loser, Wilbur Jenkins.

Conger swiveled around in his chair until his back was to Dale. He studied a memo on his rear desk and swung around with the paper in his hand.

"Do you know the news fellows at all the networks?"

"Yes, I do."

"Have they approached you about my feelings on the television debates?"

"Yes."

"What do you know about Louis Wells at North American?"

"He's supposed to be an excellent newsman, a top administrator. I had lunch with him recently. He's sharp, knows his job. I think he's ambitious, too." Dale caught himself as he was on the point of describing how hard Wells was pushing for the debates.

"Is he a friend?" In Washington political parlance that meant: "Is Wells on our side?"

"I don't know, Andy. He's very careful about such things. They all are."

"See if you can find out. His boss Fred Morgan has been cordial to me. Wells seems to be spearheading the exploitation on these debates. He's been trying repeatedly to see me. I've turned him down. North American pulled some raw stuff in the recent broadcasting hearings on the Hill. I've been told Wells had something to do with it."

"I heard a few things myself. Of course, I haven't been too close to it either. I've been in and out of Washington on the primaries and in Chicago."

"All that will slow down after the California primaries. That's the last big one."

And then it came from Conger: "You're aware how serious this debate situation is becoming?"

"Yes, I am. I must admit the East Coast seems to be much more concerned and interested in the idea than the people in the Midwest or Denver, for that matter. It's all I hear around Washington or in New York. I spent two days up there at Bones and Ropell Advertising. The way people talk up there you'd think both candidates had been nominated and had already accepted the debates."

Conger nodded his assent, and rocked back and forth in his swivel chair, twirling a pencil. There was a pause before he spoke.

"Goddam communications bastards! That's the trouble with New York. It doesn't reflect the thinking of the rest of the country. Washington's just as bad."

"I agree," said Dale.

"I haven't made up my mind on the invitation from the networks to participate in a television debate, Charlie. Find out what's behind this man Wells's activity."

"I'll try, Andy," said Dale.

Conger continued: "How do you feel about these debates, Charlie? You must have some thoughts on the matter."

I certainly do, thought Dale. But what can I tell this man? After what Little has said to me? How ironical can it get? They're the greatest thing that could ever happen to my profession, probably to me, and I have to recommend against them.

"I've given them a great deal of thought, Andy. I can only say what I honestly feel. They are a wonderful thing for the country. They will give undecided voters the finest insight into the candidates and issues that's ever been possible. But . . . they are very bad for you. Why take the chance? It's an unknown. Don't misunderstand me. You would kill the other man, no matter who. But a presidential debate is untried, unknown. Who can say what might happen? As your television adviser, I must say turn them down, as difficult as it is for me to make that statement."

"Hmmm," mumbled Conger. "Well said. Thanks." The subject was closed. He smiled at Dale. "Seeing you here makes me feel much better about the amount of TV scheduled for the campaign."

"It's good to be back, Andy. Just like old times."

Andrew Conger smiled again.

7

Sandra Nelson

A STRANGE THING happened a few days later. Dale received an excited phone call from Victor Hanson in Denver. "Charlie, remember when I said I wasn't a salesman? Well, guess what's happened? We're doing jobs for all three networks. Got the calls bing, bing, bing—three in a row. Almost fifty thousand dollars' worth of stuff."

Dale did not reply immediately. His mind went back to his lunch with Lou Wells of NA his first day in Washington. Dale vaguely remembered Wells asking him about his company, nothing more. "Who was the first call from, Vic?" asked Dale.

"North American. Some guy in Lou Wells's office. Asked if Lev Allen was free to do some shooting for them. Said they wouldn't accept any other cameraman, but if he could do the job, they'd give us some business."

"That son-of-a-bitch," said Dale.

"Who? What's the matter, Charlie?" asked Vic.

"Nothing that concerns you, Vic. Look, go through with the contracts and bids, but don't send them out. Just hold them. I'll get back to you." Hanson's enthusiasm was deflated, but nevertheless, he agreed to follow Dale's instructions.

The minute he was off the phone, Dale left for Rufus Little's office and laid the proposition bare. It was a damn peculiar coincidence that the business from the three networks started coming in after Dale got back to Washington, and while they were still trying to get an affirmative statement out of Conger on the debates. Dale, however, saw no real reason why he shouldn't accept the business, as long as Little knew it was not a payoff. "It's actually a hell of a trick to play on them, Rufe. They'll think they will be influencing me, but I assure you that is not the case. And, as I said before, we could sure as hell use the money and the business. What do you say?"

"I say no," said Little. It caught Dale by surprise.

"Look, Rufe," said Dale, "I have a stiff bank loan out in Denver. It just may be the bank boys will call at any time. That is, if my cash reserves sink too low. Would you have any objection if I set up a shell corporation in New York and ran the business under a new name?"

"Yes," Little answered. "How would you like to see all this in print some morning in Drew Pearson's column?"

"Don't be ridiculous!"

"I'm not. And it happens. Secondly, I don't want these networks to have you in their pocket in Chicago. I want to be free to use every bit of muscle out there I have. And you are muscle."

"Okay," said Dale disgustedly. "How the hell careful do you have to be?"

"There's an old saying in politics, boy. Never decide to go into the game after the age of two. If you start later than that, already you've done something they can smear you with."

With resignation, Dale called Hanson back later in the day. "Call each network, Vic," he said, "and tell them we're overcommitted.

That we can't take any more new business until after the campaign. Try and keep them on the hook. Keep that door open for me to go to work on 'em when I'm mustered out."

The rest of the afternoon was taken up with an exacting meeting on Chicago arrangements.

"How do you want to bring Conger in? By car, plane, helicopter, train, or boat?" asked Dale.

"How do I know?" said the advance man, Arthur Baldwin. "The man won't make up his mind. What do you think, Ham?"

Baldwin turned to Ham Forrest, a television producer from Hollywood who had come East to work for Dale. The two TV men had been in three campaigns together. The work load had piled up to where Dale had to have help to stay alive. Fergie had actually been the one to get the okay from Rufus Little to bring Forrest on. He would move out to Chicago with Dale and Fergie.

"We don't care how he comes in, do we, Charlie, providing nothing interferes with the parade idea. The networks have agreed to cover the parade from beginning to end, no matter how long it lasts," Forrest said.

Dale looked at Baldwin and Forrest. It would be difficult to find two more dissimilar men. Arthur Baldwin was from St. Louis. He was as conservative a man as they had on the staff, but smart, eager, and possessed of tremendous stamina. Baldwin was without nerves or emotion, and functioned in the most terrifying crisis just as he did when relaxing in his own home. When everyone else had finally succumbed to the panic and terror of the moment—an unmanageable crowd, heckling, the unscheduled delay, or seas of people pouring over the lip of a stage advancing on Conger in a solid mass—Baldwin stood like a rock, speaking calmly into his walkie-talkie, directing the men in charge of the affair. Baldwin was thirty-three years old. And a top man on Conger's staff.

Ham Forrest was sufficiently good-looking to be a Hollywood star, and he knew it. He also knew more about television production in remote locations—halls, auditoriums, planes, trains, and enormous outdoor rallies—than anyone in the country. Forrest was thirty-eight, married to a wealthy girl from San Francisco who was attractive and intelligent. Forrest, however, prided himself on his attraction to women, and swore he had never been away from home a single night without sleeping with someone. Dale believed this, having watched Forrest in operation a hundred times. It was a compulsion with him, a test of his attractiveness or his dominative powers over women—Dale wasn't sure which. If Forrest began to fear early in the evening that he wouldn't find his in-the-hay partner, he became morose, sullen, and extremely bad company. He brightened only after his new conquest was in range, at ground zero.

Actually, there was one time when Forrest failed in his goal. It was during the 1956 campaign and was one of Dale's favorite stories. Dale and he were doing a telecast with the presidential candidate in a small town in South Carolina. Forrest had arrived in the city two days before Dale, and by his attitude Dale knew something was bothering him. Forrest announced that for two nights he had slept alone. He was furious, sullen. In addition to himself, he blamed everyone from the cab drivers to the proprietor of a beauty parlor in the hotel. The last day of their visit, after the network telecast, Dale and Forrest were splitting up—Dale going West and Forrest returning to Washington with the candidate. It was approaching darkness. Only shadows of people could be discerned in the failing light. The motorcade was leaving the curb at the rally hall. As the sirens wailed and police moved out in a flying wedge on their bikes, Dale, standing at the curb and waving good-by, heard Forrest yelling at him over the noise. Dale could just barely make him out—in the still-photographer's open truck, directly behind the wire-service car and the candidate, Forrest was forcing a female photographer down to the wooden floor. The still photographers, animals all, were laughing, screaming, and applauding as Forrest, determined to "score," if he had to do it on the way to the airport in a motorcade in an open truck, subdued his prey. Later, Forrest claimed he was "just stealing a smooch from her."

And now, here in Dale's office were Baldwin and Forrest, two men who would figure heavily in everything in which Dale became involved, through to the final whistle in November.

"Well, it'd be nice to think of something unusual," said Dale. "But what the hell is there? What do you want to do—drop him out over Chicago from a space capsule? Or, we could bring him in by train, dressed as P. T. Barnum."

The three laughed. "Come on, Dale, be serious," said Baldwin. It turned out, in questioning Baldwin, that Conger did not know when or how he would arrive. No one could get an answer. It also appeared his arrival date had been set three times, only to be canceled.

"Look, Art," said Forrest, "you change that date just once more, and the networks are going to tell us to go to hell on that arrival and parade coverage. Christ, that's a big thing! Can't you lock that up now?"

"Why don't you tell Conger," said Baldwin. "I've tried."

And so it went, the three men going over item after item, move by move, to work out the steps necessary to move Andrew Conger from Washington to Chicago.

It was late when Dale got home, worn and discouraged. He went straight to the refrigerator and pulled out a large bottle of champagne. His best friend in three campaigns, Abner Shepherd of Miami, had arrived that afternoon, and Dale was going to welcome him with champagne cocktails. They had done it twice before when they'd worked for Conger, and it was now a sacred ritual. Dale stuffed a bottle of bitters in one jacket pocket, a small box of cube sugar in the other. As he took the elevator up four flights in the same apartment building to Shepherd's floor, Dale was thinking he probably wasn't going to see as much of Shepherd in this campaign as in previous ones. Everything had become so large, so specialized, so spread out.

Dale rang the bell and waited. He could hear water running in the shower. He banged the door with his elbow and left heel. The water stopped. He heard muffled mumblings and scuffings approaching the door. It swung open, and there, stark naked, stood Abner Shepherd.

"Charlie, my boy. Come in." Dale was laughing and pointing at Shepherd. "For Christ's sake, I forgot my towel," said Shepherd, and ran back into the bathroom.

"Not because you're bare-ass naked, Abner—but boy, you are a sight for sore eyes," said Dale.

"Sorry I can't say the same. I tried to get out of this tour, you know. To top it all off, everyone was sick on the jet coming up from Miami. I thought jets flew above the weather," said Shepherd.

"Only if the weather is low enough to fly over. But they should go around it. I suppose they were in a hurry to get you up here." Shepherd meticulously wrapped a towel around his waist. "Here, Father. Happy Conger Cause." With that, Dale pressed the ice-cold champagne bottle against Shepherd's bare stomach.

Shepherd screamed, snatched the bottle from Dale, and swung it wildly around his head like a billy club. "Jesus, it's cold, *cold!* Don't ever do that again!"

"Well, stop swinging it around, Ab, we won't be able to drink it for a week." Shepherd put the bottle on a table and turned and placed his two hands on Dale's shoulders, looking directly into his eyes. "Bless you, my boy, for the sentiment. When the bubbles settle in a month or two, come on up, and I'll share it with you. Bring a date. And one for me, too."

Abner Shepherd was the senior partner of a struggling new Public Relations firm in Miami. He was an excellent writer, had been with Conger at the UN, and now, once more, had been asked to serve. This time, Shepherd would be in charge of all political scheduling of the candidate. Though Shepherd was in his early fifties, he and Dale had long since bridged the difference in their ages through the deep affection and respect each held for the other. "What goes, Chazz, with Secretary of State Andrew Conger?" asked Shepherd as he walked into the bathroom again. Dale followed him in and sat on a small dressing-table stool.

"Plenty," said Dale. "How much time do you have?"

"Not that much, flannelmouth. Just give me the highlights. And . . . let's have dinner."

"You're on."

"Come on, give, son. What's the hot poop? Has the candidate given you an audience?"

"Anything new from Janet?" asked Shepherd. Dale and Shepherd were seated in a quiet corner of a favorite restaurant near the Washington waterfront.

"Nothing since the last time I wrote you," said Dale. He toyed with a cardboard wine list. "Janet's taking this hard, Ab," he went on. "I don't know. Things are mighty strained between us."

"That's nothing new. Does she want to come to the convention?"

"Yeah. That's the one thing she said in her last letter that mentioned the future. The rest of it was a real blast. Still on the same kick of me and my no sense of responsibility, no feeling toward her or the family. She sent me a bunch of bills. All kinds of new stuff she says she's doing to learn how to lead a life without me. A painting class she's enrolled in . . . a UN study group. It's lousy. I can't reach her any more."

"Well, don't you want her to come to the convention?"

"By her own admission, she isn't coming to see me. She wants a fling in the big city. Says she plans to stay with friends out on the North Shore and have a ball. I'm there to pick up the tab. What kind of a husband-wife relationship is that?"

"Why don't you write and tell her you've got a job for her only she can do? Something maybe in your suite—guarding phones—or out at the Hall?"

"She doesn't give a damn about politics, Ab, or television. Or me, I'm beginning to think. I've tried before to get her interested in TV. In my end of the business, so at least I could talk to her. But no sir. She's got her role as a housewife and a mother, she says, and that's it. She doesn't know which end of a camera the lens is on. It's a shame, too, because I've tried so hard to bring her into the atmosphere and people of my work. She wants no part of it. She says she wasn't reared that way."

"What the hell? Let her come to Chicago."

"It's okay with me. I'd love to have her there. But she won't see much of me. I'll be at the Hall day and night. It will just push us farther apart if she comes up. She'll go her way, and I'll go mine. What will that prove?"

"I don't think you know. I think you're all mixed up," said Shepherd.

"Maybe you're right," Dale replied. "I'm pooped, frustrated, and irritated. I've found it rather depressing back here this time, Ab. Every day three more guys arrive to get between me and the candidate. Everybody's an expert. Everybody's got a policy committee, a task force on this, a task force on that. I understand there are two task forces on what Conger should do on TV—one in New York, the other in Hollywood. Am I on either one of them? Hell no! Nobody knows what anybody else is doing. The staff's spread all over town in a dozen small offices. Little doesn't want anybody to know how many people he's got down here. People sneaking in and out, everything sub rosa. It's terribly frustrating. It's impossible to get a straight answer from anybody. And this goddam debate mess. Everybody pussyfooting around. Christ, it's a nightmare!"

"That, my friend, is politics. It's no better or worse than previous campaigns. What *about* these debates? Who-the-hell's idea was that, anyway?"

"North American's, I think. Everywhere I go, these network guys hound me to get a statement out of Conger, to influence him. This damn North American group with Lou Wells practically tails me with private eyes. The pressure on Conger himself must be fierce. He's had old Commander Keel back here, that PR phoney from L.A. But—and by God, I've got to hand it to him—Conger's holding his ground. He told me flatly he hadn't made up his mind, that he will not accept any debate invitation from the networks at this time. I think he's going to wait till after the convention when he's the nominee and then turn it down."

"Do you think he'll be able to hold out?"

"I don't know. You should see the mail pouring in just on the debates. Half of them telling him to accept and give the other guy hell, and the other half telling him it'll cost him the election if he accepts. I'd hate to be in his shoes."

"I wouldn't worry too much about that," said Shepherd, smiling. "How did things look to you out in the boondocks during the primaries?"

"Fine for Conger. But Jesus, what second-rate idiots I had to deal with! Penny-ante people with penny-ante ideas hitched to penny-ante budgets. No wonder we never win any governor or senate races."

"I've got to meet with Conger and Rufe tomorrow . . . about the same idiots."

"My Lord, the first day in town and you're going to see The Man!" Dale was silent, and sipped at the dregs of his cold coffee. Shepherd watched him, worried. It wasn't like Dale to be so depressed.

"What's the matter, son? You seem to have forgotten Conger's favorite saying: 'Things are going to get a lot worse before they get better.'"

"Very funny," said Dale. "Oh hell, I'll snap out of it. It's just that things sure are different this time."

Shepherd smiled, took a puff on his pipe. "A little less listenin' to you and a little more yellin' at you, eh? Maybe a few dozen too many chiefs?"

"Yeah, something like that." Charlie stretched and yawned loudly. "I'm tired, Ab. Let's get out of here. I've got another nightmare day tomorrow. I'm gonna hit the sack."

"Son, why don't you find someone to hit the sack *with?* I think you'd feel better if you went out and got laid."

"I haven't got the strength. Come on, pay the waiter."

The sun felt warm and therapeutic to Charlie Dale. After a hectic morning of further frustration and irritation, Dale left Conger Headquarters shortly after noon, changed to shorts in his apartment, and took the elevator to the sun deck on the roof of his building. Inasmuch as it was early and the middle of the week, the roof was almost deserted. He walked toward the far end, away from the snack bar, balancing a beer on his book as he kicked a chaise around to face the sun.

The roof was pleasant. Someone with imagination had decorated it to simulate the afterdeck of a cruise ship. Life preservers were hung on the fence separating the lounge area from the remaining portions of the roof. Large ship funnels, painted a sparkling white enamel on the outside and red on the inside of the funnel mouth, served as refuse cans. Over the treetops there was a lovely view of Lafayette Square, the White House, and the river basin. After looking out at the city, Dale sank into the chaise, closed his eyes, and mentally played back his frantic morning.

The day had started with a call from Conger's office asking for a report on Lou Wells of NA. Overriding Little's orders not to discuss the debates with Conger, Dale dictated a memo. In it he said that, as far as he could ascertain, Lou Wells and NA were the guiding power behind the entire debate propaganda buildup and pressure. It wasn't anything blatant and tangible, but rather, a cumulative opinion, gathered from a thousand tiny fragments of gossip, attitude, and action. So, Conger had Dale's opinion, Little or no Little. A letter from Dale's elderly mother and father in Buffalo had been disquieting. Janet had been corresponding with them, and had implied all was not going well in Denver. Dale's parents asked him for an explanation. He decided to let it ride a few days before answering. Janet wired Dale for confirmation of her trip to the convention. Dale had called her in midmorning. Once again he tried to explain to her that she wouldn't see much of him, but if she wanted to come, he said he'd love to see her. As had happened so many times in the past when Dale desperately wanted an intimate and loving talk with Janet, the phone conversation turned into a battle with each yelling at the other, trying to dominate the discussion. After Dale hung up in disgust, Fergie took the brunt of his ill temper.

"Look, buster," said Fergie, "I don't like that kind of crap from anybody. You got problems at home, leave 'em out of the office. Don't make all of us suffer just 'cause you ain't the light in somebody's eye."

"Mind your own business, Fergie," said Dale. "By the way, who gave you the shiner?"

"Mind *your* own business, big Jesus," said Fergie.

"Come on, tell me," coaxed Dale. "Maybe it'll make me feel better. Who hit you?"

"A son-of-a-bitch of an angry god from Tahiti, that's who!" shouted Fergie.

"What?" asked Dale, confused.

"You heard me. My Hunk, that's Henry Dagwiler, he was my date. He wanted to go to that new Kon Tiki joint over in Alexandria. We went all right. Drank 'em out of every gardenia they had in the place. You know the way they float 'em in the drinks?"

Dale nodded. "Proceed."

"Well, things got a little wet out. We left in fairly good shape. Waitin' for the car, Hunk started shadow-boxin' with one of those obscene monsters, those ten-foot carved things on each side of the entrance. He punches the damn Tiki over and over. Then he starts givin' it a bear hug, and shakin' it. Before I know it—whammo! A big wooden ear roars past me on the way to the ground. Caught me smack dab in my eye as it went by." She paused, a disgusted look on her face. "Why do things like that happen to me?"

"You're accident-prone, that's why," Dale answered. "Do you expect me to believe that story? Come on, did Hunk hit you?"

"How dare you say a thing like that about ol' sugar cat Hunk Dagwiler?" she shouted. "Why, he carried me to Chapel Hill as his date three times while he was there. I was Senior Queen one year, I'll have you know."

"Okay, what's next?" Dale asked, turning to a mound of correspondence.

"What's next is you're goin' to blow this office before someone hits *you*," Fergie said. "Why the hell don't you get out of here for a day or two? You're gettin' too wound up. You're losin' your jollies."

"Shepherd said the same thing last night. You know I can't leave this joint."

"The hell you can't! I'm throwin' you outta here at noon, so make your plans accordingly. I don't care if you go home to that rat's nest you live in and sleep all day. You're gettin' outta here. There ain't no appointments won't wait until tomorrow."

"What about the boys I told you to call?" asked Dale. With the load piling up and the obvious supervisory problems ahead of them in Chicago, Dale had obtained approval to bring on two more of his television production team, Tommy Tuttle and Peter Hunt.

"Don't worry about 'em—I talked to 'em," said Fergie. "They're goin' to clear themselves with their companies and get back to us tomorrow mornin'. I told 'em you wanted 'em both to report to Chicago the Wednesday before the convention."

"That's right. That sounds fine." Dale paused, looked at Fergie standing opposite his desk like a house mother, and chuckled. "You're the damnedest looking thing with that 'mouse' I've ever seen. Can't you stay sober at night?"

"That's enough out of you, Charlie my boy. You better get outta here at noon if you value your life."

"Okay, I'll go if you'll mind the store." And so Dale had left and gone to the roof of his apartment building.

It was a day of rare low humidity and bright sunlight. If Washington had weather like this more often, thought Dale, it would be an ideal place to work and live: no industry, no smoke and soot, green parks and gleaming white marble. On this day it seemed like a magic city. Now, with his eyes shut, Dale relaxed and blotted out the office, the campaign, the problems, the seven-day weeks of crushing strain and work that had passed. In a matter of minutes he was asleep.

Some time later Dale awoke. His eyes were puffy from the sun, and there were dark circles of dampness on the canvas at either side of his neck where he'd perspired. He looked at his watch and realized he'd been asleep for over an hour. Patting his face and the top of his head, he could detect a slight burn. He reached under his chaise without looking down and found the half empty can of beer. He drained it, and taking careful aim on the ship's funnel ten feet down the fence in front of him, sailed the beer can toward it. With a loud clang the can made a bull's-eye. Dale turned around to see if the unexpected noise had disturbed anyone. He looked directly into the face that for five years had haunted him more than he liked to admit. The face smiled.

"You always were a good shot, Charles. Fancy seeing you here." Sandra Nelson smiled again, and Dale sat bolt upright, wide-eyed.

"Sandy! What in hell are you doing in Washington?" stammered Dale. "I thought you were still in Paris." He turned his chaise so that he was facing her, a few feet away. "My God, am I glad to see you!"

"I'd forgotten what a sound sleeper you are," said Sandra, reaching for a cigarette Dale proffered. "I was beginning to worry about your getting a burn."

"Would you have awakened me in time?" asked Dale as he gave her a light. Sandra lowered her eyes, exhaling slowly. The smoke curled around each side of her neck and rolled past her deeply tanned shoulders.

"Maybe. Maybe not. Maybe I'd have gone down without coming over. I don't know." She looked up on the last word with no emotion in her face.

"Do you live here?" asked Dale. "Is Judy with you?"

"Yes, but she's with her grandmother in Minnesota. School's out, you know."

"Oh, yes, I'd forgotten."

Dale couldn't believe it. How had he missed Sandra the past few weeks, coming and going in the lobby, getting his mail at the desk, picking up cleaning and laundry at the valet office? But what difference did it make now? he thought. She was here, and so was he.

"What are you smiling at?" Sandra asked.

"You. It sure is good to see an old friend as pretty as you." Dale, after the weeks of work, needed the warmth of a familiar face. And Sandra's face was very familiar, particularly since it had lain next to Charlie's on the same pillow for two months through fifteen countries in Europe in 1955. "Where have you been, and what have you been doing the past five years, Sandy?" asked Dale.

"Sort of wondering when you'd mess up my life again," she said, smiling. "I came close to forgetting you—once or twice."

Dale rose from his chaise and twisted a chair around to sit beside Sandra. "I'm glad it wasn't easy," he said. "Or should I have said that?"

"I don't know, but I'm pleased you did."

"Seriously, where have you been, Sandy?"

"Mostly in Paris," she said, exhaling luxuriously. "Had a year in Munich two years ago, but except for that my office remained in Paris. There've been a lot of changes since you were there, Charles."

"I suppose so. How long have you been here?"

"About nine months. Believe it or not, we're now representing European manufacturers in Washington. That's a big switch from the days we were together, isn't it?"

Dale's mind went back to the meaningful time in his life they had been together, and so deeply in love. Memories he didn't know still existed came rushing to the front of his mind as he looked at the face of Sandra Nelson.

In the spring of 1955 when Dale's regular television show for the season had only a few more weeks to run before its annual summer hiatus, he received a call from James Finnegan, President of the Telenet network. Telenet had been asked by the Western free countries, which comprised the European television network known as Eurovision, to teach them certain production techniques widely used in the United States but little known in Europe. Eurovision was in its infancy, and Finnegan asked Dale, who worked for Telenet at the time, to leave his show a few weeks early and depart immediately for Europe and the assignment. It was too interesting to refuse. In addition to working with the countries which had television, Dale was to lecture in several countries which would commence television broadcasting within the year. Before leaving New York, Dale had wired the Telenet News Bureau Chief in Paris, listing the countries he would visit and asking him to screen several interpreters who were multi-lingual. Three applicants were men. One was a woman named Sandra Nelson, a public relations contact executive with a firm in Paris which represented several American corporations on the continent. She traveled regularly to Italy, Germany, and the Netherlands. Sandra's daughter Judy was six at the time, and was always left in Paris with an American couple when Sandra traveled. They were old and close friends of Sandra's from Minneapolis, and had known her before her husband took his own life. It was at their suggestion Sandra had moved to France, taking her daughter with her, to leave bitter surroundings and start life anew where she felt she could breathe again. Two weeks after her husband's funeral, Sandra had been on her way.

When Dale arrived in Paris, he found little to recommend any of the male applicants for the interpreter's job. A woman applicant presented problems to the traveling aspects of the trip, but Dale agreed to talk with her. It developed that Sandra Nelson had an ideal background. She spoke fluent French, Italian, and German. She had worked for an advertising agency in New York shortly after college and had written two plays for children, which had been published. Her travels in Europe for clients had only whetted her appetite to see the countries more leisurely. She lived in the Etoile district in the same pension as the Telenet Bureau Chief, and they were acquainted socially. It had come to her attention just that easily, one night at bridge. Sandra had said it sounded exciting, that she would love the assignment, and could arrange the leave of absence from her regular position. Dale introduced Sandra to the production associate and writer who were to make the trip with him. The next day the three agreed to hire her. What the hell, it was a once-in-a-lifetime trip, and as one of them pointed out, why not travel in style with a good-looking American dame for an interpreter?

Sandra wasn't that good looking. She certainly wasn't beautiful. But she was red-haired and pretty, and had a unique vitality and excitement about her. Whatever was important to Sandra became important to the three men—she made it so. They saw Europe through her eyes, grew to know her love of beauty and of people. A deep streak of religion ran through her philosophy of life, but her own brand of fatalism was the true basis of her dynamic inner strength.

Amorous advances by the associate producer and writer had been rebuffed by Sandra on different occasions. Dale, sensing the principles and independence of a girl who would accept such an assignment with three men, kept his relationship as businesslike as possible. He was the leader of that ragtail TV group wandering through the byways of Europe in a chauffeur-driven rented Cadillac, and someone had to maintain business standards.

One day Dale and she were sitting on a low stone wall bordering the front courtyard of a lovely chateau deep in the Belgian countryside. The occupant was the Governor General of the Television Authority of Belgium. The two had arrived early for a script session. While they were waiting, a house servant had suggested a walk in the gardens. Talk was easy, as Sandra had been traveling with them for four weeks. There had been no mention by Sandra, however, of her past prior to Paris. Whenever an attempt was made to discuss it, she abruptly changed the subject.

And now Sandra was admiring the charm of the chateau and its gardens, which were bordered by ancient willow trees.

"I think I could forget everything, Charles, if I lived in a place like this for a year and felt the way I do now."

"Forget what, Sandy?"

"Frank's suicide." Sandra looked squarely at Dale.

"Your husband?"

"Yes."

"Do you want to talk about it?" Dale felt a special closeness in the moment.

"For the first time, I do. Yes. In a way, perhaps it's better I don't forget. It would be too easy to love again."

"Why do you think there is something, anything, to be gained by perpetuating such a sorrowful memory?"

"Another life, perhaps. Saving the life of the next man foolish enough to marry me, unsuspecting enough not to realize what might happen. Foolish enough to let me know love again."

"Sandy, I've never known anyone who knows love in everything they see, in everything they do, as much as you do right now. If ever I met anyone who lived by love, it's you."

"I do live by it. I believe in it. But my husband didn't. I was so naïve, so unforgiving, so shocked at his infidelity." Sandy was silent. She turned from Dale toward the moat house. "I made the statement thousands of women have made before and since. I told him to leave. He said he couldn't live without me." She continued to hide her face from Dale.

The two were silent. Then Dale spoke: "It was in him to do this thing, Sandy, not in you." Sandra turned her head slowly to look at Dale face to face.

"I have so much to give, Charles. Perhaps it's too much. Perhaps I'm too loving, too trusting—" she stopped herself, then went on "—too much a woman."

"How can you be too much a woman?"

"I can love too much, and I can expect that same 'too much' to be returned by the man I love." She reached down and picked a wildflower growing at her feet in the grass. Carefully, she pulled the stem through a buttonhole in her cardigan and gently patted it into place. "Do you think you can love that much, Charles?" she said, looking at Dale with her face close to his. "Could you help me find my way back? To learn to trust, learn not to fear? I want to so."

She looks different, Dale thought. Why was her face different?

What gave her eyes the deep shine, what flattened her cheeks, what made her nostrils so pink, her mouth so soft? Where are the muscles in her face, the lines at her temples? Why is her face so soft, why does it look so different? Dale looked full into her eyes. He could almost see his own reflection. He sensed in himself what Sandra had seen that had so changed her face.

"I don't know, Sandy. I don't know if in my whole life I've ever really loved as much as I can, as much as I should, or could." He looked at her, at the face of a woman in love.

"Would you like to try, Charles? Will you let me teach you?" And, sitting on the stone wall of the chateau's garden, they kissed. They were lost to time and light. There was a oneness, a blending of the two. That evening in Liège was the beginning of their ten weeks together.

Sandra Nelson knew what she wanted and went after it in an inexplicably selfless way. In their talks before love-making, in the whispered thank-you's of lovers trying to please each other, Sandra would ask Dale what there was in life more important than love. And what brought two lovers into more complete accord than the act of love-making? Their compatibility, their intuitive reflection of the needs and wants of the other, coupled with a fierce identity and pride on the part of each, made a spirited, dynamic relationship. Their discussions were involved and often deeply philosophical.

Dale's mind did not reject Janet or his three children. He was a profoundly ethical man and could not accept the fact that he was having an affair. He told himself it was love, born of mutual hunger and need. It happened naturally, at the moment, and he felt he deserved such a relationship once in his life. Or did he, should he? he asked himself.

In the two months he watched Sandra emerge from her fears, escape from her doubts to find life again. She became a whole person and gave herself completely to him. What was the answer? Dale pondered it night after night, as Sandra slept soundly, her head on his pillow, her arm thrown across his bare chest. What should he do? Was he wrong to have these feelings? His moral conscience told him yes.

As the days drew toward the final week of the trip, somehow Sandra knew she had lost Dale. In their final parting, however, she was selfless, loving, devoted to the man who had unconsciously and unknowingly given so completely of himself. He had returned, as she had asked, the ultimate expressions, the soul and spirit of love. They had been as one together, and Sandra Nelson knew she would be less than whole apart from Charles Dale.

"Can you accept this weakness in me?" Dale had asked. "Can you understand it? Do you think less of me because I can't follow my heart and my love?"

"I love you, Charles," Sandra had said. "There is no more, no less. I am trying to make it easier for you. I asked something of you many weeks ago—to come to me. You are now asking something of me—to let you go. And I shall. I feel sorry for you, not angry. And I am a realist. With all my belief in love, I am not a dreamer. I hope you find happiness." She had touched his arm lightly.

"Good-by, Sandy. I love you." Dale had picked up his trench coat from a chair in the lobby in Paris, fighting back the tears. Was it always this way, he had thought. Why wasn't this wonderful discovery of his perfect woman embodied in Janet? Why should the mother of his children be one thing, and Sandra another? He knew he was walking away from the most important experience in his life as he hailed the taxi at the curb that sped him to Orly airport for the flight to New York.

As Dale looked at Sandra on the sun roof in Washington, he wondered if his decision to leave Janet in Denver, their lack of communication, lack of real understanding, might have originated and been in his subconscious all the time during these five years. He knew, as he brushed Sandra's tan knee lightly with the back of his hand and ran the knuckles back and forth across the smooth warm skin, Dale knew life was repeating itself.

"Look," said Dale, "I'll run down and take a shower. Then let's meet in my apartment for cocktails. I know a great place in George-town for dinner. Okay?" Dale stood up, and his body cast a shadow over hers.

Sandra looked up at him. "Isn't this where I came in, Charles?"

"No, and I won't take no for an answer. Come on, let's leave the *Queen Mary* for terra firma."

Sandra knew she shouldn't start over again, that it would lead to nothing. But Charles Dale was the man she loved. So against her better judgment she agreed to meet him for dinner.

What are we doing here! thought Dale as he looked at Sandra. It shouldn't be this fast. What's happened to me that I can forget Janet so quickly?

Sandra was stretched contentedly beside him. Occasionally she murmured softly, breathing low, guttural sounds into his shoulder. Dammit, he thought, where the hell does a conscience come from? After all, I'm only human. Maybe I better start life apart from Janet, if that's the way she wants it. He moved closer to Sandra.

"You smell the same, Sandy," he said. "It's so nice. And you feel the same." Her slender body gave to his touch as they found each other. "You feel so warm . . . so right . . . so good. It's like coming home. Hello out there." He caressed her cheek with his lips as Sandra's face lay beneath his.

"Quiet." Sandra kissed him hungrily. Their lips apart moments later, Dale chuckled softly.

"What's so funny?" Sandra whispered.

"I thought of something I said to a good friend last night."

"What?"

"Nothing important."

"If it's that funny, share it."

"I told him I was so tired I didn't have the strength to do this."

"I have enough for both of us." With exaggerated pique, Sandra added, "Or would you rather rest?"

"Quiet. I love you, Sandra Nelson."

With each week the tempo increased to a higher pitch at Conger Headquarters. More men continued to join the staff, putting ever-increasing barriers between Rufe Little, Dale, Shepherd, and the Candidate. Several social gatherings were held in various homes to introduce the members of the growing staff to one another. At each one Sandra Nelson accompanied Dale. Ab Shepherd was aware there was more than passing interest in Dale's relationship with Sandra, but said nothing. He liked her, and Dale's easy disposition had returned.

The debate pressures increased. So many wires demanding a position or clarification on Conger's part had arrived at Little's office that he decided the matter had to be discussed with Conger. Dale accompanied Little, who had put the subject at the bottom of the agenda, to the meeting.

During the long session, Dale briefed Conger on plans for the convention of the other party, went through final changes in their own convention plans, and outlined the pattern of network coverage of the five days of activity. He supplied Conger with a schedule of the other convention for quick reference and viewing. The three men again discussed the arrival plans, and Arthur Baldwin was called in to describe the particulars of time and place. The parade plans were covered in detail.

When Baldwin had left and all business had been covered, Rufe Little reached in one of his outside coat pockets and pulled out a dozen telegrams. He placed them in his lap on his crossed legs.

"I think we're at a place where something must be said about the debates, Andy," Little said. "The mileage we've made out of being silent is shrinking. From this point forward, I think it could boom-erang into negatives to your candidacy in Chicago."

"The broadcast dates for the debates are after Labor Day, are they not?" Conger asked.

"True," said Little.

"Which is after Chicago, correct?" asked Conger.

"Correct," said Little. "The press, however, is hitting the idea of weakness in the silence, Andy. It's hurting us with the chairmen of some of the state delegations. Some of them are asking questions."

"Of my staff, you two are the most involved with the debate question," said Conger, looking first at Dale, then at Little. "I want you to remember this. I never want to hear the word 'debate' again, unless I bring it up. Do you both understand?" The two men nodded slightly. "The polls have me higher than I've ever been. There is no reason to accept or discuss a debate invitation at this time. Let me see those wires." Little handed them across the desk, and Conger shuffled through the pile, barely scanning them. "The bastards! Dale, your answer to the networks is the same as Little's. There will be no comment of any kind until after the convention. Do we all understand that? And do we all understand that if the subject of debates is to be discussed, I will do the discussing? That's final. Anything else?" Conger asked, as he swung around in his chair and chucked the wires into a wastebasket.

"No, that's it, Andy," said Little. "See you at five at the Metropolitan Club."

"Check. Things sound like they're progressing," said Conger. "Stay on top of that other convention, Dale. Send me a report each day of your opinions."

"Will do, Andy. 'By," said Dale. And the two men left. On the way back to Headquarters Little was silent, preoccupied. He made one interesting comment. "Young man, we are not out of the woods on this debate mess. As you can see, it's in Andrew Conger's craw . . . and it's stuck there."

Dale heard from Janet infrequently. After a particular period of two weeks with no word from Denver, a letter arrived, postmarked Aspen, Colorado. "Betsy and Lisa came up here with me for a week of fun. It's been great fun. Lots of people here from Boston and New York. Charlie Junior's at home with Juanita—remember her? She's the girl we had in when I was sick right after we moved. The one who was such a good cook. How are you? Miss me? I'll bet. Betsy sends her love, the weather has been heavenly, and I've gained three pounds. The girls are having fun with Bill Chalmers, from New

York. He's divorced. I think you met him at the Newsoms' one year in Scarsdale. Was it a New Year's Eve party? He's been very kind and thoughtful to all of us. Bill has a small ski house, which has been yummy. The girls love to go over there on rides and for barbecues. I still plan to come to Chicago and live it up. Hope you're bearing up under the pressure. Why doesn't Conger say something about the debates? Everybody out here thinks it's stupid. He's acting so cute about them. What difference does it make? If he can't hold his own against the other candidate, he shouldn't be President. Cheers, Janet."

Dale read into the letter what he wanted to—that Janet had found a man who seemed attractive to her. He remembered Chalmers well: a quiet, intelligent, athletic type, younger than Dale. Good-looking, and a successful lawyer. An interesting turn of events, thought Dale. It relieved his conscience and made him even more attentive to Sandra that night in his apartment. Perhaps he was correct in thinking how nice it would be to have Sandra lying beside him the rest of his life. The full length of her body pressed loosely against him, his right hip tucked softly into the hollow between the top of her thigh and her flat stomach. Perhaps Janet and he should go their separate ways. It was an increasingly recurrent thought, and it scared him. Sandra felt the fleeting shiver across Dale's chest, but interpreted it as a chill. Gently, she pulled up the counterpane and kissed his cheek.

It was the Fourth of July week-end. Dale and Sandra, who by this time was a regular in the group, were invited to join Whibbley Stearns and five other couples for a three-day cruise on the Potomac. Stearns was head of a businessmen's task force in the Conger volunteer organization, a man who liked both money and a good time. In preparation, Dale rented a guitar, and Ham Forrest an accordion, both knowing that Stearns kept on board a chaplain's field organ, set up on the afterdeck of his forty-five-foot power cruiser which had been christened *The Flapper*.

The fun started right away. As the guests boarded the ship, they were greeted by an announcement posted prominently on the bulk-head. The heading read: "The Captain's Word is Law." Underneath it stated that anyone heard mentioning Andrew Conger, the convention, or the campaign would be keel-hauled!

The Friday night cocktail hour was discordant bedlam, with Dale, Forrest, and Stearns belting it out and the rest of the gang singing or beating time to the wild music. Saturday morning at breakfast, Barbara Beatty, the girl who had found Dale his apartment, and Fergie, who had come as Abner Shepherd's "date," did a fantastic hula.

There was a unique thing about Stearns's yacht. It was in excellent shape but strangely, her top speed was only three knots. Dale had been completely mystified by this and had asked Stearns at one point if this wasn't a handicap on the water, keeping way and maneuvering. Stearns's reply was, "Not a bit. Why should it go faster? Who has any place to go? Another gin and squirt?" But that evening just after cocktails, the boat came to a dead stop in the channel. Upon investigation, it was discovered that she had run out of gas.

And so went the historical Fourth of July cruise of *The Flapper*, raising hob with the normal pursuits of shipping and pleasure yachtsmen the length and breadth of the Potomac.

The final night, returning upstream to Washington, Abner Shepherd made the following comment: "Well, back to the old grind." Whibbley Stearns immediately protested that Ab had broken the Captain's word "which was law!" A court was hastily convened, jurists were selected. The court ruled "the old grind" covered all three forbidden terms: Conger, Convention, Campaign. In sight of the Washington Monument Shepherd was thrown off the stern transom into the water.

But back to the old grind it was. And the convention of the other party started the following morning in Chicago.

8

To Chicago

"Hi, BERNIE, how've you been?" said Dale into the phone.

"Fine, Chazz. What's up?" asked Bernie Lamb, listening in Chicago at the other end.

"You still registered in our party?"

"Sure. Got something you want me to do?"

"Yes, two things. I'd like you to be my eyes and ears in Chicago this week. Cover the convention for me. I'm stuck here in Washington, and it'd be a good way to break into something else I've got in mind. Could you spring yourself?"

"I think so. I'm finishing up a job for the meatpackers, but it can wait. They'll go along with me if I explain what I'll be doing."

"Good. The other thing is this: How would you like to go out with our V.P. candidate this year? Reporting to me but completely on your own creatively, to work with the guy, develop shows, and mother him through the campaign?"

"I'd love to. Who do you think it'll be?"

"Can't tell you, but if it's who we think, you would be ideal to work with him."

"Gee, Chazz, that'd be great. I'd like that very much."

It sure would be great, thought Dale. Of all people to take over the second man on the ticket—lock, stock, and barrel—Bernard Lamb would be his first choice. He was too independent and sensitively creative to phase smoothly into Dale's organization and work with other television advance men. Bernie Lamb was a lone wolf. And if this campaign followed the pattern of previous ones, the guys traveling with the second banana candidate were going to be mighty lonely.

Bernie Lamb was a television film producer in Chicago. He went from one top network show to the next, always grabbing his share of awards and improving his stature in the industry. A visit with the Lambs was invariably on Dale's schedule when business took him to Chicago.

With Bernie's writing and editing ability, his preference for working alone and being the top guy, he would be ideal to travel with the vice presidential candidate on Conger's ticket.

"That sure takes a worry off my mind," said Dale. "I don't know who I would have turned to if you'd said no. I'll keep you posted on developments. In the meantime, start clearing yourself to be out-of-pocket until November. Now, as to Chicago and the carpet-baggers in there this week—here's the scoop."

Dale advised Lamb on how to obtain his credentials to cover the Hall freely. He also explained the combined network television-coverage operation. He gave Lamb several hints as to how he could worm his way into the various control rooms to watch what was going on, and why things were or were not being done. "This week, with their convention in the same hall as ours two weeks later, Bernie, is almost like an out-of-town tryout for us. It's a perfect way to get the bugs out of our coverage. Call me once a day, more often if things come up. Try and get out there for their keynote speech tonight. I think it's old Terry Tower, the phoney."

"Fine. If I have any trouble getting in the building, I'll holler. I'll keep you advised. Sounds interesting. And thanks."

"Thank *you*, Bernie. I'm very grateful. I would have called you sooner, but the guys here were afraid we'd get picked up on spying charges. The hell with 'em. The whole thing is too vital and too complicated to take a chance on. I'll take the rap if anything happens."

For Charlie Dale in Washington, the week of the other convention was like all the previous ones, except, no matter what he was doing, he watched Chicago and the convention out of one eye. Dale's office became the center of activity, and most of the week it resembled a popular cocktail lounge. Four television sets were turned on morning, noon, and night. Staff members came and went, watching their specific interest. Secretaries dropped in, sat for half an hour, and left. Coke bottles, coffee cartons, and paper cups with the dregs of bourbon or scotch in them gathered on every flat surface. As usual, each visitor had his comments on the convention production and television's coverage. Just like New York or Hollywood, thought Dale. Everyone has two businesses: his own and show business. Dale and Ham Forrest would sit patiently through the amateur staff's dissections of the role of TV in the convention, mumble something incoherent, and forget the remarks.

Dale sent his reports to Conger, stressing after each day's coverage where he would make changes, and how their coverage would differ from what Conger was seeing.

A call came from the National Committee regarding the Women's Day plans in Chicago. Dale had completely forgotten that he was supposed to come up with a producer for a nationally televised program on their annual day at the convention. He quickly called Hollywood, talked to the woman who produced the best daytime guest-interview show on the Coast, and sent her to Chicago immediately. "If you aren't for Conger, Sadie, just keep your trap shut," Dale had said. "I don't think anyone will have time to check your registration. But I wouldn't trust the thing to anyone else. So go, girl." And she went. Into what she would always remember as the most horrifying experience of her life. Dale heard about it later.

What Sadie Vilm suffered through to get *The Old Masters Fashion Show* on the air two weeks later was sheer torture. But, because she was a professional, Sadie delivered. And the wildest political strip tease in history, complete with the wives of thirty-five congressmen as mannequins, careened onto ten million television screens.

Conger's National Committee called again, this time with a crisis on the platform proceedings. Dale sent Tommy Tuttle to Chicago to handle it and to follow through for the next two weeks on the film of the platform which would be presented at the convention.

The third day Bernie Lamb called with an odd impression of the television coverage at the other convention. "I can't put my finger on it, Charlie, but something strange is happening out here," said Lamb.

"What do you mean strange?" asked Dale.

"Well, it's something I feel rather than know. It's a hundred little things. It's so damaging, I hesitate to tell you about it. But dammit, it's bugging me, and I want to discuss it with somebody."

"Shoot."

"I think North American is favoring Governor Green all the way. Trying to throw their prime coverage spots and best pickups his way. Have you noticed it?"

"Not particularly. But why wouldn't they? He's the front-runner for the nomination. They've got to cover him, stick to him like glue. If they don't, they'll miss the story."

"I agree, but it's more than that. I happen to know they've passed on a couple of very important statements made by the other front-runners. In each case, both the other networks covered, but NA did not. Almost but not quite a blackout on the other contenders. Also, have you counted the number of exclusive interviews NA has had with Green? Every time there's a lull, they go to his penthouse for an interview."

"It may seem that way to you, Bernie, but it doesn't look that bad back here."

"That's my point. You don't know what NA is *not* covering. Out here I do. And they are covering Joe Green at the expense of other candidates they should be picking up."

"Just typically lousy NA planning," said Dale.

"Well, as I said, I haven't heard anything specific, but it's something I feel. What do you think of this Whiting guy who does all the Green interviews?"

"Pretty good. Very fair and seems objective. I wonder if he's a friend. If he is, he'd be valuable to us, because undoubtedly he'll travel with Green during the campaign, knowing him so well. Does Green have any television guy with him? Anyone special as an adviser?"

"I don't think so. There are some pros out here, but no single guy seems to be around him all the time. Incidentally, the scuttlebutt in Chicago is that our man will have to accept the debates. They're going to box him into it during the acceptance speeches out here."

"Don't be so certain. They've hit it in every speech so far, Bernie. It will continue to be a very sticky wicket, but Conger will say no. Watch that Green idea of yours with NA, and if you hear anything more about it, give me a ring. Keep an eye on Lou Wells. I want to know what he's up to out there."

"Okay. Listen, Chazz. Communication is very difficult and important here. I think you should send someone to Chicago to look into it. We ought to get on all the shortwave frequencies of the networks. You've probably seen the use of walkie-talkies right in the delegations on the floor. There are two-way radio setups to everywhere. We're missing the boat if we don't have the same thing."

"We're on top of it, but I'll get someone out to you. You fill him in and tell him what you think we should have."

A few hours after the conversation, Peter Hunt was on his way to Chicago. Dale knew full well the serious problem of effective communication at large gatherings when crowds became so dense one couldn't move. Mobs were like a trap: you were frozen in your tracks by walls of bodies. In such cases, only wireless communication provided contact with the outside world.

Governor Joseph Green won the nomination. In the interview from his suite at the hotel immediately following the demonstration in the hall, Green was asked by Amos Whiting if he had something to say about the television debates. Green said he did not, that it would be covered in his acceptance speech.

The following morning United States Senator Todd Bromley received the nomination for vice president. Bromley owned the largest sand and gravel business west of Chicago. Someone watching in Dale's office suggested one of his own pits would be a good place to bury him.

The night of Green's acceptance speech, Fergie outdid herself with preparations. She set up a portable bar, had ice, glasses, and mixes. Abner Shepherd was there, and Rufe Little. The two had dinner with Dale and then walked back to headquarters with him for the main event.

Dale watched the Green address carefully, giving his reactions and comments to Fergie as they occurred, to be included later in his memo to Conger. Green hit the debate challenge right at the top. He announced he would wage a fighting campaign and that he would take the fight and challenge to his opposition. He would not wait for it to come to him. "Therefore," Green confidently said, "I do hereby accept the invitation of the great broadcasting industry to television debates with my opponent, whoever he may be. I eagerly await the selection, here in this same historic hall, two weeks from now, so that every American will have the opportunity to write or wire his congressman and the party of his choice as to the importance of such an exchange between the presidential candidates." The hall rocked with applause and cheers. Why wouldn't they, thought Dale, as his heart went out to Andrew Conger, who he knew was sitting at home watching, listening to the Green speech. What could Conger do now? Dale looked at Shepherd, who was concerned with lighting his pipe. He looked at Rufe Little.

"Well, Rufe," said Shepherd between puffs to get his pipe going, "what do you think?"

"Just about what I expected," said Little. "I think our man may need some help with ideas on how to refuse the debates. Polls still show him way ahead. Dale, you give Ab anything he needs on it. But, Abner, start thinking." Others in the room discreetly retired, sensing the delicacy of Little's remarks.

"You're just whistling 'Dixie,' Rufe," said Abner.

"Let's whistle it loud then, whistle it loud," said Little irritably, and left the room.

Abner remained with Dale to watch the coverage of the reaction to Green's speech. The television newsmen concentrated on the debate theme, in effect throwing their own challenge at the opposition, leering at their cameras like so many procurers. In Dale's opinion, however, Amos Whiting, whom NA had assigned to cover Green throughout the week, seemed more objective than the others, more reserved in his references to the debates. Maybe he's just tired, thought Dale. One more turn of the screw, and this debate mess will be locked up once and for all.

Saturday night Andrew Conger hosted a buffet dinner at his home for his top aides. He'd been in hiding all week, making notes and gathering material from the Green convention for his own bid in Chicago. No one but Rufe Little had seen him. But now, with the Green nomination secured, a party was a good device for Conger to mingle with his staff before the move to Chicago and the nights and days of work and tension ahead for all of them.

Shortly after the party began, Conger asked Dale to accompany him out to the flagstone terrace. Conger's two sons, John and Frank, and his wife Susan joined them a few minutes later. With the suggestion that this would give both Dale and his family a chance to get to know one another better, Conger left them to return to his other guests.

John, usually called Jack, was eighteen, an attractive, outgoing teenager. He'd be excellent on television, thought Dale. Not so for Frank, who was fourteen. Frank had the unfortunate habit of hanging his head in embarrassment and wore glasses which he constantly positioned on his nose by pushing up on the center nose bridge with the middle finger of his left hand. Dale watched him do it several times. He made a mental note to drop the word to Conger's secretary Ruth Platt that Frank ought to get a pair of glasses that fitted him before he came out to Chicago. The boys excused themselves shortly, and Dale chatted with Susan at some length, more about the campaign than Chicago. Susan, with admirable wifely confidence, was positive nothing stood in the way of the nomination. Or victory in November, for that matter. Like the wife of every public figure Dale had ever worked with, Susan wanted no part of TV and said she would not appear on any television without her husband. Dale thought this was worth a serious talk with Rufe Little. Susan then discussed the decorations of the Green convention. Dale told her that as soon as the carry-out was completed, he would be involved in a completely new and different decoration plan for the Conger convention.

"Oh, that's good," said Susan. "You know, I saw those curtains they hung behind the speakers, you know, behind the rostrum?"

"Yes," said Dale. "I saw them too. And we will not have those. At least, I will say we won't have those when Andy is speaking or at the rostrum. I haven't forgotten, Susan."

"I was going to bring it up, but I'm so glad I didn't have to. There's just something about the way Andy looks when they hang those curtains, those box-pleated things behind him. And you know, almost everywhere we go, the stations use them. He looks terribly old against that background. The darkness in the folds seems like black pipes, like prison bars. It makes Andy look cheap."

"Don't worry about it, Susan. You will not see them this year. We haven't permitted anyone to use them, and won't in Chicago or on the campaign."

"It's silly, isn't it? But I feel that way, and so does Andy."

Because you've told him you think he looks lousy in front of them, thought Dale. There's not a thing wrong with drapes, or pleats, and they're almost standard in every local TV station. So now, with the king and queen poisoned against them, I'll have to travel a busload of scenery for three months.

"By the way," said Susan, "that's a very attractive girl you brought with you. What's her name?"

"Sandra Nelson. Yes, she is. We've known each other for five or six years." Unconsciously, Dale turned and looked at Sandra, who was laughing at something Ab Shepherd was saying to her as they chatted out on the lawn near the serving bar.

"What pretty red hair," Susan said. "Is Janet home in Denver?"

"Yes, I just couldn't see bringing the family back to the miserable summer weather Washington has. If things go the way they should, I won't be in Washington very much anyway."

"Oh? I thought Andy told me he hoped you wouldn't have to travel as much as on previous campaigns, that he wanted you closer to headquarters."

"That's the plan, Susan. But I'll be very surprised if something doesn't get me out on the road a good part of the time."

"You aren't referring to the debates, are you?" A new hardness crept into Susan's voice.

"Lord, no," said Dale. "Just the increase of television news coverage and the increasing use of TV all the way around." Susan looked at him without expression, no visible sign of relief at his comments.

"Yes, I'd forgotten about that. Well, I must run and see the others. Mention me to Janet when you write her. 'By." And Susan smiled warmly as she turned and went into the house.

Dale had debated in his mind whether or not he should invite Sandra to accompany him to the Congers'. At first, it seemed the normal thing to do. Everyone on the staff knew her and liked her. Several staff members and their wives knew Janet from previous campaigns but had accepted Sandra immediately. Andrew Conger and Rufus Little, however, were something different. So was Susan Conger. What did she know? The hell with it, thought Dale. My life is my life, no one else's. Nevertheless, Dale's justification for his relationship with Sandra knew periods of doubt that evening. He joined Abner Shepherd and Sandra in a sober mood.

Sandra was enjoying herself, which pleased Dale. In bed at his apartment later that night, the two discussed the staff members Sandra had met. At one point Sandra said, "How could one man attract so many nice people to work for him? I'm beginning to admire Andrew Conger."

"They're a nice group, aren't they?"

"You're so fortunate to have this association, Charles. Some of these men will be friends of yours the rest of your life."

"I doubt that, Sandy. Showbiz and most of these guys don't mix. They all go back to their tight little worlds after each campaign."

"Is that where you go too, Charles?"

"I don't know . . . I don't know. But let's not talk about that now. This is our last time together before I leave for Chicago. Kiss me, and tell me you love me." Charlie slowly pulled her head to his, and a nerve of excitement ran through him as their bare shoulders touched. Sandra kissed him. Then she looked at Dale in the darkness. "Susan Conger doesn't like me," she said softly.

"I don't believe you. She remarked to me how beautiful you were. She liked your red hair."

"Now I'm sure she doesn't. Will it hurt you if Andrew Conger's wife doesn't like me?"

"No." Charlie cupped his hand behind her head, cradling it on the pillow. "Kiss me," he said, "just like you did before, only this time with feeling."

"You nut!" And Sandra kissed him with all the feeling she possessed.

In Chicago that same night, at just about the same time, Presidential Nominee Governor Joseph Green had invited a few intimate friends up to his suite for a late champagne supper. It was an exclusive guest list. The Governor's wife Mary greeted the arrivals, announcing gaily they were to participate in a private victory toast to the fall campaign. Green's running mate, Todd Bromley, and his wife Gertrude, arrived, as did Henry Potts, Green's campaign manager, and the newly appointed press secretary, Waldo Duncan, and their wives. One or two others from the National Committee were in attendance. Fred and Benita Morgan were surprised at the exclusiveness of the group when they walked out on the large terrace overlooking the lake front, and saw the few who had been invited. Green was exceedingly cordial to the Morgans, and drew them into conversation with the Bromleys.

"There's one thing about you chaps," said Bromley, "your coverage is damn impartial, damn fair. I watched you carefully, and I daresay you gave all the contenders an equal shake. I'm certain Joe agrees with me, eh Joe?"

Green smiled at Morgan through the smoke from his cigarette. "I agree with Todd, Fred," he said. "I wouldn't ask for anything more than the same treatment on through to the end of the campaign. Television will play a large role, unless I'm mistaken."

"An even larger one if the debates become a reality, Governor," said Morgan. "I was thrilled and grateful for your reference to them in your acceptance speech. Your opponent, whoever he may be, is at the point, I should think, where he almost has no choice but to accept television's invitation."

Green winked at Morgan in a moment when Bromley's face was turned toward the French doors into the drawing room, "That's the general idea, is it not?" asked Green. "I'd hate to let your man Louis Wells down. He's done a great deal to bring them this far."

"Yes, he has," said Morgan. "We'll be working just as hard during the next convention to bring their importance to the other candidates."

"I'd be grateful if you did," said Green. "Very grateful. But, ladies, we've been talking politics too long. Come join me in a toast to our success in November."

Fred Morgan felt ill at ease in full view of the gathering as he drank the toast of victory to Governor Joesph Green's candidacy. It rather successfully committed him in the coming months. He smiled at his wife, seeking approval. Benita avoided his gaze, and Morgan noted her glass was not raised.

Later, back at their hotel, Benita Morgan, still lovely at fifty, moved next to her husband when she felt his arm on her shoulder.

"You were the best looking woman at the party," said Morgan. "I was proud of you tonight."

"Were you?" Benita asked. "Really?" Benita's thoughts were on the questioning look from her husband when she didn't join the victory toast. "You weren't very pleased with me when Governor Green made his little speech about victory in November."

"Your politics are your business, not mine," said Morgan.

"What are you doing with *any kind* of disclosed politics, Fred?" she asked. "In all the years you've had NA, I've never seen you line yourself up with a candidate publicly before."

"Don't be ridiculous," Morgan answered. "That was just good business for NA. It was a private party. We were invited, so we went. If I'd turned Green down, that would have been a tacit admission of being for Conger. I accepted to show NA's impartiality."

"What about yours?" Benita asked. "You didn't have to join that toast in front of those people."

"For Christ's sake, Bunny, forget it," Morgan answered, irritated. "I can't afford to snub either candidate. We've been through this sort of thing before. Remember 1952 in Philadelphia? That party for Bonner?"

"Very well."

"That was the same thing."

"Nobody proposed a victory toast that night."

"I don't remember." Morgan stretched his legs, both straight out, heels on the floor.

"I overheard some of your conversation with Green and Bromley on the porch," Benita said. "What was all that winking about?"

"Nothing, absolutely nothing. A private joke between Green and me about something that happened to Bromley on a TV interview during the convention."

"Just be sure it isn't too private," said Benita. "And I'd hate to think it really wasn't a joke. I'd be very shocked at you."

Morgan's arm tightened around her shoulder. He gave her a playful hug and released her. "I assure you the whole thing's meaningless, Bunny. I'd never do anything to hurt you or cause you a minute of embarrassment." He looked at her. "I love you, remember?"

When Charlie Dale and Fergie walked into their makeshift office quarters in Andrew Conger's hotel in Chicago, it was as though someone had rung a bell and said GO! It was the first round, out of the chutes, away from the barrier—call it what you wish. And the race wouldn't be over for one hundred and one days.

The nation's and the world's newspapers, magazines, radio, TV—every mass media in existence—descended on Dale in a tidal wave of strident, jabbering demands for service, interviews, or appearances for Conger in guest formats. Conger's arrival time was still confidential, which made it a complicated matter for Dale. But his main problem was being cordial and polite to the hundreds of local radio-and-TV-station newsmen in Chicago, the correspondents from Italy, from Mexico, from Japan. Each had a special and unique reason why Andrew Conger should grant an exclusive interview to his station.

Wilbur Jenkins, Conger's Press Secretary, had remained in Washington with Conger, so had Ham Forrest, whom Dale had assigned to cover the candidate personally. The press assistants Jenkins had sent to Chicago in advance of his arrival had proved wholly inadequate to meet the situation. So Bernie Lamb, and Ned Colton of the TV advance team, and Fergie did what they could to help. Dale had delegated Peter Hunt to the National Committee to coordinate all TV interviews. Tommy Tuttle was assigned to sit at the hotel with Dale, as his platform film supervision kept him close by.

Later, he would move with Dale to the TV trailer in the Convention Hall.

The days came and went in a continuous, exhausting babble of voices, a No-I-can't-deliver-Conger blur. Talk, talk, talk. Dale was hoarse by noon of each day. Every morning Dale made a frantic trip out to the stockyards to check on progress of construction and installation for TV. Then he was back to ride herd on the platform committee pickups, and to work on the long-range plans and important nighttime appearances for Conger prior to his arrival. Because all networks had their news heads in Chicago, programs were created there, but they originated in Washington, usually at Conger's office or his home.

There was never enough time to do anything altogether right. Time—time to make the trip to the Hall, time to view the footage for the platform film, time to eat, time to grab a few hours' sleep, time to sit down unhurriedly with individual program producers who insisted on Conger's appearance on their shows. Two days before Conger's arrival, and shortly before the master parade meeting Dale had scheduled with all networks plus the newsreels, Bernie Lamb announced that Wells of NA was waiting outside and wouldn't take no for an answer. He had to see Dale.

"He'll be in the parade meeting," said Dale. "Can't it wait?" he asked, looking at his watch.

"I can't get rid of him, Charlie. Says he's got to see you before."

Dale sighed, covered up some confidential schedules he had been completing, and told Lamb to bring him back. Wells walked in with someone who looked vaguely familiar. The two came up to Dale's desk.

"Hi, Charlie," said Wells. "Say hello to Sandy Jones. He's our director of the whole NA shebang out here. It's time you two met."

"Sit down, guys," said Dale wearily. "Nice to see you, Sandy. What's up?" he asked.

"The ratings on the first convention came out last night, and we got our ass whipped by Global," said Jones. "We're here to discuss the entire next eight days with you."

"Christ, guys!" said Dale. "I haven't even discussed it with myself. How bad did you get whipped?"

"Very bad," said Lou Wells. "The sales boys are steaming."

"Are they?" asked Dale. "That ain't the way I heard it. The rumble in the coffee shops along the Rialto is you guys blew it by covering Green too much. You stuck to him too closely. That's what I've heard. And by Jesus, you guys better not pull that crap on us. Unless it's Conger you're going to stick to."

"Our coverage is on the level," said Jones. "You better watch what you're saying about the way I do a political convention." Dale realized he had struck an exposed nerve, and it gave him pause.

Sandford Jones, at thirty-three years of age, was known as the hottest program producer and director in television news on any network. He was also the highest paid staff man at any of the three networks, and knew it. Jones had set his sights twenty years before, in his hometown of Appleton, Wisconsin, to be exactly where he was at the present time. He had dug, scratched, and disappointed two wives at his early age because of his love affair with money and power.

On graduation from the University of Wisconsin, Jones had made the traditional pilgrimage to Chicago, the hub of Midwest broadcasting. He started as a page at Telenet, worked his way up to cameraman, spent a summer as an assistant director at NA, and then set his sights on News. There was something more glamorous about News than the theatrical side of television. You were always where something big was happening, with important people, with important stories to be covered. Jones attached himself to the most successful "personality" newscaster in the business, and when the man was transferred by NA to the East, Sandy Jones also found himself in Manhattan. He'd made it. And today he was at the top, second only to his boss in NA's television convention coverage at a time of rating crisis.

"Look, Sandy, don't get me wrong," said Dale. "Nor you either,

Lou. I don't give a damn about either of you two guys, NA, or television, period. All I care about is that Andy Conger gets a fair shake and that what comes out at this hotel and that Convention Hall is legit."

"We're way ahead of you," said Wells. "We'd like to run a direct wire from our control room to your trailer. Okay? That way you can get right to us with important stories. Let's face it, Dale, your work here is going to be dull as hell as a news story. Conger's a shoo-in. He has no opposition. We've got to create excitement, we've got to cover battles, arguments, controversy—even if we have to start them ourselves. Or else we'll lose even more of our audience. Will you play ball with us?" Dale looked at the papers on his desk for a moment, then faced the two men.

"If it's good for Andy Conger, we do it. If it ain't, we don't," he said. "It's just that simple." Dale made a mental note to contact the other two networks for a direct wire. Wells had come up with an excellent idea, but it wouldn't be an exclusive for NA.

"That's all we ask," said Jones. "I'll order the line into your trailer."

"There's one other thing," said Wells. "I've advised my entire staff of newsmen there's a five-hundred-dollar bonus for each exclusive. They're going to be hitting you hard and often, Dale, the minute Conger gets to town."

"Fine, couldn't be better," said Dale. "We'll do everything we can to give them what they want. I'm setting up a procedure between the hotel and the Convention Hall so that we'll have advance word when any Conger VIP moves in this town. Moving from the Hall, to the Hall, from hotel to hotel outside the Hall, even suite to suite in the same hotel. Could I use the direct line to fill you in on all that?"

"That's what it's for," said Jones. "Anything you want us to know, hit the private line."

"I'll play ball with you if you play ball with me," said Dale. "There are going to be times when we will move men in and out of the hall that we goddam don't want to be interviewed, don't even want anyone to know they're in the Hall. The first time you guys swing the peepie-creepies over to them is the last time you'll hear anybody on that direct wire. Got it?" The two nodded.

"I've moved the VIP boxes and the boxes for the Presidential and Vice Presidential Nominees' families. Christ, the seating idiots had them placed where you couldn't get a shot of them, and we couldn't throw in any special light. They're fine now. Check at the Hall for the new box numbers." Dale looked again at his watch. "Guys, give me five minutes alone. I've got to make a call to Washington, and we're late for the Conger arrival meeting right now. You're going to cover that, right?"

"Damn right," Wells said, rising. "Anything new on Conger and the debates?"

"Nope."

"Okay, we'll be back later." The two men left.

Fergie came in with a batch of mail from Washington and sat down.

"Big Jesus, if they don't give us a breather or start feedin' us while we work with a tube up my you-know-what, I ain't gonna make it. We've gotta have more help."

"Stop your bitching. You're getting paid, aren't you?" Dale asked, and then he couldn't help but smile.

"I don't want the money, baby, I want to put this cotton-pickin' head down and die."

"Chin up, hush puppy. We've only got eight more days to go in Chicago. And then two thousand till Election Day. Get me Ham Forrest. He'll be at Conger's home, getting ready for that remote tonight. Call him on the private line in Conger's study. I want to talk to him privately—at his end. And keep everyone out of here while I talk."

"Yes, sir, yes, sir, big Jesus. Would somebody like to give me the number in Conger's study, or do I just make it up as I go along?"

"Call Ruth Platt at her apartment and get it. I just talked to her there. I've lost it. Conger changes it every week to keep it private."

When he reached Forrest, Dale told him about the talk with

Wells and Jones. Dale said he was coming around to the opinion that perhaps Bernie Lamb had been correct. Perhaps NA had stuck too close to Green at the expense of some of their overall coverage. "I'd like you to pass that on to Conger, Ham. At the right time. Okay?"

"Will do," said Forrest. "Everything's fine here. I've got a special makeup man for Susan. She's agreed to go on with Conger. So have the boys."

"Oh? That's great. See if Frank has new glasses. I told Ruth Platt to see he got them. I'll be watching at this end. Incidentally, tell Wilbur Jenkins I'm about to go into a meeting on the arrival parade. I have to, even though the time hasn't been announced. I have no alternative if we want coverage. Otherwise, there'll be no cameras at the locations where Baldwin's gang plans to hold their demonstrations and parade-stoppers. Also, if Conger doesn't hurry up and start from Washington, he'll never make it from the airport to the Loop. They're tearing up all the streets. They've got almost every possible route torn up now, Baldwin tells me. He's thinking of helicopters."

"You're kidding," said Forrest.

"I am not," said Dale. "When Chicago plays politics, Ham, they play for keeps. You know, nice clean stuff like ripping up all the parade routes into town with street construction. Very pleasant fellows. Don't tell that to Conger."

"You think I'm crazy? Okay, buddy, stay loose. Gotta run. They want me in the truck to look at pictures. 'By."

Dale hung up and buzzed Bernie Lamb on the inter-office. "Ready for the meeting?" he asked.

"They're all waiting," said Lamb. "I have the maps."

"Good. Let's go." The two men, with Fergie, walked to the small room off Dale's office. Into it had crowded supervisors, producers, and directors from the three television networks. In addition, each network had delivered the driver of the truck which would carry its mobile camera equipment. These trucks would precede the first car in the parade the entire route from the airport to the hotel. Representatives of the still photographers were on hand, as well as the Chicago Police.

Lamb passed out the maps. Dale sat at the end of a table which had been hastily covered with a green felt cloth by a hotel porter.

"Okay," he said. "Where are the newsreels?" There was no answer. "Goddammit, those bastards never show. Fergie, did you notify them?"

"Yes, sir. They said they'd be here."

"I'm not going to wait," said Dale. "One of you guys will have to draw position for them. Work it out among yourselves. The thing that porks me is those goddam reels never show, and then they bitch at the arrangements and claim they always get screwed. If they'd attend to one tenth of the things they're supposed to, they wouldn't get screwed."

The first item covered was the general parade route. Arthur Baldwin briefed the men on every move the motorcade would make, every turn, every step. Baldwin pointed to the positions along the route where Conger demonstrations were planned.

"Hold it," said a Global technician. "We won't be able to get a picture on that street corner. Can they move around to the north side of the building? That way we'll get a clear shot from the mobile unit to the transmitter dish we have on the hotel roof across the street. Otherwise, we'll lose the picture."

"Okay, we'll move 'em. Fergie, make a note," said Baldwin. "Now, when Conger gets to the Lord Marquette Hotel, he plans to get out of his car and accept the welcome from the Colorado delegation, his home state. There's an X on the maps where that'll take place. It'll be a big demonstartion . . . bands, palomino horses, cowgirls, the whole thing."

"No good," said Lou Wells. "Our men tell us we cannot get any pictures on that narrow side street. Any problem moving the whole damn show to Michigan Boulevard?"

"No problem," said Baldwin. "Except the Colorado demonstration will be in front of the Ohio delegation's hotel. If that's the way we get it on TV, that's the way we'll do it. Also, the motorcade will be stopping in the process of making a turn onto Michigan Boulevard. Conger's car will be at the intersection, the rest behind him, but the bikes, the TV mobile units, the security car will all have rounded the corner. It may get a little awkward trying to control it."

"We'll put extra bikes alongside the motorcade at that point," said a Chicago Police representative. "We'll also take our cue to proceed from you, Mr. Baldwin, through the walkie-talkies from your point at the demonstration to the lead bikes in the front Vee."

"Fine," said Baldwin. "It's then a straight run down Michigan Boulevard to the bridge. We'll turn there to make the circuit in the Loop."

"I thought that was out," said the Telenet producer. "My instructions are to cover you straight down Michigan to the hotel."

"If you do, ol' buddy," said Dale, "you'll miss a helluva big parade in Chicago's Loop."

"Is this final?" asked Lou Wells. "No more changes?" Dale looked at Baldwin, who shrugged.

"No more changes," said Dale. "Okay," he continued, "so now Conger's car is nearing his hotel. We bring it to the curb, with its front wheels just short of the corner, the actual corner of Coyne Street and Michigan Boulevard. There will be a mark on the curbing. Got it? Now, at that point the car is stopped. Conger does not leave the car immediately. There will be a hand mike and a public-address system at that corner. A sound engineer will guard it prior to Conger's arrival at that position. Conger will stand up in the car and talk to the mob for about ten minutes."

"Our camera truck around the corner won't get a shot of him, Charlie," said a Global man. "The marquee's in the way, or rather, the skirt hanging down from the marquee, the cloth with the hotel's name on it."

"Fergie," said Dale, "tell the hotel to remove the skirt on that marquee for Monday morning."

"We'll be blocked, too," said Wells. "We're on the far corner. We can't get a permit from Chicago to build a camera platform on the sidewalk. Without it, we can't shoot over the heads of the crowd."

"If you could shoot out the French windows of the ballroom on the mezzanine floor of the hotel across the street, would that solve your problem?" asked Dale.

"Yes," said Wells.

"Okay, it's done," said Dale. "We'll clear it for you with the other hotel. All right. Now, this is a Captain of the Chicago Police, who will brief you as to how we plan to control crowd movements. Captain?"

The Police Captain addressed the group: "The plan is to put barricades up all along Michigan Boulevard. No one, I repeat, *no one*, will be permitted beyond barricades until after the motorcade has passed that point. When the motorcade has passed, then the police will permit the crowd to fill in behind the cars. When Conger stops in front of his hotel and uses the hand mike, standing up in his car, then and only then will the crowd be permitted to break police barricades and surge across Michigan Boulevard. Up until the time Conger's car stops, all crowds will be restricted to the far side, the park side, the lake side of Michigan Boulevard. This is to keep the avenue clear for the vehicles which will precede the candidate's car. By that, I mean the bikes, the mobile TV trucks, the still photographers' truck. Even though you will see police barricades and uniformed men across Michigan Boulevard restricting people from crossing to the hotel side where the Conger car will be, please bear in mind those men are under instructions to permit the crowd to break through after the parade is no longer in forward motion."

"Thanks, Captain," said Dale. "All right, are all the crash-truck drivers here?" Dale used the term by which the mobile television vehicles are known. Some trucks were large vans, some station wagons, others specially built, still others were converted from open hearses. The drivers raised their hands. "Okay, fine. I know, gentlemen, it is very unusual to ask that the drivers attend a meeting such as this one. But after the fiasco of two weeks ago when two of you guys actually crashed into one another during Governor Green's arrival parade, I felt the men who were actually going to drive the vehicles should be here. We will now, and for as long as it takes ad infinitum, settle the position of each network's mobile-camera unit. I suggest we start by agreeing that the newsreels and stills must be accommodated. By that I mean, we have made arrangements to place the truck for the still photographers here." Dale pointed to its position in the motorcade. "It will not be a high-sided monster like the one used two weeks ago. All you men will be able to shoot, to get good pictures over the top of it. All of you except perhaps Telenet, which shoots out the tailgate of a station wagon. You're pretty low, Telenet. I don't know what you'll get on turns and curves."

"We'll manage," said the Telenet man. "We always do."

"Okay," said Dale. "Now, in your front Vee let's make five positions, like I said. Three for TV, one for stills, one for reels. Who's going to draw for the reels?" Not a sound was heard, not a hand raised. "Aw, come on fellas," said Dale. "So they never show for a meeting. So we've got to give 'em a position. So somebody's got to draw for them, and it's not going to be me." Still no one cooperated. "I'm telling you, guys, I'm not going to get into a lox-fry Monday morning. We're not going to just give 'em a position and watch all hell break loose ten minutes before the parade gets under way. We are going to settle it now, and one of you guys is going to take the responsibility of drawing for those goddam reels. Now who's it gonna be?"

The man representing the still photographers, sensing the solid wall of television personnel lined up against the newsreels, excused himself and made a call to someone while the others sat and waited. In a moment he returned.

"I will draw for the reels," he said meekly. Wild cheering, whistles, and applause filled the room. Two men attempted to pick the man up and carry him on their shoulders around the room.

"Okay, okay, guys," said Dale. "We've got a patsy for the reels.

Come on, let's get this thing over with. I got to see a Conger telecast from Washington in a few minutes. Come on guys, back to the
parade." The room settled down once again. "Now here's what
happens when Conger, his wife, and two sons leave the car and
start their walk to the hotel entrance. . . ."

And so it went, hour after hour, day folding into night, as Charlie
Dale and his staff inched their way, slowly but expertly, toward the
hour of Andrew Conger's arrival in Chicago and the opening day of
the convention.

Andrew Conger's parade was a masterpiece of television coverage.
The New York papers called it the finest television production of
its kind ever seen. None of the crash trucks crashed into each other.
Baldwin's planned periodical "mobbing" of Conger, his prearranged
surges of masses of people through police barriers, the "spontaneous"
demonstrations, all worked according to split-second timing and
were seen with beautiful closeups on TV.

Dale missed the tail end of the parade. He was in a Conger staff
car on his way to the Stock Yards and the Hall. Dale was using his
television trailer inside the Hall as home base during convention
hours, and the hotel office at other times. A volunteer driver who
knew Chicago well had been assigned to him. Dale sat in the center
of the rear seat, leaned his head back against the upholstery, and
closed his eyes. He wasn't thinking about the convention. His
thoughts were of his wife.

Janet had arrived in Chicago the previous night. She had come in
with a busload of women volunteers from Denver, and was scheduled today for duty at the main *Conger Monger* booth in Conger's
hotel lobby. The *Conger Mongers* were a women's voluntary organization, complete with two-wheel carts, umbrellas protecting their
wares, and bells and horns to announce their Conger souvenirs:
badges, hats, and whistles.

When Dale had arisen this morning after three hours' sleep, he had dressed quickly and thrown some Convention Hall admission passes to Janet, who was propped up in bed, drinking coffee.

"Here's a set for each day. Don't lose them. There's a pass for the daytime session and the evening. The kind you have will permit you to come right to our trailer where we have the television operation."

"Thank you, dear," Janet said. "I don't know how much you'll see of me. There are too many bright lights in this wicked, sinful city."

"Now, Jan, let's not . . ."

"My, what a wonderful feeling it is to be here," she cut in. "I mean, in Chicago. After Denver, it's like being in Paris. I'm glad I came."

"I am too," said Dale honestly. "I'm just sorry we won't be able to see more of each other. I'll be terribly busy. As I've told you, the only way for us to spend any time together will be if you come out to the Hall. Or late at night here in the hotel."

"Don't worry, dear boy. This is my fling. Just pay the bills when they come in. I plan to leave for Lake Forrest the minute my time is up in the Conger booth. Around four."

"Now look, dammit. I'm telling you right now any money you spend outside of essentials is on you," Dale said. "Get this silly 'fling' idea out of your head. There's a lot less money today than when I left Denver. And I'm not getting many encouraging letters from Vic Hanson, either."

"Having trouble with little Victor?" Janet asked.

"No, nothing you'd understand. But it's still touch and go, and you know it. So don't go off half-cocked to Marshall Fields or Saks. Get yourself something nice if you want to. One nice thing. I'd like to do that for you while you're here."

"Why, aren't you sweet," Janet said, taunting him. "How unselfish of you, how unlike you."

Dale looked at his watch. "I'm late. It's nice to have you here." But suddenly he wasn't sure he meant it. What a different conversation this would be, he thought, if Sandra were lying there in bed. I wonder what she's doing tonight? Maybe I'll call her from the trailer later on. "But now I've got to go. When will you be back from Lake Forrest?"

"Oh, I don't know. Whenever someone from the party drives me back."

"What party?"

"Didn't I tell you? Nancy's throwing a party for me. You remember her. Nancy Small. She and Bud were in New York a couple of years ago. We all had dinner at The Palms and went to a hockey game."

"Oh, yeah. Investment banking," said Dale. "Well, okay, I'll see you when you get back. Have a good time."

"Don't worry, dear. I will." There was mockery in her voice.

Dale's driver stopped at the VIP entrance in the rear of the Convention Hall. Dale opened his eyes, pushed his thoughts of Janet aside, and grabbed his brief case. He walked hurriedly through the throng standing at attention for the National Anthem as the convention was brought to order. It was a trick which he had used many times before, and he made the trailer quickly.

Charlie Dale's television trailer was a communications nerve center of incredible proportions. In it there was an aura of complete visual control over the very lives and destinies of every individual connected with the convention. It was an octopus whose tentacles stretched out, in the form of wires and short-wave frequencies, to every section of Chicago involved in the political pageantry at the Stockyards Hall. Nothing escaped the eyes or ears of this electronic Peeping Tom.

With a word from Dale over his direct wires to NA, Telenet, and Global, a Conger man arriving at the Hall could be instantly projected onto network TV and into forty million living rooms. A typical example of how the trailer operated took place that first night. Dale's man stationed at Conger's hotel called and said Senator Flemard had an important announcement on the Conger delegation strength and was on his way to the Hall. Dale's staff, by short wave, directed the limousine to Entrance D. Dale's staff then contacted the networks, one by one. "This is the Conger TV Trailer, Global. Senator Flemard's due at Entrance D at 9:10 P.M. He's got a hot rundown on Conger delegation strength. Do you want him?" Political panderers, peddlers of politicians to television, that's what Dale laughingly called his staff. So did the networks. The Senator arrived. A Dale man from the trailer took him to a pre-arranged position on the floor. The network roving reporters, looking more like spacemen with their portable peepy-creepy-camera back packs, whip mast antennas, and headsets, descended on Senator Flemard. The well-briefed Senator feigned surprise at the attention television showered on him. The newsmen, already aware the hot story Senator Flemard had in his human head was the only reason he had been sent to the Hall, hit the poor delegate like starved condors. Both sides, the television reporters and the Senator, played the moment for all it was worth. The newsmen appeared to have stumbled on a hot story; the Senator affected an air of concern over the invasion of his privacy. The viewers at home marveled at TV's ability to be at the right place at the right time, and were impressed with Senator Flemard's seeming ability to field probing questions expertly.

Conversely, the most important men in Conger's party in the country came and went, entered the hall and left, without so much as a single TV newsman or viewer suspecting they had left the Loop. This, too, was controlled by the television trailer. There were areas in the Hall, due to its steel construction, where transmission of sound or picture was impossible, or considerably less than broadcast quality. These were called "blind spots." Here the most confidential, controversial political huddles were held. Dale mapped out the spots with his staff, who expertly steered Conger advisers into them when privacy and the absence of the prowling television eye were requested.

The trailer, controlling every appearance and interview of a Conger supporter, devoured men and careers in its efforts to keep the networks supplied with personalities and eye-catching stories. Heaven help the individual who seriously crossed any member of the Dale staff, for television was the publicity lifeline of a politician. In the end, that line was withheld from only one Conger adviser, an individual who constantly berated Dale for the lack of coverage he obtained. The man was not an important adviser, and Dale could not "sell" him to the networks. Finally, Dale cut off *all* his coverage. The blacked-out politician eventually returned to his home state a debilitated figure, a political eunuch stripped of his power and public influence. To an incredible degree, the political fortunes of many, their position in the national party, and its national political future depended on what switch was thrown, what phone was picked up, who got the nod from Charlie Dale's trailer.

Prior to the first day of the convention, Dale's men had secretly obtained the confidential short-wave-communication frequencies of the three networks. Every word said from the network control rooms to the network men roving in the Hall was monitored in a bedroom in the trailer. Dale was also in short-wave contact with the Conger hotel to prohibit tapping of phone wires. Walkie-talkies were used in all VIP limousines by the Conger advance men, keeping in constant touch with Dale, and giving the TV trailer their progress reports and the estimated times of arrival at the Hall of the VIP's. Someone counted fifty-eight phones, thirty loud-speakers, and twelve television sets in the trailer. The sets, donated by their manufacturer, were marked either *Telenet, Global,* or *North American,* permitting Dale and his staff to monitor the coverage of all three networks simultaneously. Special "light bell" phones ran from the trailer to the speakers' rostrum area in order to alert the Permanent Chairman of the Convention, Congressman Frank Love, when show-business and political VIP personalities arrived at the Hall. The networks would be alerted at the same time, assuring maximum coverage as the various well-known figures made their ways to their special seats. Then powerful spotlights would swoop down on them in order to record, in fascinating closeups, the informal, off-the-record human-interest activity in the boxes.

The national television audience thrilled at the vivid character studies, the candid shots of national political figures in confidential conversation, who never suspected that the powerful long-range lenses of the TV cameras were sending their images into forty million homes. There was an intangible characteristic of the television camera which embraced its ability to X-ray the subject being photographed. The cathode tube searched, probed, dug into the very fiber of the person's being.

Interestingly enough, not one out of five of the candid, eavesdropping pictures, would have been possible to photograph if people such as Dale in television hadn't insisted on changing the very heart and symbol of the assembly: the state delegation standards. Prior to the intrusion and dominance of television, the state standards were tacked horizontally on poles—wide, unstable things. TV men found, however, that these signs became a cardboard curtain when the long lens cameras prowled the hall searching for candid shots of the fascinating, hurried conferences of VIP's on the floor. The two parties were consulted as to the feasibility of lettering the state signs vertically, incorporating a three-sided trylon at the top of the pole. They agreed. The television picture at Conger's convention was blocked only to the extent of the width of the vertical lettering, as opposed to the enormous flapping signs of pre-television years. The political parties found much to their joy that the vertical standards, made much stronger by the triangular design, lasted for the entire convention, whereas the previous horizontal signs were ripped off and destroyed nightly, requiring replacement each day.

These same state standards pumped, wheeled, and rocked back and forth in time to a dozen political tunes when Andrew Conger's name was placed in nomination early Wednesday evening, the third night of the convention. The nominating speech electrified the Hall. The instant the final words, "Andrew H. Conger," were uttered, Dale gave the signals for the house organist and band to let it roll and for the demonstration for Conger to pour into the aisles at the rear of the Hall.

There was the usual speculation as to how "spontaneous" Conger's demonstration was. To be sure, it was planned, but it was fun, exciting, and the delegates and television audience loved it. The National Committee, however, imposed a maximum time for it to command the floor. This was done because of fear of boring the TV audience. Years ago, a candidate's popularity at a convention had been judged by the length of the demonstration when his name was placed in nomination. This had resulted in the planned "spontaneous" long demonstration. Andrew Conger's display was no exception, but the orders from the National Committee were to clear the floor in fifteen minutes.

Skeeter Whippett had been in charge of the "enthusiasm factor" of Conger political rallies for years, both in Colorado and throughout the length and breadth of the country. Whippett, at forty-five, was a perennial cheer leader. He even dressed like one for the rallies, complete with white shirt, white sweater, white flannel trousers, and white bucks. He was blond and good looking. Tell Skeeter Whippett you wanted a wild bunch of enthusiastic kids at the Tulsa airport at 3:00 A.M. to welcome Andy Conger, and he'd have them there. Whippett was a phenomenon: inexhaustible in energy, improvisation, and ideas.

Whippett's command post for a demonstration was on the convention floor, directly underneath and in front of the rostrum, his back pressed against its base to prevent his being crushed to death. He said he couldn't operate unless he was "right smack-dab in the ever-loving-middle-screaming-thick of it." He used a walkie-talkie to his "starters" at the rear of the hall and in the balconies, for since the inclusion of TV coverage, visual stunts were also planned in the higher seats. Skeeter loved balcony and aerial tricks, for they could be carefully controlled and executed to perfection without the unknown sobriety quotient of the delegates to worry about.

Skeeter's favorite visual stunt in 1960 was an aerial device which stopped the show. At the very height of the Conger demonstration, an enormous wailing and belching replica of a Redstone rocket, complete with space capsule on the nose, inched its way out into the hall on cables strung over the heads of the delegates. It was high in the balcony, aligned with two large exit tunnels. When the rocket was one-third of the way across, the nose cone separated from the vehicle and sailed on across the hall streaming a banner which read: "OUTER SPACE IS GOING FOR CONGER." Dale had alerted the networks, and their cameras focused on it with beautiful closeups. The instant the nose cone had reached the exit tunnel, it was grabbed by waiting hands and carried around the perimeter of the entire hall to the original launching point. In the meantime, the Conger rocket made its way across and disappeared. Immediately the nose cone whistled out on the wire again, this time trailing a banner which read: "THE BIG DIPPER'S FOR CONGER." Another shriek went up from the floor. Once more the nose cone was carried around for its final journey. It came out with a huge baby-pink bonnet tied around its middle, trailing a pink and blue banner which said: "THE LITTLE DIPPER'S FOR CONGER TOO." It worked, and the convention loved it. From that point forward, Skeeter played out the string of the demonstration, but his heart wasn't in it. He had fought with Dale for two weeks, insisting there should be a fourth trip for the nose cone and a fourth banner which would read: "IN HEAVEN IT'S CONGER." Dale maintained as how there was enough worry about religion creeping into the campaign without Conger indicating endorsement from the Almighty.

Two favorite-son names were placed in nomination after Conger. With firm control from the rostrum, however, their demonstrations were kept to a minimum length, and the balloting for the presidential candidate began promptly.

For Dale, at least, it was an anticlimax. The floor manager of the Conger candidacy had done his work well. He missed his estimate by half a delegate's vote. The balloting was speeded up in the electronic calculators which projected their tallies on the large screens inside the hall. By the time the roll call had reached the Pennsylvania delegation, Andy Conger was over the top.

Secretary of State Andrew H. Conger was now his party's nominee for the Presidency of the United States.

When the booming reaction to Conger's victory had subsided,
Lou Wells of NA was a caller at Dale's TV trailer. NA had been
overly co-operative, overly solicitous since the first day. Dale wasn't
sure if they were leaning over backward to offset the rumors of their
partiality toward Green, sincerely concerned as to the quality of
their coverage in order to recoup their audience losses of the previous convention, or if they were conducting a plan to woo and
romance Andrew Conger into a statement on the debates. Wells
was his usual affable self, congratulating Dale on the Conger victory, as Dale led him to the back bedroom for privacy.

"What held up so long that seconding speech by Ralph Royce?"
asked Wells. "That was quite a stage-wait. You saw we had trouble
filling it with those interviews from the hotel."

"Oh, a stupid political crisis," said Dale, closing the door behind
them and turning down the volume on the TV sets in the rear
room. "Rufe Little made a new nonstop record from the hotel to
the Hall to cut some lines out of Royce's speech. Royce was mad
as hell. They did it right here. I stayed with them to get the changes.
Little really put the screws to Royce. Poor guy. The only thing he
really wanted to say was what Little insisted he cut. Politics stink to
high heaven."

"Do debates stink too, Charlie?" asked Wells.

"No, they don't. But it depends on a lot of things whether they
do or don't."

"How can Conger refuse?"

"I don't know. But, Lou, the polls have held. He's higher now
than two weeks ago. He has nothing to gain by them."

"He has a lot to lose by refusing them."

"Name me one thing."

"Being called chicken. No guts. Favorable public opinion is
maintained in a hairline balance sometimes. It could go to the
underdog, in which case they'd be after Conger's scalp."

"You're after it right now, Lou."

"I'm after one thing. A series of debates between Andrew Conger and Joseph Green." Wells paused, looked at the floor between his knees momentarily, and then raised his head to look at Dale directly. "What kind of assurances do you want?" he asked.

"For what?"

"For Conger to say okay to the debates? What do you need to tell him? What does Morgan need to tell him?"

"You better keep Morgan away from Conger right now."

"What do you mean? Your own press secretary called Morgan this morning to thank him for the excellent coverage NA has given Conger. Jenkins said he was calling at Conger's request."

"Jenkins is a stupid idiot. He hasn't got the slightest idea what makes TV news tick or the delicate difference between slanted news and impartial coverage. You've slanted this thing toward Conger all the way. Why?"

"We're short one man for our presidential debates, that's why. It's also why I came over."

Wells reached into a Manila folder and handed a sheet of paper to Dale. "Here's your copy of the invitation we just sent by wire to Andrew H. Conger. Want to make a little bet we'll get your man by September first?"

"Yeah, fifty bucks you don't."

"You're on." Wells left some extra copies of the wire from the three networks to Conger and departed.

Dale looked for Janet. She was nowhere to be seen. He was certain Janet wouldn't miss the Conger demonstration. She must be really having a ball, thought Dale. Dammit, I'll have one myself if that's the kind of brush she's going to give me. The hell with it!

Actually Janet Dale was out in Lake Forrest, watching the convention on TV with her college roommate Nancy and husband. Janet had mentioned to Nancy that evening she had wanted to go to the trailer in the Hall, but that Charlie somehow had given her the impression she would be in the way. Maybe she should have gone anyway; it would have been exciting. She had come all this way really hoping to be with Charlie, she admitted to herself. But, dammit, she had taken a position and couldn't just change it. Charlie had been no help at all.

But Dale had little time to think further about Janet. A call for him on Abner Shepherd's private wire came through, and Fergie handed the phone over to him.

"Thanks Fergie. Charlie Dale here."

"Ab Shepherd, Chazz. We're going to ram through the vice presidential nominations tonight. Alert the networks. Can you find Rufe and tell him to call Conger immediately? Andy's smelled something over at the Blackstone and wants to beat the opposition."

"Jesus, we'll be here till morning. Yeah, I can alert everybody. Hold on a minute."

"I can't. Get Rufe to call me, or Andy. Also tell the rostrum Conger will be calling the Chairman in five minutes. For your ears only, it will be Hughes. Stuff looks great, Charlie. 'By."

Dale made his calls quickly. Little was found, and established his home base in the trailer's back bedroom; nominators were procured, along with seconders. The opposition to Conger's choice for running-mate never had a chance. They were still trying to ascertain the correct pronunciation of their man's middle name when the first nominating speech in behalf of United States Senator Wardwell Hughes rang through the Hall. The steamroller was manned and rolling.

Dale looked at Bernie Lamb, standing near him in the trailer.

"There's your man, Bernie. Lots of luck."

Wardwell Hughes was one of the most controversial and colorful younger men in the Senate. With his wife Lucille, he had captivated Washington society, and alienated the Washington Press Corps to an extreme seldom witnessed. Hughes had never accepted an invitation to speak before The National Press Club, although he had been invited several times. He was rude to newsmen, reminded broadcasters constantly that he did not own a television set (although he did, and watched television news religiously), and was the only person Dale had ever seen who didn't photograph well even in God's own light, the sun.

"My God!" said Lamb, "I gotta light that guy for the next three months?"

"You have to do a lot more than that. You have to make him the darling of the tube and make his wife Lucille the second mistress of television, Susan Conger being the first, naturally."

"Where and how do I start?"

"I suggest you start with his Adam's apple. It looks like a grapefruit. Powder it every night on the sides."

"Oh, shut up!" said Lamb, laughing as he peered at Hughes's image on the monitor. Global was doing a feed from Hughes's suite, and Wardwell looked ghastly. Lucille looked wonderful.

"Thank God he can talk," said Lamb. "Oh well, I asked for it."

"No, you didn't. I asked you," said Dale.

The nomination went quickly under the expert guidance of Rufus Little in the Hall. It was all over much sooner than Dale expected. So this is the ticket, thought Dale. Conger and Hughes.

Someone thrust a phone at Dale. "Hello, Charlie, this is Jenkins. How fast can you get back here?"

"I can come right now, Wilbur," said Dale. "What's up?"

"The networks and press are demanding a news conference on the debate invitations. I'd like you to help me set it up. We'll hold it in your TV room next to your office."

"That's fine, and you can push it along by getting Ham Forrest down right away. He's sitting in Conger's suite. Tell him what you need. I'll be there as soon as I can make it."

"Thanks, Charlie," said Jenkins and clicked off the line.

When Dale arrived, the news conference was already under way. Ham Forrest had it completely under control. Jenkins no more needs me, thought Dale, yawning, than the man in the moon. Nevertheless, Dale was there and couldn't get out of it gracefully, so he leaned against a wall at the rear of the room, out of the heat of the TV lights, and listened.

The newsmen were reading aloud portions of the text of the debate invitation wire to Conger and slamming Jenkins with piercing questions. Challenging demands from Governor Green's head-quarters in Fairlee had made their way into the hands of the press, and their probes and insinuations were expert, even at the late hour.

"I've told you," Jenkins was saying, "there will be no statement on the debates tonight. You have my opening remarks."

"Who's Conger meeting tonight?" someone asked.

"Party leaders. The discussion is limited to the issues."

"Has he said anything which in your opinion changed his position on the debates, turning them down that is?" another newsman asked.

"No," said Jenkins.

"When will he make up his mind on the debates?" another asked. Dale wondered if Jenkins smelled this one, if he could field it. It was loaded.

"It's already made up. He is giving no more thought to the debates."

Dale relaxed.

"Do you want tonic or ginger ale?" Susan Conger asked.

"Tonic is fine," said her husband. "Is there any lime or lemon there? It would be good for my throat."

"Yes, there's lemon, dear."

"Good."

The last member of the press had left the Conger suite some time ago with the last television technician. The large drawing room was quite dark. Susan had turned out all the lights except the lamp by the end-table that held the ice and mixes and the lamp at Andrew Conger's desk. In the dimness, it was difficult to see the residue of the nerve-wracking, almost stifling press conference and family statement the Congers had survived moments before. Coils of camera cable were tucked unobtrusively behind the curtains. Huge power outlets had been stacked under tables and at the baseboards. Here and there a flash bulb was in evidence where it had been hastily dumped on a window sill by a frantic still photographer. But Susan had done her best to tidy up the room the minute the last man was gone. The two boys, Jack and Frank, had said their good-nights and left. Susan knew by experience it would be a long night for her husband. She suggested a relaxing drink together. Andy had objected, but Susan said it would do him good. "You go in and get your robe on, and I'll tidy up a bit more in the room."

Conger returned in slippers and his favorite dressing robe—red with a midnight-blue shawl collar. He went directly to his desk, looked at the stack of notes, yawned, and walked to a comfortable overstuffed wingback chair. He sat down with a sigh. Susan looked at him, legs stretched out straight in front of him, slouched down to where his chin almost touched his chest.

Poor dear, she thought, looking at his exhausted body. In the dim light falling on Conger's chair she couldn't see if Andy's eyes were open or shut. How hard he's worked for this moment. How many years have we strived for this very evening, together? Susan poured the tonic into a tall glass of ice and vodka. She stirred the drink slightly after squeezing in half a lemon. As she walked toward Andy, she thought how funny it was that the favorite drink of one of the most influential anti-Communists in the world was a vodka and tonic.

"Here you are, killer," she said softly, realizing Andy had dozed off. Long ago, Susan and the boys had nicknamed him "Killer" on a hunting trip. He looked up at her sleepily and held out his hand for the drink. He was red-eyed, groggy with exhaustion.

"Thanks, Norma," said Conger. In the early years following their marriage, Andy swore she looked just like Norma Talmadge. He used the name occasionally. "That looks good." He took a long, slow sip. "And tastes good, too. I can taste the lemon."

Susan touched his glass with hers, and while they were touching, leaned over and kissed him on the forehead. "Here's to the White House. And to the man I love."

"That's nice. Here's to the woman I love. The hell with the White House." And for the first time all day Susan felt Andy relax.

"I want you to be rested tomorrow," said Susan. "I want you to be the best-looking presidential candidate that has ever stood at a convention rostrum. Please don't work too late, Andy."

"I won't. But I want to talk. It's been a rough day." Susan sat in the matching chair near Conger. "Nice and quiet, isn't it?" Conger said.

"Lovely—peaceful. I never thought the day would end." Susan lit a cigarette.

"I'd really like this speech tomorrow to be something," said Conger. "You know, not the same old thing, not what the delegates want to hear. I'd like to do it more for TV—to set the tone of the whole campaign. I have some things I want to say."

Poor Andy wanted to talk, thought Susan. Of course he had to wind down with somebody. She knew these times at the end of a strenuous day very well. She had seen Conger in similar moods during previous campaigns or while flying home to the United States with him after important conferences as Secretary of State. Everybody needed somebody, and Andy needed her. Everything she said to him now, Susan thought, would be critical, could influence him, could sway him into fair or foul waters. Susan knew she must be careful, for in these periods of complete fatigue, Andy Conger—with close associates, with his family, good friends—was as pliable as soft clay.

"I know your speech will be special," said Susan. "You've been writing it for ten years, in everything you've said and done."

Conger straightened slightly in his chair and hunched his torso forward, placing considerable weight on his forearms as they rested on the upholstered arms of the chair. He held his drink with both hands. "There are some things I would say if it weren't for this debate furor, Susan."

"Are you going to discuss them in your speech?"

"I don't know. No, I think not. But I want you to understand why I'm not accepting them. The official invitation came from the networks tonight."

"I saw it. Ruth showed it to me."

"Well, it's just that . . ." Conger paused, shifted his weight in his chair, and continued, "It's just that it's wrong politically, Susan. I'm not afraid to debate Green. I'd take him in a minute. It's just that I will be breaking every political rule in the book if I accept."

"Whether or not you accept the debates, Andy, aren't you the one who says the best man somehow always wins? The man who's supposed to?" Susan had been the listener to Andy's fatalistic theories on political campaigns for many years. Conger's premise was that many things could be done in a campaign to heighten interest and define issues, but that forces greater than any single human were at work determining the outcome.

"Yes . . . I believe that."

"Then what difference does it make if you do debate Green, or don't? And if it doesn't make any difference, why not remove this dreadful pressure from yourself, when you think it is proper to do so, and accept?"

"Because I'm not sure they're the best thing for a campaign, or the country, as they're now being discussed. I'm not sure they won't distort issues, or cause issues to get completely lost in the razz-matazz of television. I'm not sure that what should be a serious forum for incredibly important issues and the exchange of views with Green won't turn into a cheap spectacle."

"Is that really possible?" Susan asked.

"Well, maybe I'm exaggerating. But maybe not. It's the issues that are important. Nothing else. The issues, and how well I handle them. That's how a debate between two presidential candidates can be of enormous service to the voters and contribute to our political process. But if a television debate turns out to be a beauty contest or a personality comparison, then it performs no function whatsoever. If substance becomes secondary to performance or pres- entation, then a debate on television is a bad thing." Conger stopped, sipped on his drink, and placed it on the table next to his chair. He looked up at the ceiling with a half-smile. "I wonder if Woodrow Wilson or Lincoln, for that matter, ever would have been elected if they'd had to put up with that damn cyclops of a TV camera."

"Interesting thought," Susan replied.

"All this talk about dignifying the campaign," Conger said wearily. "Agghh . . . that's a lot of pap the networks are feeding the public. Instead of elevating the importance of the office of the President, it could drag me down into the mud of a quiz show." Andy was working out of his fogged exhaustion, was finding his mind again, thought Susan.

"You don't have to make a decision tonight, do you, dear?" she asked.

"No, of course not. I merely wanted to talk to you about it. Because the debates may be the most important thing that's ever happened in politics. If this is so, I'd honestly hate to obstruct them, stand in their way. On the other hand . . ." Conger cut himself off with a shrug. "I guess what I really want to say tonight to you, Sue, is I'd like you to be patient. Permit me to be a politician here in Chicago and a selfless man who really wants to do what's right when I have figured it out. If I feel it's proper to accept the debates, I will do so."

"You're the man I love, Andy, no matter who you are or what you do," Susan said softly, looking at him. "I know you will make the right decision."

"I must," Conger said, with an edge of hardness to his voice. "I must. A great deal hangs on it. I must not make the wrong decision." Susan looked at her husband through eyes which were moist with new tears.

"Nothing hangs on it, Andy. Even if it's wrong, I will still love you as I do tonight." Conger rose from his chair, paced the room from one end to the other slowly, silently. Whatever he was thinking drew him to his desk. He picked up a pencil, made a brief note on a margin. Susan watched him, saying nothing. Couldn't he understand? she thought. What difference do the debates make, what difference the campaign? What difference, Andy? I love you.

"Whatever you do, Andy," Susan said, rising, "do what you think is best. Whatever you do it will be the right thing, because you yourself will have made the decision." Conger grunted in his preoccupation. He sat down absently in the chair, drew it forward, and peered intently at a report. Susan could see the strain of sleeplessness in his face. She walked softly up behind him, placed her right hand ever so gently on his right shoulder, leaned over and kissed his hair, her lips barely brushing the wiry gray wave above his ear. Without a word, she left the room.

Once in her bedroom, Susan was struck with an impulse to talk to Charlie Dale. Andy was deep in his concentration on the vital speech he would deliver tomorrow. Everything Andy said would be seen on television and would be affected by how well Dale was prepared for her husband's appearance in the Hall. In a matter of minutes the operator had located Dale. "Hi, Charlie, this is Susan. Got a minute?"

"Sure. Many congratulations. We've worked a long time for this, Sue," said Dale.

"We sure have. Charlie, you all set for the big night tomorrow?"

"Yes, ma'am. How's Andy feeling? I'll bet he's pooped."

"He's absolutely exhausted. That's why I'm calling you. You'll do your best for him, won't you? I mean like the lighting, the makeup, and those things? Andy wants tomorrow night to be perfect."

Susan was fishing, Charlie thought. I wonder for what?

"We're all set, Sue. I have a lighting man here from New York, special lights on the rostrum just for Andy, and his favorite makeup man from Telenet—New York also."

"Oh, that's grand. I want him to look as handsome as he should. You know, everybody changes a little in four years. Should he get a haircut tomorrow? It's pretty long."

"No, for God's sake, no. Don't let him cut his hair. Keep the barber away from him."

"Okay, Charlie, if you say so. It's just I don't want him to look like Liberace up there."

"Believe me, Sue, he won't. But the worst thing in the world is for him to get his hair cut, even trimmed, on the day of a major telecast. Honestly, take my word for it."

"Okay, you're the boss. Have you picked out his clothes?"

"Yes, Cliff Harley has them put aside." Harley was Conger's appointments secretary, and had left State to join the campaign.

"Fine. I'm not going to see any of those messy old pleats or dark curtains behind my Andy tomorrow night, am I, Charlie?" That was it, thought Dale. By God, it never failed. The last thing they brought up was always the real reason behind the call.

"You'll see no curtains or pleats tomorrow night, Sue, or any night from now through the campaign. I promised you in Washington. The only velour curtains you're ever going to see behind Andy, as far as I'm concerned, are the ones you will hang yourself when you're in the White House."

Susan laughed. "Oh, that makes me feel better. I was hoping you hadn't forgotten," she said. "Well, I guess that covers it. Thanks for all you're doing. And make it good for our boy tomorrow night."

"Our work is done, Sue. It's up to Andy now. But I know he'll be terrific."

"I do too. Good night, and thanks." And Susan hung up.

By God, thought Dale, I'm going to tell that guy at the National Committee to get off my back. The Committee had screamed to the heavens when they found out it would cost twelve hundred dollars to give Dale the new backing he wanted just for Andy Conger.

At four that morning, three men received phone calls and hurried to Conger's suite. The men were Rufus Little; George Pinnell, a close personal friend of Conger's from St. Louis; and Commander Jonah Keel, owner of a successful public relations firm in Los Angeles, and Conger's occasional tennis partner. Andy Conger had called them down to discuss the debate issue, which at that late hour had gotten the best of him.

Pinnell, who had been riding political fences so long he had pickets growing up his backbone, suggested that Conger postpone any decision indefinitely and wait to see which way the wind was going to blow. Jonah Keel, a do-gooder who somehow had wormed his way into Conger's inner circle, said they were good for the country, and made a recommendation in favor of the debates, leaving the timing of the announcement up to Conger. Conger then turned to Little, who had been rotating the invitation wire over and over in his hands.

"Well, Rufe, what have you got to say?" asked Conger.

"I say you don't debate. But I also say we got to figure out some reason why, and get it out. But after, not before, your speech tomorrow—I mean tonight. We don't want to destroy the buildup on the speech. A lot of people think you might talk debates in your speech."

"I was thinking the same thing, Rufe. Okay fellows, thanks for coming down. That is all I had on my mind. Good night."

As the three left the suite, Jonah Keel wondered if that was what it meant to be a confidant of a potential President. The meeting had grabbed him out of a sound sleep and hadn't lasted ten minutes. The heel of his slipper fell off as he stumbled into the elevator. "Goddam," he said, leaning over to pick it up.

Andrew Conger said the same thing when he was alone again. "Goddam!" He stared at the invitation wire on the desk, and slung it against the window glass; it dropped to the sill. Once more he paced the room.

Those bastards, he thought. Each one true to type. What the hell do they know? One guy says debate, one guy says don't, and old careful George says don't do either. Not a single helpful suggestion. Not even Rufe. He's so deep in hard-nose politics he can't see the signs, can't see the daylight. The hell with them. I'll do the speech the way I want to, I'll say what I want to say. By God, Susan had the only helpful suggestion I've heard all night. She was right. Do what I want to do. Be myself, say what I want to say. The hell with all of them, thought Conger. All of them, that is, except Susan. Yup, she was right as rain. Don't listen to anybody. Make this speech what *I* want it to be. And, by God, that's just what I'm going to do! At least Susan will like it, and I will too.

Conger, alert and in surprising command of his remaining strength and reserves, sat down once more. He was still working at seven-thirty when Susan, unable to sleep, brought him orange juice and tea. Conger was nodding over his pad, groggy. He couldn't drink the tea. He was like a child who had been permitted to stay up beyond his regular bedtime and become almost too drowsy to walk. Susan led him to his bed, tucked him in, and drew the blinds against the piercing sunlight.

Andrew Conger was asleep as his head touched the pillow.

9

The Last Day of the Convention

"Okay, that's fine. Now hold . . . right there," said Charlie Dale to Sandy Jones in the control room.

"How long does this hunk run?" asked Sandy.

"About five minutes. Oops! If he gestures like that too often, we'll have to pull back to include his hands." The two watched the television monitors intently. "No, it's okay," said Dale. "Just sit on him, right there. I'll alert you when he goes to civil rights. I'll want that stuff on a full closeup. Ahh, that's good, Sandy. Beautiful pictures, lovely." Jones, on a statement of Conger's which drew applause, punched up a picture of a handsome teenaged girl in the general admission seats, listening raptly to the address.

"If you'd shut up, I could do the whole thing just as good. What comes next?" asked Jones.

"I told you, civil rights. Don't talk. I want to listen for the cue. Gee, that tie he's wearing looks great!"

Dale was slouched on a high stool inches behind Jones, who was directing the television pictures from the rostrum during Andrew Conger's acceptance speech. Dale, prevailing on Lou Wells, had talked his way into the off-limit area, using the excuse that he was the only person who had seen Conger's address. For obvious reasons, there had been no advance text. Conger wanted no interpretive stories by the press before he spoke.

It was true Dale was the only person who had seen the text of Conger's speech. The day had been relatively quiet, with Conger's suite the focus of attention. Dale had made a midmorning trip to the Convention Hall to approve the special backing for Conger and returned to the hotel for a leisurely lunch with Janet.

"Sorry I'm late, Jan," Dale said on arrival at their table. He kissed her lightly on the cheek. "The goddam Chicago supply house tried to sell me the wrong color for some material. I had to battle it out with them."

"That's all right, dear," Jan said pleasantly. "Arthur and Phoebe Baldwin invited me in to the bar for a Bloody Mary. I've been sitting here only a minute."

Dale ordered for the two of them, and Janet resumed the conversation. "I want to apologize for not making it to the Hall last night."

"Oh hell, that's okay. I just thought you'd enjoy it," said Dale, hiding his disappointment.

"I know you think I don't give a damn about your work but believe me, I didn't really know what I should do. We watched it on TV. Suddenly I was very sad I wasn't with you."

"Apology accepted." Dale offered her a cigarette. "My, it's nice to have this breather. We've been going at it pretty hard for over a week. I have an appointment with Andy at three. To go over his acceptance speech."

"Is it good?"

"I haven't seen it. No one has. What about tonight? Do you think you might make it out to the Hall once before you leave Chicago?"

"I'll be there, dear. I promise." Janet laughed suddenly.

"What's the joke?"

"I was just thinking. Before I came up here, you kept telling me not to come because I'd be in the way, because you'd be too busy to see me. You said it wouldn't be right for me to hang around you at the Hall all the time, that it would make you uncomfortable."

"Well, it would," Dale answered.

"But since I've been up here, all you've done is beef because I haven't been with you out at the Hall. You've been hurt, haven't you?"

"Not in the slightest," Dale snapped. "You'd have been in the way. I merely thought you ought to see the place once before it's over. What would people in Denver think if you had to tell them you didn't even see the inside of the Hall?"

"I'm not concerned with what they will think, Charles," Janet said softly. "I'm concerned only with your thoughts."

"It's been a great trip for you," he said. "I've seen you five minutes in seven days. I guess you've had the fling you wanted. Now you can go home and tend the hearth."

"You aren't fooling anyone, Charles," said Janet.

"What do you mean by that?"

"Nothing. Eat your lobster, it's getting cold."

Dale had met with Conger in his suite promptly at three. The nominee was in his dressing gown, his work habit for the day. "I don't know how long my remarks will run, Charlie," he said. "They will not be overly long, however."

"I think that's wise, Andy," said Dale. "You noticed, I'm sure, how short Green's acceptance speech was. I'm certain he did that in deference to TV."

"Yes." Ruth Platt entered the room. "Ruth has collated a rough copy for you," Conger said. "Even I haven't read it all the way through. It's the only copy that's numbered in proper sequence. I'd like you to read it here in the room. You can sit over at that small desk and make whatever notes you need."

"Fine. It shouldn't take me too long," Dale replied. "Thanks, Ruth."

"Take as much time as you need, Charlie. Let's make this one perfect."

"Yes, sir." Dale retired to the desk. Conger paced slowly at the far end of the huge drawing room. After several moments he walked toward his desk and resumed writing. The room was silent.

Dale made copious notes as he read slowly through the document. He marked the length of each major topic or section, estimating its time in minutes. He noted each statement which by construction or buildup would evoke heavy applause or reaction. The years Dale had worked with Conger made these "cheer line" predictions unbelievably accurate. At several places Dale made notes as to a change of subject matter or summarizing statement. These were points where it would be logical to change camera lenses; either move in for a good closeup, or pull back for a wider picture, anticipating Conger's use of his arms and hands for emphasis.

When Dale finished, he looked up at Conger, who was deep in thought. Dale rose and walked toward him. He stood a few feet away, waiting for Conger to pause at his work. "Oh," said Conger, looking up. "All through?"

"Yes, sir," Dale answered. "I'll choose a couple of ties when I go out, Andy. Cliff Harley will have them, and either one will be fine for tonight."

"You're the boss," Conger said, smiling through his fatigue.

"No barber near you today," Dale ordered. "Your hair is just the right length."

"No barber," Conger replied, smiling.

"I'll meet you at the curb on your arrival at the rear of the Hall. From that point I'll be with you all the way. First you go to a restricted VIP room behind the rostrum and platform. You will have fifteen minutes there. On a signal we will leave the room, and I will take you, Susan, and the boys down to a spot behind the long entrance ramp. We will wait there for the actual introduction and entrance cue."

"I don't want fifteen minutes in some goddam closet behind the platform. I want that time here where I can work. We'll leave ten minutes later. All you need is five minutes for safety."

"That's cutting it awfully close, Andy," answered Dale, truly concerned. "What if something serious goes wrong? Will you give me ten minutes in the room?"

"Okay. But no more. I hate to wait."

"I know," said Dale. "Do you plan to rest at all between now and then? I think it would do you some good to sleep, if you can."

"I agree. I plan to finish up here shortly. Then I'll go to bed and sleep through until about an hour before I have to leave. Okay?"

"Just fine. You look a little weary. I think the rest will do wonders for you. See you tonight. And thanks for the chance to go over the speech. It's excellent."

"This means a great deal to me tonight, Charlie," said Conger, looking at Dale with the affection developed over the years of friendship.

"I know, Andy. We're going to bust our pick for you out there. You'll look like a million dollars—if you get some rest. See you at the Hall."

Later, Cliff Harley had told him no one but Rufe Little had seen Conger after Dale left. It hadn't surprised Dale that, according to his study of the speech, there was no mention of the debates. Conger was holding firm, keeping his word to his staff and himself, Dale had thought.

And now, in the control room, eight minutes into the Conger address, everything was proceeding as planned. The pictures were beautiful, and Dale had complimented Jones and Wells, who joined them during Conger's ovation. There was a slight moment of concern when the first indication of the squeal of "feedback" on the public address system made itself heard. Conger, however, followed his briefing from Dale and repositioned his head in relationship to the microphones, speaking more directly to them and leaning slightly into them while keeping his head erect. The squeal stopped and was not heard again.

It was incredible, thought Dale, that Andy Conger could look so superb on two hours' sleep which, Harley had told Dale, was all Conger had permitted himself.

The Conger motorcade had arrived at the hall early, and Dale and Harley had accompanied the candidate to the private VIP room. Conger, by habit, had paced the periphery of the room once, then settled in a chair. Dale and Harley withdrew to a respectful distance. With his chin cradled in his thumb and forefinger, Conger stared at the ceiling, infrequently consulting the notebook which contained his speech text resting in his lap.

The first time Dale observed Conger's tension, he and Harley went over to him and joked about the red phone which had been placed in the room. It was a direct line to the White House, for emergency use. Conger had said the only emergency he anticipated was not being able to read some last-minute notes he had made hurriedly in pencil. It was quiet again. No word was spoken as Dale's makeup man from New York was admitted for final touchup. Conger asked Dale for his opinion. "You look fine, Andy. Could you tighten the knot in your tie? It's a little loose . . . and large." Dale looked at Conger closely as he pulled the knot tight. That was when Dale noticed the vein in his right temple pulsing rapidly, and saw a muscular spasm hit Conger's right eyelid. The spasm was not under Conger's control and was quite frequent. In the years the two had been together, Dale had never before seen such a display of tension and nerves in his man, his Andy. It worried him, frightened him too. Dale immediately started talking.

"Uh, Andy, do you have a minute? I know your mind is on other things, but I'd like quickly to go over the physical aspects of the entrance and the rostrum. What you'll see and do." Conger gave Dale a sideways glance of irritation, the eyelid still in the spasm.

"Make it quick," said Conger.

"We leave here and go to the rear of the rostrum area, about one hundred feet behind the podium. We pick Susan up at her box behind the masking curtains. Those curtains are not behind you when you're speaking. Your special backing looks excellent. Your boys will be with a Sergeant-at-Arms, waiting at the entrance area. On the cue, you and Susan walk out and go directly to the rostrum, where the Permanent Chairman will wait for you. I will hold the boys back, about fifteen or twenty feet behind you, so the pictures on TV don't get too busy. They will be instructed to go to you and Susan when they get to the front end of the tongue. You might keep a lookout for them. But they'll go for you. At one of the times you work the right or left side of the lectern for the still photographers, I will dip in and place your speech on the lectern. There will be no timing cues from us. There are, however, two clocks on the rostrum, one indicating the clock time, the other how many minutes you have been speaking. The rostrum has its own air-conditioning unit built into it, so it shouldn't be too warm for you." Conger's spasm was less frequent now, as he became absorbed in what Dale was saying, his head nodding as he went along with each point Dale made. "The central tower position is a huge thing here, Andy. It's enormous. I don't know if you'll be able to see any of the delegates. There are four television cameras on it, a dozen newsreels, and the top bank is crammed with still photographers. The lights will be very rough from both out front and the sides. Your camera to talk into, the one directly in front of you which takes your closeups, is dead center in front of the rostrum. It is, for your purposes, at exactly the same level as your eyes. Actually, it's a little lower to favor your face when you're looking down at your notes. A special red light, larger than normal, has been installed on top of the camera. It is larger than the tally light you're used to. That is the camera you look at and speak to for your points to the television audience." Conger continued to nod, point by point, as Dale endeavored to keep the man's mind occupied with things other than his address. Dale shot lightning glances at Conger's eyelid. The spasm was gone. Inwardly he breathed a sigh of relief. His man was okay, no more panic, no more nerves. "That's about it. I will be in the control room for your speech and will guide the director from my notes."

Conger returned briefly to his preoccupation with his speech, but the moment of tension was gone. The signal came to move down to the entrance in the curtain at the rear of the tongue. Susan joined the trio as they made their way in the blackness behind the curtain. The boys were at their position. Dale saw Susan whisper something to Conger just before his name sailed out into the Hall for his entrance. Conger smiled, took her hand and squeezed it as Susan stood on tiptoe to kiss him on his cheek. Respectfully, Dale waited through this and then said, "Okay, guys, that's it. Away we go. Give 'em hell!" And Andrew Conger was walking down the long tongue with Susan, smiling and waving to the thunderous ovation from the Hall.

It was the first three-dimensional "in-the-flesh" look the convention had been permitted of its candidate for President of the United States, and they ate it up. There was a swell in the roar as Dale sent Jack and Frank Conger out and down seconds after their father. Dale learned later the pictures were beautiful on television.

Dale knew from long experience just exactly when he was, or was not "on camera," and kept his proper distance far off to the left and to the rear as he made his way to the rostrum position. Peering at the head-on camera and observing it was not taking pictures of the podium, Dale placed Conger's speech on the lectern, indicating to Conger the notebook was in position, and jumped over the guardrail separating the area from the working-press section. He made his way as best he could to the control room, three hundred feet away and five flights up, at the opposite end of the Hall. He prayed the ovation would last long enough for him to make it before Conger started his speech. It did. Conger at that point was beginning to wonder how to stop it.

"You and the boys sit down, now," Conger said to his wife over the din, dipping his head toward her. "I think the stills have enough

pictures of us. Frank Love will take you. Frank," said Conger, raising his voice to the Convention Chairman, "I think I'd better start
to think about stopping this. We may be losing them on TV. Will
you seat Susan and the boys? The stills don't need any more."

"Sure, Andy," said Love, basking in the limelight with his presidential candidate. "But they love this on TV. Don't worry about
that," he shouted. Conger, however, gently propelled his wife, Love,
and the boys from the area, one after the other, by exerting pressure on the small of their backs with the palms of his hands. Conger then turned and walked to the rostrum and raised his arm. He
slowly lowered them, hands outstretched as a signal for the ovation
to subside. It continued to pour over the front of the platform in a
wave of earsplitting volume.

For as long as Conger had been speaking in public office, nothing
had prepared him for the sight, sound, and atmosphere in which he
found himself at that moment. It was a moment suspended—a moment of ineffable thrill and excitement. The still photographers
worked him from all sides from their low platforms to the left,
center, and right of the rostrum. Delegates, shouting, marching, and
waving state standards and Conger signs, leaned over the backs of
the photographers in an effort, it seemed, to storm the candidate
and capture the rostrum area. Music from the Hall's organ boomed
above everything else, and four marching bands contributed to the
indescribable cacophony of sound. Reporters in the working-press
area to the right and left were straining, some standing on the
tables for a better look at Conger, to gain perhaps an exclusive
human-interest line for their stories. Conger waved to one or two
recognizable friends in the press corps, then concentrated on the
area immediately in front of the rostrum.

Dale was right, Conger thought. I can't see a single delegate on
the ground floor. All I can see are the balconies and general admission. God, what lights, he thought. He quickly opened the speech
notebook to the first page to see if he would have difficulty reading. No, that's okay, he decided. The reading lights on the lectern
compensated for the blinding dyna beams, spotlights, floodlights,

and "scoops" trained on him from every angle. In between the front lights, Conger's eyes saw a myriad of dancing, multicolored reflections from the hundreds of camera lenses on the central tower position. He could make out the single large red light on the camera which was dead center. He positioned his head several times, smiling all the while, to obtain a feel of talking to the camera during his speech. He noticed television had placed a monitor set on the central tower for their floor manager and co-ordinator. It had always bothered him to see his own image coming back to him. The floor manager was looking directly at him, his head encased in an enormous headset and mouthpiece. Conger took a chance. He leaned forward across the rostrum, smiled at the floor manager, and flicked his right hand twice in a turning motion, keeping it low and against the side of the rostrum. The floor manager looked puzzled momentarily, then grasped Conger's meaning and slid the TV monitor around so that the picture was out of Conger's line of sight. Goddam Dale, thought Conger, he knows better than that.

All this transpired as Conger beamed his famous and winning smile to the delegates and the television audience. The demonstration finally spent itself, lost its steam, and subsided. Organ music filled the hole in proceedings as Conger waited for the marching delegates to return to their seats in their state areas.

Charlie Dale was short of breath as he dashed into the television master-control room and collapsed, breathing heavily, on a stool behind Sandy Jones the director. "Wow, what a nightmare making my way through that madhouse," said Dale. "Okay, Sandy, from the top, letter A." From that point forward, the two men were glued to the television images of Andrew H. Conger coming to them in their electronic cubicle of communication.

As the two monitored every move Conger made at the rostrum, it became increasingly apparent the candidate was making a monumental address. Even the technical television crew manifested their admiration and interest. As in all virtuoso performances, television demonstrated moment on moment its unique and superb ability to transmit the spell of the address in the Hall to millions of viewers in their homes. Dale and Jones worked and moved as one person, completely in time and in tune to Conger's physical actions and his speech material. Minute after minute of flawless presentation ticked by, including superb cutaway shots of the audience in the Hall at exactly the correct moment. The presentation developed a rhythm all its own.

Suddenly, with no warning, Dale lost his place in his notes of Conger's speech. He thumbed backward, then forward, assuming Conger had made a cut. He was terrified at losing the continuity. He could find no reference to the words Conger was uttering. According to his notes, Conger was within half a minute of the conclusion.

"Sandy, watch it. This is an add. I don't have it. Stick with me . . . close," said Dale.

"Right." Jones straightened in his chair and alerted the crew by the direct line to their headsets to listen carefully for his cues. "What is this, Charlie?" he asked. "How long before he'll get back to the text?"

"I don't know." Dale was irritated by the noise of two people talking near the rear of the control room. "Sandy, tell those people to shut up."

"Hey, you people, shut up. Either shut up, or get out. Quiet . . . quiet," shouted Jones. The control room settled down. The only sound was Conger's words coming to them over the enormous loudspeakers.

And then it happened. It was hard to say just when Dale first realized what Conger was building up to. The new material was brilliantly constructed. Inch by inch, Conger, a master of oratory, had expertly brought his audience to the brink of his subject. Even then, the analogy he was using could have pushed the next line the other way. But it didn't. Conger squared his shoulders and looked straight into the head-on camera on the center tower position, presenting a perfect television closeup of his familiar features. He raised his right hand to alert the audience, and spoke:

"And so, in America's great tradition of free speech, and in the spirit of free competition which says for all the world to hear, 'Let the Best Man Win,' I, Andrew Conger, the candidate of this great party for the Presidency of the United States, hereby accept the invitation to television debate with my opponent for this highest office in the land. It is fitting I do so, for since the very beginning of our country's history . . ." No one in the Hall heard the end of Conger's thought. Very few heard that much.

The shock wave of disbelief was the first thing to whip through the Hall. Then the split second of transferral to the brain, the consuming thrill of the battle joined, the smell of challenge between two giants of politics, and the visual image before them at the rostrum of the man Andrew Conger who had made the electrifying statement—all these impressions flashed through the audience as Conger uttered the few words following the debate statement. Then the roar surged up from the floor, out from the walls, and down from the ceilings. The full impact of the debate H-bomb hit each and every one of the thousands who were jam-packed into the Hall.

In the control room Lou Wells let out a whoop which caused everyone to jump and actually scared Dale until he knew its origin. Wells was hysterical with excitement and triumph, jumping up and down and pounding Jones's shoulders as the ovation continued.

Good Christ Almighty! thought Dale. What has Andrew Conger done? Who talked him into it? How could he do this without consulting anyone? Me? Conger's words of weeks before came back to him. "There will be no comment of any kind until after the convention. I never want to hear the word 'debate' again." What had happened, Dale asked himself. Rufus Little will skin me alive! Who in the hell got to him? The bastard! He never talked to me, never let me know he was going to do it. What the hell, thought Dale, why should he? He's three times seven. Good Christ, the Hall is going wild, he thought, as he watched Jones's brilliant audience shots of the ovation. But what had made Conger do it? Was this going to be the pattern of the campaign, no consulting with the staff?

Lou Wells suddenly stopped his incredible gyrations and stared at the monitor, which at the moment was showing Conger, now smiling, now quite sober, standing quietly at the rostrum. As the roar continued to swell up from the delegates, the words of Governor Joseph Green suddenly snapped into the forefront of Wells's mind. When the two were in Fairlee, Green had said, "If a debate takes place during a major political campaign, one candidate or the other is quite possibly committing political suicide . . . the delicate balance of debate, the nuance of advantage over disadvantage, the dangerous courtship with political defeat." As an awesome tremor of fright broke over him and passed, Lou Wells realized he was more powerful, at that very instant, than either of the two candidates for President of the United States. He had delivered both candidates to the debates. He had carried home the bacon—two juicy, fat presidential candidates. He spun around as someone clutched him wildly from behind. It was Fred Morgan, who had left his box and had come up seeking Wells. They clasped each other's shoulders, then stood in silence as the crowd's roar from the loud-speakers continued to fill the control room. Dale's back was toward the two men. Inasmuch as Dale had no authority to be in the control room, Morgan assumed there were no Conger people within hearing distance when finally he spoke to Wells:

"We brought the son-of-a-bitch to heel, just as we planned." Wells, with his back to Dale, gestured to his rear with his thumb.

Morgan missed the significance because of the dim light. "It's a long time from Fairlee and your talk with Green tonight, Lou, but it's been worth it. Television is home free. There'll be a bonus in your salary envelope next week."

Wells grabbed Morgan's lapels and leaned into his left ear. "Charlie Dale . . . a Conger man." He gestured with his head, tilting it backward to indicate Dale.

Morgan looked over Wells's shoulder at the back of Dale's head.

"He couldn't have heard anything," Morgan said. "Too much noise. Goddam it, Wells, we've done it! Green played ball and it worked. Conger has had it."

But Charlie Dale heard every word. He walked away swiftly to a free Coca-Cola dispenser and drew a cup. Dale had no way of interpreting Morgan's comments. Out of sight, however, and on the back of his notes for Conger's address, he made quick notations of what he had just heard. What did it mean? Dale asked himself. Under no circumstances did he want to indicate he had overheard Morgan. He checked his folding money, saw he had sufficient cash, and walked over to Morgan and Wells, all smiles.

"Well, Fred Morgan," Dale said. "Didn't see you come in. Quite a moment, eh?"

"Hello, Dale. Nice to have you up here with the NA crew. I should say it's quite a moment. I never expected this to happen tonight. Did you?"

"No," said Dale. "I didn't expect it to happen at all. But Lou here did." Dale held out his hand toward Wells. "Here you are, you electronic pimp," said Dale with a smile.

"Dale talked us through Conger's speech, Fred," Wells said. "There was no advance text. What's this, Charlie?"

"Remember, you bet me fifty bucks Conger would accept the debates. You knew more than I did." Before implying his lack of being privy to Conger's debate statement, Dale had decided not to play "the game" that he knew all along Conger would announce it tonight. He was simply too tired to launch into it. What the hell, Dale thought, let 'em know it was all Conger's idea. In addition, Morgan's remarks, taken at their most innocuous interpretation, indicated to Dale something fishy had been going on. Somebody, namely Lou Wells, had been talking to somebody, namely Governor Green. Dale wanted no part of NA, and wanted to make certain the two men knew it. The money changing hands would do it.

"Oh, for Christ's sake, Dale, I don't want your money." Wells pushed back Dale's hand. "Keep it. Buy me a dinner the night of the first debate."

"Take it, Lou," said Dale harshly. "A bet's a bet. I would have taken your dough."

Wells hesitated. Morgan smiled.

"Go on, Lou, take his money," he said, smiling. "Conger people are loaded." Wells took the fifty dollars and turned toward the monitors. Things were getting sticky, he decided. Wells wanted to change the subject quickly.

"Hey, look at the picture on Camera Three, will you?" he said. "Look at that expression on Rufus Little's face."

"Shall I take it?" yelled Sandy Jones. "You want it?"

"Sure," Dale said. "Punch it up." Jones called his cues to the technical crew, and the magnificent portrait of Rufus Little in his inglorious hour of political travail sailed out into televisionland. It was the memorable candid shot of the television convention coverage.

Dale couldn't help smiling, ruefully. Little's long chin hung over the front guardrail of his box as, with lifeless eyes, he looked with disbelief at Conger on the rostrum. "Why'd you do it, Andy, why'd you do it?" he muttered. Just as Dale's mind had focused back to Conger's earlier words, so did Rufus Little puzzle similar Conger phrases. "I never want to hear the word 'debate' again, unless I bring it up." And dammit, thought Little, Conger *had* brought it up. Just a week ago. And as much as agreed with me to turn them down. At least until we got back to Washington after the convention. Little continued to stare at the rostrum. That goddam Dale told me he had everything under control, he said to himself. "Why, oh why did you do it, Andy?" Little muttered over and over in the direction of the rostrum and his candidate while, unknown to him, Dale, Morgan, Wells, and millions of other television viewers watched him staring dumbly at his candidate.

"I'd say he's in shock," said Dale. "This may be the first political campaign in which television, not Rufus Little, will dictate the outcome. Well, I guess I know what I'll be doing between now and November."

Conger, seeing it was impossible to continue over the incredible demonstration, bowed between the microphones, stepped back, and brought Susan up to the rostrum so that she would share the moment. Proudly she kissed her husband. After a proper interval he brought up the two boys, Frank and Jack. The newspaper photographers had their moment.

And still the delegates voiced their lust for battle, marching around and around the Hall. It had given the convention the spark everyone was looking and hoping for. It was strange Rufus Little didn't realize it. As one, the delegates were paying homage to their warrior, their fighter. They inhaled heartily of the odor of combat, their nostrils reacting to the pungency of a life-and-death political struggle, of locked-horn battle. Instantly Conger had become their hero candidate, not merely their candidate. He was their master duelist, who had with eminent grace come forward and picked up the enemy's gauntlet. The poor, emotionally blinded slobs, thought Dale; they don't even know whose gauntlet it is. If you told them it was Morgan's and television's own game, they'd never believe you, he thought. Alone, deflated, and in disgust, Dale walked back slowly to the TV trailer.

There was only one man in the Convention Hall who had everything to lose by accepting the debates—Andrew H. Conger.

Conger, standing at the rostrum and smothered in the personal triumph of the deafening ovation, was inclined to thank his wife Susan for showing him the values in his decision during their discussion in the early hours of the morning. But Andrew Conger, in thanking her, was selling himself short. For it was he who had the full knowledge of possible ensuing political disaster, yet his own character, his devotion to what he felt was best for the country, had made up his mind.

It occurred to no one (including Conger) that he was the only selfless person at the convention that night. There was nothing mysterious about his decision, although Rufe Little, the nation's and the world's press, Charlie Dale, and countless others would ponder it well past Election Day. Andrew Conger merely did what he felt was right. Once he knew what that was, standing up before those thousands of partisans and uttering the words accepting the debate invitation was one of the easiest things Conger had ever done in public.

When Dale reached the trailer, the noise inside was deafening. Dozens of strangers had forced their way into the tiny rooms. Someone had broken out the whiskey when Conger stopped fighting the ovation and dropped his closing remarks. The voices of the commentators coming through the monitoring sets overrode the basic screaming and shouting. Janet was there. She and Fergie, standing behind the waist-high counter between the trailer's living room and kitchen area, were acting as bartenders. Janet reached under the counter and brought up a bourbon and water for Dale. He took a long swallow, toasted his wife, and turned his head to survey the bedlam. A convention page, a twelve-year-old towhead, bursting with pride in his smart official blue blazer, was making his way through the press of people toward Dale.

"You Mr. Charles Dale?" the boy asked in a warm Southern voice.

"I am, son. What have you got?" said Dale.

"Sign here. Telegram." Dale signed. The young page accepted a coke from Janet as Dale tore open the envelope. He stared thunderstruck at the words in the wire. It was from his sister Anne in Buffalo.

THIS AFTERNOON DAD WAS HIT BY A CAR. HE DIED WITHOUT RE-GAINING CONSCIOUSNESS. PLEASE CALL WHEN CONVENIENT. LOVE.

Dale crushed the wire as he brought both hands to his temples, bent his head toward the floor, and stumbled through the noise toward the peace of the rear bedroom. A young volunteer was embracing a beautiful Conger Monger as he opened the door. He held the doorknob and looked at them silently as they exited. Alone, he slammed and locked the door, ran to each television monitor to cut off the sound, and threw himself face down on the bed. His body shook in huge racking sobs as he lay there, weeping into the stained and musty spread on the cot.

The young page had watched Dale's exit. Janet, oblivious to it all, continued her work behind the counter. After an interval the boy spoke to her.

"You know Charles Dale, ma'am?" he asked.

"Yes, why? This is his trailer," said Janet.

"He just got some bad news in that telegram. I watched them type it at the Western Union office. That's my station."

"Where is he?" asked Janet, suddenly aware of his absence.

"I don't know, ma'am. He went down that hall." And the boy pointed toward the rear of the trailer. Janet set down her drink and made her way to the door of the back bedroom. She found it locked, and knocked. There was no answer.

"Charlie, this is Janet. Are you in there?" Still there was no sound. "Charlie, are you there? It's Janet. I want to talk to you." The door opened. Dale's back was turned as he made his way back to the cot; he sat down with his head in his hands.

"Shut the door, dammit," said Dale. "Lock it," he said. Janet obeyed.

"For heaven's sake, what's the matter?" asked Janet. "What's happened?"

"Dad was killed this afternoon in Buffalo. He was hit by a car. Here's the wire!" Dale blew his nose. "God, what a way to get the news. Poor Dad. I'll bet they've been trying to reach me for hours."

"Why don't you call them? There's a phone right there."

"Where? Oh, sure. Never saw it. Have you a cigarette, Jan? I'm out."

"No. Want me to get some?"

"Please."

"I'll be back. You make the call."

"It's nice and cool here," said Dale. "I'm glad we got out of that madhouse."

Dale and Janet were in the living room of their suite at the hotel.

"Do you feel better after your call to Anne?" Janet asked.

"I guess so. Dad wasn't in any pain. They had him under drugs almost immediately. Why did it have to happen now? We were taking the whole family there this Christmas."

"There's no answer for that, Charles. He went when he was supposed to go."

"But I didn't want him to go now," Dale said and broke completely. He wept silently, head down, with his mouth closed. After some time he looked at Janet.

"I'm not crying because I loved him," he said. "I didn't know him well enough to know if I did or didn't. I'm mad because I was going to *try* to know him in these next years. We were going there, they were coming out next summer, remember? I'm sad because my father is dead, and I never had any real idea who he was, or what he was. It's so trite, but it's true. He was like a stranger. Things were hard between us. There never seemed to be any time. And I seemed to be making the same mistakes. Nuts! What makes us do these things?"

"All of us are individuals, Charles," said Janet.

"I remember when I was about six. Dad was driving us to our grandparents'. It was winter, and I was sitting in the front, Anne in the back with Mother. Dad slammed on the brakes for some reason, and I went sailing into the windshield. I hit my head, got knocked out, and cut my lip with my teeth. There was blood all over." Dale paused, then went on. "You know what Dad did? He bawled me out for sitting on the edge of the seat and not obeying his orders to sit back against the back. That's what he did. I was hurt and scared. And he was mad at me."

"Your father was very strict. You've always known that."

"Yeah, but where do *people* come in? I remember the summer he said it'd be a good idea if I learned to play golf. I was around fifteen. He made my life so miserable on the course I refused to go out with him. I've never played a game of golf since. That's why I don't play with you. I hate golf. Why did he do these things? Why didn't we have a friendship, even if there couldn't be love? Why didn't we just go somewhere, once in my life, where I didn't have to learn anything, or be good at anything, and just be able to talk to

Dad? All the sex stuff when I was young. I remember so many times asking Mother. She'd say 'Ask Dad,' and Dad would say it wasn't important. Around and around and around. I never knew him. And then I made this pledge to myself, just about a year ago, that from now on I was going to work at knowing him better. 'Cause a lot of it was my fault too, I guess. And now he's gone."

"You knew him a lot better than you realize. And he left a great deal with you, whether or not you recognize it."

"All I know is that Dad is gone, and I didn't know him." There was a knock on the door. Dale indicated to Janet with a nod of his head to answer it. It was Fergie.

"There's a milk plane at two A.M. boss. You want it?"

"I guess so, if that's the only one," he answered.

"Okay," said Fergie, "one seat on the two A.M. You can pick the ticket up at the airport. Limo leaves the lobby at one." She closed the door.

"This is the sort of thing we should go through together, as a husband and wife," Janet said.

"I know, I know," Dale said with irritation. "But I don't want you to have to go from here to Buffalo, then all the way back to Denver. It'll be miserably hot in Buffalo—it always is. I appreciate your feelings, and I'm grateful, but I think I'll do this alone, then go on to Washington. The kids need you. You've been away a week now. You better go back before you spend all my money." Dale turned his head away. He stared absently at the face of Andrew Conger, looking out at him from a red-white-and-blue poster on the wall.

Janet rolled her husband's lighter over and over in her hands. Finally she looked at him. "I've heard some rumors about you and a girl in Washington," she said. "I'm sorry to bring it up now, but if you're packing me off to Denver I have no choice." Dale continued staring at the poster. "Seems you've been seeing a lot of one girl, someone you've known a long time. That you've taken her to Conger's house, and on a three-day house party on someone's boat. Thanks a lump!"

Dale turned and looked directly at Janet. "The girl's name is Sandra Nelson. I've known her five years. Met her in Europe on the long trip. It was what I guess is called an affair. When I came back it was over. Nothing more. I couldn't have been more surprised to run into her in Washington. She's a friend. I relax with her. She's been good for me back there."

"It may have been all over, but it seems it's started up again, doesn't it?" said Janet. "What the hell is happening to you? Have you lost all sense of right and wrong?"

"Not a bit. There's nothing to this thing with this girl. I was lonely, teed off. I ran into her again. We were good friends before, so I see her every now and then. If you're learning to live apart from me, why shouldn't I take a little instruction myself? Two can have a ball as easily as one, you know."

"Don't be silly. I just said that to make you jealous."

"Is that why you've only written me three or four times since I've been gone? Since May? And one of the times is to tell me about you and some guy up at Aspen? And then I say, okay, come to Chicago. And where have you been, I ask? Out on the goddam North Shore with all your Finch pals. While we're in here sweating out Conger's nomination for President."

"Don't start feeling sorry for yourself, Charlie. If you do, I'll spit right in your eye. I said I was sorry. Let's have a few minutes without yelling at each other before you have to leave. Mix me a drink."

"I'm for that," Dale said, rising and going to the portable bar. "Forgive me. I'm tired . . . Dad . . . everything. I shouldn't have blown my stack."

"When do you have to leave, dear?" asked Janet, as Dale continued his packing.

"In about an hour or so. They'll call me from the desk."

Janet was lying on her bed in a negligee. She was relaxed but troubled as she watched Dale's swift movements in and out of the two rooms. Dale's wide travel experience had made him an expert packer: swift, neat, complete.

"You better take a shower before you leave. You'll feel better," Janet said.

"I will. Last thing. Could you make me another drink, or shall I?"

"I'll make it," said Janet, rising. Dale continued to pack, and was leaning over a suitcase when Janet came to him with the drink. She looked lovely—clean and fresh, he thought.

"Thanks, Jan. You smell nice." Her negligee fell open. He looked at her soft breasts, took a sip of his drink, and placed it on a table.

"You look nice, too." She pressed her body against him, increasing the pressure of the full length of her thighs against his, hard and with meaning.

"Mind your manners, you hussy. Do you want me to make love to you before or after my shower? Because that's what I want to do very much. Right now."

"What has cleanliness got to do with good earthy sex? It's never bothered you before."

Dale barely touched the silk of the negligee on each of her shoulders. It slipped silently to the floor. Janet tilted her head up, lips parted.

"Janet, Janet, it's been too long! Help me. Everything's all messed up—"

She smothered the last words as she kissed him, and led him toward the bed.

"Well," said Dale, "I hope you've had a good time in Chicago. That's why you came here, isn't it?"

"My, it's been lovely," Janet answered with satisfaction. "And the last few minutes were the loveliest." She stretched as she lay beside him.

"You still thinking of running home to mother?" he asked.

"If you see much more of this girl in Washington, big boy, that's where you'll find me. I don't go for that kind of stuff."

"I know. I don't either."

"Your high and mighty morals must be giving you a bad time about now."

"They are. I'm not prepared to say how I feel—or what. I'm confused."

"When will I see you again?" Janet asked after a long pause. She trailed her fingers down his thigh.

"I suppose when it's all over. Maybe. If you're interested."

"Get rid of that girl, Charles. Or you'll be sorry."

"I like her very much. She's good for me."

"So am I. Want to see just how good again?"

"Well," said Janet, "I'm sure glad you came back on the campaign."

"You are?" Dale asked in surprise. He closed his large suitcase with a groan.

"Yes—to protect Conger from the debates. You've really done a superb job."

"Very funny," Dale replied with annoyance. "And very cruel. All I can say is as far as I know he didn't consult anyone. And it wasn't in his speech when I saw it this afternoon. Rufe's going to take me apart limb by limb when I get back to Washington. You watch. He'll accuse me of working on Conger behind his back." He checked the drawers in his bureau to be certain they were empty.

"He'll do no such thing, if I know Rufe Little," said Janet. "I'll bet you anything Conger told only one person that tonight he was going to accept them."

"Who?" he asked, snapping shut his small bag.

"Susan."

"Jesus, you're like every woman in the world. Romance will out, love is all. The power behind the man. Conger doesn't talk things like that over with Susan. This was a political decision."

"I'll bet she knew," insisted Janet. Dale dismissed her comment with a snort.

"When the boy comes, tell him to bring this stuff to the Michigan Boulevard entrance. I'll stop at the desk and tell them you'll be here until tomorrow noon. Don't pay the bill. Tell them to send it on with the Conger staff bills to Washington." He closed his two brief cases and came to his wife.

"It's been wonderful, Jan," he said. "Give the kids my love, and don't forget to go to the bank and check those stocks. Give me the exact number of shares and purchase dates. No maybes. It may all have to go into the business."

"I will," Janet replied. "Oh dear, I wish I were going to Buffalo with you."

"I'll be there only a few hours. You know you belong in Denver. Give the kids a big kiss. And don't forget to get them a prize before you leave tomorrow. They'll be heartbroken if you don't."

"I won't forget. . . . I don't know whether I can stand not seeing you for almost four months. Goddam you, Charles Dale, you come back to Denver as soon as you can. Do you hear?"

"Where else is there to go?"

"Don't kid me. You watch what you're doing back there—after hours!"

"Down, girl," he said, leaning over her. He kissed her lightly. "Chin up."

"I'll send flowers to your mother. Tell her all of our thoughts are with her and give her all my love." Janet clung to him.

"I will. I have to go. 'By, dear. Keep the Faith." Her husband turned and was gone. Not even a National Political Convention could suspend time, or life, or death. Dale lurched into the cab which sped from the curb for Midway Airport.

The trip to Buffalo was depressing and a strain. But Dale was pleased he made the effort, for his mother was grateful and relied on him heavily. He was constantly at her side. It made him happy to feel he was needed. There was little or no time, however, for sleep.

Dale's sister Anne announced she was a volunteer worker for Governor Joe Green. Anne despised Conger. She seemed to be more interested in criticizing Dale's television coverage of the Conger convention than comforting her mother. He supposed it was understandable, but it irritated him. "I did my best. No cracks, please," he said to her harshly.

Ironically, the one item of his father's the family was certain Dale would want to take back to Washington with him was his father's set of matched golf clubs. It came as a surprise when he told them he had never resumed the game.

No one seemed particularly anxious to drive Dale to the airport. He called a cab and said his good-by's at the house.

It was breathlessly humid, blindingly hot, when Dale arrived at Washington National Airport. He took the limousine to his apartment. On entering, he drew the venetian blinds shut. Then he made himself a cool drink and started to unpack. After removing his suits, he stopped. "The hell with it," he said aloud. "Hello, mattress. Hello, sacktime."

Dale put the night chain in place at the door, threw off his clothes, and collapsed on the bed.

The convention is over, he thought. Now all I've got ahead of me is the whole goddam campaign—and the debates. The hell with all of it, he thought.

Dale slept continuously for twenty-three deep and untroubled hours. When he awoke, he was ravenously hungry, and made himself a sandwich with stale bread.

Then he went back to bed and slept another ten hours.

10

One Hundred Days Until Election

"MANY TIMES the local committee will be at odds with what we want for Conger," said Arthur Baldwin, addressing his raw recruits who were to be the political advance men for the Conger campaign. "Whenever possible, find a compromise—but never one which you know by policy is unacceptable to the Secretary of State."

"What do we do if there isn't any compromise and the local people refuse to budge?" asked someone in the rear of the room.

"Call us in Washington. We'll do everything to smooth out the problem. And remember this: We'll always back you up—if you're right." Baldwin's men laughed.

There would be many a day before they would laugh that hard again, thought Charlie Dale, listening to Baldwin as he waited his turn to address the men on the political rally and presentation aspects of their job. Arthur Baldwin had brought his team of space-men into Washington immediately following the convention. They had come from every corner of the country, from every walk of life. Among them were lawyers, an anthropologist, sons of Fat Cats, political science Ph.D.'s, accountants, salesmen, public relations men, a doctor, and two farmers. For several days Baldwin had put them through their paces, indoctrinating them into the folkways of national political campaigning. There were few veterans. One or two had worked in previous campaigns and had been hired at the in-sistence of the White House or the National Committee. For most of them, however, this was a new experience.

These were the men who would fan out across the face of the nation and deliver millions in audiences to Andrew H. Conger at perfectly arranged and timed whistle stops, prop stops, bumper stops, shopping-center stops, and the giant evening rallies. They will lie, cheat, wheedle, con, and spend money like it was going out of style before the campaign is over, thought Dale. But they will deliver the crowds to the candidate, if they have to hire them at a dollar a head to do it. I wonder, thought Dale, which ones will falter, become lushes, which will be the strong and which the weak? How many will get in our hair at rallies, or dig TV and our problems? Who will be the phoneys, who will be the guys who deliver?

"To review," said Baldwin. "When you get to a town, never see the local meeting or events chairman first. Always see the top local political contact before you see anyone else. Be sure everyone under-stands that, after you have drawn up the minute-by-minute itiner-ary, there are to be no, I repeat, *no* changes. Make courtesy calls to all major officials of the party in the area. Include senators, governors, congressmen, National Committeemen, state and local chairmen, and local and state Conger chairmen. Remember at all times you are a personal representative of Andrew Conger. So act like one."

"How do you act like one?" someone asked. Another laugh filled the room.

"If you don't," said Baldwin, "you'll find out soon enough how to act like one. Names are important, names of everybody. Get the names of every person connected with the affair and their titles. Shoot them back to Washington immediately so we can get out the 'Thank you' letters." Baldwin consulted his notes. "We'll skip the procedure for impromptu speeches and talks for now. Charlie Dale here will tell you about them later, but keep in mind it's better to have the candidate stand on the hood of a car to address them than haul up some monster platform that never gets filled. And in that car we want a local policeman in plainclothes as the driver. No volunteers, no young eager beavers. It must be a member of the local law force, in plainclothes, a guy who will spend all his time watching the road and the crowds, not watching what Andrew Conger is doing. If this type of guy is not available, get a paid driver, preferably checking his political registration before you hire him." The men chuckled again. "To review the receiving-lines problem and receptions. No reception longer than forty-five minutes should be scheduled prior to a major nighttime event. In this time, about six hundred people can go through the line and meet Andrew and Susan. In a larger reception, where it is the main event of the stop, you can figure about eight hundred to a thousand people an hour through the line." Baldwin stopped, closed his notebook, and looked at the men. "If you make a serious mistake twice, just take the plane home from wherever you are. I don't want to see you again. Don't come back to Washington. . . . And now, Charlie Dale, who handles TV, rallies, and a lot of other stuff, has a few things to say."

Baldwin presented the men with a review of Dale's past political experience and named several network shows to his credit. Dale made his way to the front of the room.

"It's good to see all you guys, and I am sure we will be looking at each other under very different circumstances before this is all over," he said. "We'd like you people to know one or two important things about operations in my area." Dale gave the men a rundown on the television aspects of the campaign and its importance to every public appearance. He explained where television control began and ended. He told them of the importance of timing in the candidate's schedule; that once air time was purchased the candidate had to be delivered for the telecast. "As far as inside a hall is concerned," he said, "my men will take complete charge of every single item and element included in the area from the speaker's stand or podium back to the wall behind it. This takes in almost everything the TV cameras will see when they shoot the head table, the platforms, the candidate speaking at the rostrum. You guys have everything forward of the podium, except the area between the podium and the head-on, or center, camera position. That pit, that hole in there, is ours, although usually you'll find a row or two of press tables filling part of that space. The press section is yours to set up, but we may be forced to ask for changes in it if we can't get what we need for good pictures. Our men will let you know when this occurs." Baldwin laughed. "Yes," said Dale, "our men waste no time in letting you know."

Dale covered the arrival of the candidate at a meeting or telecast. "We supervise curb to curb," said Dale. "That means we meet Conger at the curb on arrival. We are there to open the door of his car, so he sees a friendly face no matter where he is. We then take complete charge of the candidate, if there is television, from that point forward until after the affair. We then deliver him back to the curb to you men. Our responsibility is finished. You take him from there."

"Does he always leave from the same place he arrives?" asked a voice on the side.

"Mostly, yes, but not always. Don't count on it. But, what the hell, that's all decided before his arrival. You'll know. If you don't, you've blown it." Dale continued to brief the men, who found television's and broadcasting's role completely mystifying. They were fascinated with the procedures Dale outlined.

"Two final things," said Dale. "Never take anything for granted. I had a governor once—he shall remain nameless—who was in charge of a meeting. There was a big framework and scaffold in the middle of a football stadium where the candidate was speaking. I asked the governor what it was, and he said it was a pictorial pyrotechnic display. You know, one of those old-fashioned things where someone lights a fuse, the fire goes up and around the scaffold, and pretty soon a wobbly American flag begins to emerge from huge clouds of yellow or white smoke. Well, this scaffold had silhouettes of the two men on the ticket on it, with an American flag in the center above some horrible local campaign slogan which had been turned down by the National Committee for official use. Anyway, he assured me this was what all the wood and stuff was. And he wanted it lit on the entrance and ovation of my man. Well, my man was making his entrance on national television, and Baldwin explained to you that's the way we always like to do it. So we're on a full network hookup. My candidate comes in on schedule. Everything goes fine, he and his wife make it up to the speaker's stand, and we have beautiful pictures of them. We're on the air, mind you. But the guy who's supposed to light the pictorial display is late on his cue. I signal my man to wait a few seconds, let the ovation roll on, knowing we want pictures of this pyrotechnic thing for our large TV audience. We wait. Nothing happens. So I tell the candidate to go ahead and start to talk. He gets the crowd quieted down with hand signals and opens his mouth for his first line. At that moment ten thousand tons of the loudest fireworks I've ever heard exploded over our heads in the stadium. The candidate was terrified. I think he thought his opponent was attacking him. So did I, for that matter. I was stunned, to say the least. It went on for at least five minutes. I can assure you Andrew H. Conger still remembers that night, and hasn't let me forget it either. Which all proves one thing. I goofed. I took someone's word for something. I believed a governor, a stupid thing to do. Never believe a governor. I should have checked with the fireworks guys themselves. They would have told me they had some noisemakers out there. It was my mistake. It taught me a great deal. Never take anything for granted."

Dale then told them the story of the time he borrowed a white ten-gallon hat from a member of a cowgirl band and rushed onto a stage and spoke to the audience of a late-evening rally in Oklahoma. The chairman had failed to show up, the crowd was sitting on their hands, so Dale took over. He waved his hat, looked down at the thousands of glum faces, and said, "As the Senior Senator from the great state of Oklahoma, I want to hear an old-fashioned Ponca City welcome for my best friend in the Senate, Andrew H. Conger." The audience was stunned momentarily, then raised the roof with their enthusiasm and applause. The reason was the Senior Senator from Oklahoma that year was not in the same party as Andrew Conger. The implied endorsement by their good and faithfully serving Rustlin' Bob Bennett brought them to their feet in a roar. "So, when you're in a jam," said Dale, "don't be afraid to improvise. You'd be surprised what you can get away with if you have to. Let the juices flow, men. What the hell, you're just like forty-eight-hour men with a circus. By the time they find out what you've done, you're in tomorrow's town." Baldwin coughed. "Well, of course, always remember you're working for Andy Conger," said Dale. "But improvise when you're really in a jam. Thank you."

"Take a memo to Conger, Fergie," said Dale. "I think our TV group is firm enough now to give him a rundown on who is doing what."

"Copies to . . . ?" asked Fergie.

"Rufe Little, Wilbur Jenkins, Arthur Baldwin, Cliff Harley, Ab Shepherd, Josh Holden in New York, and my own people. Maybe you better send a couple over to Lucas Farmer, PR head of the National Committee. Okay? 'AC from CD. Subject: Television Supervision and Production. Paragraph. It is proper at this time to advise you of the team which will be supervising and producing your television and public meetings. For your information, I am also listing the men we have assigned to Hughes. They will travel exclusively with the vice presidential candidate. In case of emergency supervisory needs on your TV, however, it is understood they are available for assignment to you. New paragraph.

" 'I will head up the operation, supervising TV for you and Hughes. Paragraph.

" 'Assigned exclusively as your personal traveling production adviser and producer is Ham Forrest, whom you know and trust. Paragraph.

" 'Working ahead of your meetings and other TV commitments will be the following: Tommy Tuttle, a top man who will function as an advance man and producer-director; Peter Hunt and Bud Rust, new men to us, but well experienced in remote and traveling TV shows. They will be advance on-the-road TV producers. In addition, I have three producers in New York on standby. They will go out on an "as needed" basis. I am hoping to obtain the services of Billy Dee as your traveling sound man. He is the best in the business, operating his own firm in Hollywood. It is safe to assume he will be with us. Paragraph.

" 'In September I plan to ask Rufe Little for approval of Hans Kleinert as a traveling lighting consultant. We would use him on the debates and major television appearances. Paragraph.

" 'Your usual makeup man, John Lowell, will be available to you again this year for all network telecasts. Plus the debates, naturally. Paragraph.

" 'Functioning as supervisor of a TV desk here at Headquarters (receiving all reports from advance men, directing assignments of telecasts, routing the men physically around the country, and co-ordinating our office with local stations and their needs) will be Ned Colton. I have worked with Colton before at a network level of production and program management. He is tops. Colton will co-ordinate the above elements for Senator Hughes also, and reconcile the needs of both candidates to available personnel. Paragraph.

" 'On the Hughes staff will be Bernie Lamb, whom you met in Chicago. He will be personal traveling consultant, functioning as Forrest does with you. Two advance producer-directors will service Hughes, as well as a traveling sound man for public-address and audio supervision and maintenance. Paragraph.

" 'The above supervision will be co-ordinated with needs at the National Committee. Paragraph.

" 'Our contact at the advertising agency, Josh Holden, will function through me.'

"That's it, Fergie. Are the guys ready?"

"They're chewing their fingernails in anticipation, bossman," Fergie answered.

"Drop sick. Bring my notes. Let's go."

The men were gathered around a small conference table in one of the available meeting rooms at Conger Headquarters. On entering, Dale passed out a copy of the Television Production Manual to each person. "This is not all new, guys," he said, "but rather has evolved over the years. I've rewritten it completely to conform with our present staff structure and personnel. You'll see an important new section on local stations and TV news coverage—how to get the most out of it in each city Conger visits. A lot of our problems have disappeared as local stations have become more familiar with remote production. You know: airports, lousy halls, outdoor stuff. Four years ago many stations didn't have a remote truck. Now it's old stuff to them. Any telecast outside of a studio, however, is a potential problem. Something can always go wrong. So use the check-off lists indicated in the manual." Dale arranged his notes and lit a cigarette. Then he continued.

"You all know the difficulty we used to have with the newsreels in years gone by. Well, that's all over now. We're one big happy family. However, don't forget: Always give them a platform which does not connect or touch the television camera platform. When they slam down those damn film magazines while they're changing film, I don't want our TV camera platform to shake, I don't want Andy Conger looking like a bowl of Jello. So keep a space, even two inches is okay, between TV and newsreel platforms. With the new high-speed film the reels use, there's no battle any more on how much light to throw on the rostrum. If we come up a little bit, they can shoot any picture television gives them. One hundred and twenty-five foot-candles is plenty for them, and for us." Dale then went into the subject of wardrobe, proper shirts for television, un-obtrusive ties, and makeup. "You who have been with Conger before know we travel a West Coast makeup man for all important network telecasts. If you're stuck and the man isn't available, you may have to improvise. After this session, Ham Forrest will brief you on how to obtain the correct makeup tones and base powders in any local drugstore. But if the man's on network, don't worry. The Hollywood guy will automatically be scheduled to the event."

Dale covered the technical manual cover to cover. He discussed the positioning of cameras, their optimum lengths from the rostrum, the relative position of the camera's lens to Conger's eyes, and what to do under circumstances where there was but one camera in the hall for use in a telecast.

"Ned Colton wants me to explain the situation with 'pool pencils.' These are the wire service guys who will usually demand of Wilbur Jenkins they be permitted in the same studio as the candidate when we are originating from a TV station. We insist they function on a pool basis, that is, three or four guys drawing straws to cover for the entire traveling press corps. Most of them know their place, will not move if you ask them not to, and will stay in whatever prescribed area is indicated to them. There are a few, however, who are wanderers. We know who they are. Ham Forrest can fill you in on them. What goes for pencils also goes for the stills. The photographers will also insist a still pool group be permitted inside the studio while you're on the air. These guys are one giant pain-in-the-ass. As you know, I am firmly convinced all still photographers are throwbacks to a pre-Neanderthal society. *Life* guys are the worst. They will feign deafness, pull out thirty-five different colored passes going back to the Al Smith campaign; they'll do anything to be where they are not supposed to be to get the exclusive shot. If they give you trouble, just call a security man or a cop. Throw 'em the hell out."

Physical arrangements were discussed. Dale explained the importance of the fifteen-foot aisle behind Andrew Conger at the rostrum in order to remove the possibility of "leg-kickers," or "nose-pickers." The proper background to be placed behind Conger was discussed, and Dale went into detail regarding Conger's dislike of pleats, folds, or gray drapes. "We all know they are fine," he said, "but Andy doesn't like 'em, Susan doesn't like 'em, so we don't like 'em. They are not to be used during this campaign."

The custom-made time-cueing device for Conger's speeches was then demonstrated by Ham Forrest. It consisted of two small black boxes connected by one hundred feet of cable. One box was to be placed on the speaker's rostrum, the other in the press section, the wire carefully laid in between. The box on the speaker's stand had varicolored glass panels on the face of it. The other box consisted of a set of toggle switches. By placing a stopwatch on the press table in front of him, the television advance man, while sitting in the press section, could relay time cues to Conger who could be as far away as one hundred feet. If Conger were to get a five-minute cue, that is, five minutes until he must be finished with his remarks, the TV man flicked the toggle switch on his box marked "Five Minutes." The corresponding "Five Minutes" glass panel on Conger's box right next to his speech pages, lit up. The TV advance men liked it for it did away with hand signals. Conger liked it because it meant he never had to take his eyes off his speech to receive clear and accurate time cues.

The men were checked out on their walkie-talkies and were told of the procedure to follow for televised news conferences. "Remember," said Dale, "these are basically for the working press, national and local. Never, but never block their view of the candidate or the candidate's view of them, for the question-and-answer format of a news conference depends on unobstructed visibility between the questioner and the candidate. Set up your newsreel positions to the right and left of the press corps, never in front of them. A televised news conference is supposed to begin with the entrance of the candidate to the podium. However, if he is late, and there will be times when this is unavoidable, put little Wilbur Jenkins on as a pad or fill. Let him give his regular daily briefing to the traveling newsmen from the lectern. The local viewers eat it up 'cause it's all trady and inside stuff, like what time their bags have to be in the hall in the morning, changes in the schedule, blah, blah. It's a good fill when Conger is late. Remember it."

Studio telecasts were covered in more detail. The standard entrance for Conger and Susan was explained, the responsibility of the TV men for the routining and production of all pre-shows using local talent and imported stars were discussed. Dale then summarized.

"It's difficult to define all the things you are supposed to be during this campaign. Most importantly, you are a confidant of the candidate and will see him more often and more intimately than many of his policy advisers, for you will always brief him alone in the dressing room before speeches and telecasts. The man will come to rely heavily on you for information you do not possess. He will ask it of you simply because you are the only person available. Get it for him, no matter what you have to do. Don't be embarrassed about making him up in front of his wife. She's used to it. I have touched earlier on the aspect of you guys being the 'friendly face' for our hero. This is an enormously important aspect of your job. Put yourself in his shoes for a moment. Let's say it's Syracuse, New York. You have a studio telecast which will be seen on the entire East Coast that night. Afterward Conger has a rally in a downtown hall to be televised locally. He's been campaigning in three states already that day. It's been raining off and on. He's tired, his throat is sore, and he's running behind schedule. The daily schedule calls for him to arrive in Syracuse and go to the hotel for two hours' rest and staff work. Here, he would get a breather, change his clothes and freshen up for the evening appearances. But that's all out now because he's late. The plane lands. He cuts his remarks short at the airport, gets behind a police escort weaving in and out of rush-hour traffic at eighty miles an hour and screams to the television studio. A thousand or so people are jammed around the entrance; no plans, no advance notice, just the curious and the fanatic party loyals. It's dark now, beginning to rain again. The Conger car roars up to the curb. The candidate's stomach is in knots. He knows he's late. He wonders if the staff got his clothes out of the plane and to the studio. He wonders if he'll make it on the air on time. And he wonders who the hell has everything under control so all this can happen smoothly. That, my friends, is where you come in. Be at that curb when the car stops. I repeat, be at that curb and smile, goddammit, even if he ain't gonna make it on time and everything's going to hell in a handbasket! Open that door and smile. Tell him hello, and tell him everything's under control. 'Cause if you don't and I hear about it, I'll break your goddam necks. That's one of the biggest reasons you're out there in the boondocks, to be the friendly face in a strange town that tells the man everything's okay—that you've got it under control. And don't forget it. And don't forget he's married, that his wife is going along with the biggest gag known on the face of this earth, an American Presidential Campaign. See that she's not neglected, that she's taken care of, gets to the right room to watch the telecast, and that people from the television station leave her alone.

"As a windup, here's a practical but corny thought I've always kept in mind from about the second week of a campaign forward. Your job is the care and feeding of Andrew H. Conger. Treat him like the thoroughbred he is. Baby him like a race horse. More than anyone else connected with the campaign your job is absolutely to guarantee his well-being, his appearance, his actual disposition and campaigning personality. If he's got a cold, your telecast suffers. If he's tired, if he's irritated, if he's smothered by local idiots, if surprises hit him because of your poor advance work or your improper briefing, if his suit needs pressing, if his tie isn't tied correctly, if his hair makes him look like Gorgeous George or a G.I. recruit after his first boot shaving, your telecast will suffer. And Andrew Conger will suffer. For it will affect what millions of people think of the Andrew Conger they are watching that night on their TV sets. Remember this, more people will see Andy Conger on just a New York State television hookup than ever saw Abraham Lincoln during his entire life. More people will see Conger on a coast-to-coast network telecast than saw Franklin Roosevelt in a year, two years, for all I know. Keep those things in mind. If Conger's fly needs zipping up, tell him. If he's too busy, zip it up yourself. If you're both too busy, call a stagehand. It's important. That's all I have. Thanks guys. It was a good meeting."

In New York, Fred Morgan of North American was holding a meeting at the same time as Charlie Dale's. Unlike Dale's session, it consisted of one other person, Lou Wells, and was strictly confidential. The subject was NA's care and feeding of Governor Joseph H. Green.

The day before the three television networks had met to determine the production responsibility for the first debate. Morgan's luck had held, and NA had won the production toss. This meant NA would produce the first debate, the other two networks assuming responsibility for the second and third. Previously, Morgan had hinted to Green that if NA did not win the toss, they would continue to do what they could in the news-coverage area. Green had guilelessly replied by asking Morgan to send him a brief on the research behind the NA documentary on the need of a Secretary of Communications. For Fred Morgan it had been a pleasant conversation. And now, with NA ramrodding the first debate, both Wells and Morgan were in a state of extraordinary good humor.

"Looks like somebody up there likes us," said Wells to Morgan.

"And Joseph Green down here," said Morgan. "There's something I want to go over with you. Let's sit where we can be comfortable." The two men moved to the couches surrounding the coffee table at the end of Morgan's office. "Cigar?" asked Morgan, reaching into a new humidor on the table.

"No thanks, Fred," said Wells. "When did you take up cigars?"

"After the conventions. My goddam doctor insisted I cut down on cigarettes. Lou, I want to be very candid and straightforward with you in this discussion. I ask that everything we discuss be in strictest confidence."

"You have my assurance, Fred," said Wells, wondering what Morgan had on his mind.

"Several months ago we dreamed of the situation we now have at hand. Namely, that both candidates would accept the debates, and we would have the occasion as a fantastic public relations weapon against the do-gooders. We have a little less than three months before Election Day. And every one of these days should see a story on the debates. I want to make sure you haven't forgotten the importance of this aspect of using the debates."

"I haven't forgotten. I have assigned a man in the Washington Bureau and a man here to stay on the story exclusively. We have a series of documentaries planned which will lead up to the first debate, and the Public Affairs Department is about to submit a proposal which outlines programs for airing through November fifth."

"Good. I can't overemphasize the importance of this thing for public opinion. I say this because something tells me it's going to get a lot worse before it gets better. I mean, I think the powers against us are about to shift emphasis from the scandals, which are fading, to our actual programs. I have reason to say what I do. I think we're about to see a well-planned, long-range blast on a national scale, perhaps from Washington, on the so-called mediocre stuff we're telecasting in prime time. You know, the violence, brutality, delinquency wail. I can hear it swelling up from the Potomac and rolling in from across the Hudson now."

Wells started to speak, then stopped. How long did Morgan think any network could get away with the stuff they'd been cramming down the public's throats? he thought. The hell with the rigged quiz shows. They were Bible lessons compared to the brutality and sadism of the murder and mayhem, shoot-'em-up shows.

"The debates will be our answer to the criticism, Fred," said Wells lamely.

"They'll do a good deal. But that won't be the cure-all. Other things must be done. Now here's what I have in mind, and there are 'ifs' in it. But you and I must reach an understanding on this. And then go forward." Wells nodded. "Let's say," said Morgan, "that Green makes the White House. I happen to think he will. I haven't told you, Lou, but I attended an exclusive private dinner with Green in Chicago. I'm sorry I couldn't work you into it, but it was out of the question." A good dig, thought Wells. The man's already buying his house in Georgetown.

Morgan continued. "So I have become quite close to Green. Let's put it that way. If he makes it, he will offer me the new Communications spot in the Cabinet." Morgan diverted his gaze from Wells. He worked at scratching out a stain on his trouser leg as he spoke the next lines almost as a throwaway. "And when I get the offer, I will accept it." Wells decided silence was the best choice at that moment. He was correct. "If I do this," Morgan said, "two things happen; one definitely, the other probably. The first is that North American will need a new president for at least four years, perhaps longer. If I read the Indian signs correctly, and I'm pretty good at this sort of thing, the new man should not come from the shoot-'em-up side of the network or from sales. If we took either of these areas as a source for the chief executive, it might get goddam embarrassing for NA in congressional hearings if these same guys had to defend what they had been making and selling. Now the second part. If I am sitting in Green's cabinet in the White House, I don't want to have to sit there and defend North American morning, noon, and night. It's going to be tough enough if everything goes well, but I don't want it worse than it has to be. So, my one big out will be that there's a new team, a new look, a new policy at NA. I want to get the jump on Global and Telenet because the knives will be out, you know that." Wells nodded as Morgan amused himself by puffing out full, rich smoke rings. "My inclination, Lou, is that if Green goes all the way you should be the next president of North American. Does that interest you?"

As slow and labored as the buildup was, Wells couldn't believe it when he heard it. He kept himself under rigid control, permitting himself nothing more than a half-smile as he said, "Nothing in the world interests me more, Fred."

"I was sure you'd say that, and I'm very pleased at your reaction. So, it boils down to this. You become president of NA *if* Green makes it. Now, interestingly enough, we have production control over the first debate, which should have the largest audience of all of them. Get it? Need I say more?" Morgan's face hardened. He leveled his eyes at Wells, and spat out a piece of cigar leaf.

"I get it," said Wells with assurance. "There must be any number of little things. I will personally produce and supervise the debate and will keep on the alert for what I can do."

"Get as tough as you want. Remember, these debates are under the absolute control of the networks, not the candidates or their representatives. Let's talk again before you meet with the Conger and Green people. Do you have the presentation thoughts of Global and Telenet?"

"Well, yes. Generally they're leaving it up to us, and will take the cue for their debates from what happens in ours, what the public reaction to it is."

"Just remember this. We've purposely hit for no less than eight debates, one a week starting in September. Finnegan, Fenton, and I are in total agreement on this. If we lose two or three, what the hell. I couldn't care less. All we need is one, Lou. Just one. The first presidential face-to-face debate in history. So don't be too picky on the number. Let the two candidates fight it out between themselves. We're home free with just one."

"Just one," said Barbara, watching Ned Colton fix her a gin and tonic. "I've got to go up to my room."

"What do you mean?" asked Colton. "I thought you were staying for dinner. We're having a communal barbecue."

"What are you cooking?" Barbara asked.

"Steak, what else, baby?" said Colton, nuzzling her neck.

"I'll stay."

The doorbell rang. Fergie entered with a load of men's suits, shirts, and socks. "Just call me Anna May Wong, Chinese laundress. No charge for bachelor service," she said, dumping the bundle into a chair. "Don't mind if I do, Ned Ol' boy. Heavy on the tonic. I've got more sewin' for you poor babies to do tonight."

"Would it be all right if Shelton Flagg comes for dinner?" Barbara asked.

"What, again?" said Ham Forrest, buttoning the cuffs of a clean shirt as he walked from his bedroom onto the porch of the ground-level apartment. "Please, Barbie, he's on the Green staff. What will people say?"

"They've already said it, smartie," said Barbara. "Rufus Little has talked to me, and so has Ab. We reached an agreement."

They sure had. Barbara Beatty, in her constant quest for someone to pay the cost of her twilight years, had met Shelton Flagg, Managing Director of Communications for Governor Green. Flagg had successfully managed the radio and TV for two upset victories in New England, one a senator, the other a governor who had snaked into a stronghold held by the enemy for eighty years. Flag was from Philadelphia. He spent his summers at Martha's Vineyard, and was a bore on the subject of the influx of tourists in recent years and how tourism had disturbed the tranquility of his bachelor's island retreat.

It was against Rufe Little's Queensbury Rules of Politics for a secretary from Conger Headquarters to be seeing a man on the Green staff. Barbara, however, had struck a pact with Little and Shepherd. She had fallen in love, she told them, and explained it wasn't that easy to find a man—at her age. If she continued to see Flagg, she promised she'd compromise herself to the extent of getting as much information out of her intended as possible. She wanted her man, at any cost, and it came high. Barbara Beatty became the Mata Hari of the Conger campaign, carrying back to Shepherd, Baldwin, and Little veritable jewels of information after her nocturnal gymnastics with Flagg.

"Well, we've got enough food. Tell Flagg to bring a jug next time he comes. He's so tight he squeaks," said Colton.

"It's just the way he was brought up in New England," said Barbara defensively. "Inwardly, he's a very generous person."

"Does he give a lot, Barbie?" teased Forrest. "Huh, does he give, is he generous in bed?"

"You stop that, Ham Forrest," shouted Barbara. "Shelton Flagg is a gentleman, and I am a lady. If I weren't so hungry, I'd go eat alone."

"Apologize to the lady, you ape," said Fergie, looking daggers at Forrest.

"Listen," said Forrest, "we took this apartment to get away from women telling us what to do. But I apologize, Barbara. Go in and wash some glasses. The others will be here shortly."

The Charlie Dale television advance team, consisting of Peter Hunt, Ham Forrest, Thomas P. Tuttle, and Bud Rust along with Ned Colton, had deposited themselves in an enormous cavern of an apartment at The Sunshine, a fading monument to the flower of southern hospitality. The boys had chipped in and rented a five-bedroom suite that was gargantuan in its proportions. The building was fifty years old, and Suite 99, at the end of a long ground-floor hall, was to live in infamy years after the Conger campaign was over. It was their Nantucket without sand, their Malibu without grunion, their Bermuda without bikes. The boys went through a dozen new toothbrushes a week, what with so many unexpected guests.

The men came and went on their assignments out of Dale's office, striking off in the dead of night on survey trips and production assignments like an advance cadre of Reconstruction Day drummers. And throughout the campaign, Suite 99's transient occupants became the "lost little children" of Fergie, who mothered them as her own. She straightened out their tangled love-lives, sewed on buttons, administered hot mustard-plasters, did emergency food shopping, and rode herd mercilessly on the housekeeping help of The Sunshine to bring some element of cleanliness and order out of the fifty years' accumulated dirt in the corners of every room. She comforted and soothed the smashed hearts of a dozen female Washington residents who were caught up in the whirlwind of physical activity in 99. She bucked through the boys' cash advances at the National Committee and became a fierce terrier at the disbursing office when reimbursement on an expense account was a day late.

"Fergie, can I talk to you about San Francisco?" asked Tommy Tuttle, who had been sitting in the corner, quietly cutting his toenails.

"What about it, dream boy?"

"Talk to Charlie, Fergie," asked Tuttle. "About me. You know how badly I want to cover that rally out there. He says Peter's going to do it. That ain't fair. I got friends in San Francisco." In Dale's office some of the boys had seen the top-secret schedule for the first week of the campaign, even though it was two weeks away.

"Everybody's got friends in San Francisco," chimed in Forrest. "I don't now how Peter got so lucky, but you'll have to stand in line behind me if he doesn't do the Embarcadero rally. Why, for Christ's sake, there's a ten-boy curry at India House out there which is named after me!"

"To say nothing of probably several children," chimed in Fergie. "How do you keep your gals straight, Ham?" she asked, smiling.

"I thought you wanted to do Dallas," said Tuttle. "Isn't that where you've got that six-foot blonde stashed away?"

"Aw, come on," said Forrest. "It's just that I have too many friends. I won't be able to visit with all of them in this campaign."

"Is that what you call it, 'visiting'?" asked Fergie.

"Careful, girl, or you'll have to apologize," said Forrest. "Where the hell are Charlie and Sandy? They're late, and he's the guest of honor."

"They'll be along," said Fergie. "Old Crash got held up at the office as per usual. Rufe Little called him over on something just as he was leaving. Little's still suspicious of our fearless leader, and Conger's okaying the debates."

Tommy Tuttle looked at Fergie. "How serious is this Sandy thing getting, Fergie?" he asked. "What's with Janet in Denver?"

"I don't know, and I don't care. What he does is his own business," Fergie said.

"People are beginning to talk," said Tuttle.

"You mean people like yourself," Fergie slung back at him. The doorbell rang, and Dale and Sandy were ushered in with a loud chorus of "Charles Crash, our leader, our leader." Sandy beamed at Dale, who laughed when they called him "Crash." The nickname had stuck after a series of one crisis after another in which Dale had given out order upon order to the men and Fergie to "do it on a crash basis." The group left the entrance hall and walked toward the porch.

"Sorry I'm late, guys. Had to see Rufe Little. And an enemy in our own camp." Someone handed the new arrivals their drinks, and the party was under way.

Dale had several known, and a few unknown, enemies on the Conger staff. Dale was being his executive best: decisive, rough, positive. He was short on protocol, a stickler for perfection, intolerant of mistakes or ignorance. He was tops at his job and knew it. He couldn't understand how anyone else could remain on the staff without the same degree of knowledge and efficiency. Dale worked at the speed of a three-stage rocket, hour after endless hour, day after exhausting day. He was intolerant and outspokenly critical of those staff members who left at six, their work undone. They were on the staff because of some inexplicable loyalty to them by Conger, a relationship they had exploited to obtain their campaign status.

Dale's real fury, however, was saved for the self-styled television impresarios, the know-nothing amateur "image" and show business experts, who were legion in a political campaign. The most dangerous of the type were those who had at times the ear of the candidate. A lawyer who really thought he knew lighting, makeup, staging, wardrobe, textures, foot-candle readings, lenses, production techniques, writing, and music could be found on every campaign staff. They changed with the year and the candidate, but a specimen of the species was always on board. This year it was George Pinnell, one of the three men Conger had consulted in the early dawn of the day of his nomination in Chicago. Rufe Little's orders to Dale were, "Be nice, go along with him." Which, as far as Dale was concerned, beautifully described a professional politician. Pinnell was a heavy contributor, had the candidate's ear, so he became a cross Dale bore throughout the campaign.

Pinnell had decided that Andrew Conger, while waiting to be introduced and seated on various platforms, was holding his hands in his lap in an effeminate way, crossing his legs too stiffly, creating an altogether unpleasant picture of a presidential candidate. There was something unnatural, abnormal, in Pinnell's concern about Conger's physical appearance. At various times Pinnell had complained of the nose-hairs in Conger's nostrils, his eyebrows, the hairs growing on the top rim of each ear. It was a possessive, bitchy, female approach to Conger's mannerisms and appearance. Dale was not comfortable around the man, and few were. He wondered what Andy Conger saw in him. Perhaps it was merely that Conger could relax completely in his company, that their dissimilarity actually fostered the friendship. It seemed strange, though, that Andy Conger would have as a friend a lawyer who said he admired T. C. Jones, the gifted female impersonator, more than any other artist in the American theater.

Dale talked to Pinnell, promised he would mention the mannerisms to Conger, and took his leave as soon as possible. By the time he reached the street, Pinnell's comments were gone from his mind.

Andrew Conger made several forays out of Washington in August, prior to the official opening of the campaign in September. These trips for isolated speeches served many purposes. They provided the candidate with an accurate barometer on the major issues of the campaign. A "grass roots" reading on the acceptance of the party's political platform was obtained. Equally as important, however, was the opportunity gained to break in the traveling staff, the physical and television advance teams. Dale selected the largest TV rally in the August period as a training camp for his new men. Dale himself remained in Washington while the team went into the South to cover the rally. Ham Forrest was in charge. The night before the rally Dale received the first of what were to be countless practical jokes between the men in the field and the Washington office. The fun would continue through Election Day.

Forrest was worried about the size of the crowd. So was Arthur Baldwin. Dale told them to pull out all the stops and build an impressive pre-show or warmup show. Money had been allocated for regional entertainers, but the boys were still worried about Conger's ability to fill the hall, which was too large. A searing heat wave had hit the South, driving crowd estimates still lower. It was after midnight when the call from Forrest came through to Dale in his apartment. Later, when the boys were in the Pacific Time Zone with Conger, calls arrived straight through the night, with an around-the-clock group of girls assigned to the office.

"Hello, Charlie, didn't wake you, did I? This is Ham."

"You know goddam well you did," said Dale. "What's up?" he asked, yawning as he reached for a cigarette.

"Everything's going fine, except the pre-show. How'd you like a chorus of a thousand voices?"

"Is it any good?"

"What do you mean, is it any good? It's sensational. We've heard it. It's an organized chorus, they sing together all the time. They have their own robes, everything. Fabulous stuff they wear."

"Sounds great to me. Do you have enough time to publicize it?"

"We'll use radio and sound trucks all day tomorrow. There's one little thing their leader has requested, Charlie, and I wanted to clear it with you."

"What's that?"

"Well, they take care of their own robes and hoods, and everything. And if they agree to participate in the rally, they want permission to burn a fiery cross at the auditorium's entrance. Okay by you?" Forrest asked, having difficulty controlling himself. Dale broke out in laughter.

"You bastards," said Dale. "I don't need any KKK chorus at a Conger rally. If they want to burn Green in effigy, tell 'em it's a deal." Forrest laughed and gave Dale an encouraging picture of the local television co-operation and coverage. "Good night, Crash. See you Friday."

Emergency conferences with Andrew Conger became daily occurrences as the tempo increased. On a typical day Charlie Dale was leaving his office for a planning session and luncheon at the National Committee when, five minutes before he was due across town, the candidate's office called urgently. The Secretary wanted Dale to join him for lunch in fifteen minutes. Could he make it? Dale ran toward the elevator, shouting his change of plans to a pursuing Fergie.

As Dale entered Conger's office, Ruth Platt greeted him. "Hi, Charlie. My, you made good time."

Dale gave her a brotherly peck on the cheek. "Hi, beautiful. What's the crisis today?"

Ruth gave Dale a bored look and said, "Clothes. His tailor's here from New York. The Secretary's selecting four or five suits for the campaign. He wanted you to be sure they were okay for TV."

"Who are these other people?"

"Fat Cats. A small private luncheon, you know? Rufe Little set it up. He's over in the corner with that big chemical guy from Utah. Can't remember his name. His wife's nice, though."

Dale participated in the study of the fabric swatches. Susan Conger joined them, made her preferences known, and returned to her role as hostess. Conger, the tailor, and Dale, leaning over the massive desk, continued to eliminate fabrics.

"Charlie," said Conger in a low voice, "could you take some drink orders for these people? The whiskey and mixes are in that long sideboard."

"Sure," said Dale. "You got a white jacket that'll fit me?" he asked, laughing. "Where's the ice?"

"There's a refrigerator built in the sideboard," said Conger. "Incidentally, I'd like to talk to you and Rufe after these other folks leave."

"I'm free," said Dale. One was instantly "free" if the candidate called for him.

The luncheon was pleasant. Dale was introduced all around. There were four couples, one from Los Angeles, one from New Hampshire, and the two from Utah. Dale enjoyed the break in his otherwise hectic day.

When the group left, Dale and Little settled down with Conger at one end of his magnificent conference table, an historic piece which had a history of use in high Washington offices dating back to 1840. Little and Dale waited for Conger to speak.

"Your first meeting with the Green people on scheduling is tomorrow?" Conger asked, looking at Dale.

"That's correct," said Dale. Conger was referring to the problem of reconciling the political itinerary and travel schedules of both candidates to a common date for the first debate. The situation actually would boil down to finding a city to which Green and Conger could fly in order that both might appear on the same telecast.

"This isn't going to be easy," said Conger. "One of the problems is the information which will be given away to the other side in trying to find the date and city. I'll be goddammed if I'm going to give them my travel plans for the next two months just to pick a city for these debates."

"Whatever happened to the split-city idea?" asked Little. "You know, like "Person to Person," or with that split-screen stuff—one man in one city, the other in another?"

"The networks have withdrawn that format for the first debate," said Dale. "They think it's okay for the later ones, but think it would be bad for the initial telecast."

"Let's get two things straight," said Conger, looking at Dale. "There may be only one debate. And, we do the withdrawing, not the networks. They are not controlling these telecasts. The candidates are."

"I am not sure that's the way they see it, Andy," said Dale. "They're going for a face-to-face format for the first one."

"I'm going for the White House," said Conger. He shifted his weight in his chair, irritated. "These debates will be what I want them to be, along with my opponent. It's going to be a pain-in-the-ass to bust open the schedule for even one of them. But . . . I guess it has to be done. Get this straight, however. I accepted these debates because I was in a box—there was no way out. But, I am going to hold the line at one debate, no more."

Christ, thought Dale, wait until the networks hear this.

"In these scheduling meetings with the other people you are to drag your feet," said Conger. "As long as you can manage it, make it impossible to arrive at a city or date. The longer we stall, the later it becomes in the campaign, and the fewer dates will present themselves for the debates. I am very sincere, Dale, about this. I've been conned into the idea of the debates. I will concede that. But I am not going to be pushed into more appearances than fit my plans. So we do one, but no more."

Rufe Little carefully removed an ash from his cigar by rolling it around the lip of a porcelain ash tray, in the center of which was the seal of the office of Secretary of State. "I think we better soft-pedal the public or press awareness of our stand, Andy," he said. "Why not, if we're asked, say we're going ahead in good faith. That we're reserving a decision on subsequent debates until after the first one? If we do that, we'll satisfy everybody but won't be giving away our intentions. Also, chances are we better start meeting with the Green people on the first date, and this plan wouldn't prevent that."

"If we don't start meeting soon," said Dale, "there may not be any debates."

"Which would be just fine with me," said Conger. He grinned ever so slightly. "Oh, I know we've got to agree to one date," he said. "But each possibility, each city, each indication we may be able to work something out, should be as tough as pulling teeth out of a mountain lion. Make it difficult as hell all the way through. Agree to nothing. Use me, Little, as the excuse to defer any decisions. This is a feet-dragging operation. We've got the money for paid political programs which we can control. Every minute I'm on television with my opponent, he will be gaining stature, visibility. I don't care what anyone says about my command of TV. I can only be hurt by debate."

"We see these debates as a gift from heaven," said Shelton Flagg, Managing Director of Broadcast Operations for the Green Campaign. "Imagine it. Eight hours of free prime time in the evening offered to us on a silver platter. Actually, in our minds the free time is secondary to the opportunity for Governor Green to articulate the great issues of the campaign in debate."

"To say nothing of the publicity," said Dale. "You care about everything television can do to bring your man up in the popularity polls. Christ, as of the day you start your campaign, there will be twenty-two states your man has never been in, never set foot in." Flagg winced at the truth of Dale's words.

It was the third time the Green people and Conger representatives had met to hammer out the date and city for the first debate, making sure while doing so that "the enemy" didn't acquire any valuable information about the rest of the political moves on the grand checkerboard of national campaigning. At the meeting in a private dining room at the Mayflower were Charlie Dale and Abner Shepherd of the Conger staff, Shelton Flagg and Murray Smith of the Green group. Flagg was to disappear after this meeting—and for the rest of the campaign—into an elusive mist of endless sessions with the network heads endeavoring to obtain free time for Green. Dale didn't see him again until the evening of the first debate. Flagg was an old-time broadcaster, a man whose mind had not been able to make an easy transfer into the mysteries and intricacies of television. He had no knowledge of television costs or production, and left those details entirely to Murray Smith, and Green's advertising agency. Flagg, trading constantly on his relationship with past presidential candidates, had tried to force himself into the inner circle of Green's advisers. Unfortunately, he was out of step with the times and tempo of modern campaigning. There were many situations in which Flagg found himself that caused him to long for the peace and quiet of his backwater executive job in Philadelphia. Flagg's one target, based on figures he garbled mentally and vaguely remembered from past campaigns, was the enormous cost of campaigning on TV. He relentlessly hammered at the networks for gifts of time. He obtained several free half-hours—sustaining periods opposite high-rated shows on the other networks. Result: no audience for Green.

"I made the statement because our first date could be affected by subsequent dates for further debates," said Flagg.

"Look, Flagg," said Shepherd, "before this meeting you were going to nail down three possible dates in three possible cities. I have my schedule, and I have those possibles to throw on the table. Are you prepared to do the same?"

Flagg consulted his papers and whispered something to Murray Smith, Green's newly appointed television adviser. "Uh, Murray Smith here," he said, "has recently joined us. You're aware he'll be handling TV, all phases of it. I haven't had time to go over the cities with him. By that I mean whether or not they have proper production facilities to handle a telecast of this magnitude."

"Let's leave that up to the networks," said Smith. "Our job is to deliver the candidates. Their job is to deliver the facilities. Isn't that the way you see it, Dale?" he asked.

"Exactly," said Dale. "I've advised our people against a couple of impossible locations, where I know there aren't proper facilities, but outside of that it should be up to the network. In this day and age it is not necessary to limit our thinking to merely New York, Los Angeles, and Chicago. There are many fine local stations whose studios and facilities could accommodate us."

"We've been all through that," said Shepherd impatiently. "I've got other things to do besides sitting here to get a lecture on TV stations in the United States."

"That may be what it boils down to, Ab," said Dale. "Not only the studios, but the physical plant to handle the press and the camp followers."

"If we can pick a city and date which will place Green and Conger in the same city between Labor Day and Election Day, I don't care if the networks have to rent the Ringling Brothers' tent for a studio," said Shepherd.

"The networks will have to satisfy me on their ability to produce a top-quality show from the city we select, or I will recommend against it," said Smith.

"We're down to only one network, fellas," said Dale. "I thought you knew. North American won the toss a couple of days ago. They go with the first one. Which may also be the last one."

"Heaven help us all," said Smith. "We'll have Lou Wells in bed with us before this thing is over. He'll end up a candidate running for President."

Murray Smith is no fool, thought Dale as he looked at him, smiling at the comment. Dale didn't know too much about him, only a few impersonal surface facts, meager information. Smith was from Boston, had been in television and theater production for a number of years, and had no deep personal tie or relationship to Governor Green. The story Dale had heard was that Green's advertising agency had been unable to satisfy the candidate with one of their men. Green had asked for a comprehensive search to find the right man, no matter where he was. Murray Smith was the result. He appeared to be in his early thirties, younger than Dale but poised and sure of himself. He had style, and a gracious manner which appealed to Dale. His head was small for his body, but his forceful manner and the deep crow's-feet at his eyes belied his youth. Only his blond hair without a trace of gray gave a clue to his age. Smith's hands were long and graceful, and a ring of one of the military services adorned the third finger of his right hand.

Murray Smith demonstrated a good knowledge of production and visual techniques. Dale made a mental note to get together with Smith for dinner, away from phones, as soon as it could be arranged. He realized already that if the two couldn't work together efficiently and arrive at production decisions independently of North American, there would be deep trouble ahead on the debates.

"I think we can handle Wells," said Dale. "We'll put a leash on him." Smith grinned. "Okay," continued Dale, "what's the first date you guys are throwing at us?"

"Well, we've got our three," said Flagg, "although two of them aren't too practical. But it's all we can get." He and Smith huddled over their notes. "The first date is September eighteenth, a Monday." The two looked up at Dale and Shepherd.

"Hmmm," said Shepherd. "We're dead there. Besides, that's too early. Our man will never buy that. Where will your man be on that date . . . East, Midwest, or Far West?"

"Oh, no you don't," said Flagg. "If the date is out as a possibility, we decided we didn't have to disclose locations. Remember?"

"I stand corrected," said Shepherd. "Just thought I'd try. My apologies," he said facetiously. "Good God, after the past five days that's the best you can come up with?"

"What have you got?" asked Smith, putting the ball back in Conger's court to disclose vital information as to the candidate's future campaigning whereabouts.

"Let me see," said Shepherd. Unconsciously, he was sliding his chair away from the conference table, back to the opposite wall. Dale slid his chair at the same time, eyes glued to the Conger schedule. It was a practice which had become standard at each meeting—Dale had laughed aloud the first time he had caught himself doing it. The session would begin around a table, each side comfortable in the free give-and-take of information vital to the discussion. As the meeting progressed, however, and it became increasingly important to consult the confidential travel schedules, each side would begin the slow retreat to opposite walls of the room. Invariably, the session was concluded in the atmosphere of a Quaker meeting: the Conger men lined up along one wall, holding their schedules tightly against their chests like so many Las Vegas gamblers; the Green people sitting upright in their chairs, lined up against their wall, looking like British counting-house clerks. The conference table, suddenly bare of conferees, loomed strangely between the enemy camps, a wooden no-man's land in their war of political secrecy. "Where will your man be October sixteenth?" asked Shepherd, throwing the question like a winning bid to a partner in a championship bridge tournament.

"For the first one?" asked Smith, surprised. "So late?"

"For the first one," said Shepherd. "Our man will be in the Midwest, if that will move things along faster."

The Green men now knew not only where Conger *would* be October sixteenth, but just as importantly where he would *not* be.

Flagg, looking up from his schedule, spoke: "Interestingly enough, that is an available date for us. But not for the first one, Ab. We could only do four debates before Election Day if we started that late. Doing one a week, that is."

"That may be three more than there will be," said Dale. "Could your man be in Chicago October sixteenth?"

Once again the secretive glance, this time at a schedule of committed political meetings. "No," said Flagg. "I can't tell you why, so don't ask me. But he cannot be in Chicago." The Green men were silent as they shuffled through another set of files. Each side had done this a dozen times while the other side watched patiently. It was a pantomime accompanying each date or city offered. "Our man will be in the Midwest," said Flagg, finally. "I think he could be in Cleveland, October sixteenth, and still keep his commitments the following day."

"Cleveland?" asked Dale. "If he can make Cleveland, why can't he make Chicago? The previous day being Sunday, I should think he could make either one."

"Can your man make Cleveland?" asked Smith, looking at Shepherd.

If I don't settle on one date, thought Shepherd, we'll be here till November. What the hell, I'll give on this one. "Yes," he said, "we could make Cleveland. But why not Chicago?"

"I said, don't ask me," Flagg repeated. "Do you want to consider Cleveland and October sixteenth for a debate? I dislike it intensely. Green will never buy such a date for Number One. I will recommend strongly against it to him."

Does Green give a damn about your recommendation, Dale thought, looking at Flagg. From what I hear, Flagg, you can't get five minutes a week with Green. "What about the third date?" asked Dale. "Do you want to hear ours?"

The third possibility, even later than October sixteenth, was discussed and discarded. Flagg refused to disclose Green's plans on the date offered by Shepherd, so it became a standoff. Provided with the possibility of Monday, October sixteenth, and Cleveland, Ohio, the meeting broke up, each side to return to their principals with the information.

Charges, demands, countercharges, taunts, and accusations were to fill the air for days to come over this one possible date and site of the first face-to-face debate. While Green fumed over Conger's steadfast position that this would be his first available date for debate, August was drawing to a close, and the campaign kickoff loomed over the horizon to the East.

It would be weeks before any agreement would be forthcoming from Conger on the Cleveland date. Governor Green, however, feeling the debate possibility was slipping away from him entirely, accepted the date without warning in a news conference. There was continued silence from Conger Headquarters. Feet-dragging was indeed the order of the day. A planned leak from the Conger staff implied Conger might rescind his earlier availability position on October sixteenth, and Cleveland.

11

August in Washington

"WHAT CAN YOU SAY to Susan Conger, Mr. Dale?" asked Pearl Hayes, Chairman of the Women's Division of Conger's National Committee. "What can you do to make her mind us, make her behave?"

"I can't do anything, Pearl," said Dale. "Susan Conger has very definite ideas as to what she should and should not do on television. I respect her position in this."

"Well, I don't," said Hayes. "There are millions of women involved in this campaign. They need a leader, an image. That image should be Susan Conger. How can she be so selfish as not to provide us with our female symbol?"

Christ, thought Dale, these same bitches are here every four years; only the faces change. Where do they come from? What do they do when they're not playing at being men, smelling up offices in Washington, and demanding the impossible? Shrieking, screaming, strident, overly masculine dames, frustrated at home or thrown out by exasperated husbands, only to end up in Washington acting and sounding like so many political fishwives.

Pearl Hayes came from Oregon, and she was a type. She could have been president of a women's club—national president, that is. She'd settle for nothing less in the hawklike possessiveness with which she attacked her every interest. Or she could have been head of the Movie Censorship Board in her home community, or chairman of the Committee for Better Salaries for School Bus Drivers. The compulsion to direct, to assert herself, to dominate, would cause Pearl Hayes to gravitate to causes the rest of her life. At the moment the Conger campaign fulfilled her needs. She wanted to run Susan Conger the same way she did other causes.

Pearl Hayes looked ridiculous behind the massive dark walnut desk, like a little girl playing nurse or school teacher. Only the stakes were much higher, and the consequences of Pearl Hayes's actions toward Andrew Conger's wife could be disastrous to the careful and slow plan Dale had conceived through which he hoped to convince Susan Conger that a few necessary television appearances would be in good taste, and a painless experience. If this broad so much as says one word to Susan, thought Dale, I'll jam that stupid fruit bowl she calls a hat down her throat.

"I believe Susan Conger has given you an excellent symbol through her actions at Conger's side these past years of public life," said Dale. "She's one of the most selfless people I know. I believe her reasonable desires for privacy during the campaign should be respected."

"Do you agree, Mr. Dale, the once-a-week women's daytime program with Susan Conger is a good idea?" asked Mrs. Hayes.

"I do," said Dale.

"Do you agree it will bring millions of women across the bosom of the United States a more accurate picture of our little Cinderella?" Mrs. Hayes asked.

"I do," Dale repeated.

"Then how can you sit there and say my request for eight days of her time in an entire campaign is unreasonable? And how can you not go to Andrew Conger demanding he permit his wife to participate in this project?" Hayes asked, jutting her chin at Dale. A thin sliver of brilliant sunlight cut through the Venetian blinds and spotlighted the fine black hairs which Mrs. Hayes was either too lazy or too proud to pluck from her upper lip.

"I don't demand things of Andrew Conger," Dale answered with disgust. "Your idea is good, Pearl, but it simply will never come to pass. You will not get eight days of Susan's time. You will not get two days. Susan has ruled out any appearances on her own. Conger will not force Susan into anything against her wishes. He, too, has a certain respect for his wife," Dale concluded bitingly.

"We are aware of their feelings toward each other, Mr. Dale," Hayes said haughtily. "How am I going to get this project for the Women's Volunteer Organization? I must have it. I will have it! Will you deliver Susan Conger to me, or will I be forced to contact Andrew Conger directly, indicating I could obtain no satisfaction from his television men?"

The other women in the room, as if at a signal, cast their eyes down to their laps, up at the ceiling, onto notes—anywhere to avoid witnessing the stupidity of their female chief. Dale, without emotion, no expression on his face, looked at Pearl Hayes. Then, softly, he said, "You can tell Andrew Conger anything you want to tell him, Mrs. Hayes. Why don't you arrange to have breakfast with him sometime this week and talk the whole thing over with him? Perhaps if you presented it to him personally, he would see the wisdom in your request. After all, he's just as practical a person as you. And interested in just as many women's votes."

"Mattie," said Hayes, turning to a court follower, "call Mr. Conger for a breakfast appointment. Tell him I want to discuss Mrs. Conger's once-a-week daytime program. We must have it!"

My God, thought Dale rather sadly, the stupid broad believes me. He wished he hadn't made the suggestion. For Pearl Hayes never was to have breakfast with Andrew Conger. Conger's office had long-standing instructions that no calls from Pearl Hayes were to be brought to his attention during the campaign. Dale was very well aware of this.

"Listen, Big Jesus, maybe you don't have a heart, maybe Andy Conger doesn't have a heart, but somebody's got to take care of this little old lady at the end of the hall," said Fergie. "She's been here since eight o'clock this morning. I took her to lunch, jammed a Manhattan down her to stop her crying, and now she's back again. Please, please, Charlie, will you see her?"

"Fergie," said Dale, sitting at his desk between two mounds of requests for Conger's appearance on television shows, "if I don't tackle this stuff right now before the meeting on network stuff, I'm lost to it forever. There are requests in this pile that have gone unanswered for three weeks. I can't let it go any longer. Have one of the volunteers talk to her. What does she want?"

"She's got a campaign song," said Fergie.

"So have five hundred other people we've been nice to around here," said Dale. "Get a release, a copy of the sheet music, and the record if she has one, thank her, and put her name on the 'thank-you' list for a note from Conger. I can't see her, Fergie."

"She's been sittin' like a puppy dog, outside Conger's office all day. She has a battered-up old black phonograph in her lap. She won't go away."

"Feed her and tell her to come back in four years."

"I told you, I've already fed her, smart boy. The hell with you." Fergie slammed Dale's door as she left, and Dale returned to the stack of unanswered requests. As he came to each one, he made a mark in the upper right-hand corner, signifying one of the three standard replies to requests for Conger appearances. The first was a polite "no." The second was one which stated Conger might be in the city of the TV station which originated the request, and they would be advised if the candidate's final travel plans were to make an appearance possible. The third letter said the request was being forwarded to the candidate with a favorable recommendation. While Dale was reviewing an invitation from Milwaukee for a local Sunday night panel show, the door to his office opened wide, the doorknob slamming against the inside wall.

"Mr. Dale, may I present Miss Eunice Merkel? This sweet, dear thing would like you to hear a campaign song." Fergie pushed a little shrunken woman into Dale's office and motioned her to a chair.

"How do you do, Mr. Dale," said the Grandma Moses of Tin Pan Alley, the oldest song-plugger Dale had ever seen. "I am very appreciative. If you are busy now, I could come back later. That wonderful Andrew Conger is so busy making his plans to deliver this fair land of ours into a decade of peace and productivity, he couldn't see me today. His staff has been very kind to me. Mr. Conger didn't have room for me in his waiting room, so they brought a chair out into the hall where I wouldn't be any bother to anyone. It was drafty by the elevator, but my, it's nice to be here in Andrew Conger's Headquarters. I feel so safe."

Dale looked at Miss Eunice Merkel. She must be seventy-five, he thought. She was not five feet tall and was dressed in a red hat, white shoes, and a blue dress covered with stars. On the upper left shoulder of her dress was pinned a giant Conger button, which said, "LET'S SEND A.C. TO D.C." The button had become quite popular as the weeks went by, until the opposition manufactured several thousand which used the same words but in a slightly different way. They were quite suggestive, playing on the A.C.-D.C. idea. The official ones disappeared overnight.

As Dale watched in horror while Fergie plugged in the phonograph, he noticed Miss Merkel's shoes were actually white sneakers. With a pen Miss Merkel had drawn a neat "A" on the toe of one, a "C" on the other. Her eyes twinkled as she reached into a filthy, dog-eared manila envelope and withdrew several sheets of music and two half-hour rolls of sound tape. Dale remained silent. So it was a tape recorder Fergie had hooked up.

"Miss Ferguson has been like a mother to me since early morn," said Miss Merkel. "I came here directly from the bus station. Yesterday I was in Kansas City. They liked the song out there very much."

"Thank you, Fergie, you may go now," said Dale, darting a look at his maternal nemesis. Fergie left the room, smiling broadly at Dale over Miss Merkel's shoulder as she closed the door. Miss Merkel immediately bent down and unlocked the tape recorder. She swiftly positioned the spools, talking all the while. "I couldn't get to see you at the convention in Chicago, but I was there. My yes, I haven't missed a convention in forty years. After the convention, I got myself a bus ticket and went to California. Nobody would listen to my song out there except a nice man who used to be in movies and has something to do with Mr. Conger's rallies. He said he saw me at the convention in 1948. My, it was flattering. He remembered." She paused, then went on: "California already had a Conger song. I played the song for a nice young man in Pueblo, Colorado. He said it reminded him of a song called "Ragtime Cowboy Joe." He's wrong—tempo's different. But he said I should come to Washington." She expertly threaded the tape through the machine. She snapped on the power switch. "I have one hour of the song, done twenty different ways. We can listen to the first half-hour reel. Then, if you want, we can play the second half-hour."

Dale felt as if he were walking the last mile. Zella Ferguson, employed as his master protector against such occurrences, had forced him into a situation he had been spared through five campaigns. Charles Dale was trapped in his office with a nut, and there was no escape.

"Did you compose this song, Miss Merkel?" Dale asked hesitantly.

"No, my grandson did. He's a member of ASCAP." The music tape whirred forward as Miss Merkel searched for the beginning of the version she wanted Dale to hear. "The band on this 'take' is the house group at the Band Box in Chicago," she stated. What kind of a kook do I have here, thought Dale. She looks like Whistler's Mother and talks like Ella Fitzgerald! As the eight-bar introduction to the lyrics boomed out of the speaker, Miss Merkel jumped up, spread her legs in a cheerleader's stance, and snapped her fingers in perfect rhythm, swinging her hips.

Dale was jolted by the sensational marching song which filled his office. It was as catchy as "Happy Days Are Here Again," as easy to whistle as "I'm Looking Over a Four Leaf Clover." After the first chorus, Dale motioned to Miss Merkel to lower the volume. "Have you played this for anyone else in Washington?" he asked.

"Nobody but Miss Ferguson has talked to me," she said. "I haven't been able to open my machine before this moment."

"Do you have any plans for the next hour or so?"

"Only to play this music for you. It will take an hour to hear all the versions."

"Good. Excuse me while I make a call." Dale asked Fergie to get him Rufe Little. Dale went over to the tape recorder and turned up the volume. An instrumental version, so bright and peppy he found himself marching in one spot, spun off the tape. The light blinked on Dale's phone, and he dumped the sound.

"Rufe, this is Charlie. How fast can you come to my office? I've just heard the official song for the Andrew Conger for President Campaign. I've found it, and it's great!"

"In our opinion, there are several possible formats or combinations of formats which might be used," said Charlie Dale to Andrew Conger. "In addition, there are sophistications of each one. I'd like to cover them quickly."

The meeting took place on the screened porch of Conger's home at dusk. It was the final night of the three-day Labor Day weekend. Andrew Conger had asked for the session late the previous Friday, minutes before Dale and Sandy Nelson left for what they thought would be three days at Virginia Beach. As it was, even with cutting the holiday short, the two relaxed and enjoyed the time away from Washington. Dale slept ten hours the first night, eleven the second. The days were full of sun, lazy walks, the nights wondrous with unhurried love-making. The two made plans to meet in

Paris after the campaign. Dale saw his life commencing to parallel his love for Sandy. Denver seemed like another world. And Janet's warning in Chicago was forgotten. They were silent on the drive back to Washington, each alone with thoughts of the future.

Dale dropped Sandy off at her apartment, changed his clothes, and arrived at Conger's house a little early. Muffled voices projected from Conger's study as his houseman ushered Dale into the superb drawing room, the scene of countless important, international, name-studded social gatherings. Dale lit a cigarette and was settling back with a handsome book on Peruvian art when Rufe Little and Abner Shepherd joined him. They could hear Conger ushering his undisclosed guests to the front door; then they were summoned out to the comfort of the patio. Conger was dressed informally in a sport shirt and slacks and looked cool despite the warm evening. His feet rested on a footstool as Dale talked.

"The first would be the classic formal debate," Dale began, "with or without a live audience in the hall. On a one-hour basis it could be a ten-minute opening statement for each candidate, fifteen minutes each for rejoinder, and a five-minute closing statement by each man."

"Too dull," Conger said softly, adding, "I think."

Dale continued. "The second format could be the formal debate but with audience participation, that is, screened questions from the audience of the evening. It could be a formal opening statement, then the free section of screened questions, possible rebuttal, and a closing formal statement from each candidate. Number three would be a completely freewheeling face-to-face discussion. The two principals plus a neutral moderator who would be used merely to maintain order and toss out the first item for discussion."

"When is the first meeting with North American and the Green people on this?" asked Conger.

"Day after tomorrow," said Dale.

"Send me a memo on it the minute it's over," said Conger.

"Yes, sir," answered Dale. "The fourth possibility would be a panel discussion, Q and A. If we are forced to compromise on your dislike of the formal debate idea, a sophistication would be a combination of the formal opening and closing approach, with either face-to-face freewheeling as a center section or questions from a panel. Neutrality of the panel might be guaranteed by permitting each side to designate an equal number of panel members."

"Where's Jenkins?" asked Conger, referring to his press secretary.

"Had to get a statement out for the A.M.'s," said Shepherd. "On the farm issue crisis."

Conger guffawed. "Who the hell cares about that?" he said. "Dammit, I wanted him here. He's going to have to carry the hod if we end up with a panel of newsmen on this thing." There was a silent pause in the darkness. "Sorry, Dale . . . continue."

Dale could no longer see Conger's face. He did, however, talk in his direction. "A modification of the pure panel approach would be the panel-interview type telecast. Each principal would be questioned separately by the same panel, with a guarantee that the same issues in essence would be posed to each candidate. This format lends itself especially well to the split-city idea with candidates in different cities. If there is to be more than one debate, there is no reason the formats cannot be varied from debate to debate. Our evaluation of the formats, however, should be based on this hypothesis: in the possible formats open to us, there must be one or a combination of formats which will maximize the strengths of our candidate, and at the same time exploit the weaknesses of our opponent."

A long discussion followed concerning Conger's strengths and Green's strengths and weaknesses. Naturally, Conger's weaknesses were not covered. There were those who thought he had none. Dale, having observed his public appearances intimately for eight years, knew differently but remained tactfully quiet.

"With your preference for the Q and A aspect of press conferences, Andy, I should think we should give that element in our format serious consideration," said Little.

The Green weaknesses were discussed further, and it was agreed the format which would best point up Conger's strengths would also, fortunately, draw attention to Green's weaknesses. The panel approach, however, would have maximized both, in their opinion.

"According to the memos I've received from you, Dale," said Conger, "and the scraps I get from the network people and the press, I think we will be forced to accept in some fashion the formal debate idea. However, Charlie, be certain you make the majority of the time on the air devoted to Q and A from a panel. Do you think Green will buy this?"

"I don't know, Andy. I hear they want the formal debate all the way through, with prepared and rehearsed statements, a minimum of unrehearsed rebuttal, the right to refer to notes and texts . . . the old-fashioned formal debate."

"They don't do that even in intercollegiate debate any more," said Little. "They have teams, cross-examination, run them more according to courtroom procedure. What about cross-examination, direct cross-examination by one candidate to the other? You'd kill him, Andy."

There was a pause before Conger answered. "I'm not so sure." He spoke softly as his mind considered the thousands of ramifications of the decisions being reached that night. Dale's gaze wandered to three fireflies dancing outside the porch screen. Crickets were setting up a counterpoint to the historic discussion. Conger yawned loudly. "Even if we participate in the selection of the panel, it'll be loaded against us if it's press."

"If I may say so, Andy, I think the seriousness of the occasion will prevent pure hatchet questions," said Shepherd. "In the event any reporter is stupid enough to try one, I should think a loaded hostile question could be turned very much to your advantage. What the hell, you've been doing it for years in press conferences, and you love it."

"Sure . . . sure," said Conger, impatiently. "I understand. It's just that with the international play these debates are going to get . . . didn't you tell me, Dale, they will be telecast in Europe the next day?"

"That's correct, on video tape," said Dale.

"That's my point," continued Conger. "A hostile question can bring on an emotional situation. In order to silence the man down in the heat of the moment, I could commit myself, maybe even the country, to an untenable position. Well, I'll just have to guard against that if it happens. Goddam these debates anyway." Conger yawned again.

"It's getting late," said Little. "I think we better break this up. You've got a damn important three-day swing this week, Andy, and then next week is the kickoff."

"I know. We'll conclude with this point," said Conger. "The shorter the debate and the more formal it is, the more it operates in Green's favor. Therefore, to break him down, to cut through the preparation he might make prior to the debate—the rote answers, the quotes, dates, and notes—I am going to take the position that the first debate should be a combination of very short formal presentations at the opening and close, with a long section of questions from a panel as the main body of the exchange. Rebuttal must be included in some form. And—Dale, you check this out with the Madison Avenue boys—unless they come up with violent opinions in the negative, I will accept one debate only, and it will be two hours in length."

"Two hours?" screamed Lou Wells at Dale. "What the hell are you trying to do to us? Put us out of business?" He slammed his pencil down, pushed his chair away from the table, and tilted back on the two rear legs as he looked at the ceiling. "We can't clear two hours of prime time. This is blackmail!"

"What are they going to talk about?" asked Murray Smith.

"If your man doesn't know how to fill two hours, really just half that time—his half—on the issues involved in this election, he's lost it already," snapped Dale.

The format meeting was confined to the three men, plus a free-lance stenotypist taking notes for all of them. In reality, each participant kept his own notes. NA, however, had established a practice at the earlier meetings of mimeographing copies of the transcript and forwarding them to those in attendance.

Dale was asked to present Conger's preferences. He had decided to hurdle the two-hour bombshell first, before getting into their internal format thoughts for the telecast. "Do you realize the program and time clearance problems—I repeat—on a two-hour telecast?" asked Wells.

"Do you realize the audience to such a debate?" countered Dale, his voice rising. "Hear me out, please. My man as of now has not accepted the one date which has been discussed by both parties and seems to be a possibility. It is my off-the-record opinion he will accept it. My man, however, has repeatedly said he wants but one debate. There hasn't even been a discussion in my staff of more. Therefore, *if* there is to be but one debate, if that's all my man will buy, why not make it a blockbuster? Why not make it more than historic? Let's make it a monumental occasion." Dale felt he had done well to put the emphasis on the importance of the telecast, keeping their minds off the real reason for fighting for the two hours—to wear down Green.

"We've had no discussion of a debate longer than an hour," said Murray Smith. "We've stuck strictly to the invitation concept of the networks."

"There must be more than one debate," said Wells. "We'll accomplish nothing with one debate. The people will learn nothing. It will be a waste of time."

"You know that's not true, Lou," said Dale. "But, if you feel strongly about it, then let's call the whole thing off. We're trying to work out a debate. Call it the first debate if it makes you feel better. But we insist it be two hours in length."

Wells, fuming at Dale, looked at him silently. He scooped up a cigarette pack, lit one, and said, "What other sterling thoughts do you have from Andrew Conger?"

This is it, thought Dale. I'll do it now. He pushed his chair back, closed his manila folder of notes, and stood up. "There's no use meeting with you, Lou. If this is your attitude toward our sincere efforts to work out the debates, the hell with it. I've got other things to do. So has Andy Conger." Dale turned to his brief case.

"Wait a minute. . . . Sit down," said Wells. "If I offended you, I'm sorry. That goes for Conger too. We'll work it out. Sit down." That son-of-a-bitch, said Wells to himself. This hairless, snotnosed son-of-a-bitch. I'd hammer his face into knackwurst if he blew the whistle on these debates.

Dale stopped, turned halfway toward Wells, and looked at him over his left shoulder. "Are you ready to hear the rest of our suggestions?" he asked. "Without editorial comment from North American?"

Murray Smith looked at the two men. What goes on here? he wondered. Wells's remark wasn't *that* sarcastic. What is Dale driving at? Smith had only one set of orders from Green: *Don't lose the debates.* Wisely, he had kept silent during the exchange. Now he wanted to get onto a new subject quickly. "Have you people considered the pure formal debate?" he asked Dale, hoping to smooth over the moment.

"Yes, we have," Dale answered, resuming his place at the table, ignoring Wells and concentrating on Smith. "This gets into my next point. We've had, as I'm sure the Green people have, long discussions on the various forms of debate open to us. Nothing I say here is final. For instance, there's been so much in the press about these things being compared to the Lincoln-Douglas series. The networks, in their ads and in their press releases, have been beating that drum to death. We think it's dangerous. We think the audience may be disappointed, may already be oversold on what these things will be. We'd like to ask the networks to soft-pedal the Lincoln-Douglas comparison. And, for the same reason, we believe a telecast which embraces the formal, classic debate form for its entirety will precipitate further comparison. Therefore, we are against formal debate as the sole approach to the entire time period of two hours." Wells winced again, but held himself in check.

Again, Dale had used an argument which bore no resemblance to the real reason Conger was against formal debate. Conger wanted the free-wheeling question and answer section, and Dale hoped this suggestion would come from someone other than him.

"You mean like Q and A?" asked Wells, "instead of all formal statement and rebuttal?"

"Exactly," said Dale. "Another point I make, with all due respect to my candidate and the other man, is that we feel a formal debate will be dull as dishwater. We'll be losing audience from the first minute to the last."

"I can't go along with you there," said Smith. Aha, thought Dale, a strike. Smith continued. "We feel anything less than a formal debate will turn it into a quiz show, a 'Meet the Press' spectacular, just another show. As a matter of . . ."

"Murray," Dale cut in, "you've got to get one thing through your head. There is no 'just another show' aspect to the first forum in the history of American politics which presents both presidential candidates in a face-to-face encounter, a face-to-face exchange on the issues of a presidential campaign."

"Good point," said Smith. "It sounds like you people expect the first one will be face to face," he added hopefully.

"We do," answered Dale.

"Do we all agree to that? If so, I'd like to lock it up right now," said Wells.

"I can't lock it up here," said Dale, "but it will be recommended. Has been, as a matter of fact. I think Conger will buy it."

"I know Green will," said Smith, smiling at Dale.

"May I reprise?" asked Dale. "We recommend a two-hour telecast, a combination of formal debate procedures, to satisfy the public's impression of what these things are supposed to be, and freewheeling Q and A from a panel, the latter comprising the main body of the two hours."

"Any restriction on subject matter?" asked Smith. "Foreign, domestic, defense?"

"We haven't discussed that point," said Dale. "But with Q and A not screened in advance, I don't see how there could be."

"Who comprises the panel?" Wells asked.

"As big a nightmare as it would probably be to select them, we think the answer is a panel of newsmen," said Dale.

"That's great," said Wells. "I like that. We would draw the finest men from the broadcasting industry, the best reporters at all the networks, for the panel."

"In a pig's patootie you will," said Dale. "If there's a panel of newsmen on this debate, they will be drawn from all media: wires, dailies, broadcasting . . ."

"Now wait a minute," yelled Wells. "Wait a goddam minute. This is broadcasting's show. All the way. Any reporters permitted in that studio will come from radio and TV, period."

"I'd like to be around when you say that to Wilbur Jenkins, our press secretary, who has to live with a hundred and twenty-five of those animals every day, or to Waldo Duncan, Green's press chief. Right, Murray?"

"Right," said Smith. "Wells, you're smoking a weed. The one consolation on this panel nightmare will be that *we* won't have to decide how they're to be picked, or pick them. The press secretaries can have that little hot potato all to themselves."

"Amen," said Dale. "Lou, let's pass on that for the moment. I'd like to discuss the issue of audience versus no audience."

"In a minute," said Wells. "I think it's only fair we hear out Murray on the total proposal from the Green camp."

"By all means," said Dale. "How could we have forgotten that?" he said, grinning.

"I was wondering when you nuts were going to recognize there are two political parties in this country," said Smith. Murray went on to enumerate their optimum format ideas. They reflected the evaluation the Conger staff had given to Green's strengths and weaknesses in the meeting with Conger. Smith said they leaned toward the formal debate, wanted one hour as the length, and strongly urged that, in the best tradition of the American town meeting, and the Lincoln-Douglas exchanges, there be an audience to the encounters.

Dale admired him. They had hit every one of Green's strengths, right on the nose. The audience question was disposed of quickly. No one could come up with a formula to prevent "stacking" or "packing" the hall, so they threw it out. Smith, in his own mind, liked the idea of a panel of newsmen. He hesitated, however, to go too far in the meeting. More than once Dale discerned a consistent hesitancy in Smith's ability to articulate his opinions pro or con an issue. He wondered if it came from his lack of exposure to political television—politics in general—or was it because he didn't know his man Green as well as Dale knew Conger. Perhaps that was it, Dale decided.

"Look at it this way, Murray," said Dale. "No matter how the press panel is selected, it preponderantly will favor your man. Ninety per cent of the working press is for Green. Even Conger knows that."

Smith narrowed his eyes and looked at Dale, half grinning, through his cigarette smoke. "I'm not so sure," he said. "I'm not so sure."

"Balls!" snorted Dale.

The group broke for lunch, Dale and Smith diving for phones in their separate suites to check developments at their respective offices. The meeting resumed and lasted until midafternoon. Item after item of format, panel, debate, rebuttal, was discussed, carefully dictated to the stenotypist, and marked for review with the candidates. The selection of the moderator became a major topic. It was ultimately resolved to recommend a professional broadcaster for the important spot, as opposed to an educator or personality high in the public's eye. The dangers in using an amateur were too grave for such an historic telecast, it was decided, and any high public figure, almost by definition, could not be expected to be politically neutral.

Wells concluded by pressing Dale and Smith for decisions from their candidates. "We're only a little more than a month away from the date your two men have been discussing," he said. "We are only about two weeks away from deciding what sort of physical shape this telecast will take. If we go the two-hour route, a combination of formal opening and closing, Q and A from a panel in the middle, no audience . . . uh . . . oh yes, a moderator, try for unrestricted subject matter, when can you guys get me an answer?"

"A week maybe," said Smith.

"I have no idea," said Dale. "My man hasn't agreed to the date yet. Until he does, he'll see little urgency in locking up these other things." Dale looked at his folder and reached for his cigarettes to put them in his jacket pocket.

"I'm goddam sick and tired of Conger seeing little urgency in these debates," snapped Wells, his voice rising. Dale raised his head, looking at him. "I'm sick and tired of Conger's feet-dragging approach to every damn issue. I'm pissed off with him thinking he can narrow down a monumental idea to one stinking debate. Well, he can't. I think he has one hell of a nerve asking the broadcasting industry for two solid hours of prime evening time. We had a certain time in mind, for the American people, in the best American tradition, and your goddam Conger and Conger staff—and you— have screwed it up to where it's almost unrecognizable. I'm sick of it. We're running this show, not Conger." Wells was screaming now. "We're running this, do you understand? Do you understand?" he repeated, leaning far over the table. He spat out his words, eyes flashing. Dale was stunned by the outburst.

"Shut up, Wells," said Dale softly. "You don't know what you're talking about." Dale stood up, facing Wells across the table. "There are two men running this debate. Their names are Andrew Conger and Joseph Green. Nobody else is running it . . . nobody, do you understand that?" In spite of himself, Dale's emotions swelled up. He felt his throat pulse as the blood surged to his head. "Not me, not Smith, not you, not NA. We are here to service these guys . . . to make what will be the biggest ordeal of their lives a little easier, make it run, perhaps, a little more smoothly. That is all we are doing, nothing more. You haven't got one cotton-pickin' thing to say about these debates, Lou Wells. You're a service man, waiting for Andy Conger and Joe Green to tell you to check the lights, put some air in the tires, wash the windshield. Get that straight, and remember it. If you don't, you're in for a hell of a lot of surprises —and grief. You make *me* sick!" If I don't stop now, thought Dale, I'll say some things I shouldn't, and maybe I'll paste him.

Wells glared at Dale. I'd like to bust this big bastard right in the mouth, he thought. But I better shut up. If I don't, I might let slip something I shouldn't. I'll break you, Charles Dale, said Wells to himself. Nobody can talk to me that way and get away with it.

The two men looked at each other, unmoving, for a long moment.

"Fellas, it's getting a little hot in here," said Smith. "Let's call it a day and go back to our nice candidates and get nice Lou Wells his answers."

It broke the tension. Dale laughed; Wells exhaled heavily and turned away from the table. He brusquely mumbled his farewell and left. Dale and Smith were alone.

"I guess Lou has changed his mind about a statement to the press. They're still outside," said Smith.

"Yes, I guess he has," Dale said, smiling.

"I'm glad you said what you did to him, Charlie," said Smith. "If you hadn't, I would have."

12

Crisis in the Capitol

THE HOURS ticked by toward September 12, the campaign kickoff date. Days blended into endless nights at the office. "Press" and "Traveling Staff" tags were issued to personnel who would accompany Conger on the road. Demands for Conger's appearance on panel shows and guest programs reached a ridiculous peak. Phone calls began to filter back to Dale's Washington office from the television advance men in the field. It became more and more difficult to see Rufe Little, obtain any response from Conger. Dale accepted the fact that it might be a long time before he would have his precious fifteen minutes with Conger to get the vital answers needed to his memo of the network format meeting. He sent the memo off, as requested by Conger, stapling the small red flag to the top right-hand corner, signifying *Urgent*.

The planning days were at an end, the rehearsal was over—ready or not. The Big Show was about to begin. Abner Shepherd's head spun with the home phone numbers of State Chairmen, facts and figures on plane schedules, road mileages from A to B, instrument-approach airports. Arthur Baldwin's men were over the horizon too, sending back their flat, dry reports to the Political Advance Desk: major issues in Omaha, drought conditions in the Dakotas, unemployment figures from Toledo, shortest route from the airport to The Westerner Hotel in Reno.

August had seen hundreds, probably thousands, of partisans don the red-white-and-blue colors for Andrew Conger. They had enlisted, for the duration, in the "Great Battle of the Sixties," as the Conger National Committee labeled the campaign. And now, daily, the regiments marched out to that battle to man their political combat stations in every corner of the country. Dale wondered how many would bog down when the smoke had cleared, come to a soggy halt in the first air-conditioned bar, or cure loneliness through a delicious delay in the nearest motel sack. Only time would tell.

Dale knew from past experience that a campaign staff develops a hyper-focus on its candidate. The staff members become nameless, faceless servants to a cause, slaves to an ideal, prisoners of Their Hero. It was not easy to remember that these people were mostly volunteers. They had wives, children, businesses at home. They got sick, tired, frustrated, scared, lonely. Some would find themselves in over their heads, others would be bored with the menial tasks through which they served the candidate.

Rufe Little also knew that a headquarters was made up of human beings, a staff composed of people. He had this thought on his mind as he called Dale to his office two days before the campaign kickoff.

"Sit down, young man," he said to Dale. "You and I are going to have a talk. About you."

Dale, curious, selected a chair at the edge of Little's desk. "What's up?" he asked.

Little's phone buzzed. He took the call, then advised his secretary to hold any future ones until he was finished with Dale. He walked around his desk, and sat in a matching chair, a few feet from Dale, facing him. He methodically crossed his legs, cradling one thigh with both hands and lifting it on top of the other, almost as if his leg were an inanimate thing which had no motor power of its own. With his head tilted slightly to one side, he spoke. "How's your business out in Denver, Charlie?"

"Lousy, Rufe," answered Dale, still confused as to the purpose of the talk. "I'm not sure we'll make it. I got a letter from the bank the other day, and they're calling on our loan. We're on the ragged edge of going under."

"I'm sorry to hear that."

"Yeah, me too. Perhaps I made a mistake. I left a guy in charge who was predominantly creative, knew nothing about business or sales. I felt it was the thing to do in order to protect the orders we already had in the shop. But I'm very worried. It looks bad."

Little reached into a humidor on his desk for a cigar. "How are things at home?"

What kind of an interrogation is this? thought Dale. What's this man driving at? Watch it, Charlie boy, watch it. He'll get you every time. "Fine, I guess. Everyone seems to be healthy, the kids have had a good summer. Janet writes cheerful letters. I'd like to get out there for a visit sometime this fall."

Rufe meticulously immersed the end of the cigar in the flame of his huge butane lighter, rolling it around and around as he drew the first pure smoke through its length. He exhaled a long, powerful jet stream, carefully controlled by his compressed lips. "Remember Herman Sayle? You met him in the primaries . . . State Chairman. We replaced him last week."

"Oh? He was your own man, wasn't he? Didn't you put him in to clean up the mess down there?"

"I did. He's gotten himself mixed up with some woman. He called me to say there may be a scandal and a smelly divorce. He thought he'd better quit, to protect Conger from getting tarred with his brush. Unhappily, we let him go."

"That's too bad. You had a hard time finding a good Conger man, as I recall."

"I did." Little paused, looked directly at Dale a long moment. "Remember Harold Mills, over at the Volunteers? Ran the club organization section?"

"Sure. Nice guy. What about him?" What are you getting at Rufe? Dale wondered.

"Fired him yesterday. Told him to go home and forget he was ever on the Conger campaign."

"What'd he do wrong?"

"He got mixed up down here with one of these Dumb Dora female hicks that come out of the boondocks, get a job in Washington, and end up sleeping with every man in sight to get ahead. We got reports from some important people in his apartment building. This chippy had moved in with him, shackin' up. Mills has seven kids at home. We caught him padding his expense account. He's run up bills all over town, and this Dumb Dora hick, with Washington ga-ga fever sticking out all over her, is now pregnant as a mare in April."

"That's a shame. Sort of disgusting. What's all this got to do with me?"

"I want you to leave this Sandra Nelson woman alone until the campaign's over. I don't want you to see her again. Bust it up. Get out of it."

Dale's first impulse was to get up and walk out. But he knew it wouldn't accomplish anything. Why was it always Rufe Little who slammed him with ultimatums which affected him so personally, so emotionally? "You seem to have a passion for telling me what I can and cannot do, Rufe."

"Maybe somebody has to. If everything is so fine at home, why are you fooling around with a woman back here?"

"That's none of your business. What I do away from the Conger campaign, this office, is my own business, not yours."

"Everything you do between now and November is my business."

"Did this come from Conger?"

"Of course not. I'm running this show."

Susan Conger had called Little regarding the talk going around about Dale and Sandra two weeks previously. Little had brushed it off as not serious. Susan had phoned again, a few hours before Little decided to call in Dale. He didn't want it to get to Conger. Susan had threatened to bring her husband into it if Little didn't take action. "This is my own idea," Little re-emphasized. No use setting Dale against Susan Conger at the outset of the big push, he decided.

"Rufe," said Dale, leaning forward, his weight on the arms of his chair, "I have few cut-and-dried principles by which I run my life. One of them, however, is that it belongs to me, no one else. This girl and I have known each other for years. I almost married her six years ago. I may marry her after the campaign. Are you silly enough to ask me to refrain from seeing someone who may be my wife?"

"I am telling you to break it off. There will be no scandal connected with the staff of Andrew Conger."

"And what if I don't?"

"You will."

A thousand thoughts flashed through Dale's mind: Janet, Sandra, his future, his company, his children, his mother in Buffalo, all these and more. He knew what he had to say. He sighed, tapped his thighs with his fingers, and looked into Little's deepset, weary blue eyes. Dale spoke. "Okay, Rufe, the hell with it. It's been one miserable frustration after another anyway. I've had it. You don't want advisers, executives. You want 'yes men'—clerks. I don't believe in any organization that dictates what a man should or shouldn't do away from the office. I've always been against these goddam corporations that interview a guy's wife before they hire the guy. The hell with it! I quit. I'll be out of here at five tonight. Ham Forrest can take over for me."

"You'll do no such thing, young man. You are one of the top advisers to a winning presidential candidate. You're a member of the inner ring. A man in that position never leaves a campaign. He knows too many palace secrets."

"If I stay, I am going to see Sandra Nelson as often as I want to."

"You are going to stay . . . and you are not going to see Miss Nelson. Is that clear?"

"You're making the same kind of noises you did in Denver . . . in your hotel room. I didn't like it then, and I don't now."

"I'm not concerned about your feelings toward me. I am only concerned about Andrew Conger's campaign for the Presidency."

"In a pig's ass that's all you're concerned about. You're concerned about yourself, the same way you were in Denver." Dale breathed in and out heavily, twice. "Okay, Rufe, I'll stay. You've left me no choice."

"You wouldn't know what to do if I did."

"Careful, Rufe, don't push me too far. I said I'd stay. I'll settle the thing with Sandra Nelson as soon as I can. I won't see her until after the campaign. But I'm doing it for Conger, not for you. You wouldn't know right from wrong if it came up and bit you in the face. The only decent man, the only real *man* in this whole stinking campaign is Andy Conger himself. So . . . I'll see it through until November. But give me a wide berth after that. Don't ever call me, don't ever have anything to do with me. You'll never see me for sour apples within a hundred miles of a political campaign again as long as I live."

"Steady, son, you may regret that statement. Don't be so final. Leave yourself some room for retreat. Five years from today you may need Andy Conger a lot more than he needs you."

That's really it, isn't it, Rufe, thought Dale. The Creed of the Political Hack: Always Leave Enough Room to Crawl Back, to Suck Back In. I've finally got your ticket, Rufe Little. I didn't have it in Denver, but I have it now. You're afraid, afraid to go it alone. Oh, you've got guts, and you're tough as nails when you're dealing with those not your equal. You've got guts, all right, when you're manipulating those who have no alternative, those who are pushed to your wall because they're not their own master. Terrified, beholden, helpless political appointees, frightened convention delegates whom you could destroy with one phone call to the right person. That's your meat, isn't it, Rufe? When a career, a reputation, rests on your tenuous patronage power, oh, you're tough, you're really ruthless. This is your muckhole. Keep it, Rufe.

"You want something down here," Dale said, driving hard. "I don't. I've never wanted anything in Washington, Rufe, and I don't want anything now. I don't owe you a damn thing. You owe me a great deal. But just leave me alone when this thing is over. I don't see how you can look at yourself in the morning when you shave. How can you stand it? I'm so sick of the backbiting, the groveling for crumbs at the candidate's gate, of watching you guys weigh seven thousand alternatives before you can muster up enough courage to go to the bathroom. I'm fed up with the fence-riders, the pilot fish, the parasites, the bloodsuckers. Christ, if guys ran their own businesses the way politicians operate down here, American industry would go bankrupt in six months."

"I think we better break this up, son," Rufe said softly.

"It isn't nice to hear, huh? You and your smoke-filled rooms. Dead air, dirty air, that's all you guys can breathe. There's no fresh air left in this town. Thousands of spineless politicians sucking in the dead, lifeless air already fouled by tens of thousands before them—all breathing, over and over, the same lifeless, stinking dead air. Hanging on, hoping to catch The Big One." He paused, stood up, and looked down at Little. "I'll do what you say. But not for you. It's for Andy Conger . . . and myself."

"I wish you'd put yourself in my position for a minute," said Little. "It's my job."

"I guess I'll always like you personally, Rufe. But your line of work disgusts me." Dale left the room.

Rufe Little didn't give a damn why Charlie Dale was staying or who for. The matter was closed. Actually, he liked Dale and was trying to save him. He picked up the phone and dialed a private number in Dallas. The Natural Gas boys were six hundred thousand short on their campaign commitment. "We've got to go for more, fellows," he said into the phone, "a lot more."

"Another cup of coffee?" asked Sandra.

"No thanks, I've had plenty," said Dale.

"Pour me some. I want to take it over to the couch. And I want to hold you, and kiss you, and thank you for the nicest night I have ever had in my life. I want to be as tender to you as you were to me. I love you, Charles Dale." Sandra leaned across the small dining table and kissed him softly, dreamily, slowly. "I can say it completely, selflessly now." She took him by the hand and led him wordlessly to the couch, setting her coffee cup on the coffee table. "May I tell you you are the most wonderful lover a woman ever had?"

Dale grinned. "You inspire me, Princess. Let me tell you what happened yesterday. It won't be . . ."

"Shhhh . . . don't talk. Lean back. That's it. Close your eyes. Don't move." Sandra cradled Dale's head against her breast, arms locked around his chest. Dale, however, was deeply troubled.

Maybe I should have told her last night, he thought. But he hadn't been able to. He knew he'd been selfish. He knew he'd planned it so that they would have one more night together.

After leaving Rufe Little's office, he had walked around Washington for an hour. It was an unusually cool evening, with that magic half-light, that amber afterglow of dusk, bathing the lush, deep green of lawns and trees in an ethereal haze. He had decided to get it off his chest with Sandy before his two-day trip to New York, rather than after. And he was leaving at noon the following day. He called Fergie, told her he'd leave for the airport directly from his apartment, that he wouldn't be in the office in the morning. Then he called Sandra and told her he wanted to see her for dinner, and that he wouldn't have to leave early in the morning.

Yes, it had been a lovely night, Dale thought. He didn't want to cut it off. But now it had to be done. She had to know.

"Sandy," he said softly, his eyes closed, motionless in her arms, "I can't see you from now until after the campaign." He felt her arms stiffen around him, ever so slightly. She leaned down and nuzzled his ear.

"Why—honey—why?" Her words were slurred and muffled as she nipped playfully at his ear with her teeth.

"Rufe Little has forbidden it."

"What do you mean he's forbidden it? How?" Sandra pushed Dale gently off her body, sat up and reached for her coffee.

"We had a talk yesterday. He made me promise I wouldn't see you. I tried to quit. He wouldn't let me." Dale looked at her, his eyes seeing something very precious and dear to him. "I'm sorry. I don't know if I can do it. But I must try. Evidently people are beginning to talk. He's afraid of somebody like Drew Pearson getting the story."

"Are you?"

"No, I'm not."

"Do you want to see me between now and November?"

"Yes . . . I've already said I don't know if I can stand not seeing you."

"Then why do you put yourself through this pain? Why do you build this strain for yourself?"

"I'm not. Rufe Little is."

"You're wrong, Charles. You are doing it. You don't have to go through it. You can leave the campaign if I mean as much to you as you say I do."

"I can't do that, Sandy." Dale rose, went over to his pack of cigarettes. He offered one to Sandra. She shook her head. He sat in a chair, not looking at her.

No, I can't leave the campaign, Dale thought. Not after what my actions in coming back here have caused in Denver. Forgetting Janet, I've put everything I want out there in jeopardy by my decision to join Andy. I can't remove the only justification I have. And what *about* Janet, he asked himself. I guess by now most of her respect for me is gone. Whatever remains would leave instantly if I were to bail out of the campaign. Why is Janet's respect important? he asked himself. It shouldn't be if I don't care. Sandra was looking at him with irritation.

"Are other people going to run you for the rest of your life?" she asked. "Are you always going to win the battle but lose the war?"

"I don't understand you."

"Do you know what love is, Charles? I do, and I am glad I do. If I lose you this time, it's for good. Never again."

"You're not losing me, Sandy. It's only for two months, a little more. Can't you give me that?"

"Can't you permit love, for once in your life, to show you the way? Can't you let the beauty of love tell you what to do, instead of Rufe Little, Andrew Conger, or, more accurately probably, his wife Susan?"

"What's she got to do with this?"

"I told you once I didn't think she liked me. She doesn't like anything that's honest, spontaneous. Everything is for the impression it will give—the perfect marriage, the perfect husband, the perfect wife. Phooey. Life isn't like that. It's all too perfect. Susan Conger isn't that perfect—nobody is."

"I've never heard you talk this way."

"You've never walked out on me before because a presidential candidate's wife doesn't think love is important."

"I think you're very unkind to Susan. You haven't the slightest idea she's to blame for this. It's Rufe Little himself lowering the boom on me because he's afraid of a scandal. That's all there is to it."

"Are you afraid of a scandal?"

"For Andy Conger, yes. Not for myself."

"Charles, how can love hurt anybody? Don't you understand? Through your lack of love you've hurt me once before. I didn't think I'd ever get over you leaving me in Europe." Sandra paused and looked down at her hands. "The scar was deep. A human being is born with only one set of emotions. And you have ripped mine, torn them dreadfully. I've worked hard to repair the damage. I've loved this summer. I've loved you so, being with you. I can only take my cue from the way I feel about you." Sandra looked up at Dale, hands folded simply in her lap. "Five years ago you hurt me in Paris. And now it's the same pattern in Washington. But there will be no third time. I can't permit it to happen. I couldn't go through it."

"You don't have to go through it, Sandy. Why are you so selfish about this?"

"I'm not selfish, Charles. I'm trying to show you that Rufe Little is your straw man this time. In Europe it was Janet." Ever so softly, Sandra added, "Love is a very important thing. More important than your job, the White House, being President. Love must be the pure shining thing that guides the lives of all of us. It has guided mine up to now. The only happiness I've ever known has come to me through love."

"You're being very idealistic, Sandy."

"No, Charles, oh no. I'm not angry with you if you can't see by yourself what I'm trying to show you. I feel only sorrow. If you really loved me, there wouldn't be a choice, a moment's hesitation."

Janet isn't this selfish, Dale said to himself. She'd understand. She already has. Janet wouldn't put me in a box like this. She'd roll with it, go along with me. Maybe Janet understands me better than I understand myself.

"If you love me," Sandra said softly, "it would be the easiest decision of your life."

"I don't want to lose you, Sandy," Dale answered. Why did I say that, he asked himself. Why?

"You want me around when you need me, but not when you don't. What about my need for you? Will it always be this way . . . you thinking only of yourself?"

"I'm thinking only of you . . . you know that." But I may be lying, Dale thought. If I only had more time to know myself, my emotions. I want to be sure I want you around even if it's not convenient. I want to be sure it's more than just satisfying my need today.

"Were you thinking only of me," asked Sandra, "when you decided to tell me all this after last night, not before? So you could spend last night with me, enjoying yourself? So you'd have a beautiful memory after you walked out?"

"That's a cruel thing to say."

"I've risen above your cruelty. Because I love you. In a way, I'm glad we had last night. Yes . . . I'm glad."

Dale noticed her eyes misting with tears. And suddenly he felt his own composure slipping away. In spite of himself, he could sense the swelling up of emotion in the back of his throat. He couldn't bear to see Sandra cry.

"I'm so miserable, Sandy," he said, turning his head away. "How can I be this cruel to you? I'm so lonely, so unhappy. I don't want to bring this sorrow to me, or to you. I don't know what to do. I'm confused. I'm terribly lost." He turned to her. He was weeping openly. "I should be strong, but I'm not. Can't somebody help me? Can't you help me?"

"You've got to help yourself, Charles."

Dale dropped to his knees and buried his face in her lap, smelling the familiar scent of her perfume. He wrapped his arms around her legs. Sandra unconsciously stroked the back of his neck.

"Isn't there someone who understands?" asked Dale. "Don't *you* understand? What is the answer? How can this happen?"

"The answer is in you, Charles."

"I'm so alone—so alone."

At that moment Sandra Nelson was no longer afraid of losing Charles Dale. For he had said he was alone. It was very clear to Sandra she had already lost him.

In Dale's meetings in New York he had difficulty concentrating on the intricacies of the preparations for the campaign kickoff telecast. Midmorning of the second day he could contain his thoughts of Sandra no longer. He seldom called her at her office, but he did so now.

"I'm sorry—Miss Nelson is no longer with our Washington office," a pleasant voice said to his operator.

"Yes, she is, operator," said Dale. "She's confused. I'll make the call station to station and talk to this party."

"Go ahead, please."

"I'm calling from New York. Would you connect me with Miss Nelson's secretary, please?" There was a click and the voice said, "Hello?"

"Is this Miss Nelson's office?" asked Dale.

"Yes, it is. Or *was*. This is Miss Horner speaking. I was Miss Nelson's secretary. Are you calling for her?"

"Yes, I am. May I speak to her? This is Charles Dale."

"I'm sorry, Mr. Dale, but Miss Nelson left this morning for Paris. She has been transferred back to that office."

"You mean she's gone? For good?"

"Yes. She and her daughter went over this morning. By air. Would you like her address in Paris? I could give you that."

Dale stared dumbly at a youngster's photograph on the desk he was using to make the call. In the labored script of a child the inscription in the lower right corner of the frame said, "*I love you. Sandy.*"

"Hello, Mr. Dale. Hello?" the secretary in Washington said.

"Uh . . . yes. Uh . . . No thank you. I have no need for Miss Nelson's Paris address. Thank you."

13

September and the Campaign Starts

"READ IT TO ME, Fergie." Dale leaned back at his desk in his chair, closed his eyes, and listened.

"It's to CD from AC," Fergie started. " 'Subject: Political Meetings, first week. Sound Systems. New York. Bad mikes in Times Square. They stuck in my face. Too high. Detroit. Beautiful p.a. Best I've ever heard. Get the name of the mikes and the equipment. See we have it everywhere.' "

"Christ!" said Dale, "here we go again." The memo from Andrew Conger was a weekly rundown from Conger's point of view of Dale's operation on the road. Whenever Conger hit an ideal setup, it was always, "Get the name of everything, and see we have it at every stop."

"No wonder it was perfect in Detroit. He was in a brand-new hall. Go on, Fergie."

" 'Denver. Couldn't see your new man Tuttle when he gave me my cue. He did not brief Susan properly on who would seat her at airport platform. Wind bad. Couldn't see cameras. Had to talk directly into sun. Very bad.' "

"Of course it was," said Dale. "That's so we had the sun at our backs for TV, and on his face. It'll do him good to get a suntan anyway. Remind me to do that memo on his use of a sun lamp from now on through to the first debate."

Fergie continued. "The next city is Salt Lake. Conger says, 'The Governor made an excellent introduction to my speech. Get a copy of it. Send it out as the standard intro for the campaign. Cameras too high. Susan said all they could see on TV was the top of my head. Let's have no more crappy stuff like that.' " Fergie then added, "He's got a note here at the bottom. It says, 'Reports excellent on kickoff telecast. People say it was one of our best. Let's have more like it.' "

Dale laughed and leaned forward. "More like it! He's out of his mind. We couldn't do that again if we tried."

The opening telecast had been a masterpiece. Dale had obtained Conger's approval on a coast-to-coast television profile of a national campaign in the age of jet flight. It was the new look in campaigning; the compression of time and space. Conger was anxious to convey this total approach to his campaign and his own boundless energy with a stunning kickoff program.

It was just that. The telecast was titled, "Coast-to-Coast: The First Day," and started in daylight on the East Coast. It ended that same day, still in daylight, in Los Angeles, providing a breathtaking picture of the pace Andrew Conger was going to set for himself and his staff between then and November. Early in the morning, Conger was taped on his departure from Washington Airport for New York. A huge "workers' breakfast" rally at the Astor Hotel on Times Square was the climax to Conger's triumphant and colorful ticker-tape motorcade into the city. It was carried "live" by two networks and taped for use in the evening telecast. By helicopters the party left downtown Manhattan and went to Idlewild, where they now entered Conger's chartered jet. Propellor-driven "feeder" planes had been used from Washington so that La Guardia could be used for the New York arrival instead of the remote Idlewild.

Everything had gone according to schedule. When the huge silver monster carrying Conger to Detroit on his first leg west lifted from the runway, he was one minute ahead of estimated departure time. It wouldn't always be so. A labor rally was staged at the Detroit airport, followed by a motorcade into the new mall along the river for a noontime office-workers' outdoor meeting—all of which was taped and used in the evening telecast. Conger then flew on to Denver, for a rousing midafternoon airport meeting, short but colorful in the best tradition of the Rocky Mountain Empire. It was the usual home town sendoff for the conquering hero, complete with cowboys, bucking broncos, six-shooters, covered wagons—the whole works. At one point Dale had considered going out to do the pickup in order to see the children—yes, Janet, too—but his overall supervision of the telecast dictated his presence in the master control room in Chicago, from which the entire telecast was controlled. Conger then flew on to the West Coast, racing the sun. Dale was determined to get the shot of the plane touching down at Los Angeles International Airport, to symbolize the end of the flight which started with the takeoff at New York, all in daylight hours. His men were concerned about the time needed for the plane to taxi from the runway to the speaker's area at the ramp. Dale came up with the idea of picking up the vice presidential candidate, Wardwell Hughes, who at that moment was speaking before a huge rally in Louisville, Kentucky. On the air they took pictures of Conger's plane landing, followed it briefly as it nosed toward the ramp, then cut directly to Louisville. Bernie Lamb was producing the telecast, and had prepared Hughes carefully. Lamb was in direct voice contact with Chicago, where Dale could see both pictures—the preview shots of the Conger plane in Los Angeles approaching the camera area and Wardwell Hughes in Louisville. At precisely the correct moment, when the unloading ramp had been rolled up to Conger's plane and the door unlocked, in that predictable delay before the head, shoulders, and finally the body of Andrew H. Conger would step into the California sunlight, Dale shouted to Lamb, "Okay, Bernie, give him the cue." With that Lamb indicated to Hughes he should introduce Conger immediately. Hughes had been briefed to be prepared to cut into his remarks at any time in order to introduce the top man on the ticket, two thousand miles away. The contrast between the darkness of night in Louisville and the brilliant sunshine in California was striking. The picture of Hughes already out on the trail, addressing a packed evening rally as Conger's plane landed, gave the proper impression of a vigorous campaign in depth across the face of the country. Wardwell Hughes sang out his Conger introduction. The Louisville hall roared its approval. At that instant, Dale switched the picture to California, where the welcoming crowd at the airport was beginning its swell toward a thunderous ovation. Conger appeared and spoke for five minutes "live" to conclude the telecast. Everyone, including Murray Smith, agreed it had indeed been a thrilling telecast. Smith called from Houston to tell Dale he had all of his men watching, and that they thought it was excellent production. For the first time in all his years of campaign activity, Dale found himself beginning to like immensely a member of the enemy camp. He wondered what Rufe Little would think of his emotional treason.

"Give Andy's comments to the boys when they call in, Fergie," said Dale. "Type 'em up for Colton to have at his desk when they report. Also, keep trying to get Vic Hanson at my shop in Denver. Here's a memo to Rufe Little. 'To RL, from CD. Subject: Debates. Rufe: I think it is time to hire a lighting director named Hans Kleinert who knows AC's problems. He lit our convention in Chicago, where AC looked great. This man should be traveled, stay with AC on the road for perhaps a week before the debate, phasing in with his peculiar lighting characteristics before the move out to the debate city. AC is tough to light under any circumstances. Every person must be lit differently. Some people have white skin, others ruddy complexions. Some skin is almost transparent, some opaque. Some people have few or no planes in their faces, giving them an inanimate quality. Others have faces which look as if they've been chiseled out of stone, with a thousand different planes that catch the light beamed from theatrical lamps. So, tone, animation, texture, contrast to hair color—all these things—affect what a man looks like on TV. Our man is critical. Please authorize the expenditure necessary to travel this top Los Angeles lighting director I have in mind. We would also use him on major network telecasts throughout the campaign. Please advise.' That's all Fergie," said Dale. "Get that off to Little as soon as you can. I want to tie this Kleinert up before he gets committed in Hollywood to fall production. Or to Governor Joseph Green."

Chartered planes for political candidates were flying palaces, thought Dale. The airlines, cocking a public relations eye toward Washington, vied with each other for the plum of transporting presidential candidates. In reality, the scheduling offices in the candidates' headquarters did their best to give each major air carrier an equal opportunity. With the load of booze, exotic fruit, and other extras the airlines put on board for such flights, it was a wonder the planes could leave the ground. Public relations men supervised the flights from the cabin. Extra stewardesses (the prettiest in the fleet) were supplied, to the delight and gentle indoor calisthenic activity of members of the traveling press in the press plane. The press plane usually contained more "extras" than the candidate's plane, for it carried the men who wrote the tens upon thousands of words a day describing the campaign to their wire services, daily papers, weekly magazines, radio, television, overseas clients. Who could say how many mentions of Constitution Airlines found their way onto Page One of the *Herald* because their correspondent traveling with Andrew Conger demanded of the stewardess, and always received, five cocktail onions in his vodka Gibson?

Conger's jet resembled no typical passenger craft. More than half the seats were ripped out and replaced with secretarial work areas:

desks protruded from the walls; electric typewriters clicked out the next speech of the day, the next release to the press. Mimeograph machines operated at thirty-five thousand feet, spewing out copies of necessary material at a rate considerably slower than the speed with which the jet ripped through the heavens. Ottomans were located casually throughout the forward staff section, facilitating conversation among four or five people. Staff members wrote reports, dozed fitfully, conversed, chatted with the stewardesses—all to the accompaniment of the constant rhythmic clatter of the typewriters and the cyclical whir and whip of the mimeo machine. And all forward of the soundproofed bulkhead separating the troops from the leader and his queen consort.

Behind the bulkhead, at the rear of the plane, was an airborne villa of incredible splendor. It was in this area that the various airlines threw caution to the winds in their attempts to impress the presidential candidates. Plush custom leather, hand tooled and sometimes monogrammed with the initials of the candidate, luxuriously covered every piece of furniture. Magnificent custom-fitted bedspreads and linens, again monogrammed, embraced the beds, which were retracted in the daytime, but used for short naps or evening flights. Every electrical traveling appliance conceived by man in his search for creature comforts away from home was to be found somewhere in the floating suite: a good percentage were in the bathroom. Electrical massage chairs for Monsieur and Madame were standard equipment. Airborne FM radio and television were also standard equipment in the lairs of the political pashas.

The candidate seldom came forward from his celestial sanctuary to mingle with the troops and honored guests. In this day when jet flight comprised a high percentage of total campaign travel, a senator seeking five minutes with the candidate might be forced to fly from Miami to Seattle in order to obtain the audience. The length of the flight could well be the only free time the candidate would possess that day, or for the next ten or more days. Naturally, the senator would have to fly back to Miami at his own expense after his five-minute chat.

When flying into a state not previously visited, it was common practice for that state's political bigwigs to join the candidate prior to his initial appearance. The candidate would be briefed on local conditions, made aware of last-minute popularity polls, and local issues. Once again, however, in the Jet Age of politics it was sometimes necessary for the State Chairman of Oregon to fly to New York in order to ride back and triumphantly enter the state with the candidate.

It would certainly be a shattering experience for the defeated presidential candidate, Dale thought, when, after the election, he found himself standing in waiting rooms, unmoving lines, and at drafty turnstiles with the commoners, waiting his turn to board a conventional passenger aircraft. Not the least of his deprivation would be the absent Cadillac, which in the campaign days had whisked him out onto the field to the very foot of the boarding ramp.

Dale knew several candidates who never did get over it, practicing great lengths of management manipulation in their future business positions to perpetuate the luxury of their personal private plane. They simply couldn't kick the habit.

Staff members also used the charter flights for urgent conferences. When Dale had to get an answer from a member of the staff which accompanied the candidate on his trips, and the issue involved more than could be discussed in a late-evening phone conversation when the party was back in his hotel rooms after the usual evening rally, Dale would then fly to a city, pick up the party, and travel from city to city conducting his business. It was necessary frequently to practice this in order to brief Conger on major telecasts scheduled shortly in the future, and to obtain decisions from him which could not be transmitted through other staff members.

On one such flight, Wilbur Jenkins left his journalistic flock in the press plane in order to talk privately with Dale in Conger's plane. Issues had arisen over the servicing of the press at the first debate, and Dale had caught up with the traveling party.

"There will be various security areas, Will," said Dale. "Different colored passes for different grades of security. There's no use working it out now until Conger decides he's going to go to Cleveland on October sixteenth. We have to see the physical plant—the building—before I can tell you exactly who will be permitted where. What you should tell me mainly, so that I have it in mind, are your requirements. We'll take care of all national and international press not traveling with you. The station will handle local press. I'll send you memos as that firms up."

"Good, Charlie," said Jenkins. "I get kinda far away from it, you know, with the traveling. I'd sorta like you to handle as much of the press stuff as you can."

"I will if you'll back me up. And I mean all the way. We'll be making important decisions minute by minute. Whatever we decide, you must understand, is the best I could do."

"I'll back you up. Just keep me posted."

"I'm going to hold you to this, Wilbur. There won't be time for arguments or changes when you descend with your press horde, and Green with his, on top of the press of the world which will precede you into the debate city."

"I understand," said Jenkins. Dale knew he didn't, but let it pass. "We'll need approval of pool still photographers in the actual studio," said Jenkins. "I've been talking to Duncan of Green's staff. We think four stills can handle for everybody. We'll also need immediate darkroom facilities. The pool stills will have to empty their cameras of film in front of witnesses, to prevent any hanky-panky. You know, holding back a roll which turns out to be exclusive stuff the next day."

"Right. What next?"

"Pool pencils will also need clearance into the studio. Again, Duncan and I think four will be adequate for everybody." Dale nodded. "The press rooms must have full wire and telephone facilities, and must be in the same building as the telecast. Otherwise, the guys will scream."

"The press room will be in the same building as the telecast if that is possible, Wilbur. If it isn't, they won't be. This is what I'm talking about. You've got to go along with me on this sort of thing."

"Okay. But try real hard to work it out. These guys are tough enough to keep in line without adding to their beefs."

"Will most of the press move from the hotel with The Man when he moves, or will they come over to the studio earlier?" asked Dale.

"I don't know. Normally, they'd stay with the candidate. On this telecast, however, they may want to come over ahead of him in order to do color stories, behind-the-scenes stuff."

"As it stands now, you won't be permitted in the control room, Wilbur," said Dale. "No matter where we originate from, our approach is to keep everyone out not directly connected with the telecast."

"That's fine with me. I'll be too busy with my guys." Jenkins pulled a slip of paper out of his pocket, and consulted it. "Do you know an Amos Whiting, a TV news reporter from KZVI? That's in Fairlee, Green's home town."

"No, I don't. Why?" asked Dale. "I know who he is."

"He traveled with us a couple of days last week. He's an independent cuss, doesn't give a damn for anything or anybody. But honest. Seems to give our man an even break, too. We had to wait for him twice to make the press bus. The other guys were sore as hell at him. Anyway, one night he got drunk as a skunk, came by my room late and knocked on the door. Wanted to talk to me. I let him in. He wanted to know where you were, if you were going to be with us while he was traveling with Conger. I said I didn't think so. He wanted to tell you something about North American and the debate. He wouldn't tell me. Said I wouldn't understand."

"I wonder what it was."

"I don't know. He said he could hang North American if he wanted to, and talked about some deal between Green and NA that Lou Wells was mixed up in."

"I'll be damned," said Dale. "I'd like to talk to him. I overheard something at the convention between Wells and the president of NA, Fred Morgan. It didn't make much sense, but I wrote it down.

I've got it back in my apartment. Maybe Whiting does have something."

"I dunno," said Jenkins. "He was pretty drunk. You know, guys like to make you think they've got a hot story, that they know inside poop you don't know. It usually comes out when they're stoned . . . want to be treated like a big shot. Whiting's close to Green, you know. He might have been just pulling that stuff on me, letting me know he was a close buddy of the other man."

"The kind of thing I overheard, and what Whiting may have been trying to say, is up awfully high, Wilbur. And very damaging —if it's true. I wouldn't know how to go about checking it out. Jesus, it could backfire horribly."

"I wouldn't either. It's dangerous. I just wanted to tell you about it away from the press boys. That's why I wanted to have this talk with you. If Whiting shows up for the debate, you might ask him about it. He's back with Green now. You might keep your eyes open."

"Wilbur, since the night Andrew Conger accepted the debate challenge in Chicago, my eyes have been open as far as I can stretch them."

The expected controversy arose between Arthur Baldwin's physical advance men, concerned over the size of crowds in halls and at meetings, and Dale's operation, fighting for every minute of television coverage they could beg, borrow, or steal. Only as a last resort would Dale buy the time to televise their candidate in local meetings. It was a game his men played with local station managers throughout the country. Ned Colton would shout with glee, his high laugh ringing through the office, as he successfully conned another station in a large city to carry Conger's address free. Dale, as well as Colton, knew full well the local stations had an eye on Washington and the Federal Communications Commission, which would hold them accountable after the campaign for their "public service" contributions of a political nature. But it was fun, and free television coverage accounted for an incredibly high percentage of the total number of telecast hours Andrew Conger enjoyed during the campaign.

"Goddammit, Dale, we're worried about the crowd," Baldwin was saying, calling in from Spokane. "You and I had a deal on Spokane. No 'live' TV for the rally. You're going to kill our crowd. These people are dead on their ass up here. If you guys televise the meeting, half the people will stay home to watch it on TV. Conger's going to blow his stack when he sees those empty seats."

It was true Conger would scream if there were empty seats. Dale had never known anyone, including the biggest names in show business he had worked with in his long career, who could take a house count as fast as Andy Conger. In the midst of the ear-splitting bedlam which accompanied his entrance and walk to the rostrum, time and again Conger, smiling all the while, would lean over to Dale and say, "House only three-quarters full. Tell Baldwin I want to see him after the meeting." He had an eye like a chicken hawk when it came to cutting through the smoke, haze and floodlights to count the last empty seat up in the blues.

"We're only following orders, Art," said Dale. "We were told to step up TV coverage. If you're in trouble up there, I'm sorry."

"Anybody tell you, specifically, to televise the Spokane rally?" he asked.

"Yup."

"Who?"

"Andrew Conger."

"Shot down again," said Baldwin. "You guys have got to stop takin' orders from the candidate. He's only running for President of the United States. I'm trying to fill a goddam dirigible hangar in Spokane." They both chuckled.

"I've got a list here, Art, which just came in from Conger," said Dale. "It's got a mess of cities on it. He wants full TV coverage in each one."

"Oh, God!"

"Are you sitting down?"

"Go ahead, shoot."

"First one is Omaha."

"Jesus!"

"Next one is Milwaukee."

"Christ!"

"Next one is Nashville."

"We're dead. We've had it. Gotta run. Conger's finished his speech. Call you from Boise. 'By."

"Hi, Daddy, this is Betsy. I'm in Denver." Dale's oldest daughter was calling him long distance. It was midafternoon in Washington.

"Betts . . . how are you? Gee, it's good to talk to you." The call took Dale by surprise.

"It's raining here."

"Can you speak a little louder? I can't hear you over all the noise back here."

"Sure," said Betsy, raising her voice. "How's that?"

"Fine," said Dale. "Gee, you sound great. How are Lisa and Charlie Junior?"

"Oh, they're okay I guess. Nobody's sick."

"How's your riding coming? Jumping yet?"

"Not yet—but almost."

"I've tried to reach your mother a couple of times lately, but there's been no answer at the house. I guess she's been out a lot. Do you have a maid now?"

"Not always. That's why I'm calling you. Juanita's been sick. She can only come two days a week. So I'm baby-sitting now for Mother the other days."

"Why baby-sitting for Mother?"

"Well, it's about your company. Mother's down there most of the time."

"That's fine, Betts. I told her to use the office any time she felt like it."

"Well, I'm not supposed to tell you, Daddy, but it's more than that."

"What is?"

"Mother's being down there all the time. She's working there every day. Trying to straighten it out."

Straighten what out? Dale asked himself. Janet doesn't know anything about my business. "What's she trying to do, Betts?" he asked.

"Well, as I said, I'm not supposed to say anything to you, but I think you should know. She's working very hard, every day. I don't know what's wrong, Daddy, but Vic Hanson isn't there any more. He's disappeared."

No wonder he hadn't been able to reach Hanson! Dale shook his head sharply at the shock of Betsy's words. "Where is Mother right now, Betts?" He lit a cigarette with one hand.

"At your office. She's there every day. She's trying awfully hard, Daddy. And she's so worried."

"Well, I'll take care of that when I talk to her. I appreciate your call. It's been so good to talk to you. Give a big hug and kiss to Lisa and Charlie for me. Don't you worry about anything. It will all work out fine." Dale was impatient to talk to Janet.

"I hope so, Daddy. We love you very much."

"Fergie," Dale yelled through the door to the outer office, "get me my office in Denver." This is going to be sticky in more ways than one, thought Dale. He hadn't talked to Janet since Sandra had gone to Paris. Alone at night, he had spent many hours trying to put the pieces together, trying to be Charlie Dale, as Sandra had said. He thought more than once of calling Paris. Each time he had reconsidered. He wanted time to think. Dale had written a couple of short notes to Janet, mostly on money matters and the coming school year. Betsy would be changing schools, and he wanted to be certain Janet helped her through the transition. Nothing personal to Janet, however, had found its way into Dale's letters. He was in an emotional limbo; a middle ground of doubt, exhaustion from the campaign, and personal insensitivity. But what was going on in Denver? And where had Vic Hanson gone? What a strange way to find himself talking again to Janet. His wife, who didn't know the first thing about his business, was the person to whom he had to turn for information concerning his own company.

"Hello, Janet, this is Charlie. How are you?" he said into the phone nervously.

"Charlie? Is that you? I'm fine. Who told you I was here?"

"Betsy. She called me. We had a nice talk. Is she all set for her new school? I forgot to ask her."

"Oh yes, she's very excited. We went over the other day and had a nice chat with the Headmistress. She may not be able to stay the whole year, though," Janet added inexplicably.

"Oh?" asked Charlie. "How so? I thought that money was put aside."

"It was, and she'll probably be okay. I said *maybe* she'll have to drop out."

"What's the matter, Jan? Something wrong? What happened to Vic Hanson?"

"I don't know. I got a call from the bank one day. They said they'd been trying to reach him, as he'd missed a payment of the big loan. Then they got some checks from Phoenix drawn on the company. They were large amounts, under Vic's signature. They asked me to come down."

"Who'd you see—Mr. Barnett?"

"Yes. He talked with me. About three weeks ago. I thought you had enough on your mind in Washington without worrying about all the problems out here. Mr. Barnett and I talked it over, and he thought maybe I could sit on the finances closer if I came in regularly. The books and things are pretty screwed up. Mr. Barnett was here two days last week with me."

"Are you telling me that Vic has flown the coop . . . and with some of my dough?"

"Something like that . . . yes."

"Why that son-of-a-bitch! I'll kill him!"

Dale remembered Hanson's passion for playing poker. What was it Hanson had said? "I lost this week, but I'll make it up next." Christ, he had probably used Dale's money to pay off debts!

"Don't say I didn't warn you," continued Janet. "But in the meantime, Mr. Barnett and I have been trying to keep you out of receivership. It's really quite a mess."

"Good God! How do you know what to do? How do you know where to start? You don't know anything about the film business or bookkeeping, for that matter."

"I do too."

"Oh? Does someone have a line on Hanson's whereabouts now? Have you stopped payment on everything?"

"Oh, Lord yes. That's all taken care of. We think we know where he is. That money's gone. The thing now is to keep The Dale Organization from going under. I've cut the payroll to the bone. I've kept your film editor, Bill Davenport, so we can finish the production already in the shop. I let the cameraman go. We settled his contract, and have a first refusal on his services if we need him."

"Good . . . that sounds fine. What about new business? Anything coming in to help?"

"I think that should wait until after the campaign. I've written each of your clients a letter—I'll send you a copy. It simply says the company and you are too busy right now to bid on, or solicit new projects. I think it will satisfy them, and keep us alive in their minds until you can return, if you do. The way we see it out here is to take whatever dollars are available, cut our overhead to the bone, work on unfinished production, and try to skin through. Maybe we'll make it, maybe we won't."

Dale made notes as Janet talked. From them, he could write her that evening with further thoughts. "I don't know what to say. I don't know how to thank you."

"You'll find a way." Janet paused. "Are you seeing that girl?"

"No. As a matter of fact, she's in Paris." Dale wondered if he could say it, what he would feel like. "Maybe it *was* just an affair. Maybe not. She's a very fine person."

"She must be to attract you the way she did."

"I'm still pretty confused—but I'd like to see you. I, uh, don't suppose any visit would work out soon. If we're strapped for money I don't think you can fly back here. I've got to sit down and talk with you. Maybe something will break on a Conger trip. I almost came out for that airport rally on the kickoff day. Did you go?"

"Oh, yes. You didn't think the children would miss that, did you? We had a fine time. All the mothers and kids. They had a station wagon-caravan—they called it Tailgate Day out here—to get a crowd out in the middle of the afternoon. It was a mob scene. We were miles away from Andy. Listen, as long as I've got you, I want you to answer some questions for me."

"Fine. Go ahead."

Janet went through a list of business details which needed immediate decision. Dale was surprised at her rapid grasp of his company's affairs and projects. One by one, he gave Janet her instructions, feeling complete understanding on her part of each issue involved. "Anything more?" he asked after a pause.

"No, I guess that's it. Well, we'll be here, plugging away. If we go under, you can't say we didn't try. I'll watch our correspondence, and anything vital I'll shoot on to you. Onward and upward. This is a lot of fun down here."

"Our" correspondence she had said, thought Dale. After all the years Janet hadn't fitted into his life, was it possible, Dale wondered, that now there was a beginning of a common purpose, an understanding? Could this be a bridge across their dreadfully strained relationship?

"Fine, girl. I better ring off now. But . . . once again I want to say how proud I am of what you've done. And grateful!"

"You haven't said that before, Charles. I mean the word 'proud.' You're doing great back there. We read about you all the time. Take care of yourself. And it would be yummy if you could get out, even for a day, if you want to come. I haven't forgotten that last night in Chicago."

Dale chuckled. "I'll try, Jan. Honest, I will. And I do want to see you. I want things to work out for us. They must."

"If you want them to, they will."

"Say hello to the kids for me. And don't work too hard. Bless you for what you're doing."

"Thanks, dear. I should run. Bill Davenport's waving his arms at me. Says there's a crisis in the dubbing room."

"What in the hell are you doing out here?" asked Dale of Lou Wells.

"I've got a crisis," answered Wells, "and your office said this is where I could find you. I need some answers. By the way, what are *you* doing rattling around New England in a Conger motorcade? On these Maine cowpaths you're about as far away from TV as you can get."

"Same thing as you. Get in the car. I'm here to get decisions from Conger on the network shot we have on Global Tuesday night. Only way to get at him was to force a promise out of Cliff Harley I could ride in Conger's car between two bumper stops today."

"Are all motorcades like this? I'll be killed!" moaned Wells.

"You've been riding in a car too far back. These motorcades are like a game of Crack the Whip," Dale added knowingly.

Why Andrew Conger, in the modern age of communication-in-depth offered by radio and television and the press, still thought there was any value in a motorcade was beyond Dale's comprehension. But he assumed it was the same old story: pressure from a State Chairman. So today, here was Andy Conger, crawling in and out of his car every fifteen minutes or half-hour, following a hair-raising cross-country race from the previous stop in order to stay on schedule. The gathering might be five hundred people, a thousand, or three thousand. Mostly children let out of school, waving their American flags. Susan Conger loved these informal meetings, said it made her feel close to the real people of America. To everyone except the candidate and his wife, motorcades were a nightmare, hatched in the witches' cauldrons of Detroit's auto factories.

Conger motorcades always ran behind schedule. There were too many variables when the advance men checked out the running times. Consequently, if a reasonable forty miles an hour had been planned for the day's motoring, after the first stop the speed of the lead car was usually increased to sixty miles an hour. At the opposite end of the weaving, bobbing caravan, as many as forty cars back, the speed became ninety miles an hour in order to stay with the pack. Dale never understood this principle of forward motion. But invariably, the tail end of the motorcade was forced to maintain a horrifying breakneck speed in order to keep up with the considerably slower-traveling front end. Women members of the press closed their eyes as their bus careened around corners. Towns became a blur. When this mechanical land-snake halted, the screech of brakes could be heard for miles. But the outriding motorcycle policeman somehow kept the chrome-trimmed behemoth from devouring itself each time the lead cars stopped.

Mysterious things happened on Conger motorcades. Staff people were locked out of cars. Inexplicably, drivers would lock their automobiles during Conger's speech. When the staff occupants assigned to the car by number, veterans of the rapid takeoffs from such "bumper stops," would dive for the car door, they would find to their horror it was locked. Other times the staff people were locked *in* their cars, more correctly kept prisoners by their drivers, who seemed to be operating from a set of instructions printed in Moon Talk and sent to them via registered rocket from Outer Galaxy Nine. Still other members of the staff would return to their assigned car to find *no driver*. This was the worst horror of all. The driver, likely as not, would be in the local sandwich shop licking an ice-cream cone, oblivious to his chauffeuring responsibility. Or he would be at the speaker's stand clawing at Conger for an autograph. In such cases, he would inevitably be swept along with the crowd as it followed the candidate to his car. When Conger literally waved good-by to him at the curb, the misplaced driver would have the sickening realization that he was a long way from where he was supposed to be—driving an automobile in the now departing candidate's motorcade. In such instances, if the driver had been forgetful enough to leave the keys in his car, he would be forced to watch it depart on schedule, in its proper place in line, driven by one of the Conger staff assigned to it as a passenger. Many drivers, excited by the appearance of the presidential candidate, waited until after Conger's speeches to relieve their bladders. When it was time to move, they simply were on their way to a bathroom.

Strangely enough, however, Dale could not remember any automobile which ever ran out of gas or got a flat tire, the two things one would naturally assume would plague all motorcades.

Of all inventions known to politics, none could compare with a Conger motorcade press bus. It was a rolling, free-loading, mobile booze palace, immune to state laws. It resembled a luxury gambling ship, anchored beyond the reach of the law three miles offshore. In dry states, however, the three miles was sometimes reduced to three feet, the distance between the side of the swaying saloon and the state police outriders escorting the air-conditioned distillery through their backward state.

The press floated through mile after mile of brilliant American countryside, dazzling in its fall colors, in a kind of dazed exhaustion: asleep, terrified, hung-over, out cold.

There were hidden talents to be found in many airline stewardesses. Dale remembered a campaign in which a stewardess from the south named Tallulah Bankhead Beane had been the difference between survival and death during a grueling three-day motorcade which rocked and rolled through one-hundred-degree heat, fog, a tornado, and a dust storm before its termination. Tallulah Bankhead Beane was a ball of fire. The press loved her, adopted her as their own. She became a captive Fatima in their bus, forced to accompany them everywhere. She led them in community-singing mile after mile. She would stand on a large suitcase and do the Charleston as the bus careened over hill and dale at close to one hundred miles an hour. She mixed their drinks, administered Bromo Seltzers, cooed them to sleep with Southern lullabies. The last Dale heard of Tallulah she'd been made a supervisor of stewardesses; grounded now, no longer able to give so much pleasure to her wards and passengers. Tallulah Bankhead Beane—the greatest political cruise director of them all—grounded!

Conger was delivering Motorcade Speech A at the current stop, with Wells and Dale sitting in the car until it was concluded. "Yeah, these damn motorcades are an institution, Lou," said Dale. "They're murder on the press—and the staff. What kind of a crisis has made you chase me all the way out here? Must be pretty serious."

"I have two. When are we going to get an answer from Conger accepting that October sixteenth date? That's the first problem. The second is that I must hold a production meeting damn quickly, or we'll never make that date. But I can't hold the meeting and give out any construction orders on the set or deadline notices until I know what date we're going to go."

Dale was silent. Wells did have a problem. Conger's strategy was causing every conceivable type of difficulty in preparing for the debates. "We're having a staff session this Sunday, Lou, in Washington. Conger's coming into the office all day. I expect to get your answer then. I'm positive he'll announce his acceptance of the October sixteenth date for the Monday A.M.'s."

"Then I'll be safe if I schedule a production meeting Monday in Washington?"

"Well, as safe as anything can be these days. If you want to take the chance, I'll practically guarantee you'll have your answer by Monday. You'll be holding your meeting with an okay from Conger on October sixteenth. The main subject this coming Sunday is bound to be the schedule. It's got to happen. They'll be forced to firm up the debate date in order to firm up his plans for the weeks around it. Incidentally, it's off the record we're working that far ahead."

"I understand. It goes no further. Will you try and get another answer for me Sunday? Ask Conger if he prefers to stand or sit for these debates. I've asked Murray Smith to get the same info. Our decision on this will dictate the entire design approach for the set. If you can get that out of him Sunday, we'll be way ahead when we meet."

"I'll try, Lou. Although I can't promise. If I see him, which I should, I'll do my best to get an answer."

Charlie Dale never saw Andrew Conger that Sunday. He waited for twelve hours, hoping for his five minutes with the candidate. It was part of the picture of the constant frustration, the inexcusable inefficiency which wore down the staff to gibbering robots. Dale could only conclude that the things which kept Conger from seeing him were more important than the debate. Whatever they were, thought Dale, this was the story of the campaign. Everything ultimately had preference over television, particularly the debate.

Dale watched political hacks come and go all day. Ruth Platt assured him time and again, as did Conger's Appointments Secretary Cliff Harley, that he'd get his five minutes. Rufe Little assured Dale that Conger would announce his acceptance of the October sixteenth date. Neither occurred.

A two-hour session with dull, overfed State Chairmen settled four personal appearances in as many cities. In the four meetings combined, Andrew Conger would appear before perhaps one hundred and fifty thousand people, one-tenth the audience enjoyed by a children's religious television show at nine o'clock Sunday morning. Dale knew he was in trouble when Arthur Baldwin and Abner Shepherd came out from a meeting on two upcoming weeks and said Conger had thrown out their proposed plans, canceled the entire schedule, and asked for a new approach to those specific areas and states. In the newspapers the following week columnists would, likely as not, report Conger's revision of his plans as new master strategy emanating from the Conger command. A television commentator would label the new plans as an example of the flexible, hard-hitting strategy of the Conger brain trust. Balls, thought Dale, if they only knew.

Dale waited disgustedly but patiently to see his man. It was "Play it by ear, fellas, play it minute by minute. We're flying by the seat of our pants, guys, you know that." The columns, the fish stories, the think-pieces which would be written about The Master Plan.

Hell, there wasn't any. The campaign was a ship without a rudder, a horse without a bridle, a car without a steering wheel. A huge, inconceivably expensive, man-devouring directionless glob which slipped, slid, and jerked its way hopefully toward the White House.

There never was any time. The advisers had no time with the candidate, the planners had no time with him, the researchers had no time to present their findings even though they previously had miraculously obtained time to get approval for the research. The candidate had no time for any of them. It was hit the crisis of the moment, the first card off the top of the panic deck. Good politicians were opportunists: opportunists made good politicians. Seize the issue of the moment, the advantage of the hour. Jump on it, build an attack on the opposition. Plan a trip to the vulnerable city or state— slam, slam, slam the opposition. Then wait for the smoke to clear, make an assessment, pick up the pieces every week-end, and start all over again.

The changes in the itinerary. The constant changes. No long-range planning. No careful, thoughtful periods for productive reflection. As far as Dale was concerned, any presidential candidate who was smart enough to plan four weeks ahead—*and stick to his plan*—would win a presidential campaign hands down and going home.

No plan, no plan. It was like kids playing with dynamite, babies with matches, ten-year-olds with a Redstone Rocket. The rocket on this Sunday, however, was the debate. The single telecast of the debate might have an audience of one hundred million people. But Charlie Dale couldn't get five minutes with Andrew Conger who, come hell or high water, was going to find himself in front of that cyclops of a television camera being X-rayed on the debate stage, no matter how many political hacks sucked up his time on how many Sundays.

Sundays. A day of rest for the candidate. That's a laugh, too, Dale thought. The poor guy. From the moment he opens his eyes on Sunday after a grueling week of campaigning, the vultures are on him. And I'm one of them, thought Dale. I'm one of them. Something must be done to cut down the torture a presidential candidate endures.

And so that particular Sunday came and went. Dale worked fitfully at his office, Fergie checking Ruth Platt and Cliff Harley every so often for a reading as to when Dale could see the man. He never did.

"Hasn't your man ever heard of television?" Murray Smith asked, not looking at Dale. He tapped his cigarette ash rhythmically into a china saucer. Dale said nothing.

"Goddamn it! When is Conger going to stop this feet-dragging? He's killing himself," said Lou Wells. "He's a laughing stock. Do you think you'll get an answer this week?"

"I don't know, guys," Dale said dejectedly, shaking his head. "I just don't know. I promised you we'd have it for this meeting. We don't. There's nothing else I can say. Let's go on with the meeting. I don't think I'll have another crack at my man until next week-end. If we can arrive at a list of *must* decisions, I guarantee you I'll get them if I have to fly to Hawaii to meet with him."

The three men were meeting in the North American suite at the Sheraton-Carlton. It was a three-room arrangement the network had rented to expedite the debate meetings with the candidates' representatives. Wells had felt the three rooms might prove useful if each party wanted to confer in privacy to arrive at decisions or call their staff headquarters during the long sessions.

Dale was in a depressed mood when he arrived. The comments of Smith and Wells had irritated him further. This first production meeting was his best opportunity to kill—once and for all—the possibility of any drapes or pleats being used in the basic design approach to the debate set. Because of his inability to get his answers from Conger, however, the two men were lined up against him before the meeting even got under way. This is going to be a black Monday, thought Dale.

"We have to go ahead," said Wells. He ran down a checkoff list of twenty or so items, answers to which were needed from the candidates. Finally he added, "Charlie, what do we do about the standing or sitting problem? I've got two designers in New York right now going out of their minds—afraid they'll be handed an impossible deadline."

"I'd like to hear Murray's thoughts," said Dale. "If we agree, I'll take a chance."

"My man wants to stand," said Smith. "He likes it better. It's more like his press conferences. He tells me he thinks better on his feet."

"I'll make the same recommendation to my man," said Dale. He preferred Conger to stand for the same reasons Smith had enumerated. "I'll take the rap if I'm wrong, but I'm sure my man also will want to stand."

"Fine," said Wells. "We can go ahead on that then. I'll have sketches down here Thursday of three basic approaches to the physical debate staging. Will you men be in Washington?"

"I'll probably be here," said Dale. "Although at this stage of a campaign I can't guarantee anything, as you've just found out. Murray?"

"I think I'll be here, unless I'm in Los Angeles," Smith said.

"Aha," said Dale. "Governor Joseph Green is doing something big on TV in Los Angeles Thursday. My, that's nice to know." Dale smiled. Smith's face remained a blank.

"I'm going out there on other business," said Smith.

"Sure, I know," said Dale, playing him. "Like a major nighttime rally on the full Global Television Network, maybe?"

"C'mon, fellas," said Wells. "We've got work to do. As for the set, because most people have it in their minds this debate is going to be much like the classic Lincoln-Douglas exchange, but we know it isn't, we think the design approach should be very formal, to play off visually against the informality of the format. We also think it should be visually patriotic in some way, that there should be some historic symbolism to remind the viewers of the magnitude of the occasion."

"How about a heraldic design center stage which has two six-shooters crossed on a field of frustrated staff advisers?" asked Dale.

"Or two blood-dripping stilettos crossed on a field of broken campaign promises," Smith suggested, chuckling.

Wells ignored the byplay between the two, and continued. "Our design department will be working on approaches reflecting those thoughts, and they will be sent to Cleveland."

"For our approval," said Dale. Wells let the barb slip by, and Dale added, "I must say I'm against too formal a design approach. I think it might overpower the candidates. We don't want to make this thing so formal the audience will expect our men to come out in sandals and togas with laurel wreaths in their hair."

"I couldn't agree more," said Smith. "If anything, I think we should lean toward a warm approach to the set, wood tones and textures, something which will present these men in human terms."

"Those are my sentiments exactly," said Dale "Let's face it, this debate is going to be an ordeal for these men. They're going to be tight—nervous. I think everything visual should offset that personal physical tension."

"How about something with soft folds or drapes? You know—warm-toned fabrics hung vertically?" asked Wells. "There are some very warm fabrics we're using these days on our news shows, beautiful textures. They hang beautifully. And are exciting to light with slashes from spots. You can get exciting effects, and the drapes provide a maximum of flexibility when light is played on them. Valuable for last-minute adjustments."

"Hmmm . . . interesting," said Smith, doodling with his pencil, "but let's not have any last-minute adjustments."

This is it, thought Dale. Wells brought it up for me, thank God. But it's now or never. "Lou," he said, looking at Wells, "do you remember Conger's acceptance speech at the convention?"

"Of course," said Wells. "Who doesn't? I'll never forget it as long as I live. When I heard that man accept our debate proposal . . ."

"You screamed like a man who had just won ten Irish Sweepstakes," said Dale.

"So did I," said Smith, grinning.

"I'll bet you did," said Dale. "Where were you that night, Murray?"

"We were at the Kona Kai Club in San Diego. Green went there for two weeks after the convention. It was a fabulous place. I got there the day of Conger's acceptance speech. You should have seen the joy in Green's camp that night. It was still early out on the Coast. We had quite a celebration."

"Well, you, Murray, might not have caught this," continued Dale, "but I think Lou was aware of it. We had a certain standard backing behind the rostrum from the beginning of the convention straight through Wednesday night. This permanent backing was vertical curtains, box-pleated and hung in heavy folds. It was changed before Andy Conger spoke—at a cost of twelve hundred dollars!"

"What's he got against drapes?" asked Smith.

"I remember now," Wells cut in.

"There's nothing the matter with curtains or folds behind my man as far as I'm concerned," said Dale. "But I must tell you no one will ever see Andrew Conger on television during this campaign speaking in front of them. It's a very strange thing," Dale added, "this dislike of curtains. There's no logic connected with it. I'll be very honest with you. It started with Conger's wife. For some reason, and she has a right to her opinion, she doesn't think her Andy looks well in front of velours hanging in folds. It's something about the shadows deep in the folds, the vertical black lines. But that's beside the point. Through the years she's convinced Conger this is a very bad backing for him. He's now at the point where he believes it one hundred per cent. I've seen Conger walk into a local TV station. You know, the standard gray velour drapes usually are the only backing they have. I've seen him blow sky-high the minute he sees them. It makes no sense, I admit. But these are the facts of the matter. I simply cannot approve any such approach to our debate design. My man sees red. I'm hired to see such things don't happen."

"Isn't he being a little overboard on this thing, Charlie?" asked Smith.

"Of course he is," said Dale. "But why fight it? Do you have a strong preference for curtains?" he asked Smith.

"No, but my man looks fine in front of them. And they do have a warmth to them," answered Smith.

"I agree," said Dale. "But let's get the warmth in some other way, through some other material such as wood-grain, or even a tightly stretched nubby cloth or weave. My man doesn't object to cloth behind him. He objects to the vertical folds, the black lines."

"I understand," said Smith. "I'll go along with Charlie, Lou, if it'll help matters. Let's find something else."

"So we agree," said Dale. "We're looking for something to give us warmth behind these men as they appear on the telecast, but we kill the idea of loose drapes or folds." Dale and Smith nodded their agreement.

You two may be killing velour drapes, said Lou Wells to himself. But, Charlie my boy, you have just given me something Fred Morgan and I have been looking for. If something as simple as this will irritate your man to the extent you say it will, you better prepare yourself for a surprise. Yessir, this may be just what we've been looking for. It will put you in the doghouse, just where you belong!

"I'd like to keep an open mind until we see what the designers come up with," said Wells. "I've made notes of your comments, Charlie. I assure you I will keep them very much in mind."

14

Autumn in the West

"HELLO, CHARLIE . . . ? This is Cliff Harley. You're going to have to talk loud, or I won't hear you over the noise out here. Can you hear me?"

"Yes," said Dale, shouting into the phone. "I can also hear Conger on the p.a., speaking in the background. Where are you?"

"In a phone booth at the airport in Billings, Montana. Andy wanted me to call you. When we land in Seattle tonight, he's going to announce at his news conference he's accepting the October sixteenth date in Cleveland for the debate. Did you get that?"

"Yes. That's fine. I'm glad you called. Thank God, it's settled."

"The Secretary wanted you to know before he made the announcement . . . thought you might want to make plans. Incidentally, he asked me to tell you he's sorry about last Sunday—in the office—you not seeing him. Things just got jammed up. I showed him your memo on the 'must decisions' yesterday. He wondered if you could come out to Colorado Springs this week-end. We'll get in there late Saturday night and rest there Sunday."

"Will the same thing happen as last Sunday?"

"Don't be ridiculous. He's asking you to come out. He's told me to block out as much time as you need."

"I'll be there." At least I didn't have to chase him to Hawaii, thought Dale.

"Do you want me to put you down for a room Saturday night at the Broadmoor, Charlie?" Harley asked.

"Yes. Make it a double room. My wife will be with me."

"Will do. Gotta run. Ham Forrest wants to say something. He's right here."

"So long, Cliff. See you Sunday. And thanks for the dope." Dale listened to Conger concluding his speech as Forrest came to the phone.

"Hey, Charlie, old buddy," said Forrest, "how do you get out of this chicken-shit outfit?"

Dale laughed. "How're you doing, Ham? The man giving you a bad time?"

"Jesus, yes. I heard Cliff saying you were coming to Colorado Springs. Has that new portable sound system equipment arrived yet?"

"Nope. It was due here last Monday."

"Dammit! I hoped you could bring it out to us. The old man is screaming about the lousy sound we've had at airports and in the motorcade stops. There's been some cable cutting too, Charlie."

"No kidding? I thought we were through with that sort of thing."

"In the cities . . . the big ones. That's where it's happening. The sound man, Billy Dee, tells me he's lost audio because of fresh, clean cuts in his power lines. At big city shopping centers. Billy Dee's been wonderful. I don't know what we would have done without him along. Boy . . . we've had some near disasters lately. He's saved us on every one of them."

"That's what he's there for, Ham. I'm glad he's doing so well. Tell him I appreciate it."

"He'll want to spend some time with you at the Broadmoor. He thinks this stuff he calls sabotage has got to be brought to someone's attention." There was a roar of applause in the background as Conger ended his remarks.

"Listen, Ham, you'll be with Conger tonight before the rally in Seattle, right?"

"Check. It's a complicated entrance. I'll be with him. If you've got something, make it quick."

"I do. Tell him that in the debate meeting Sunday I'll need at least an hour. Also tell Cliff Harley that . . ."

"Okay . . . okay. Gotta run. Party's pulling out. 'By." The line went dead.

Goddam, goddam, said Dale to himself. Gotta run, gotta run. That's the story of this campaign. Why can't anyone ever complete a conversation? Why isn't there enough time? Why does every piece of important business have to be conducted in a phone booth at a noisy airport five minutes before the candidate is pulling out?

Phones, phones, phones. Staff members of a political campaign had phones growing out of their ears. Because the pell-mell campaign trips of the candidate never stopped for anything once they started, all business, even of the highest importance, had to be conducted before, during, and after the candidate's speeches and public appearances. Special phone lines, at the most incongruous locations, were the first items covered by Arthur Baldwin's physical advance team. Not only did a temporary phone represent the lifeline back to headquarters and civilization for the Conger staff man, but, equally important, the phone symbolized the press coverage Andrew Conger would or would not obtain from that particular speech. At a safe distance from the phones marked "Staff" was sure to be a bank of press phones. In the Western time zones these phones meant the difference between whether or not Andrew Conger would hit Page One of the *New York Times* the following morning. The deadline on filing, naturally, moved up to an earlier and earlier hour in the day as the campaign party moved westward. In the areas where there were four hours difference due to discrepancies in Daylight Saving, filing stories became a major headache for the traveling press.

Once a political campaign hit the trail, communication indeed became the major obstacle to efficiency and decision. Baldwin's men, on the spot, became the human umbilical cord to the traveling party. If Dale, for instance, wanted Ham Forrest to call him from The Dalles, Oregon, Dale's office contacted Baldwin's advance desk next door at Headquarters in Washington. The advance men were under mandatory orders to call in to Washington fifteen minutes before the candidate's arrival at their location. At that time all urgent messages for the traveling party were relayed to Baldwin's advance man, who passed them on to the proper individuals immediately upon landing.

The Conger traveling party was a piece of society in limbo, cut off from its natural environment. It was schizoid: darting into association with the public for the candidate's public appearance, then withdrawing from all contact with the outside world for hours on end until the next stop. Sour racket, thought Dale. A hell of a way to run for the Roses.

"Fergie," he yelled above the din in his office, "get me reservations to fly out of here Friday for Los Angeles. In the morning . . . nonstop. I want to arrive there about noon. I'm going to cover that rally at the Garden. Also, get me a flight from L.A. to Denver, any time after midnight Friday night. Put a call in to Lou Wells at NA. And, oh yes, get me my wife Janet . . . at my office in Denver. I want to talk to her right away."

"There's no doubt about it. You guys are getting sloppy," said Dale, looking at each man. "I came out here just to observe, and I'm damn glad I did. Here are the notes I've made. Don't hesitate to interrupt me. We haven't much time, and there are things that must be corrected immediately."

Dale was addressing his TV advance team after the huge network rally in the Los Angeles Garden. It had been in his mind for some time to check the boys on their operation on the road. He did not advise them of his arrival on the Coast, but elected to show up at the hall midafternoon, unannounced.

The rally was over, and the hall was thinning as people made their way unhurriedly to the exits. Tommy Tuttle, television producer of the rally for Dale, had broken down his light box, which cued Conger on his timing, and had collapsed his traveling lights and secured them in their traveling cases. Ham Forrest, who accompanied Conger on the road, also listened, his trench coat draped cape-fashion over his shoulders. Hans Kleinert, the lighting director, sat patiently, a clipboard in his lap. Billy Dee, the able union sound engineer who accompanied the candidate and supervised all public-address systems, rubbed his hands together briskly to rid himself of the dirt from his cables and stood at the edge of the gathering. Dale hiked himself up, sat on the edge of the center camera platform, and spoke to the men before him.

"It's inexcusable, Tommy, not to have made your inventory of the hall's available equipment earlier. What's the use of having Hans come all the way down here when this hall doesn't have a sky ladder? How can he place lights when he can't get to them?"

"A hall this big without a ladder?" asked Tuttle. "Who'da thunk it?"

"Nobody, but it doesn't have one. In the future, hit available gear earlier in the day. Next, the aisle behind Conger was cheated too narrow. I don't care who made you do it, or why. It wasn't wide enough. We had a nose-picker on the tube, and we also had some fat hack with the loudest pair of argyle socks on I've ever seen. If he reached over and pulled them up once, he did it a hundred times during the telecast. All this grew out of Conger's left ear as he talked. So, dammit, don't let anybody con you into a narrower aisle. If the camera position is lower than Conger, sometimes you can get by with the narrow aisle. But only then. Next point: Senator Smear's intro to Conger was way too long." Senator Smear was a private nickname Dale's men had given a notorious party orator, whose entire career had been built on slander and innuendo against members of the opposition. Dale loathed him personally and despised his tactics.

"That son-of-a-bitch," said Tuttle. "He promised me."

"With a guy who's running for President, the only intro I buy is one line, regardless of what anyone, including Conger, wants or tells you. It goes like this: 'It gives me great pleasure to present the next President of the United States . . . Andrew H. Conger.' Anything more than that is garbage—a stage wait. And the introducer does not, I repeat, does *not* have to introduce Susan. She always makes the entrance with Andy. If they don't know who she is by now, we've either blown it, or Conger's living in sin."

"What are you gonna do, Charlie?" asked Tuttle. "Senator Smear promised me—even showed me a copy of his intro in advance. It couldn't have been more than fifteen seconds long. And yet the fat, slobbering bastard talked almost three minutes on the air. I'da like to die when I saw the look on Conger's face."

"I was standing next to him," said Forrest. "It's a good thing nobody heard what he said. Even Susan couldn't calm him down."

"There isn't much you can do," said Dale. "The only thing is to know your man. If you have the least doubt about his holding his remarks to your prescribed length and content, you will have to go back to the old game of moving all the clocks forward before air. In the early days we had to do it all the time. What you do is move every stinking clock forward five minutes. Then you rush up to the guy who's introducing Conger, ask him to set his watch with yours—take a timecheck. Then you get him up at the speaker's podium one minute to air . . . by *his* watch. It's really six minutes before air. At exactly straight up on his watch, you give him the signal. He drones on and on with what you knew was going to be a long introduction. All this time he thinks he's on TV. But hell, you haven't even started yet. When you get down to your TV time, give him a cut. He'll be happy as a clam at high tide, thinking you were graceful and didn't give him a cut signal in the middle of his remarks. After about six minutes the man is bound to be at the end of his intro anyway.

He'll wind up, give a hell of an intro to Conger, and sit down. His Conger intro will come the minute you hit the air. The man you sandbagged because of his verbal diarrhea won't find out he wasn't on TV until the next morning, when his secretary asks him why he wasn't on the Garroway Box from the rally. By that time, you're in tomorrow's town. So, that can be done. Be careful, however, when you do it. And be sure the man you do it to ain't a real good buddy of Andy Conger's. Next: wardrobe. What's the matter with his shirts, Tommy?" Dale asked Tuttle. "Who's laundering them—Susan?"

"Dunno," said Tuttle. "I'll watch it. Can I get Cliff Harley to buy some and keep them with Conger's stuff?"

"You buy them, and give them to Harley to keep for television only. Next point: Ham, I'm surprised at you. When you led Conger out of his dressing room, you were damn near too late getting him at his position for his entrance. What happened? That's inexcusable."

"Phone call to Washington," said Forrest. "He didn't pay any attention to me. I was waving, making signs, pointing at my watch. He kept smiling and nodding at me. But he also kept talking on the phone."

"No more phones in that room. I'll pass the word to Rufe Little and Baldwin's men. It's too dangerous. Next point: We lost the man on his long entrance down the center aisle of the hall. The shots were great while we had him, but we couldn't see him, couldn't pick him out of the mob. Next time, build a ramp down his entrance path about six inches or a foot high. That way his head and shoulders will stick up above the crowd. So will Susan's."

"Fire Department stopped us," said Tuttle. "We wanted to do that. They said it was a hazard . . . said someone might trip and fall when leaving the hall after the rally."

"Did you try a payoff?" asked Dale.

"Nope. Should have," said Tuttle.

"Right," said Dale. "They can be bought."

"In L.A.?" screamed Forrest. "You're crazy!"

"Well, always try," said Dale. "Next point: How in hell did the stills get up on the platform behind the candidate while we were on

TV? What in God's name is going on these days? We have never, I repeat, *never* permitted still photographers, or anyone else, behind the candidate when he's at the rostrum before or during his speech."

"Wilbur Jenkins," said Tuttle. "He's the heavy. I yelled bloody murder, told him everything you've just told us. It made no difference. Jenkins said he had a commitment to *Life* and some other buys to get reverse shots, to get what the hall looked like from the candidate's point of view."

"Does he have any idea what those goddam animals looked like on TV?"

"I've tried to tell you, Charlie," cut in Forrest, "Wilbur Jenkins doesn't have any ideas about anything. He should have been left on the Iceland desk at the State Department."

"I'll talk to him," said Dale. "I want to know immediately if it happens again. How did the fist fight start with the stills on Conger's entrance? Jesus! . . . We had a hell of a time keeping it out of our pictures."

"A local still accidentally hit a traveling still's camera with his elbow while he was getting his shot," said Tuttle. "That started it. Just a misunderstanding."

"Okay. Next point," said Dale, referring to his notes. "The plain-clothes men clearing the way for Conger and Susan on their entrance were much too close to the candidate. In order to shoot Conger we also had to shoot the gumshoes. It looks bad—and is. Also, tell them not to hold out their arms to keep the crowd back. On the tube it looks like Big Brother's coming. Let the crowd mob the man. It ain't going to hurt him, and he loves it. But, we always need those plain-clothes guys ahead of us. Please, however, make sure they walk at least twenty to twenty-five feet ahead of the candidate. Billy Dee, you were on the ragged edge of feedback squeal on the public-address system all night. When it happened the first time, why didn't you back off? Once is understandable, but no more."

"I didn't have nothin' between full on and full off up there," said Dee. The others laughed in their exhaustion. "That was the screwiest sound panel I've ever seen. The minute I backed the sound off the eensiest bit, I couldn't hear nothin', not even in my headset. So I just crossed myself a couple of times and kept it full on, prayin' it wouldn't squeal."

"Was there a house soundman up there?" asked Dale. "Couldn't he check you out?"

"He was asleep, dead drunk when I arrived, and he's still up there, dead drunk and sound asleep. I didn't even find anyone to show my union card to. They was all dead drunk."

"They'd be far from dead drunk if Governor Green were speaking," said Tuttle.

"Amen," said Forrest.

"Okay, guys, we're not here to discuss the union movement in the United States," said Dale. "Oh . . . on Conger's arrival at the rostrum, Tommy, did you brief Senator Smear to wait for him there?"

"I did," Tuttle said, "but he didn't."

"Did you also tell him to be sure and escort Susan to her chair? To wait for her?"

"I did . . . but he didn't."

"Well goddammit, Tommy, you've got to change your line, or something. That is a must, all you guys know that. You've got to put the fear of death in those guys. Tell them we'll see that Conger puts them on the District of Columbia Subcommittee on Public Transportation if they don't behave."

"A better approach than that, one I always use," said Forrest, "is to tell 'em if they're a good boy, Conger's going to make them Secretary of State. Oh, they love that. He's going to have about five Secretaries of State so far."

"Last but not least," Dale said, "is this. Andy Conger did not take his cues for getting off the air from us. I am stunned by what I saw happen tonight. How long has that been going on, Ham?"

"About ten days, off and on," said Forrest. "I don't know what's gotten into him. He's always been so careful about being cut off the air, about always getting off on time. I can't understand it."

"Did you give him everything normally?" Dale asked Forrest. "All the signals?"

"Just like always—but he didn't follow them. I knew he got the signals, because I saw his eye flick to them each time. I'm certain he got the cutoff signal too. I could see the reflection of the light in his face . . . just barely."

Dale considered Forrest's comments for a moment. "God, if this is happening, we're in for a lot of trouble," he said softly. "It's never happened before."

"Do you suppose he's getting the big head?" asked Forrest. "Thinks he doesn't need us any more?"

"Maybe," said Dale. "Maybe. I haven't seen him that much to know." Looking at none of them, he added, "God help us if you're right."

"You mean, God help Andy Conger, don't you, Charlie?" said Forrest seriously.

Dale ignored the comment and looked at his watch. "That's it, guys. I have to run. Actually, it was a good telecast. We've had a lot of compliments on what you've been doing. I do feel, however, you're getting a little lax. Keep these things I've said in mind. You've got the word on October sixteenth in Cleveland for the first debate? I'm going to pull Tommy Tuttle off the road, and he'll report to Cleveland a few days before the telecast. Just in case I need him. Ham, you stay with Conger right straight through. If he sits down somewhere the day before, Sunday, you come on to Cleveland. This will all come to you in memos, but that's my plan. Hans, you'll be in Cleveland, too. C'mon, Tommy, run me out to the airport. I've got to catch a midnight plane for Denver. See you in Colorado Springs, Ham. Good luck, guys."

Sunday on the road with Andrew Conger had a pattern, a feel all its own. It was the only day of the week the staff wasn't called by six in the morning, as per the campaign's mimeo'd itinerary and timetable, which usually listed a breakfast meeting for the candidate. Normally, his audience for such fumbling, eye-rubbing appearances was composed of party workers, precinct captains, and the like. The staff usually attended along with the still-weary press corps, if only to gulp down a cup of horrid coffee and a stale roll before the mad dash to the airport and frantic departure for the grueling daily schedule. On Sundays, however, the halls of the hotel occupied by the staff were quiet, as the occupants on either side of empty corridors slept their lovely sleeps of utter exhaustion.

Local Sunday papers were placed outside each door. Dale often wondered how many of the staff took time out from their intense and grim campaign existence to read the comics. Now and then a door would open, and an adviser would make his way down the hall, tucking his shirt in at the waist as he walked. Such a person obviously had been summoned unexpectedly by the candidate because of a pre-church crisis. Occasionally, the muffled hum of a mimeograph machine could be heard. Probably grinding out a statement which had to be distributed to the press. Likely as not, the girl operating it would be standing at the machine in a house coat, hair in curlers.

Lost and confused local residents were almost standard props on Sunday mornings. Invariably, they were looking for a relative on the staff, and, in the jumble of room assignments, would knock on the wrong door, much to the fury of the staff occupant, who doubtless had left a call for one o'clock in the afternoon.

In the hotel area assigned to the staff, the strange hushed stillness pervaded every room, every activity, every necessary conversation. For the candidate was getting his rest. God knows he deserved it, to say nothing of his wife. In their desire to give Andrew Conger one more minute of blessed sleep, people almost tiptoed. Dozens of rooms away from Conger's suite, someone leaving the door to the hall open from a room where a conversation was in progress would be severely admonished: "Don't you know Conger's still asleep?" Typewriter keys assumed an entirely different sound, as if they were wearing socks in deference to the sleeping prince. On more than one Sunday, however, the staff felt rather ridiculous upon learning the candidate had been awake and up since eight o'clock, working at his desk on a major address.

Such was not the case, however, at the Broadmoor Hotel in Colorado Springs on this particular Sunday. Charles and Janet Dale slept through the crisp, clear, early hours of this day of rest, as did the candidate's staff. And Andrew Conger, the shepherd of his political flock, also slept. He would get up only in time to attend the latest possible church services with his wife, a mandatory ritual which hypocritical Americans had thrust upon every political candidate since ratification of the Constitution had guaranteed them the right to free selection of their national leaders.

It was late morning before Dale and Janet were seated at breakfast in their room. A veteran of many campaigns, Dale dressed immediately on rising, even though his time with Andrew Conger wasn't scheduled until afternoon. Janet watched contentedly as her husband put the cream in her coffee.

"That's enough, dear," she said. "It's thicker down here than at home." She reached into a pocket of her pink lounge robe and offered Dale a cigarette. "Isn't it beautiful after that rain? The mountains are so clear. And look at the new snow on that ridge."

"We went through a couple of cloudbursts last night that were unbelievable. I don't often have to stop the car like that."

"If you'd stayed out here this summer, you'd know all about them."

"Touché. It was a good idea not to bring the kids down. It was great seeing them yesterday, but it's better for me if we have what we can of this day to ourselves." Dale looked at his watch. "I've got to go over my notes sometime before I meet Andy. This is a hell of an important session. I've been waiting weeks to get some of these answers."

"Charlie Junior was so sad to see you leave last night. Did you hear him ask you to quit and come home?"

Dale looked at Janet before answering, remembering the night that Sandra had asked him to quit the campaign. "It's been very tough, I guess, on the children," he said. "Such a long time away from them. God, how I wish it were all over. And the panic and pressure have just barely started."

"Watch yourself, Charlie. Don't let it get under your skin."

"I won't. But I'll be damn glad when this first debate is behind us. You have no idea of the magnitude of this thing. No one has, including Andy. He could win or lose the whole campaign in those two hours on October sixteenth. It's almost too important—I mean, there's a frightful danger here of overemphasis—distorting all the values and the real choice the voters must make. Oh well, it's got to be done now. I have a session with Rufe Little and Ab Shepherd before the Conger meeting. We'll get a lot of agreements before we see Andy."

"Are they here too?" asked Janet.

"Everybody's out here. This is the first opportunity to appraise the campaign so far. Andy's been swingin' now for three weeks. It's time to take stock. That's why he sat down here . . . away from the idiots and time-wasters in Washington."

It was a pleasant, peaceful interlude together. Janet ordered another pot of coffee and read the paper. Dale worked at his notes for the meeting, occasionally looking up and asking his wife a question relating to his business problems or the children. It was still some time before he was scheduled to meet with Little and Shepherd when there was a quiet knock at the door. Dale raised his voice slightly and said, "Come in."

Cliff Harley walked into the room. He looked clean-shaven and relaxed—but very tired. He smiled upon seeing Janet and greeted her warmly. Then, with a look of apology, he turned to Dale. "I hate to break this up, Charlie, but The Man wants to see you right away."

Dale looked at his watch. "Now?" he asked. "It's only one o'clock. We weren't supposed to meet until three, I thought."

"I know," said Harley, "but he's changed all his appointments. There's a crisis, and he wants you to have your time before the day goes down in flames."

"Okay," said Dale. "Jan, call Little and Ab and tell them to meet me outside Conger's suite. I'll be there in five minutes, Cliff."

"Conger wants to see you alone. No Little, no Shepherd," Harley said. "Make it as fast as you can. He's waiting. Nice to see you, Janet." He turned and was gone.

"Goddammit" said Dale. "This is one meeting I didn't want to have with him alone. I wanted Little and Shepherd with me to back me up on a couple of points." As he talked, he whipped a tie out of his suitcase and gathered his papers into a Manila folder. "There are some things I haven't even had a chance to go over with Little," he said, knotting his tie. "Well, I can't help that now. Whatever we decide, that's the way it'll be." Janet watched the tension mounting in her husband. These poor people, she thought. How do they stand it?

"Will you work on my space out of Denver tonight?" Dale asked. "I haven't had time to do anything on that either. Here's the folder on the possible flights to Chicago, nonstop. You'll see a check mark after the two I've requested. Try to get me on the late one, if you can. I don't know how long I'll be with Andy. Why don't you stand by, and I'll come back here. Oh . . . call Ab and tell him to call Little and explain what's happened. Find out if they'll be free later." He turned and smiled at his wife. "Wish me luck."

"You'll do better alone than with the other men there," she said. "Tell Andy the gals in Denver are working hard for him." Dale was gone, walking toward Conger's suite. Harley met him in the outer "buffer" room and sent him into the living room, which was warm with brilliant sunlight, and commanded a superb view of the mountains behind the hotel's grounds.

Conger was seated at a large mahogany secretary which had been placed in front of the French windows at the far end of the room. It provided him with a pleasant work area, and still left much of the room free for callers and conferences. The candidate greeted Dale, and motioned him to the conversational area comprised of two couches on opposite sides of a low coffee table and two matching wing-back chairs.

"This is a nice suite, Andy," Dale said, as he spread his notes out before him.

"It's Sue's and my favorite," said Conger. "We come here a lot when we want to get away from everybody."

"Did you have a chance to stop by the ranch?" Dale asked.

Conger frowned. "No, dammit, there wasn't time in the schedule. The rain delayed us last night. Charlie, there's something wonderful about this part of the country. When I come back I can even smell it . . . in the air. Especially after a rain."

"Janet and I love it out here. She came down with me," said Dale, watching Conger yawn as he spoke. He went on: "The reports from New York on the network rally Friday night are excellent. You had the highest rating so far in the campaign, and the number of sets in use were very high."

"How'd we do against the competition?" asked Conger.

" 'The Underworld' show beat you, but you grabbed a fat share from the other network, and you ate into 'The Underworld's' regular audience. Sets in use at this time are considerably higher than they were on the kickoff telecast. The reports from Washington were that the pictures were excellent and that you delivered an effective address." Dale paused, then added, "Naturally, we were all sorry you were cut off the air."

"Was I?" Conger asked with surprise. "I didn't know that. How much was I cut?"

"We went out on the long applause after your cheer line on America never knuckling under to an aggressive power. Ham Forrest tells me he's sure you saw the time cues clearly. Did you get mixed up—did we do something wrong?"

Conger yawned again. "No," he said, shaking his head back and forth trying to clear away the fatigue, "it was my fault. I saw the time cues but ignored them."

"If I may say so, Andy, it's the first time that's happened on a network telecast. It's a lot better if we can go off clean."

"I know, I know," Conger said impatiently. "I was mad at that fat bastard Franklin and his goddam garbage-long introduction to me. I thought you fellows had that sort of thing under control. I had to get through some of my advance text for the traveling press, so I just kept going. Can't your men throttle those goddam long-winded bastards like Franklin?"

"That's one on us. We blew it. No use hashing over it, but our buddy Senator Smear promised he'd limit his intro to fifteen seconds. What else can I say? I'm sorry."

"Forget it," said Conger brusquely, irritated by the information there'd been negative reaction to the cutoff in the East. "This is an order. Franklin never appears on TV with me again during the campaign—ever."

"Yes, sir."

"But that's not why you're out here. How are the plans for the debate coming?"

"Fine. Slow, but fine. Certain preferences of yours should be settled now before we go much further. I have a list of things, and I'll cover it as quickly as possible."

"Take all the time you want, Charlie," said Conger, leaning his head back on the high wing of the chair. "I have sensed a great swell of excitement and anticipation, under this campaign focussing toward the debate. Am I correct? Do you feel it?"

"Yes, I do. And I'm interested to know you feel the same thing," Dale said seriously. "I believe that already they've become almost too important. I can't overemphasize the incredible spotlight and audience the first debate will command. I could tell you otherwise to put you at ease, but if I did, I would be doing you a disservice. The debate will hold the attention of every voter in the United States. The estimates on television's audience alone go as high as one hundred million viewers."

"That's why I wanted to meet with you alone. From this point forward, whenever possible, this debate is between you and me. I want you to memo me on every meeting, every decision, every thought or opinion you have."

"I can start right now, before we get into my list, by saying I strongly recommend you use a sun lamp every day between now and the first debate. I hoped the other two guys would be present just to back me up on this. I feel it's very important, and others agree with me."

"I won't use one. Out of the question. It's silly, and phoney."

"It really isn't, Andy. And I'm sorry you feel strongly about it.

Forget it. Maybe you can get some color in the motorcades. There's very little contrast between your face and that shirt you're wearing." Conger smiled, as he always did when Dale talked to him as "talent," as a performer. He looked ill at ease, and was.

"Okay, Charlie," said Conger, "that's enough of that. What's next?"

Dale smiled, shaking his head slowly from side to side. "Honest, Andy, it's important. But the hell with it. Well, first I have assumed you would prefer standing to being seated for the debates . . . when you are speaking. I take this cue from the fact that you've never sat for a news conference."

"Correct. I think standing would be better. How far am I separated from my opponent? On the stage?"

"I don't know yet. We haven't seen any set designs. Do you have any feelings on this?"

"Not seriously. But I do feel there should be some separation, a good feeling of physical separateness. I don't want the other man crowding me—at my elbows, in the corner of my eye—while I'm speaking."

"I'll keep it in mind and keep you advised. Before we leave design, I assure you there will be no pleats or curtains behind you on this telecast—or any other." Conger smiled and said nothing. "We have arbitrarily taken the position there will be no audience. We see no way to equally and safely apportion the seats for each candidate's supporters in such an audience section. I personally feel the audience is all over the country, at home, in front of their TV sets, in groups of two or three people. That is your audience. I feel an audience in the studio would split your allegiance, as it tends to do at a rally. For the debate, our camera approach is entirely one of you and your opponent working to separate cameras, concentrating on the audience viewing at home. Also, in the same meeting, we knocked out any private forums. This debate will be presented by the television industry."

"Are you having trouble controlling it from my point of view? Are those NA bastards giving you a bad time?"

"Yes . . . and no," said Dale. "I'm on top of it, but I have to watch them like a hawk."

"Don't be afraid to call for help if you need it. Don't let those bastards walk all over you, Charlie. There's a lot at stake. Do you need help now?"

"No, I don't think so. But I'm not afraid to blow the whistle if I do. I'll know more in a week or so."

"Fine. What's next?"

"I need your thoughts on sponsorship. The networks have presented their position as follows: 'There is historical precedent for sponsorship. The conventions are sponsored, the Inaugurations in January have been sponsored, and important trips by the President have been sponsored.' "

Conger reflected on Dale's statement. He rubbed his forehead between his eyebrows with his index finger, shutting his eyes as he did so. "I think the continuity of the debate issues would be destroyed by commercials of any kind," he said.

"They're only talking about a fifteen-second mention at the opening and closing of the two hours, Andy. No commercials once it starts. Just a tasteful mention that so-and-so is bringing the telecast to the public."

"I'm against it. How do you feel?"

"I'm dead against it," said Dale. "If television can't donate two hours once every four years without ringing up the cash register on a sale, the industry is doomed."

"How are they doing on clearing the two-hour period?"

"It's coming fine. It looks as if it'll be eight to ten. Couldn't be better. The next item's on format. We've had several discussions on how to select which candidate speaks first. And the feeling is whoever speaks first should also speak last. Little says he's discussed this with you."

"Those are my feelings. I want to speak last on the debate, have the last word on the air, get the last lick in with the audience before we go off. Is this what Little said you'd settle with a coin-toss?"

"Yes. It seems too simple, but it's probably the best way. We thought we'd toss a coin in Cleveland when we meet there Tuesday. If I win, I'll elect to have you speak first and last."

"Fine. That's the way I want it. Does the other side understand there are to be no notes, no written texts, no reference material brought to the telecast? It was under those conditions we both accepted the debate invitation."

"Yes, sir, they do. It was discussed at a meeting in Washington. With your feeling about limiting the number of debates, the next point I have is whether or not there is to be a restriction on subject matter. Domestic, foreign, and the like?"

"Why not make the first hour on domestic issues, and the last hour on foreign policy?"

"That's excellent."

"Do you see anything wrong in that approach?"

"No, sir, I don't. You've said all along that the campaign will be won or lost on the foreign policy issue. Therefore, even if you don't win the toss on speaking last, you will be closing with strength on foreign affairs. The moderator would be the timekeeper, and simply state it was time to go into the second half of the debate and announce the new subject."

"That's the way I see it. Let's lock that up. That'll be it." Conger put his slippered feet up on the edge of the coffee table. "Next," he said, looking at his wedding ring.

"This sounds silly, and I apologize in advance for taking up your time with it. In the case of this debate, however, it's damn important. I've had a run-in with George Pinnell as to which is your best profile. I just want you to know I don't agree with George, and, if we win that placement toss, we'll place you so your best profile, in our opinion, can be favored with your primary camera. I'm not going to tell you which one because I don't want to inhibit you. But we've discussed this before."

"We have, and I know which one," said Conger, smiling. "It's not the one Pinnell thinks is best. Go ahead without letting him bother you."

"I have a memo here covering the various approaches to the rebuttal and rejoinder principles," said Dale, handing Conger his copy. "I know you feel strongly there should be the opportunity of rebuttal on every statement, and I agree. Perhaps you could look this over in the next few days, and get word to me which pattern you prefer. It gives you a picture of the various alternatives insofar as time values are concerned. For instance, if the statement is five minutes, perhaps the rebuttal should be two minutes. Then it could go back to the first man for a rejoinder, a counterrebuttal of one minute. That sort of thing. It's covered in this memo, with ten or so time possibilities." Conger nodded and closed the folder, placing it on the floor beside his chair.

"Is the NA crew predominantly for us or against us?" asked Conger.

"What do you mean, Andy?"

"Do you know the political registration of the technical crew, the cameramen, the technicians who will be used on the debate?"

"No, I don't. I doubt if the actual crew to be used has been selected, down to the last man."

"I want you to ask NA for that information. Let's start out knowing our enemy."

"This could hurt you Andy," said Dale. "These guys, as you know, are all union, and if they felt you were suspicious of them, it could backfire. If I ask NA for this information, the word will get out."

"Let it," said Conger. "If anything goes wrong, I want this information in my possession before the debate starts. So get it for me."

"It will be embarrassing, Andy."

"Get it."

"Yes, sir." Dale paused, obediently made a note, and referred to his papers. "As long as we're on the subject of the crew and the production of the debate," Dale continued, "we have a decision to make on whether or not reaction shots are to be permitted during the telecast."

"What do you mean?" asked Conger.

"When you are making a statement, talking at your lectern, is the camera permitted to go off you and take a picture of the other man's reaction to what you're saying? And vice versa. If the other man is talking, should the camera ever leave him to take a picture of you listening to him, reacting to what he says? You may want to agree to the right to make notes during the telecast of what the other man says. That's not bringing notes to the debate. The feeling of NA is that the audience expects reaction shots, and they are insisting on the right to leave either candidate whenever they desire to do so, in order to take a picture or reaction shot of the candidate not speaking."

"What is your opinion?"

Dale paused, shifted his weight forward, cocked his head, and looked slightly past Conger—beyond his left shoulder—as he collected his thoughts. "It's difficult to put into words, Andy. I have very strong feelings against the use of reaction shots. I would say the same thing if I were working for the other man. There's nothing biased or partisan about my position. I feel this is not a show in the sense of show business, not a popularity contest between two men for a new Cadillac. It is an occasion of the most profound importance. Every word said by you or the other man can influence a voter one way or the other. I feel it is wrong to rob you, or the other man, for that matter, of the opportunity for visual emphasis of your point of view by removing the camera from you at that precise moment. My reasoning goes like this: If you're saying something which is of sufficient bite or importance to provoke a reaction from your opponent, then, by definition, I feel the camera should be on you. That's the very time the audience at home should see your face. That's the convincer, your day in court to score against your opponent. I agree that when a debate is held in front of a live audience in a hall, the person sitting in the audience has his personal choice of watching the debater speaking, or the other man listening. But, when he takes a look at the man listening—for his reaction to what the speaker is saying—he also has the speaker in view. The speaker is never lost to his eye. He stays in the frame.

I have asked NA if they can physically position the cameras and lecterns so that when a reaction shot of one man is taken, we shoot across the other man speaking at his lectern, don't lose him entirely."

"And? . . ."

"They don't think it's possible. I do. I am dead against depriving either candidate of the right to make his most telling points to the camera. I feel the television cameras should be scrupulously objective reporters, not editors. In addition, what television director has the clairvoyance, the knowledge of the political issues, the sophistications, the nuances of logic and statement structure, to be able to discern the exact moment at which he should cut away from a presidential candidate? I defy any director in the business today to say he'll do it without bias, without injury—albeit unintentional —to one candidate or the other."

Conger listened thoughtfully as Dale spoke. He remained silent for a moment after his television adviser had concluded. "Is this a big issue?" he asked.

"Very big. So far I have kept silent. NA says they will take reaction shots whenever they feel it will help the telecast. Whatever that means. That in this day and age of television the audience expects them. I say the audience expects nothing from the first presidential debate in history until they see it. The camera should be a viciously honest, reporting, eye-witness pencil—nothing more."

"I agree," said Conger. "Keep me posted. Naturally, we won't take a walk, but make careful notes of everything said about the matter. And who says it."

"I'll do what I can to get what we call a 'two-shot,' a picture which keeps both candidates in the frame at all times, even when they cut away, as they insist on doing. Lou Wells, the head of News at NA, is the heavy so far. He says they are controlling the telecast, and will do what they feel is best."

Reflectively, Conger tapped his fingers on the arm of his chair. "This whole debate situation seems to be an issue of fighting for control, does it not?" Dale nodded in agreement. Conger continued. "Control all the way up and down the line. Control in everything, every item of everything. Listening to what you've been saying, Charlie, it appears to me it's two against one as we start. The network and the other man."

"I'd hate to go that far, but I must admit it's been rough," said Dale.

"Do I control more of the two hours with a freewheeling exchange with my opponent, face to face, in the style of the Lincoln-Douglas debates, or do I control more with a news panel as the major backbone of the presentation?"

"A few weeks ago," said Dale, "you felt you'd feel better with the news panel, that a format using a panel would bring out most of your strengths, and most of the other man's weaknesses."

"Now I'm not so sure," said Conger. "Perhaps there's a better format." He paused, then added, "For me."

Dale was surprised and shocked at Conger's switch in signals. He got the feeling that this was the real reason Conger wanted the meeting alone with him—that all along he'd been meaning to bring this up. And bring it up with the men absent who were not directly involved with television.

"I know there's a feeling the classic Lincoln-Douglas approach may favor my opponent. I also realize there is strong sentiment the working press must be represented. I have no control, however, over the questions from the newsmen. They could be all hostile—or all friendly, for that matter. But that's a risk, a gamble. In a classic form of two hours of pure debate, face to face, freewheeling—perhaps even direct interrogation of one candidate by the other with just the moderator as a timekeeper or referee—I think I might do better, control a higher percentage of the total time period. What do you think, Charlie?"

"My instant reaction is favorable. I think if you announce this at a press conference, you will stun the opposition. More importantly, however, I think you will come off better in the telecast with this format. I somehow get the feeling the more this takes the classic form of a Lincoln-Douglas debate, the better off you will be. I think the idea of direct interrogation of one candidate by the other is excellent. No one in between. Just the moderator to keep score of the length of statements. On rebuttal and rejoinder. I have a feeling you can get more penetration of attitude and issue that way than with any other approach. Why put a news panel in to clutter it up? There must be just as good a way to get spontaneity, conflict of point of view. It seems to me it would be exciting to slug it out toe to toe. It sure would separate the men from the boys."

"The only danger is in its getting to be a shouting match below the dignity of the future President," said Conger. "I think the seriousness of the occasion, however, will offset that possibility. Would it be difficult to shoot down the news panel at this late date?"

"Not at all," said Dale. "There's been no public statement on the format that I know of. I think the networks will have mixed feelings. On one hand, they won't be able to merchandise their favorite pretty-boy newscasters, but on the other, they will be able to pull out all the stops on the publicity—describing it as a classic presentation of the historical Lincoln-Douglas debates. I think they'll be delighted. And I think the other man will be too. I strongly recommend you jump the gun and announce it as a condition of your debate appearance. Oh, I know we're supposed to clear it with the other guys first, but they've broken every rule in the book. Why not announce that you see no reason to hide behind the skirts of the nation's press corps, and feel certain Governor Green would not want to be accused of this either. Jenkins will have a hot potato to handle for a few days, calming the beasts in the press compound. But that's all."

"I'm not appearing on this debate for the press, Charlie. Let's get that straight. This is television's show—all the way. If this campaign proves one thing, I think it will show the emergence of television as the dominant factor in the American public's vote-deciding process. I think this campaign marks the beginning of the end of the print media's hold on the ability to influence the voter. The debates will push television far out in front, more than can be measured until it's all over." Conger smiled, pleased. "I like this switch to the free exchange without a news panel. I like it very much. You work out the statement with Jenkins for my approval. We'll release it to the press this afternoon for the Monday A.M.'s. Anything else?"

"No . . . except take care of yourself." Dale started to rise, but Conger motioned to him to remain seated.

"I have something, Charlie. And it must remain confidential. I don't want to discuss it with anyone on the staff. No one." Dale looked at Conger intently. Slowly, Conger rubbed one hand against the other as he spoke. "There will be only one debate. I will accept no more. Which is why we have spent this time together. And if you need more, let my people know. There will be but one debate. On October sixteenth—in Cleveland. I am going to announce my decision on this tomorrow."

"It would make my job a lot easier if you could hold off on it until Thursday, Andy. I've got the survey in Cleveland all day Tuesday. They'll be at me like wild cougars if you've made the announcement before the survey. I think a lot of things we'll be deciding would blow sky high if they knew there was only going to be one debate. They'd cut me down with anything they could get their hands on."

Conger smiled. "I appreciate what you're going through, and I'm grateful. I know it won't be easy. All right, we'll hold off. But act accordingly. You can assume I'll announce it Thursday. Things are going too well to agree to more than one of these trials by television."

"Fine. That'll make everything okay. I probably won't see you for such an uninterrupted period again until the day of the debate. If I must, I'll contact Harley. But I'll be busy as hell between now and the sixteenth. From now on, it'll be the crisis of the moment. I'm going to Cleveland tonight, stay there a day or so on the survey of the debate, and then on to Philadelphia to make up the campaign train. Do you have any thoughts on that?"

"No . . . Nothing different from past years. But, God, haven't they invented any loud-speakers that are better than the ones we had all the trouble with before—from the rear platform?"

"Interestingly enough, there are some new ones. And we plan to use them."

"Get as much light on me as possible under the canopy on the rear platform. We'll be campaigning later in the afternoon than we did in past years. I'll be speaking from the train many times in darkness. Get all the light on me you can."

"Fine. Will do. One thing: Do you plan to bring Sue with you to the debate studio? It will make some difference in the planning of our physical arrangements."

"No. Sue will stay at the hotel. I'll come to the studio by myself. You and I will probably ride over together."

"Very good," said Dale. He looked at Andrew Conger, head back in the chair, chin slightly raised. God, this man is exhausted, thought Dale, even at this hour of the afternoon. Bone weary, so tired a full night's rest doesn't make a dent in his fatigue. Dale reflected on the endless talks, meetings, and conferences which would be held, the momentous decisions which would be reached before Andrew Conger's head knew a pillow again on this, his day of rest. And Harley had mentioned a crisis. Conger seemed preoccupied, engrossed in his own thoughts. Dale didn't want to break the spell by interrupting. Conger brought his head down, and his eyes fell on Dale. "I was just thinking," he said, "of the meeting eight years ago, almost to the day, when you and I were in Colorado Springs. Remember?"

"Very well," said Dale, smiling. "The Senate race."

"It was a beautiful afternoon, a Friday, I believe." Conger was talking to himself more than to Dale. "We'd come down from Cheyenne, and the rally was in the little town square. There were kids running all over, the trees were turning gold and brown, and I spoke in a little band shell kind of thing. I remember a whole bunch of students from Colorado College lined up after my speech."

"Remember the traveling stills who pleaded with you to walk across the square to the bazaar some church was holding? You were mad as hell, but they insisted. Those pictures they got with those elderly people, and those great faces of the women with those pies and jellies. . . . They were the best pictures taken during the campaign."

"Yes . . . I remember. Sue thought it was terrible. But, you know something? I knew some of those people. There was the wife of a blacksmith who's been on the ranch for years. And a woman who used to come out and cook for us in the fall. I've got one of those pictures with me in the Stetson the 'stills' put on me hanging in the upstairs study in Washington." Conger's eyes were bright, his body became animated. "What do you say, Charlie, let's have a drink. How about a vodka and tonic? Just one. It'd really hit the spot, wouldn't it?"

"You're on. Here, let me make them. You want any lime?" asked Dale, moving toward the cocktail tray.

"No thanks. That was eight years ago, Charlie," he said, not turning, talking to the wall. "We've been through a lot together. Some big ones. Some rough ones. It was very different then. Why, in that Colorado Springs speech I'm not sure we had even radio covering us. No television, no newsreels . . . just talkin' to the people."

"You had radio. I remember settling a fight between two local stations as to where their mikes would go on the funny little rostrum in the band shell."

"I miss you, Charlie, sometimes, on the road. It seems odd not seeing your face at the meetings, at the stops."

"I feel strange myself not being with you. I envy Ham Forrest. It sure is different this time. This campaign is a monster. I just couldn't handle it from the road any more, Andy."

"Of course not," said Conger. "This debate is the most important responsibility you have. You belong wherever the debate takes you." He paused. "Forrest does well, but it's not the same. There are a lot of new faces."

"Tell you what," said Dale. "After the debate I'll take a breather from Washington, and come out and travel with you for three or four days. I like to check up on the boys anyway. It'll do me good to get out in the weeds again. You know, my favorite towns: East Jesus, Montana; Scattersand, Nebraska; Nowhere, Oklahoma."

"Hope this debate won't throw you too much of a curve in Cleveland."

"We'll make it all right. I agree that the debate will be a little more complicated than that speech in the band shell downtown, Andy, but we'll make it."

Conger smiled, raised his glass. "Fine. Cheers, Charlie . . . cheers."

"Cheers, boss. Give 'em hell." And Andrew Conger relaxed. He had stolen eight minutes to relax and have a drink with an old friend.

"Tell me the story about the three old ladies in St. Petersburg, Charlie. You know—the three ladies who came up to you just as I was entering the ball park? That's one of my favorites. Tell it to me again."

"I knew it would happen," said Dale. "Little is mad as hell Conger's thrown out the question-and-answer element in the format. Wants to know why I gave in on killing the news panel. Says every paper in the country will be down on him. Goddammit, I can't control who does or doesn't attend a Conger meeting."

Finally, thought Janet, he's unwinding. He'd been so quiet when he returned to the room. And how quickly he'd suggested they go to a nearby stable and rent the horses. Somehow he needs this very much, she thought, looking up at him, the mountains already in shadow behind him in the slanting afternoon sun.

It was true Dale had been silent, uncommunicative, on his return to the suite. It seemed terribly important to him to change into the riding clothes they'd brought from Denver and leave the hotel as soon as possible. With barely a glance at the horses, Dale had selected a Morgan gelding and suggested a Palomino mare for Janet. He seemed preoccupied, withdrawn, as they left the town behind them. They chose one of the trails at the base of the mountains behind the hotel. It was only when the buildings were out of sight that he seemed to come out of his shell. Upon rounding a gentle curve, he pointed ahead to a flat promontory, a spot of lush green grass at the side of a stream, shaded by brilliantly colored trees.

They cantered to the quiet, secluded spot and dismounted. Dale tethered the horses to one side as Janet stretched out contentedly on her back, facing the foothills below Pike's Peak, glistening in a white mantle from the previous night's snowfall. Dale lit a cigarette for her, then walked to the water's edge. He stared into the stream a long time. Then he turned and told Janet of his time with Conger and his subsequent session with Wilbur Jenkins on the debate release for the press. He described his meeting with Rufe Little and Shepherd, and how he had taken the full brunt of the changes Conger had requested. Little had implied that Dale had "gone it alone," with no regard for previous staff decisions and recommendations.

"I didn't go off on my own at all. I listened to what a presidential candidate had on his mind, and I happened to agree with him. Conger's smarter than all of us put together. He hit it right on the button, and I agreed. And it's final. The statement is being mimeo'd now. Little and Shepherd are just miffed they weren't in on it. I can't help that. I suppose right now they're in there trying to change Conger's mind. Jesus! . . . Can't one single thing remain firm around here?"

Janet watched Dale pace at the edge of the stream. "Your meeting with Andy accomplished everything you expected, didn't it?" she asked.

"Yes. I've got a nightmare ahead of me in Cleveland. . . . But the session with him was good. I could almost see him unwind with my naked eye. That poor bastard. How in the hell do they go through it? He ended up by asking me to tell that silly-ass story about the three old ladies in St. Petersburg. You know, the ones who had the bottles of cough syrup they said could have cured Wendell Willkie? Andy laughed till tears ran down his face . . . and I'll bet he's heard me tell it ten times."

"You're good for him. I'm glad you're in this campaign."

"Thanks for saying that, but I'm not. Oh, I guess I am. But the egos, the pressure, the changes, the infighting! . . . It gets to the point I can hardly control myself. On top of it all, I've got this mastodon of a debate ahead of me." Dale stopped to watch a squirrel rustling in the leaves at the base of a tree nearby. "By the way, thanks for taking care of the plane reservations, Jan. And Shepherd said you were very helpful screening those people who somehow got to his suite."

"You don't know what it means to feel a part of what you're doing," said Janet. "In campaign after campaign, I sit on the sidelines, or attend meals with you while you talk of places, dates and issues, and people who sound as strange as if they were from another planet. You have no idea how isolated, how intense you become, how separated from what you're doing I become—and feel. Everything's so confidential . . . so inside. It's the only time I never know what to do, when to laugh . . . or talk . . . or shut up. God, if I was a help to Abner, I'm delighted."

"You were. Very much so," said Dale.

"And let me tell you, Charlie, it's been swell to get away from the kids for a while. I'll admit Denver isn't quite the cowtown I thought it was, but getting down here, even this close, to talk to some adults again, people from the East that I've known, it's been such a good day."

"For someone as jazzy as you, that's quite a statement. I thought you'd have brought Denver to its knees by now."

"I've been busy down at the store—remember?"

"How true. Do you like being a career mother?"

"I love it. But get your fanny back at that desk as fast as you can, hear?"

"Will do," said Dale, smiling. He became serious. "Boy, this crew registration thing Andy wants from NA! It can be a terrible boomerang. How in the hell can I get the political registration of every goddam NA crewman without hurting Conger? I just can't think of a way. Why is he so suspicious? If I told him what might be going on between Green and NA, he'd really flip."

"Do you think it's wise not to tell him?" asked Janet. Dale had also told her of Amos Whiting's remarks to Wilbur Jenkins.

"It's a risk I'm taking," said Dale. "I can't see how it will help him to know if it's true . . . or untrue. If it's true, I don't see how we can capitalize on it, except to walk off the debate and charge collusion between Green and NA. That's a hell of a serious thing. It would shatter the country, stun the public. If it's untrue, it would only irritate Conger, put him on the defensive, make him even more suspicious than he is, going into the debate. I just think it's better to try and handle it without his knowing. If I'm wrong, Jan, I'm really wrong." Dale paused and watched the quiet water. Janet's mare rattled her bridle as she tugged at a leafy bush, still green. "But this political registration thing is entirely different. Conger has asked for this. I'm duty bound to deliver it to him."

"You'll find a way."

"Oh, I'll get it somehow." Dale paced once more, talking all the while. "All this effort . . . all this fierce intensity, this dedication. And, lets face it, it's probably the same on the Green staff. Yet millions of people couldn't care less. Millions won't even get off their dead asses to vote! What does it all mean? What does it prove?"

"You just do your best, old boy, and then go on to the next thing."

"But what is the next thing? What do I go on to?"

"What do you want, Charlie? Are you interested in our marriage? In me?" Janet asked, looking full into his eyes as he stood facing her, arrested momentarily in his pacing.

Dale met her gaze. He stood with thumbs tucked in the waistband of his frontier pants, shoulders slouched, his weight on his right leg. And then, looking away, he spoke quietly:

"I want to go home, Jan. With you. I want to go home and sleep for a year. I don't want to talk to anyone but you and the children for a year. I'm tired—tired of fighting. Tired of driving others, driving myself." Dale still kept his eyes on the ground. "I had a blow-up with Rufe Little a few weeks ago in Washington. I said a lot of things to him I shouldn't have said. That's not like me. I really like Rufe, and I know I hurt him. Some day I'll find the right time to tell him how sorry I am. But why did I hurt him? I hope it's because I'm tired of keeping up with other minds that want money, power, success, my spot, just a little bit more than I want it."

Janet tried to interrupt but Dale went on. "Something's happened to this country, Jan. We're experts in everything but ourselves. We're trying to hit the moon when we can't even find the true values on this earth—trying to find a way to sustain life in outer space while we destroy life here. We are becoming a people who are soulless, suspicious, mistrustful of one another. Yelling, coarse, grabbing, running, screaming, get-'em, get-'em people. Why doesn't someone, somewhere, yell, 'Stop! Stop, slow down?' Why doesn't somebody blow the whistle?" He looked across to his wife.

"I know what you mean," Janet said. "Darling, I want to help you find what you're looking for. I don't really care about power or money or success. But I do care about love and about you."

Dale walked over to her and took Janet's hand in his. "I've been a fool, Janet. I want to come home. I want to be in our own house where I can love you quietly for a long, long time."

Janet felt her eyes glistening. "I know you can't really come home until the campaign's over. But let's go home now. Tonight."

Gently, he pulled her to her feet. For a long moment the full length of his body pressed against hers. Then they moved apart. "Come on. I'll race you back."

"According to the week-in-review wrap-ups," said Fred Morgan, lighting a cigar and looking over at his wife Benita, "Green is coming up fast. Polls don't show it, but there seems to be a public acceptance of Green out on the campaign trail. A ground swell may be starting."

Benita said nothing. She continued to work at the Braille transcription of a Dickens novel. Benita donated considerable time to the work of transcribing important literature into the raised dot characters. In the room's silence she raised her head. She absently twirled her stylus on the corner of her slate as she studied her husband.

It had been a lovely Sunday spent with friends on Long Island Sound on a racing yawl out of Oyster Bay. It would be their last cruise of the season, for already there had been a crisp autumn nip in the air. As the magnificent sky over the harbor and the low hills had blurred into black, pierced by twinkling lights across the Sound, they had left for home. It had been Benita's idea to work an hour in the study, and Fred had joined her for coffee and reading.

Fred's involvement in the political campaign—or what she knew of it or suspected—troubled Benita deeply. She had given him every opportunity to reveal his discussions with Governor Green, but, for the first time in all their years of marriage, he had been uncommunicative about his activities. She had heard snatches of conversation between her husband and Lou Wells regarding North American and Green. What she had heard had shocked her. Her questions had drawn nothing but noncommittal answers from him. She was convinced Fred was involved far more deeply than he had admitted, she was convinced her husband had become involved in something she didn't like at all. She hoped Fred had sense enough to stay clear of any compromising relationships.

"What is this thing between you and Governor Green, Fred?" Benita began. "Ever since that night in Chicago you've been so tight-mouthed about it. Are you still seeing him when you go to Washington?"

"Sometimes," Fred answered, not looking up from his paper.

"You're not trying to swing anything his way through NA, are you?" she asked, throwing it out in a quiet voice.

"Of course not," Morgan answered. "What makes you say a thing like that?"

"I don't know. I feel it. You've been distant about the whole thing. I've overheard you talking to Lou Wells, and then Green . . . and then mentions of the debate. It would be a terrible thing, Fred, if somehow you felt you had the right to place all your facilities at the disposal of Green. You have enormous power—you know that. You could almost break one or the other of these two men. This is the first time we haven't both been inclined toward the same man. But even if I liked Green instead of Conger, I couldn't conceive of sitting by while you manipulated NA or your programs to favor a candidate."

If Fred Morgan had one love in life beyond his passion for North American, it was Benita. He did not answer, and his over-long pause gave him away. With a sharp movement, Benita raised her head, and removed her glasses. She folded the two earpieces together as she looked with love at the man she'd been married to for twenty-three years. Then she spoke.

"If I thought you were involved in anything as evil as that, Fred, I think I'd leave you."

15

October in Cleveland

"Paging Mr. Charles Dale . . . Paging Mr. Charles Dale. . . . Will Mr. Charles Dale please report to the Passenger Service Counter of United Airlines."

Dale heard the message as he walked toward the baggage area in the Cleveland airport. In a matter of moments he was on the phone to Murray Smith. "You son-of-a-bitch!" said Smith.

"What's the matter? Sorry I'm late. Socked in at O'Hare in Chicago for five hours," said Dale. "I thought I might have to take a train. How are you, Murray, and where are you?"

"I'm in the Sheraton-Cleveland Hotel, you bastard," said Smith. "Get your ass in here. I've been on the phone to Washington—to the Coast and Green—about that goddam change your candidate made in the format, throwing out the news panel. Why the hell don't you warn a buddy?"

"Oh . . . That! Is that what you're pissed off about? We just thought it might make for a better telecast. You know, onward and upward on TV, and all that sort of thing."

"Horse crap! Get in here. We've got a lot to decide between ourselves before we see Wells or anyone from NA. They're screaming at me to go over to the studio. I've stayed right in this stinkin' room waiting for you all day."

"I'm taking the limo in, Murray. I'll give you a call when I get there."

"I'll be in the bar, you traitor. You welcher."

"When is that stupid candidate of yours going to go with something—stick with an agreement?" asked Smith, looking at Dale across their table in the cocktail lounge.

"You're talking about the next President of the United States," said Dale. "You know goddam well this change is good for your man. You were the first guy to toss in the idea of a classic debate format, à la Lincoln-Douglas. Don't kid me. You guys love this change, now don't you? Don't you? Come on . . . admit it."

"Well . . ." said Smith, "originally we did want this. But lately the press has been so down on your man we were beginning to relish the idea of the news panel."

"Do you have an okay on the change from Washington?"

Smith hung his head in mock shame. "Well—as a matter of fact—yes."

Dale laughed. "You bastard! All this yelling and screaming, and I'll bet Happy Joe Green leaped through the phone giving you an okay."

"Do you have any more changes you're going to spring on us?" asked Smith.

"No more that I know of. Of course, I haven't seen the candidate for almost twenty-four hours. That's a long time to let him roam free without a television man at his elbow."

"A very long time . . . in this campaign."

Wait till Conger announces only one debate on Thursday, thought Dale. He reached for his condensed notes of the Conger meeting. "You and I have, indeed, some things to go over," he said. "I've got some alternatives on the form the two hours can take in straight face-to-face exchange. It'd be nice if you could get on the horn first thing in the morning and get some opinions from somebody. That way we can hit NA with a solid front."

"Shoot," said Smith. "I'm all ears, Darryl."

"We think the two hours should be split between domestic issues and foreign policy. Probably domestic the first hour, foreign the second. To hold the audience. The moderator switches the subject matter and acts as a timekeeper." Dale handed Smith a sheet of paper. "Here's the way it might work out. On a coin-toss the candidate who leads off the first hour—the guy who speaks first—speaks last on the first hour. Then, in the second hour, the candidate who spoke second on the first hour, and didn't get the final lick in on domestic issues and have the first closing statement of that hour, speaks first on the second hour—and last. You'll notice the way I've figured it out, an 'A' for one candidate, a 'B' for the other. If you follow A and B through, you'll see how it comes out even—and fair. Here's another sheet, with statement, rebuttal, and rejoinder principles worked out in the body of the new format. This hasn't been approved by Conger, but—"

"There you go again," said Smith.

Dale smiled. "Aw, come on," he said. "This does have the approval of the staff tycoons. I met with them after my session with Conger. I wanted to show it to you, so you can start it in the mill. When we get back to Washington, we can lock it up quickly. I also would like to get it in the hands of Wells tomorrow, so they will have some idea of our approach."

Smith studied the two sheets for some time. "This is interesting," Smith said finally. "I like it. There's only one thing a little vague. In the middle section, after their opening statements, and after each man has his five-minute rebuttal, do they go into rejoinders with

time limits on them, or is there a period where it's toe to toe—the
two candidates questioning each other on issues literally face to
face?"

"That's what we propose, Murray. No participation by the moderator of any kind. He has no question on cards, nothing like that. He
lays out, becomes merely a timekeeper, and lets the two candidates
have at each other. He blows the whistle in time for the two five-
minute closing statements of the first hour. Ditto the second hour."

"You know why I like it? 'Cause it's simple. And it keeps the
goddam press off a television debate, upon which they don't belong,
if you'll pardon my phrasing."

"Amen," said Dale. "This is what Conger's thinking has come
around to. We started discussing that issue, namely: Is this for the
press or for the television audience? We've come to the conclusion it
should be television's show all the way. And, with a news panel,
there is no realistic way to limit the members of the press on the
panel to broadcasters. So we decided the thing to do was to toss out
the panel."

"My people—my man—are going to like this," said Smith.
"Maybe I can get an okay tonight. They're on the Coast again. With
the three-hour time difference, I may be lucky and get an answer."

"Okay," said Dale. "Let's leave that for now. We like it too . . .
very much. Here's some more decisions from The Man."

Smith had bought the format, thought Dale. Looked like Andy
Conger was going to get his chance to try and wear Governor Green
down in two hours after all. "Incidentally," said Dale, "on that format, we thought the simplest way to decide which man speaks first
would be a coin-toss, no?" Smith nodded, and made a note. Dale
continued. "No sponsorship. We're firm on that. Also no audience."
Smith winced, as if he'd been stabbed.

"Oh, dear . . . and I had such foolproof plans for stacking the
hall. Oh, well. . . . Okay. We'll buy it. We don't want sponsorship
either."

"No prepared texts brought to the studio," said Dale. "No reference materials, no notes of any kind at the outset of the debate.

Notes, however, may be made while the debate is in progress. I've already covered no press panel. The podiums. Not too close together. Conger doesn't want to feel crowded. He wants elbow room. I'm going to ask you to play ball with me on this, Murray. And I'll do what I can for you. I say this because we're going to approve reaction shots of the candidates only if both candidates are kept in the picture—not one photographed at the exclusion of the other. In order to do this, the podiums can't be too far apart, or the shot will be too wide."

"I agree with your reasoning," said Smith, "but we couldn't care less about reaction shots. As a matter of fact, we like 'em. But . . . if you're going for this 'two-shot' idea, I think the lecterns will be close enough for our approval. I don't want too wide a gulf between the two men. It'll destroy the rapport, the feeling of physical relationship."

"That's exactly what we want," said Dale. "I think we'll be okay if NA stays out of the picture."

"They won't."

"Conger's wife will not come to the studio. He'll come alone."

"Ditto Green."

"I think we should have some high stools behind the lecterns in case they want to rest, relax off their feet while the other man has the floor. Two hours is a long time."

"Let's ask NA to bring out three or four different pairs for us to look at," said Smith. "Also, I think, in the lectern should be incorporated a well for a water glass, a low railing to keep pencils from rolling off, and perhaps a small light."

"I'll be anxious to see what designs NA shows us. But . . . I believe the lectern should be closed in front, like a dock—a British court dock—which would act as a modesty shield."

"Glad you brought that up," said Smith. "I'm going to insist on such a design, and I meant to clear it with you weeks ago. These guys shouldn't be standing up there visible to the TV audience from head to toe. They should be shielded by the lectern. We go along with you all the way on that. Oh dear . . . Happy Boy Green ain't gonna like his audience being taken away from him," Smith reflected.

"You show me the plan that'll work to prevent stacking, and I'll show it to my man," said Dale. "But that isn't our real reason against an audience. We feel the debate is for the audience at home—period. If there had been TV back in the days of the Lincoln-Douglas debates, those stupid sod-busters wouldn't have sat around on barrels and logs to listen to them. They would have been in their homes—pardon me, *log cabins*—watching it on TV."

Smith chuckled and stroked his chin. "You've got a point," he said. "I'll buy it. But my man sure loves to see his flock, his campaign congregation, sitting there before him."

"My man ain't exactly an introvert," said Dale. "Oh . . . I checked with my man, and he definitely wants to stand. So I'm home free on that gamble."

"Good," said Smith. "I haven't got too much to add. We have few major differences outside of the use of reaction shots. You know, I bet the average person would be amazed at how similarly these two men are approaching the physical aspects of the debate, and the format. They're not at loggerheads at all about it. Only as to the number of them. I won't press you for the real reasons why your man has come around to the classic debate form without the news panel. I'm sure I know. But I can understand easily why we want as many as we can get, while you want as few. Your man's still ahead of us in the popularity polls."

"True. Do you know Cleveland, Murray?" asked Dale. "I don't."

"I thought this was your home town."

"No. Buffalo."

"As a matter of fact I do. I went to Western Reserve a couple of years, then transfered to Harvard. What do you need?"

"A nice, quiet dinner with good wine," said Dale. "I'm beat, and I've got a raft of calls to make to the guys when I get back to the room. Conger's out West too, so the boys will be checking in late."

"There's a place called The Tavern not too far from here. Cleveland has no night life, no restaurants. It's one of those cities that's been out playing golf since World War Two, while the whole damn town has gone to hell in a handbasket."

"I don't care where we go—but let's go. We better line up some places for the gang the week of the debate, though. Are there any clubs around?"

"There's a place called The Hermit Club. It's close by somewhere. I've got a couple of buddies from Reserve who are members. I'll get some guest cards."

"Fine. Take me to a steak, Fearless Leader. Quickly. And because we have foisted these dreadful changes on you so mercilessly, I'll do the buying."

"Are you willing to pay the price?" Lou Wells asked Smith and Dale. "NA is prepared to spend a hell of a lot of money out here to make this plant acceptable to you, but why the hell you couldn't go from Chicago, I'll never know. The press are going to scream. You must accept the fact that this isn't big-time out here."

"You know, Lou," snapped Dale, "I think North American is more interested in accommodating the press and grabbing the publicity on the debate than in accommodating the candidates. Already, we've spent the whole morning here and half the afternoon walking around and around, around and around, to be sure the press will be happy with their arrangements. I'm the first one to say they have to have a place to work, but, Jesus, let's sit down and get to the damn production of this debate."

"Lou," said Smith, "I'll tell you what. We'll give you the second debate in Chicago, the third debate in Washington, and the fourth one in Los Angeles."

"I'll give you a fifth one in New York," said Dale, "if we can just sit down and see something from your people on the first one." Hello, Thursday, thought Dale.

It had been a tiresome survey for the two men. They had been up early, and by nine o'clock were plodding through the labyrinth of rooms, halls, scene docks, storage areas, studios, and control rooms of WTSR-TV, the North American affiliate in Cleveland. In attendance were Sandy Jones, the North American director from New York assigned to the debate; several supervisory engineers from NA in New York; two engineering installation executives; five men from NA Press Relations and Publicity; three production supervisors; representatives of the Ohio State Police and Cleveland police force; representatives of a private protective organization which would have internal control of the building on the debate day; four executive personnel of WTSR, including the station manager. Initially, the group was taken on a grand tour of the entire plant, then back over certain portions. Then Smith and Dale asked to be guided alone by a local man. The two retraced their steps in certain areas a third time without the brass. They assured themselves of the workability of the floor plan and work areas for the press. "Why we didn't have Waldo Duncan and Wilbur Jenkins meet us out here I'll never know," said Smith at one point when the two were forced to make a decision— far beyond their experience—on facilities for the pool photographers' darkroom area. Various degrees and zones of security throughout the building were agreed to, certain necessary personnel being permitted in one area but not in another.

The physical location of the building was excellent. It was located in a minimum-traffic section on Cleveland's nearby lakefront. The plant was on a short street which paralleled Lake Shore Drive. The WTSR building itself was isolated, surrounded by what looked like acres of cinder parking lots except on the one side that bordered the street. The men were told the structure had started life as a streetcar barn, only recently had the tracks in the cinder areas been removed.

The basic design of the building made it a giant columnless and windowless sound stage, sectioned into offices, engineering and sales areas, and the studios for actual television production. Insofar as security was concerned, the law-enforcement officers and the private agency were delighted with the ease with which they could seal off and isolate the structure. Morley Haynes, WTSR's station manager, stood nervously at the outer fringe of the group of visitors as they decided whether or not they would commit themselves to Cleveland as the location.

"I like it," said Smith. "The idea of originating in a city away from the sophisticated jazz of the large television production centers appeals to me."

Dale mentioned that aspect could work both ways, good and bad. "I'm not referring to production, Murray," he said, "but to the wild enthusiasm that could generate out here, with the two presidential candidates in the same city the first time in history. These Buckeyes are liable to explode and cause plenty of headaches for everyone. But I see no reason, insofar as television production and the WTSR plant are concerned, not to originate here. I'll go with Cleveland."

Haynes mumbled something as to how splendid that was. He immediately turned to a local publicity hack to hit the wires with the story. Three NA press men leaped to muzzle him; no stories would go out without prior approval of NA in New York.

"And approval of Jenkins and Duncan," said Dale. "You guys better get in the habit damn quick of remembering the candidates, the people this debate is for, or there are going to be some mighty sore knuckles around here."

And so it went until after lunch when Dale demanded they get on to the real purpose of the trip to Cleveland—debate production. The men sat in folding chairs, placed in a half-circle in the center of the cavernous Studio Three which would be the scene of the debate. Only those connected with actual production of the telecast were present.

"We have every indication this first debate will enjoy the largest audience in TV's history," said Wells. "If we seem overbearing, if we seem overly concerned about this point or that element, I assure you it is only because of our desire to satisfy the enormous audience this telecast will experience."

There's another reason, thought Dale. You'll know Thursday, Lou, old boy. It's the *only* debate that's going to take place. You damn well better make it good.

Wells continued. "Conger once again has caused a complete change of signals. For two weeks our designers have been working in New York on a basic approach to the staging which included the placement and participation of a news panel. Now you've thrown that out. So we start all over again. I have the set designer, Frankie Alton, here again. You met him in Washington. He's here to get every decision relative to design that Conger or Green have made. May we hear them?" Wells concluded, looking at Dale and Smith.

As the North American technicians listened, the two men ran down the list of physical preferences, and the decisions reached since the previous meeting. Smith voiced the physical arrangements, Dale the format approach. Wells asked for a review of the areas of difference between the two candidates. Dale articulated these, ending with his absolute position against the reaction shots planned by NA. "And Green is just as adamant on the other side," he said. "All our other differences have been resolved."

"I have a note here from someone asking me to check whether or not your men want on-the-air monitors so they can see themselves as they are being televised."

"No," said Dale.

"Yes," said Smith.

"That makes it tough for engineering," said Sandy Jones. "They'll have to wire up each monitor separately to the closeup camera. Why doesn't Conger want one?" he asked, turning to Dale.

"Why not ask Murray why Green wants one?" answered Dale.

"Okay . . . why?" asked Jones. Smith shrugged his shoulders. "Don't know. He just likes it."

"I'll tell you why," said Dale. "Green has got a couple of Broadway, Actors Lab-type guys coaching him on his hand gestures and use of his best profile. Green wants to check his acting lessons on the tube as he goes along. You know—learn-as-you-go, do-it-yourself demagoguery."

Smith frowned, jutting his chin out at Dale in mock anger. But he remained silent. The meeting continued, with NA recommending as the debate's moderator Weldon Parkhurst, a top NA News and Public Affairs commentator. Smith and Dale assured Wells that Parkhurst would win an early approval.

The Cleveland survey offered another opportunity for Wells to test the strength of Dale's feelings against the use of drapes or curtains. He didn't miss it.

"In New York we find an overwhelming preference for the classic set Frankie Alton designed, using curtains in classic folds, gracefully spaced in a broad semicircular arc behind the candidates. If it meets with viewer-approval on the first debate, we also feel the drapes will offer the simplest design for the other networks to duplicate in subsequent debates. Keeping in mind your feelings, however, Alton will now show you the other set design, the one using wood textures, which you requested, and then show you how the drapes may be hung from the top of it, quickly. I say this because we at NA plan to bring a full set of drapes to Cleveland. A studio does strange things to design. We'll have the hard flat set which you prefer, Dale—Smith says he has no preference—and we'll . . ."

Dale cut in. "Smith may not have a preference, Lou, but he has said repeatedly he will go along with me on Conger's dislike of drapes. Why do we keep bringing them up? What's the point? I am never going to approve curtains on the first debate—or any other debate. Now that's final. You're wasting your time, the designer's time, and our time with this constant harking back to a design approach I cannot—*and will not*—approve."

Smith remained silent. Poor bastard, he thought. Someone at NA must have it in for him. Fortunately, his man Green was coming up smelling like a rose through the whole argument. He'd look great in front of drapes.

"We're not putting this debate on for NA," Dale stated with irritation. "It's for the candidates, not for NA. Rembember that. What are used will be those things which make the candidates most comfortable, not those which NA wants—which satisfy the frustrated egos of aesthetically ambitious NA executives. Get that through your head, Lou. I mean what I say."

"Have no fears, Dale," snapped Wells. "As long as the debate is under my control—and it is completely my baby, no one else's—the set used will be the one you people want." But Wells had his answer. Dale was still after control. He wasn't giving an inch on the drapes. A plan was forming in Wells's mind. He would discuss it at the correct time with Fred Morgan. It called for making Morgan the heavy. "To answer your question, however, Frankie Alton thinks the drapes best portray the feel of the importance of the occasion without the literal use of columns. I agree with him, as does Sandy here, and several others whose opinions we value highly at NA in New York."

Dale looked at Wells, not replying immediately. This was going to be it, he thought. He's going to do it with the curtains. He's going to send Andrew Conger right up through the light grid, straight up and out through the roof girders, and spring these goddam drapes on me the day of the debate. Well, we'll see about that. There must be some way to sandbag him, corner him. Dale noted it on his pad, speaking as he did so. "Several weeks ago I made a statement at one of these meetings: My man will not appear on the first debate if vertical folds—curtains—are used as a backdrop behind him. The statement still stands. We insist on this control. Now I want to get on to something else—a request of NA. My office will need a list of the names of every North American employee involved in the tele-cast. We want the name *and* the address of every technician directly involved in the telecast."

"What're you going to do?" snapped Wells. "Check their political registration?"

"Don't be ridiculous," said Dale. "Conger wants to send them a personal 'thank-you' to their homes. Nothing more. But I will need that list no later than Monday morning, October sixteenth. This is a personal request from Andrew Conger."

"Might as well give me a copy, too," said Smith. "I can't have Charlie's man sending the crew mash notes without them getting something nice from Happy Joe Green."

I'm off the hook on that one, thought Dale. He made the decision to ask merely for the names and addresses, hoping Conger would for-get his request in the heat of campaign and the debate preparations. If, by some fantastic circumstance, he did ask Dale for the political registration of the men, Dale decided to add the registrations willy-nilly—eeny, meeny, miney, moe—opposite the list of names. He privately concluded it would do Conger immeasurably more harm than good to press the network for the political registrations.

"Well, under that situation," said Dale, "maybe we don't need it after all. But . . . I guess I better deliver for my man. He asked me personally for it."

"You'll get it," said Wells. "You and Smith will toss a coin in Washington as soon as you both approve the format, is that correct? To see which man has the opening and closing statement in the first hour, which, as I understand it, controls the other candidate having the opening and closing statement in the second hour."

The men nodded. "How does NA plan to handle the stand-in problem out here in Cleveland?" asked Smith.

"WTSR is going to run a contest to find two look-alikes for Conger and Green. They'll be given an all-expense trip to the Inauguration, and meet the candidates the night of the debate."

"In a pig's ass they will," said Dale. "My man is not a prize in a local contest. He ain't meetin' anyone but Green the night of the debate. What Green does is his own business."

"I'm agin it," said Smith. "Bring some people out from New York. Send us their publicity photos in Washington this week. I can tell by that."

"Ditto," said Dale.

"Anything else?" asked Wells.

"Yeah. . . . We're catching a plane for Washington. Right now," said Dale. "Somebody call a cab for us. You ready, Murray?"

On the flight into the Capitol, Dale and Smith relaxed. The stewardess slipped them two extra martinis when she saw their staff baggage tags bearing the candidates' names. It was a smooth flight, and the two continued to talk shop all the way in. Dale asked Smith's sufferance on the problem of the drapes. "Couldn't we control it up to a certain point on the clock the afternoon of the debate, Murray, and then say that from that time forward no changes of any kind will be permitted without our prior approval?"

"That ought to work," answered Smith. "Actually, we're much

better off with our wood tones and textures of wood grain in that other design. Why don't we let Wells play his little game—hang the drapes for us to look at. We'll turn 'em down, and then, as of such-and-such a time, tell him that's it?" Dale agreed, and felt he had solved an enormous problem.

"I got a crazy message when I called Washington from the airport, Charlie," said Smith. "Get this. We hired a public-address guy we didn't really know anything about to travel with Green. He had a personal relationship with someone high-up on the staff. The guy comes from the Southwest somewhere. Phoenix . . . Tucson maybe. Anyway, about two weeks after he's joined the traveling party, his wife shows up. So he starts paying her way on all the flights, and they travel together everywhere. Well, Mama Green, sweet and simple Mary, takes a shine to the guy's little wife. The gal starts to ride in Mary Green's car in the motorcade, sits with her in Green's compartment in the plane, works into acting like a personal secretary, traveling companion. We get a note to stop charging this soundman for her travel, and she gets put on the staff roster of the official Green party. Comes then the bombshell. Seems this morning we get a call in my office from the guy's *real* wife, sitting home in Tucson and not hearing anything from her husband in a month. She's frantic and wants to know what's happened to him. How about *that?*"

"What'd you do?" asked Dale.

"Well, it seems this gal whose been traveling with him is an honest-to-God hooker." The two men roared with laughter. "He picked her up in one of the towns which was an overnight stop when he first joined up. So what do we tell the wife of our presidential candidate? That she's gone soft for a hooker? What do we tell the press? What a situation! We fired the guy, and told him to take his 'wife' with him at the noon meeting today. Now I need a replacement fast. I mean, like tonight. I haven't the slightest idea where to turn. My office says they can't scare up anybody who can move that fast, and who's good. Do you have any ideas?"

Dale took out a piece of paper and his pen. He wrote down the name and home telephone number of a friend of his in Hollywood. "Call this guy. Tell him I suggested you get in touch with him. He runs the best sound company in the country. Tell him what you need. He'll have a man with Green—a good man—in twelve hours."

"You've saved my life, friend," said Smith. "I appreciate this."

"Forget it," said Dale.

"I'll call him first thing when we land. It'll still be early on the Coast." Smith placed the note in his pocket. "I've got another continuous problem with Green, Charlie. It's very personal. Could I talk to you about it?"

"Sure. My lips are sealed."

"We're trying some new makeup on my man. Using a sun lamp. Almost bake the stuff on him. It makes Green look great. Tan, ruddy, chiseled. But it makes him perspire like mad. At the temples. And up here, across the lower part of his forehead." Smith stroked his face to indicate the areas. "Is there any anti-perspirant you know of that will stand up under the heat of the lights and the makeup? I've got to find something. It's terrible."

"I don't know what makeup you're using, Murray," said Dale, "but a couple of years ago I got a call from the National Committee. There was a Senatorial candidate running somewhere in New England, a hell of a good guy. He won, as a matter of fact. But he perspired terribly. You know, like Murrow. He had no control over it. Maybe it was nerves, but he had this incredibly profuse flow of perspiration every time he went on TV. This prevented use of any close-ups of him on TV because of his perspiration problem. Cameras had to stay wide. Anyway, the committee asked me if I'd get into it, see what I could do. I called a guy who is very senior in the Make-up Artists Union in New York—it's Local Seven Ninety-eight. I'll give you his name and number back in Washington. He told me about something he'd adapted from the theater. Seems a lot of people have this trouble. He found a dehydrating agent—aluminum chloride, I guess it was—which has been used by surgeons for years, and can be taken internally, orally, in pill form. They use it to dehydrate themselves during long and exacting surgery to cut down perspiration which could cloud their vision. Surgeons also use it to prevent their hands from becoming moist and slipping on surgical instruments. Anyway, that's what he told me. But it dehydrates you fantastically when taken internally. Surgeons gulp water continuously to make up for the deficiency. I didn't like the idea of asking this senator to take a pill internally, either. So this makeup expert got some aluminum chloride liquid. We simply mixed the dry pancake makeup with the liquid instead of water, and used this mixture as makeup on the areas where there was heavy perspiration. It stopped it completely. We got a mild shrinking of the skin, tiny wrinkles from the dehydration, but they couldn't be seen on camera at all—even in the tightest closeups. The senator told me he had a slight sensation of super-cooling—nothing more."

"Sounds like that's for me," said Smith. "I never heard of it before."

"I wouldn't want you to use it without expert advice. Don't even experiment with it until you can talk to this guy in New York. I'll get you his name."

Dale looked at his watch to see how much time remained of the flight. It was interesting, he thought, how close the two were becoming. Their friendship had begun to cross over the intangible barrier of political ideology, candidate allegiance.

In the preparation of this debate, for the first time in American campaign history the staff members of one candidate had been forced to communicate, to reach agreements, to confer with the representatives of their opponent. None had been thrown together more intimately or continuously than the television advisers. It was almost as if they were "seconds," Dale thought, in the great classic tradition of the duel of honor. The mid-twentieth century modernization was that these "electronic" seconds picked television stations as the dueling ground, and inspected their masters' weapons in the form of TV cameras instead of swords, or pistols. Charlie Dale and Murray Smith, comfortably sailing through the night sky, to report once again to their principals, their Master Political Duelists—their Candidates.

Dale decided to level with Smith now on his dogmatic attitude toward the use of curtains on the debate set.

"Weeks ago, Murray," he said, "I went beyond the pale in terms of stupidity on this use of curtains behind my man. You must think I'm a nut to be carping about them as much as I do. So let me explain."

"You already have," said Smith. "And believe me, Charlie, I wish I could take a stronger stand. But I can't. It doesn't mean that much to me."

"I know. That's why I want to explain it." He paused and snapped off the reading light above his head. "Sure they're going to bug Conger, make no mistake about that. But you know he won't take a walk. I wouldn't permit it, no matter what I say to Wells or anyone else in public. But these curtains have become a symbol of who the hell is controlling this debate, as far as I'm concerned. NA thinks *they* are. They insist on it. I maintain this debate must be under the control of the candidates. How the hell do we know what crazy-ass ideas some network might come up with four years from now? And slam 'em at a presidential candidate?"

"You're right," said Smith. "It's very serious, this question of whose in the driver's seat."

"Every inch of the way it's been fight, fight, scream and yell for what we know these men want and need. Television networks don't know a goddam thing about politics. But, by Jesus, they think they do."

"They're really so naïve about the whole subject," added Smith, "that I wonder where they get the idea they have the right to tell the political parties what to do?"

"I've never ceased to be amazed by it. You'd think each network president, or whatever ghost writer in PR writes his speeches, had been chairman of one of the National Committees for fifty years, the way they sound off. Every time I pick up one of the slick magazines and see another article by a network tycoon telling the political parties how to run their campaigns—streamline them—or how to change completely the way they conduct their conventions, well

. . . all it does is prove how politically unsophisticated broadcasters really are."

"To think *they* think the politicans give one good goddam what the broadcasters want, or think!" Smith replied. "It gets back to the same thing. Broadcasters should be chaste, scrupulously honest reporters, not producers or innovators when it comes to politics."

"Somehow," said Dale, "we must get this debate thing into a posture where the networks come to the candidates and say, 'Okay, fellas, what do you want?' Until that happens, any presidential candidate, now or in the future, will be exposed to the baseless whimsy of the network idiots. For Christ's sake, Murray, how do we know, if we don't establish control, that in future campaigns the networks won't insist on the two presidential candidates appearing in red-white-and-blue Uncle Sam suits, complete with top hats?"

Smith laughed softly. "Your point is well taken, Charlie. Because I can't do anything about it, I'll keep my trap shut. But I promise you I'm with you all the way. The only place to vest control is with the candidates."

Dale lit a cigarette and glanced sideways at Smith. If ever the time were right to disclose his concern about North American's favoritism toward Green, it was now, he decided. Tonight, on this plane, he resolved, may be my one and only chance. He reached into his brief case, thumbed through the files at the bottom until he found the notes of the scrap of conversation he had overheard between Morgan and Wells in the control room at the Chicago convention. Somehow, for some inexplicable reason, Dale felt he knew Smith sufficiently well to discern in him any attempt to hide the truth. Furthermore, he felt it wouldn't hurt to jolt Smith with his suspicions at this date so near the debate telecast.

"Murray, you've asked me to keep several important confidences tonight. I'd like to ask you to keep one. So serious I hardly know how to discuss it. I don't think I would bring this up if we weren't on a plane. I'd be afraid you might walk away and never come back. You may find your opinion of me considerably altered after you hear what I have to say. Can I trust you on this? Completely?"

Smith nodded solemnly.

"I don't know whether to just tell you . . . or ask you," said Dale. "I don't want to embarrass you, don't want to spoil our relationship. I feel so very strongly that if we don't stick together on this debate, we may never get it on the air. On the other hand, I feel compelled to discuss this thing with you in order to explain what could be my necessary actions and attitude in Cleveland when we come back for the actual telecast. So don't feel you must make a comment."

Smith nodded again, his face grave. "I'll understand," he said. "Let me be the judge of that—after I've heard what you have to say."

Dale referred to his notes. "When my man announced he would participate in the debates in his acceptance speech the last night of the convention, Fred Morgan of NA came into the TV control room . . . where I was with Lou Wells. It was dark, and he didn't know I was there. Lou did, but not Morgan. He said, and these are his words: 'We brought the bastard to heel, just as we planned.' He then said to Wells, 'It's a long way from Fairlee and your first talk with Green to tonight, Lou, but it's been worth it.' He said some other things about a bonus for Wells and about TV being home free. Then he said, 'Green played ball, and it worked. Conger has had it.' Neither Morgan nor Wells have any idea I overheard this conversation. Then, a few weeks back, I learned from a member of our staff that one of the traveling press approached him with the information there'd been a deal made between Green and NA, and that Lou Wells was mixed up in it. He said he could hang NA if he wanted to. This press guy hoped his path would cross with mine sometime during the campaign. I haven't seen him. And the guy was dead drunk when he ear-banged the guy on our staff and slobbered out his story. That's the end of it. I'm not asking you for any information. I am merely telling you I am on guard because of what I've heard. If I see any manifestations of it in Cleveland as the debate takes shape, I'm going to scream as loud as I can. It will be very gory. I'm liable to be cut and bleeding myself."

Smith remained silent, pondering Dale's shocking remarks. Dale watched him closely, leaning forward in his seat to observe his face and eyes. Not a nerve flicked, not a muscle tensed insofar as Dale could see. Smith took a final and lengthy pull on his cigarette, calmly snuffed it out in the ash tray in the seat arm, and shook his head from side to side as he exhaled slowly. "I swear to you I know of nothing between Green and NA," he said softly. "If I thought it were true, I think I'd try to get out."

"I didn't ask you for that, Murray," Dale said to him. "I appreciate your honesty. I have nothing more to say. You'll hear no more unless there's a crisis. Come on, we've got enough time for a couple of games of gin. I've got cards in my brief case."

16

The Campaign in High Gear

"My Gawd, big Jesus, this place has been a madhouse since you left," said Fergie.

"I've only been gone four days. Why do you think I hired you, Scarlett?" said Dale. "To keep on top of situations just like this. In your own hush-puppy way." He paused and riffled through the pile of file cards on his desk. "Are these in order of importance, chronological, or what?" he asked her.

"Just take the top card off the stack," she said. "One at a time."

Dale read, fighting his lack of sleep the previous night. His plane had been held over Washington for over an hour because of thunderstorms. It was well after midnight when he reached his apartment. Propped on his pillow was a note from Abner Shepherd, advising him of an early breakfast meeting on Conger's paid political television programs. Conger had called Rufe Little, asking for a step-up in his TV. Recent polls indicated an even stronger television influence over uncommitted voters, considerably stronger than newspapers. Conger was now asking for TV every night, regardless of his previous concern over reducing the size of the crowds at his evening meetings. A decision had been reached regarding a paid half-hour nighttime network telecast two days after the debate. The time was to have been filled with a panel of prominent men endorsing Conger's position on major campaign issues. Now it would be Conger himself. Dale recommended that a half-hour be constructed on video tape of the whirlwind campaign activity leading up to the debate. For three weeks a mobile video tape unit, an enormous, rolling TV production studio, had been following Conger, under contract to the National Committee. The mobile unit taped the most colorful of his meetings for paid five-minute spot programs, or programs which could be used in the local area after Conger had proceeded to other states. Dale placed a call on the recently installed radio-telephone in the electronic bus. He gave the crew chief orders to report to Ham Forrest, who was with the candidate, for particulars on the new production assignment. Before reaching his office, Dale had solved his third crisis of the day.

The card Dale read was clipped to a confidential rough copy of a revised travel schedule for Conger. Fergie had underlined the dates of October 13, 14, and 15. Prior to this new revision, Andrew Conger had been left free on October 14 and 15 to rest and prepare for the debate. Now, however, the days were committed to a man-killing schedule on the West Coast. "Son-of-a-bitch!" said Dale, looking up at Fergie. "Look what they've done to that poor bastard. God knows what this will do to his performance on the debate. Get Shepherd. Tell him I'm on my way to his office."

Dale exploded at Shepherd as he walked toward his desk. "What in the name of all that's holy are you trying to do to this man? I've pleaded and pleaded with you to keep him free before the debate. You promised, Rufe promised, Conger promised. How can you do this to me . . . to him?" Dale cried, in honest anguish.

"Simmer down, Charlie," said Shepherd, exasperated. "Goddammit, don't pin the blame on me. It was The Man himself who insisted on the additions. We all reminded him of your recommendation on the two uncommitted days. So don't blow your stack at me."

"Can we rescind this decision. My God, he's in the East—still on the train Thursday night. Why does he go out to the Coast for just two days? Can't he stay in the East . . . come to Washington, or something . . . and prepare and rest for the debate? Can we get to him and talk to him?"

"No, it's too late," said Shepherd. "I just made the last call a couple of hours ago. They're private Fat Cat meetings and a crisis in California."

"Well," said Dale, "don't blame me if I have to carry him to the podium, prop him up, and feed him pep pills to keep him awake for the two hours we're on the air. I think you guys are killing the man. Murdering him."

"Can't you get it through your stupid head the candidate is doing this to himself?" shouted Shepherd.

"I know . . . I know," said Dale softly. "I'm sorry, Ab, it's just that all the preparation, care, and feeding we can give this man to prepare him for this nightmare debate isn't going to mean a damn thing if he's exhausted, if he hasn't had time to unwind, get his wind, and think—think about the debate." Dale smiled, ashamed of his undue criticism of Shepherd. "I know it isn't you guys. But, dammit, when the hell is somebody around here going to blow the whistle? On Conger, I mean? He gets all worked up, thinking about this crisis, that state, this finance problem, and wham—he throws ten extra meetings into what is already a man-killing schedule. Someone has to be strong enough to say *no* to Andy."

Shepherd looked up, squinting above the smoke from his pipe. His head was cocked to the side as he said, "Got any candidates for the job? On a temporary basis . . . like one day's employment?"

So Dale's contender in the gladiator match of all time would not arrive in Cleveland until late Sunday night. And the meetings preventing his necessary rest and preparation consisted of behind-the-scenes political manipulation in California (one state instead of the

fifty that would see the debate) and Fat Cat fund-raising sessions in
Portland, Oregon, and Denver. So, at the most, Conger's debate preparation was sacrificed to add political strength to his candidacy in
three out of fifty states, all fifty of which would be glued to their TV
sets, hoping the candidates' performances would add wisdom and
insight as to how to cast a ballot on Election Day.

"I'll give you a clue, Rufe," said Dale to Rufe Little. "There may
be some very big fireworks in Cleveland come the actual night of the
debate. I may need all the backing up you and the rest of the whole
staff can give me. I hope we won't have to suck The Man into it. It'd
be shattering if Conger had the remotest idea some hanky-panky
might be going on between Green and North American."

Rufe Little looked at Dale, disbelieving what he had heard. Dale,
still not completely convinced his suspicions were justified, but sensing something powerful at work behind the scenes, had decided to advise Little of his concern.

"I'll back you up," said Little, "if you're right. Seems to me we
better set a deadline, if it ever gets to the point we want to pull
our man."

Dale said, "Make it three in the afternoon."

"Okay," said Little. "If I don't hear from you by three, we go
through with it."

Dale considered the time once more, quickly ticking off the various
rehearsal elements, production schedules, and possibilities of error in
the hour. "I don't see how anything serious could happen after that,
Rufe, except what they might pull while we're on the air. You know,
stuff like unflattering reaction shots of our man, bad camera angles
on him, picture distortion. I can't conceive of them going that far,
even if my suspicions are correct."

"If we pull The Man too late, I think it would backfire. The press
would interpret it as cold feet, spoil-sport, nit-picking. We must pull
him in sufficient time to hold a full-blown press conference, a complete airing and explanation of our actions. If we're at the mercy of

press interpretation, up against the time the telecast is supposed to hit the air, we'll never get our day in court."

"I'll buy the three-o'clock deadline, Rufe. You'll be in Cleveland, right?" Little nodded, reaching forward on his desk for a memo.

"I have here a piece of research which interests me," he said. "Seems as though this Hans Kleinert man you hired as a lighting expert is not registered in our party. Don't we have enough troubles without you hiring theater people who are for Green? I mistrust those show-business people."

"I don't believe it," said Dale. "Hans Kleinert is a professional— and a loyal Conger man. Even if he weren't, he wouldn't let politics interfere with his professional standing. He'd do the best job he knew how."

"We've gone through every registration file possible," said Little. "I want you to get rid of Kleinert. I've told you before how touchy the patronage problem is, let alone the job a lighting man in the other party could do on our man the night of the debate. I thought you checked this, Charlie, before you hired him. How do we know who he's for?"

Dale looked at Little with sorrow. You poor bastard, he thought. You can't trust a single living soul, can you? If someone isn't regis- tered in Conger's party, he's a traitor. Very quietly, Dale said, "You're wrong, Rufe. I don't care what your research says, this man is not an enemy, and I'm not firing him." Dale reached for a phone. "I'm call- ing my office. They'll contact Kleinert on the Coast. He's home for a couple of days between assignments. You accuse him—directly— on the phone. I wouldn't want the shame or blame for it on my hands. We'll sit here until he calls us back."

Dale's mood of uncompromising trust and confidence in Hans Klei- nert was a mystery to Little, an irritation. Time and again, Dale had brought on the friction between himself and Little with his positions of no retreat, no equivocation—all blacks or whites, no grays. In Little's world of compromise, expediency, mistrust, and suspicion, Dale was a stranger with whom communication was impossible. For the two men did not speak the same language. The light blinked.

"Hello, Hans?" asked Dale. "This is Charlie. Did I wake you?"

"No," said Kleinert. "Melisse and I are sitting here having breakfast. I was just telling her about the great pictures in San Francisco. You know, she's a very severe critic, Charlie, and she says those were the most beautiful pictures of Andy Conger she's ever seen in her life. What's up?"

"Uh . . . it's a silly thing, Hans, and I don't want you to take this personally. I'm in the office of Rufus Little, the campaign manager for Conger. He says you're registered in Green's party—that you're not carried on the files of Conger's party in your district. I've tried to tell him you're not a Green man. Now I'd like you to tell him. I'm putting him on the phone. His name is Little."

No reaction came from Kleinert, so Dale passed the phone, his eyes never leaving Little.

"Hello. . . . Kleinert?" Little asked.

"Yes, sir, what can I do for you?"

"Well . . . you know these things are strictly formalities. To keep us in the good graces of the National Committee, you know," Little said.

"No . . . I don't," answered Kleinert. "What National Committee?"

"Forget that part of it, then," said Little. "You're not registered in Conger's party, and we can't have people like that on our staff. I have instructed Dale to terminate your services, unless, of course, you have registered so recently there's been a delay in the transferral of this information in your district in Los Angeles. It's strictly a policy decision, you understand."

Kleinert paused before answering. "No, I don't," he said. "I'm not a Green man, Mr. Little," he said. "And I'm not registered in his party. Also, I'm not registered in Mr. Conger's party. I'm forty-five years old, Mr. Little. I have never registered with any political party, and I have voted in every presidential election since I was twenty-one. I am an Independent. I believe the man is more important than the party. I make up my mind on the abilities of the man." He paused again, and Little started to speak. Kleinert cut him off. "This time, Mr. Little, I have decided Mr. Conger is the best man. Have you ever met an Independent, Mr. Little? There's nothing unclean about us, you know, or unprincipled. We cherish our vote. We don't pull the party lever at the top."

"You're not registered with either party?" asked Little. "I'm not sure we can accept that at the National Committee. I'll have to look into it. For the time being, however, at least through the debate on October sixteenth, you stay on. Here's Dale."

"He's an Independent," said Little, handing the phone to Dale. "I don't like that."

Dale cupped his hand over the mouthpiece. "Is he for Green?" he asked. "Is he registered in Green's party?"

"No," said Little. Dale looked dead into Little's eyes, his expression one of absolute disgust.

"Hello, Hans," Dale said into the phone. "As I said, it was just a misunderstanding back here. I'm terribly sorry about it, but I wanted to straighten it out immediately. This is a firm commitment for your services through Election Day in November. Mr. Little agrees to this. And, oh yes, I looked into the matter of a fifty-dollar increase in your fee per telecast. That's been approved too. You have anything for me?"

Again, Kleinert paused before speaking. Then he said, "You didn't have to say all that, Charlie. I'm sorry I put you on the spot. I've never registered with either party. It never got me in trouble before."

"You're not in any trouble, Hans. It's the people back here who are mixed up. Give my best to Melisse. Call me when you get to Miami. I've got some things to pass on to you. So long."

Without another word, Dale turned and left the office.

On schedule, Andrew Conger announced his decision to participate in but one debate. The political bombshell struck a direct hit on the Green campaign staff, stunning them for several hours. They received it as the latest curve thrown by a candidate not to be trusted—but one who had to be debated. Conger had surmised correctly. Green agreed to the startling condition, and Smith was quick to call Dale with his own violent denunciation of Conger's tactics. Dale wondered if Conger's decision, over which he had no control, might militate against their close relationship. Cleveland would be mighty hostile if Smith joined with North American.

The full force of the Conger statement hit the broadcasting industry with staggering impact. Even in Fred Morgan's earlier realistic appraisals of the frequency and number of debates, he never seriously thought there would be less than four. As far as the other two networks were concerned, for weeks they had been occupied with their plans for the subsequent encounters between the candidates which would be televised over their respective facilities. Charlie Dale felt the full violence of their fury and disappointment. The only member of the Conger staff known to broadcasting on a first-name basis, the three television networks held him personally responsible for depriving the industry of their great show of virtue. It was as if Dale had shot Santa Claus, robbed the poorbox, struck a blind man. Global and Telenet discussed the idea of discarding North American's position as producer of the first debate. Realistically, however, they knew the responsibility must continue to rest with NA. No other facility could possibly enter the picture at the late date and meet the deadline requirements on construction, arrangements, and security. Reluctantly, and with great envy, Global and Telenet released a weak statement of confidence in North American. Lou Wells breathed a sigh of relief only slightly deeper than Fred Morgan's when the crisis had passed. The two still had control of the debate. Andrew Conger was still their pigeon. With certainty, Lou Wells had a leg up to proceed with the plans which could catapult him to the presidency of North American.

For the first time in the campaign, Dale felt the deep, bitter resentment from the networks which would continue on after Election Day. Only time would tell if his loyalties and beliefs in Conger were to affect his future. He mentioned it to Janet one evening when he called her. It was fortunate, he said, that his small organization in Denver, which now looked as if it would survive, was not at the mercy of the vindictive memories of broadcasting's important programming executives.

"No one can hurt you, Charlie," Janet said, "unless you let them. I am so happy we are out here, that this will be our home when it's all over."

"I am too, Janet, but I may get cut up pretty bad in Cleveland. There could be some bloodletting out there. I can't tell you the reasons. If you read about it in the papers, or hear about it, don't worry. My job out there is to protect Andrew Conger, not myself. I'll be doing my best for him, that's all."

"I know you will, Charles," said his wife. "Don't let them get you down. I'm not worried. Good night, dear. I love you."

True to his promise, Dale was joining the Conger campaign train for Conger's morale, and for his own sake, to see for himself how the candidate and his preparations for the day of debate were coming.

"Track Thirty-two," said the station master in Philadephia to Dale. "You're going to have a long hot walk if you go out now," he continued. "They won't be backing it into the station until about five o'clock this evening."

"I've got to get out there right now," said Dale, looking at his watch. "I'm supposed to meet some sound technicians at eleven o'clock. How do I make it?"

The day was blisteringly hot. If anything is worse than Philadelphia on Sunday, it is a hot Philadelphia on Sunday—in a steaming railroad marshalling yard. If this is late Indian Summer, they can have it, thought Dale as he picked his way down a roadbed of ballast brown with rust. The handles of his bags were moist in his chafing palms.

There was little activity in the yard at that hour of Sunday morning. The silence heightened the grip the heat held on the area, and not a breath of air stirred. God, Dale thought, we'll perish if they don't have the air conditioning on, as he approached the rear platform car of the Conger campaign train—The Sixties Special, as they had named it.

In the train the power was on, but the air conditioning was not. A thermometer read 115° in the narrow passenger corridor leading to the compartment assigned to Dale as the broadcast control center for the train. This compartment was as close to the candidate as security and practicality would permit. Andrew Conger would live, work, and make his speeches from the last car.

Dale doubted if there had been any significant innovations or changes in campaign trains in thirty years, the time sound-systems came into general use. In the first place, the railroads were so shackled by federal and state regulations governing their every dimension, every piece of rolling equipment, every modification, that there was no freedom for changes that were dictated by advances in equipment design. Public-address systems were still a mystery to an industry which—in the Jet Age—lit a kerosene lantern as a safety device to protect millions of dollars' worth of rolling stock hurtling through the night at ninety miles an hour. Time and again, after three or four days of painstaking work installing the wires between Dale's control center and the candidate's rear platform car—dirty, difficult work under the trucks and around the axles of the ageing carriages—some nameless, brainless railroad supervisor would, without the slightest warning, uncouple Andrew Conger's car in the dead of night for servicing, thereby severing as many as fifty of the electronic lifelines. This would mean frantic activity at daylight to restring the lines before the first speech of the day, or facing the wrath of Andrew Conger, suddenly deprived of the electronic extension of his articulate powers.

That day one delay after another, forced by ridiculous railroad featherbedding and regulations, put Dale's installation plans far behind schedule. Early in the afternoon a horde of Conger volunteers descended on the sweltering cars. Their assignment was putting up the political decorations—bunting, banners and posters—which would adorn the inside walls of each car. They swarmed over the steaming metal snake, successfully impeding the progress of each technician working against his own particular deadline. A torrential thunderstorm struck the yards, further delaying work. As in the case of so many projects involving a combination of frantic volunteer and professional effort, however, the work was finally completed. As the train backed slowly into the station to wait for its important guest, everything was in readiness.

"Who moved my rear platform?" Conger shouted to no one in particular as he came through the door. "Who moved it? That's the largest crowd we've had so far! It's inexcusable to move the train while I'm still speaking. Somebody moved my rear platform!" he repeated in frustration.

"Just a foul-up, Andy," said Dale, straightening up off his haunches where he had crouched with Ham Forrest behind the rear windows during Conger's speech. "Get the band stuff on immediately, Billy," Dale shouted into the intercom back to broadcast control. "We're rolling early. The candidate dumped his standard closing when the train started to move." He paused momentarily. "That's it. I hear it. Fine. I'll be back in a minute." He replaced the light-bell phone. "They haven't pulled out on you early in a long time," Dale said, turning to Conger.

"Well, goddammit, let's not have any more of that. Especially with these huge crowds. Get the estimate from Jenkins for me. Tell him to play it up with the press. We're going to have a good day. Nice to have you on board, Charlie."

With Susan in attendance, Conger and Dale had breakfast in the car's dining lounge. Final arrangements for the debate were discussed. The format, with its option of first and second speakers in the two hours of domestic and foreign issues was approved, as were the pattern and time values of rebuttal and rejoinder. The candidate and Dale discussed the proposed format for the national telecast on paid political time two days after the debate. Dale explained that it would give Conger maximum exposure with little or no effort, as the backbone of the half-hour would be video tape, shot from the mobile unit, with Conger merely ad-libbing transition descriptions from one sequence of an enthusiastic crowd to the next. In effect, it was a personal political travelogue, with Conger's pre-taped speeches carrying the political message, and Conger giving the audience his impressions of the people and the country as the recorded material swung from one section of the land to another. "If this works well, Andy, and you're happy with it, we should do another one just like it near the end of the campaign," said Dale. He watched his man sip his morning tea, dropping a tablespoon of honey into the cup, followed by a wedge of lemon. Years ago Dale had suggested this mixture to Conger. It was well known by vocalists and opera stars. The combination had enormous therapeutic values for one constantly using his voice, especially outdoors, unconsciously straining to overcome location noises and background disturbances. "I suggest you stay with the honey through the debate, Andy," he added. "It'd be a bad time to have a raw throat. According to your schedule, they've crammed you right up to Sunday, the night before. Is there any way you can knock off that last day and rest?"

"The party's in trouble financially," said Conger. "I told them I'd do those Fat Cat meetings. I know your debate's important. I'll have to take a chance on my own energies."

And preparedness, thought Dale. "It will be a dangerous time to gamble, Andy. There's no second go at it. One hundred million people watching . . . and only one roll of the dice."

But the matter was closed in Conger's mind. He turned to Jenkins as he walked into the dining area. "What's the police crowd-estimate at that last stop, Will?" he asked. "Looked pretty good to me. Nice to be up here among friends again."

"Yeah," said Jenkins, "these people in New York State like you."

In New York, high up on the executive floor of North American Broadcasting, Fred Morgan and Lou Wells plotted their next move in the privacy of Morgan's office.

"To cover the set design situation first, Fred," said Wells, "there's

no doubt in my mind we have something here which will rattle
Conger, irritate him to an unknown degree. Charlie Dale is really
fighting for control. I know it. But he has harped on the drapes
at every meeting. He says he won't approve the use of drapes under
any condition, that his candidate will take a walk if they're used
on the air."

"Which we know won't happen," said Morgan. "And so does Dale.
He may be worried more than anything else about his own slot with
Conger if his man sees the drapes. You know—dropping the ball."

"I'm sure there's some of that, but I'm also certain it's not going
to help Conger if we hang drapes on that set. He'll be teed off at
Dale, teed off at us, and we'll have broken through whatever composure he might bring to the studio."

"Is Green's TV man suspicious?" Morgan asked.

"No. He knows nothing. It's better he function in ignorance." He
paused, then went on: "In order to prevent any last-minute switches,
Dale has insisted no changes be made in the set or staging after
three in the afternoon. What I thought could happen is, you delay
your arrival at the studio until after that time. I'll go along with
whatever Dale wants prior to your arrival. You walk in and order
me to put up the drapes. That's all there is to it. I've kept my
word to them . . . and you call the shot."

"You're certain Governor Green's people have no feelings against
drapes?" Morgan asked.

"Positive," said Wells. "Their man Smith says he couldn't care
less what the backing is—that Green looks good in front of
anything."

"Okay. We'll do it your way. Drop me a memo which says I
shouldn't arrive at the studio until after three—that you're respecting
the wishes of the television representatives of the candidates in
asking me to remain absent until that time. You meet me when I
arrive. I hope I make it. I'm not due to leave Rome until Saturday
noon. That ought to give me enough leeway."

"That takes care of what we can do *before* we hit the air, Fred,"
said Wells. Morgan's eyebrows went up in surprise at the implica-

tion. He waited for Wells's explanation. "We've had a hell of a running battle about reaction shots of the candidates at their lecterns. You know—shooting one man while the other's talking. Trying to get good human-interest reactions, expressions, possibly note-taking and the like. Dale's dead set against them. And his reasons are valid. Smith wants them used, assuming Green will break even because of his photogenic qualities. I have insisted that, as the producer of the telecast, that the final decision rests with us."

"And? . . ."

"I think we should use them," said Wells. "Naturally, I'll have to make certain my director cuts away an equal number of times from each candidate. Even so, there should be a way to favor Green." He paused, looking at Morgan. "And no one can lay a finger on us, no one can blow a whistle for those two solid hours that we're on the air."

"It's risky," said Morgan. "There could be a nasty playback on it. If you're careful, and think you can carry it off, go ahead. I don't want to know anything more about it. You're right, though. It could kill Conger on the tube."

"The only possible danger I see is if there were going to be more than one debate . . . and the next network were to handle Conger in a more kindly fashion. Then, by comparison, we might have to face some adverse public comment. But that can't happen, Fred, because it looks like there's only going to be one."

"Rufe says that if Conger's popularity drops another percentage point in the private poll, he's going to recommend more than one debate," said Abner Shepherd, sitting in Dale's office. "Our hero's slipping, Charlie," he continued.

"Oh, no!" groaned Dale. "Don't say it. You mean I might have to go through all this again? More than once? My God, I'd never make it!"

"Rufe says The Man got a kick out of seeing you on the train. You're good for his morale, son."

"What the hell, I told him in Colorado Springs I'd try to join him sometime for a couple of days. I saw a chance, got my answers on the debate format, and left. I hate those damn trains."

"What do you think of the pre- and post-debate survey Little wants to do? On viewer-reaction to the candidates?"

"Well," said Dale, "I hate to say this, but it fits into Little's thoughts re more than one debate. It'd be a hell of a barometer to base the decision on. I think we ought to get some indication as to how Andy affects the uncommitted voters watching. How big is the controlled sample—a thousand people?"

"Something like that. They'll be interviewed between now and the debate. Then they'll go back and interview the same people after the debate—with different questions. If there's a swing to one man, or the other, they'll catch it."

Fergie entered the office, her eyes flashing. "Charlie, you just can't sit there gammin' with old man Shepherd when we're in such trouble. You're goin' to hairlip the campaign if you don't get to this stuff before lunch. Do you know three people have been waitin' all mornin' to see you? Nobody can confirm our space in the hotel in Cleveland. Nobody will give me a copy of Conger's goddam schedule Saturday and Sunday. Nobody knows where Ham Forrest is. There are eleven urgent offers for Conger on TV before the debate. They've got to be shot down. Kee-rist, what a mess!"

"Turn 'em all down, Fergie," Dale said quietly. "Do that, then come back."

"You ain't got no conception what's goin' on around here," Fergie said. "This big slob comes in here and louses up your office while long-distance calls are comin' in from New York, Miami, Hollywood, Pittsburgh, Cleveland, and God knows where . . ."

"Who's trying to get me?" asked Dale. Shepherd rose to leave. "Stay, Ab. Don't mind Fergie. She's always like this."

"Son," said Shepherd, "never buck the pent-up spleen of a bitter woman. They'll get you every time. See you later," he said, departing.

"Dammit, Fergie," said Dale, "he's my friend. He came in here
to talk to me, and you insulted him. What the hell kind of assistant
are you?" he bantered.

"Balls!" said Fergie. "You'd talk till midnight if I let you." She
sat in the chair Shepherd had vacated. "Seriously, big Jesus," she
said, her voice under control, "I think we're goin' to go under.
The pressure is more than any of us can take—leastways me. I
just can't stan' to see us sinkin' deeper and deeper in the hole. How
do you do it?"

"You taught me, Fergie," Dale said, smiling. "Just take the top
card off the deck. Remember?"

"Damn you. It ain't always that easy. I had two Fat Cats this
morning who insisted they be permitted in the studio in Cleveland
for the debate. What do I tell 'em?"

"Tell 'em no. Tell everybody no. Tell those guys waiting to
see me I'll see them now. Cancel my lunch date. I'll eat here at
my desk. Let's move on that pile of wires as soon as we can. Are we
set on plane tickets to Cleveland? Ham Forrest is going to call you
from the next train stop. I just talked to him."

Fergie stood up, arms akimbo. "Why, goddammit to hell, don't
you tell a person?" she shouted. "We been tryin' to talk to Ham all
day yesterday and today."

"Why didn't you ask?" said Dale jokingly. "Honestly, Fergie, we
can't get anything done around here unless you communicate your
needs to us. We're—"

Fergie cut him off. "That's enough outta you, big Jesus. I just
think I'll go out to Cleveland and stay in the sack the whole time."

"You do, and I'll snitch to Andy Conger!"

Somehow they lived through the mounting tension, the increased
demands on their waking hours, and the accelerating pressures. Never
again would any of them experience the human, flesh-crushing
load of this presidential campaign. Dale made a solitary vow to force
his time in Cleveland into a pattern of reasonable rest at night. If
one person in Cleveland needed to possess every possible faculty
given him by his Creator, it was Charlie Dale.

Dale was never to get his rest. On arrival, he was an exhausted man. He checked in at the Sheraton-Cleveland Hotel on Public Square, leaning heavily on the front desk. A call to Murray Smith's room at the Statler-Hilton Hotel, which had been assigned to the Green party, returned no answer. Dale sat in the lobby, head down, with his eyes closed, as Fergie sought vainly to locate Tommy Tuttle, the Conger advance man Dale had taken off the road and ordered to Cleveland. He looked with disinterest at the sheaf of phone messages, wires, and registered mail Fergie plopped in his lap. How am I going to get through this? he asked himself. Everything was going wrong. Nothing was coming through on schedule. He had called the station and asked for Lou Wells, who supposedly was in Cleveland supervising the mounting of the master debate set which Dale and Smith were to approve at noon. There was no Lou Wells in Cleveland, no debate set. Dale wondered if it were intentional on North American's part. Were they delaying to a point of no return, to an hour or a day at which point approvals were meaningless, where any suggested change could not possibly be effected and still make air time?

From the moment Dale sat in the lobby of his hotel until the split-second the debate hit the air three days later, the tension and pressure mounted in an ever-increasing spiral. No one escaped. The fear of blunder, of a wrong decision in the crush of an impractical deadline, became enormous. Every technician lived with the strain. Routine pre-planning procedures and techniques of television production were magnified a thousand times in the taut atmosphere of the now famous studio. Set-dressing, studio temperatures, furniture and working props, water glasses, shadows, color values, note pads and pens, lighting adjustments, floor covering—all these were to become subjects of the most infinite and minute scrutiny. Nothing escaped the microscopic inspection of Charlie Dale and Murray Smith.

Early working press arrivals, employing any ruse to gain access to the studio and its environs, were a constant annoyance. The private protection force was called to duty forty-eight hours early because of the traffic around and in the building. Saturday, the Mayor, at a well-attended non-partisan civic luncheon, dubbed Cleveland the nation's first Debate City. He announced preparations under way for public viewing of the debate—outdoors and indoors—in the city's major pedestrian-traffic areas. Slowly but surely, hour by hour, the country's total interest and curiosity focused ever more sharply on a windowless concrete cube, sixty by ninety feet square, on Waterview Court near Cleveland's lake front: Studio Three at WTSR-TV, the historical scene of the first presidential face-to-face debate.

This singular event in politics and in communication, of such far-reaching consequences to personal political power, leading to fame in victory, or rapid obscurity in defeat, distorted the judgment, warped the efficiency and composure of every person connected with the debate. Tempers ran short. Experience, clouded over with fatigue and strain, no longer mattered. At times it became impossible to make a decision, any decision. Time was always a factor, the plain and simple commodity of time. Time to make the decision, time to make the vital change, time to argue, sell one's point of view, convince the other side. Time simply slipped through the fingers of the men fighting for the best on-the-air presentation they could deliver to what would be the largest audience in television's history.

Murray Smith, arriving late from Texas, seemed irritated far beyond his usual pleasant disposition. Conferring in Dale's room at the hotel, he insisted that a wire be sent to the network immediately demanding to know why North American had not delivered the set on time for their approval. In the wire, he stated that he and Dale would go anywhere—at any time of the day or night—in order to insure them the right of approval before it was too late to make a change. Inexplicably, Smith snapped sharply at Dale when they were working out the wording of the wire.

"Easy, old buddy, we're in this together. Or at least I thought we were," said Dale, wondering if Smith had finally been made a conspirator against Conger.

"I'm sorry," Smith said quickly. "My nerves are worn to a

frazzle. I could barely extricate myself from the traveling party to get back here. I've got a lot on my mind, Charlie."

"We both do, Murray. But, Jesus, let's hang together. It's our only hope against North American—our only chance to get something acceptable to our men on the air. We must keep control."

Smith was silent, head down and brooding. His manner disturbed Dale. It had been ten days since he'd seen his counterpart on the Green staff. The tension was exacting its toll from his friend on this, his first national campaign. Dale worried how Smith would get through the next few pressure-filled days. "Is there any way we can split the load? Do you need anything from me?" He said it to indicate he still valued the bond of friendship between them.

Smith looked at him squarely and shook his head. "No, Charlie, but thanks. I've got a very tough personal problem."

"Would it help to talk about it?"

Smith sat down on Dale's bed. He placed his Scotch on the night table and searched for his cigarettes. Dale, leaning across, offered one to him. "Thanks," said Smith. Preoccupied, he lit it in silence. "I've got a daughter, Charlie. She's six. Tomorrow morning at Boston General she undergoes a serious heart operation." He looked up at Dale, his face lifeless, drawn and colorless with fatigue and worry. "Oh, my wife Liz understands why I can't be with her. We talked it all out from Dallas last night. We've been married ten years —and we're very close. But little Missy . . . Melinda . . . it's hard for her to understand why I'm not with her when this important thing is being done. I'm the one that took her to all the specialists, talked and talked to her about it. I've been with her every step of the way. And now it's going to be done—tomorrow. And here I am, stuck in Cleveland, Ohio. Where everything's going wrong. I couldn't possibly leave."

"Why not?" asked Dale softly, with honest sympathy.

"I can't get anyone here to carry the ball for me. Who'd speak for Green?"

Dale looked at him a long moment, then said, "I will, Murray."

"You? That's impossible!"

"Why?" Dale asked. "Get your ass on a plane to Boston—right now. Give me some numbers where I can reach you. I'll cover for you. I think I know as well as you do what you will and won't buy when we finally see the set, if we ever do before air time. I won't commit you to anything, but I can sure as hell represent your thoughts and opinions. If we haven't reached common ground on this stuff by now, we're dead anyway." Dale watched him consider the proposal, stroking his upper lip with his index finger.

"I could be back by late afternoon, Charlie. It's just if I could be with Missy when she goes up, so she could see me. . . . And stay with Liz till she's out of the woods. What have we got to do here between now and then? I'm so bushed I can't remember anything."

"Nothing, really. Except this lox-fry on the set. If it arrives and they put it up, I'll go over and see it. You leave some emergency numbers with me, or call me from the hospital with them. If the set's not acceptable to *me*, I'll tell you why. I'll also tell you what it looks like in terms of what I know you want for Green. Outside of that, tomorrow is mostly nuts and bolts. Arrangements, arrival routes, facilities for press, and the timetable of rehearsals. Oh, I think we get the various colored passes tomorrow. And, if the set arrives, I assume they'll start hanging lamps immediately. But it'll be a far cry from final lighting. If they get into lecterns and stuff like that, I'll put it off until you're back. So go, dammit. You're needed in Boston more than you are here. I'll cover for you as fairly as I know how."

"You've made quite an offer, Charlie. And I'm going to accept it. Thanks."

Dale phoned Janet on Sunday. He was so full of frustrations, he thought he'd explode.

"You know what those bastards did?" Dale said to her. "They woke me up at two o'clock in the morning and said the set would be up at three. They were holding an official meeting at the time, and I was required to represent Conger. I could have killed them. I hadn't been to sleep more than three or four hours. The guys from our Conger mobile TV truck had called me about a fire. We lost all the video tapes for Andy's telecast next Wednesday—after the debate—and the truck was a total loss. Andy will have to do the telecast from scratch. The truck burned right down to its axles."

"Oh, Charlie, what a shame!"

"Honestly, the whole damn week-end's been that way. In the wire Smith sent to the networks, when he was so mad about the set not being up on schedule for us to approve, he said we'd go anywhere at any time—day or night—so they made me get up and go over there at three goddam o'clock in the morning. Jesus, I was mad!"

"You sound all worked up."

"I am. 'Cause when I got over there, they had the goddam curtains up, the velours—you know, the stuff like what's behind the President when he speaks, but what Andy hates. And Susan. So they got me up to have me look at something they knew damn well I wouldn't approve. God, I was mad. I turned it down cold, told them I was acting for Murray Smith too. They didn't believe me, so we called him in Boston. Poor guy had just walked in the door of his house. Well, at least we killed the drapes, then and there. North American still insists it's their first choice, and that we'll have to look at it tomorrow morning with full lighting on it. And the ridiculous thing about the whole situation is that the other set is terrific. Just what Smith and I wanted. It looks like a million bucks. Just the right combination of warmth and dignity for the two guys. You'll like it when you see it. God, I'll be glad when the traveling party gets here. It's been a nightmare sitting on this powder keg alone. If they only could have sent Wilbur Jenkins or someone to handle the press. They've hounded me until I've gotten to the point I've had to simply turn my back on them. And that's bad—for Conger, I mean."

"He got a huge welcome at the airport when he arrived here this afternoon," said Janet. "They're probably leaving about now."

"Well, it was a terrible mistake to schedule him so heavily this week-end. He should have been sitting right here in a hotel, wood-shedding the debate, doing his homework. And resting. He needs the rest as much as the preparation—probably more. . . . How's the bank behaving on the Dale Organization loan?"

"Fine," said Janet. "Everything's under control. The contract for the training film helps—a lot. It's not much, but the money will probably tide us over until you get back. The bank is very under-standing. They're all Conger men. They want to help, and know what you're going through."

"The hell they do. Nobody does . . . except maybe you."

"That was a wonderful thing you did for Murray Smith."

"Anyone would have done the same, Jan. He came back in great spirits."

"Well, twenty-four hours from now the debate will be over," she said. "I want you to know how much we want this to be a success for you—and for Andy. I know how much of yourself you've poured into it. And it will be tremendous. I just know it."

"It's not just me. Hans Kleinert, for instance, will work all night tonight with the network lighting man. Everybody's working just as hard and long as I am. I include the Green people."

"Just remember, Charlie, we love you very much, and we'll all be watching tomorrow. You need your sleep. We should hang up. Call me after the debate, if you get a chance."

"I'll try. I just wanted to talk to someone tonight and get a little of this off my chest. I'm all wound up. It's been such a madhouse. But now I think I can sleep. Good night, dear, and I love you."

But Charlie Dale couldn't sleep. His mind turned over and over on the hundreds of loose ends still requiring attention the following day, the day of the debate. Janet had said she'd be watching. Dale's mind leapt to the millions upon millions of Americans, along with his wife, who would also be watching. Lying in bed on his back, his stomach tightened. In the darkened room he fished for his four-hour sleeping pills, which he now placed beside his bed every night, and took two of them. Desperately, he waited for the few hours' sleep the pills might afford him. Tomorrow was the day.

It's already tomorrow, he thought. Gradually the pills took effect. He could feel the waves of sleep as they began to break over him.

And then his phone rang. He let it ring again and again, hoping it would stop. It didn't. He picked it up groggily. "Hello," he slurred.

"This is Cliff Harley, Charlie. The Man's in the hotel. Safe in his room. I thought you'd want to know."

"Yeah . . . That's fine. I'm glad you called. Thanks, Cliff. I'll touch base with you tomorrow on the debate plans. Good night."

The Man's in the hotel, thought Dale. Safe in his room. Thank God. He's here.

And Charles Dale slept.

17

The Day of the Great Debate

"CLEVELAND INDEED has been honored as the host city for such an historic event," the announcer's voice said over the radio, as the four men listened attentively, driving into Cleveland from Chagrin Falls in their regular car pool. It was Ernie's day to drive. He had a German FM radio in his car which, they all agreed, was a duzer. Ernie turned the volume up slightly as the announcer continued: "At this very moment, Secretary of State Andrew Conger is at the Sheraton-Cleveland Hotel, resting after his late arrival last evening. Governor Joseph Green is in his suite at the Statler-Hilton, and we are told he has not yet awakened. In but minutes less than twelve hours from now, these men will converge in a television studio in our city for the most important political event in the history of the United States."

"Hey, Ernie," one of the men yelled above the radio from the

back seat, "let's cut out a little early tonight, huh? Molly'll kill me
if I'm late gettin' home. Can do?" Ernie's head nodded affirmatively
as he leaned in to the radio-speaker to catch the words of the
announcer. "What about you other guys?' said the voice from the
back seat. "Shut up. We'll all leave with you," said Ernie. "Our
office is closin' a half-hour early so's everyone can get home."

Riding in on Cleveland's rapid-transit system from Shaker Heights,
two men studied the front page of their morning newspaper, the
Cleveland Plain Dealer. Its usual conservative makeup had been
scrapped for the day. A screaming double headline read: "CON-
GER, GREEN ARRIVE." Then, under it, "TONIGHT'S THE
NIGHT!" The commuter nearest the window pulled down the shade
against the low-slanting, brilliant sun. He spoke to his friend. "How'd
you like to be in their shoes, huh? I wonder if this is going to be
good or bad—for either of them." His friend said, "I dunno,
Howard. . . . But God help our TV repairman if our set isn't
back tonight. I sent it out a week ago to get a new tube. Goddam
Erna and her League of Women Voters. She insisted we get it
fixed before tonight. It was promised last Friday, then Saturday. If
it doesn't come today, I think Erna'll go right out and buy a new
one. I'll kill her if she does."
The man near the window said, "I'm stuck at the office, damn
it. We've got a stupid deadline on a presentation. But I understand
somebody's bringing a portable set in. So I'll see the debate somehow.
I want to see what happens to these guys under pressure. We've got
the same pressure several places in the world right now, you know."
"I'll have it right in my house if that goddam set isn't back."

Deep in the Cuyahoga Valley which bisected downtown Cleveland's squatting industrial complex of steel mills, iron-ore docks,
and oil refineries, a milkman dropped off his usual order at the
watchman's shanty at a plant entrance. The protection employee
standing in the open door greeted him. "Hi, John, gonna watch the
old debate tonight?"

"Yeah, we're going to a coffee klatch in the neighborhood. Some people for Green are throwin' it. I ain't made up my mind yet. But what the hell, a little coffee, a little Danish . . . nice way to watch the debate. I wonder what's going through them two guys' minds right now."

"Accordin' to the radio, they're still asleep. It must be gettin' to be a big affair over at that television station. They just called up for more of our men. That's the second time they've added protection."

"They don't need you guys over there. All they need is a referee and a bell."

Outwardly, the city of Cleveland looked no different than it did on other crisp October mornings. Here and there a lazy haze of mist and smoke from burning leaves hung over the shallow valleys. Otherwise, the city was clear in the autumn air: brilliant and sparkling. Lake Erie picked up the rich blue of the cloudless sky, shining like a sapphire through the yellows, reds, and oranges of trees which bordered its shores. Clevelanders awoke, dressed, ate, and went to work. Bus riders, automobile riders, streetcar riders, and those fortunate enough to walk, made their way toward their offices. Planes arrived and disembarked passengers at Hopkins Airport. Trains crawled into the cavernous downtown Terminal. And the good citizens of Cleveland, in hundreds of thousands of homes, offices and factories to the east, south, and west of the Lake worked into the tempo of the day. Regardless of who they were, where they lived, or what must be accomplished on this Monday, October 16, these diverse and busy people had, for the only time in their lives, an absolute common interest: The Presidential Debate at eight o'clock.

Along with the usual number of traveling businessmen in Cleveland on a Monday morning, there were several thousand additional visitors. The nation's and the world's press was gathering there by the hour. Over fifty television technicians from New York and Chicago augmented the regular staff of WTSR-TV. At the Statler-Hilton Governor Green's special advisers from Washington were checking in. And at the Sheraton-Cleveland, although Andrew Conger was still sleeping, his staff was not.

"Fergie," said Dale, "read the wire back to me."

"Right now?" she asked. "My eggs will get cold."

"You heard the man," said Ham Forrest. "Read it, golden girl."

At Dale's request, the three were having breakfast in his room. Forrest was in attendance after but four hours' sleep. He had come in with Conger the night before. He placed a serving plate over Fergie's eggs as she rummaged in a brief case for her notes. She extricated the copy of the wire with a flourish.

"It's to Lou Wells, care of WTSR-TV," she read. "And it goes: 'Re Debate, October sixteen. When rehearsal concluded Sunday night I felt podiums were still too close together. As placed by you, it is my opinion that the physical closeness will inhibit the candidates and give them a feeling of being crowded. I feel strongly that the close proximity of the lecterns will militate against the debate aspect of the telecast. The difference in the political philosophies of the two candidates should be visually manifested by a suitable physical space or separateness, something which does not now exist. I am asking you to reconsider moving the lecterns to provide a wider space between them. Please advise. The upstage backing and set design using hard flats and wood textures and grain is excellent in my opinion. It has our enthusiastic approval. Signed Charles Dale.'"

Fergie threw the copy on the floor and dove for her eggs.

"Thanks," said Dale. "Now you have some idea of what this damn telecast has boiled down to," he said to Forrest. "That's why I wanted the three of us to meet. Every minute of the day must be carefully planned for each one of us. No blind spots. No duplication."

"When do I sleep?" asked Forrest, yawning.

"Tomorrow," said Fergie. "Just like us."

"I want to go over this list with both of you," said Dale. "First of all, how's the man been doing on the road, Ham?"

"Tired," said Forrest. "He's beat."

"So is Green," said Dale.

"But Andy's real tired, and he's getting sloppy," said Forrest. "He's forgetting things we've told him for years. His gestures are sloppy, he's fighting the mikes, straining his voice when he doesn't have to, pounding the lectern too hard to make his points. He's not working the whole hall any more. He's slipped into a bad habit of just working the right half of the hall."

"Put the stuff down on paper for me," said Dale. "I'll go over it with him when I brief him."

"I hope you have better luck than I," said Forrest.

"Okay," said Dale. "As soon as we're finished here, I want you, Ham, to go to the studio and cover. I'll be over as soon as I can, but definitely before eleven. That's the time those bastards are going to show us the set with drapes . . . all lit with final lighting."

"Drapes," shrieked Forrest. "My God, our man will go—"

"I know, I know," said Dale. "I've been fighting it all along. It's too long a story to go into now. I've got it under control. They will be killed, *for all time*, at eleven. They hang over the other set—the one Smith and I have approved. NA wants the drapes. This is very important, what I'm saying now. We have an agreement—NA, Smith and myself—there will be no changes in anything made after five this afternoon. We light for two hours—from three to five. No changes, by no one, will be authorized after five o'clock. We've had a hell of a lot of trouble with NA—nit-picking by Wells and Sandy Jones. So Smith and I have insisted the set be locked up by three, with nothing changed after five. You, Ham, will remain in the studio from that time forward through the telecast. Fergie will give you every number where I can be located. You are to call me immediately if anything is changed—if anything smells wrong to you."

Forrest nodded. "Some hanky-panky going on?"

"I don't know," said Dale. "Maybe."

"I say something smells rotten in Cleveland," said Fergie. "I don't know nothin' about TV, but I wouldn't trust any of these monkeys out here. They're a bunch of shifty rascals."

"Next point," Dale said. "I have an agreement with Rufe Little that three o'clock is our deadline to yank Conger if we don't like what we smell."

"My God, is it that bad?" asked Forrest.

"Maybe," repeated Dale. "So we're committed to the debate after that time. Fergie, do you have those two lists of the North American and WTSR technical personnel?"

"Yes, boss."

"Give me both of them," he said. "This is confidential, Ham. Andy asked for the political registration of the crew. So I dummied up a list. I was damned if I'd make everyone on NA's payroll hate him by going to Lou Wells for the information. If The Man asks you for it when you're with him, I've got it."

"Okay," said Forrest, nodding. "Jesus, this is bigger than all of us."

"Amen," said Fergie. "You'd think it was Christ debating the Devil."

"I know a few people who think it is," said Dale, chuckling. "When you get to the studio, find Hans Kleinert," Dale said to Forrest. "He's been there all night working with the NA lighting director, Rudy Wolff. You've got one camera fired up over there right now—from eight until noon. From then on, we have all four cameras straight through air time. Find out if Kleinert is pleased with the way things went."

"Where do you want me, big Jesus?" asked Fergie.

"You go over with Forrest and guard the private phones in our office area. Don't leave them. I may have to get you in one hell of a hurry if signals get changed around here. Give me a reading on studio temperatures when I get there, Fergie."

"Off the same thermometer?" she asked.

Dale nodded. "Now, Ham," he said, shifting his chair toward Forrest, "we're still going around and around on reaction shots of the candidates. You know, cutaways—for color—for human interest. I will lose the battle, that I know. But I'm going to go down fighting. I don't happen to believe in them. I want you to make yourself up some sort of a tally sheet, and have it ready for tonight when we're on the air. You'll be in the control room somewhere. Not back with me, but some place. I want you to have a stopwatch and time every damn reaction shot that's taken—and how many. I'm going to keep book on Lou Wells, if nothing else."

"I don't quite get you," said Forrest.

"I'll explain it to you going over in the cab, lover boy," said Fergie. Dale reached into his dispatch case and drew out an envelope. Inside were the security tags for the WTSR building and studio. "Here's your pass, Ham. It will permit you to go anywhere. And Fergie, you get the same," he said. "I've got to brief Wilbur Jenkins now, and give him his press passes. Then I'll be with Rufe Little. He will disburse all the passes for the traveling party and the VIPs for their viewing lounge. Why anyone wants to come over there, when he can sit right here in his room and be comfortable with a drink in each hand, I'll never know."

"Any booze at WTSR?" asked Forrest.

"None," said Dale. "After Little, I will be with Cliff Harley. I don't plan to see Conger until around six-thirty tonight. I'll leave the studio about six, come back here, shower and change, and then go up to Andy. I'll ride over with him."

"What's the studio-rehearsal timetable as you have it?" asked Forrest.

"Well, there's what I've given you, plus a sheet Fergie has from NA. It's subject to change—the lighting rehearsals and stuff. There's a briefing around noon by Wells. At that time he'll give out final rehearsal schedules and times to move our man within the building."

Forrest looked at his boss quizzically. "Charlie, you really are worried about North American trying to sandbag Conger, aren't you?" he asked.

Dale thought a moment before answering. "Yes. I am," he said, "but I have no proof. It's just a hundred little things they've done, some before we got here, but mainly Lou Wells's nit-picking and interference since last Friday. It's like a soft shell, a puffy curtain. I can't seem to get through it . . . or see it. But it's there. All around me. Like I'm being silently led to the slaughter. Or, rather, Andy Conger is. Fergie's reported several shocking things to me— stuff she's heard around the studio." He paused and looked at the two, so widely dissimilar in background, experience, and nature, but who had given so much of themselves for him and for Andrew Conger. "I think the three of us must be on the alert at all times. As I've said, Fergie's home base should be at our private lines in our office space. I'll need you for a hundred things, Ham, before I arrive with The Man. But, from that point on, you stick with Andy. Lord knows what crisis or panic I might have to bail out at the last minute. I'll feel safe to operate only if I know you're with Andy. So I'll bring him to our offices and turn him over to you. Then I'll come and get him when it's time to move him down to the studio floor. In between, buddy, stick to him—like glue."

"Is John Lowell here?" asked Forrest, referring to Conger's regular makeup man, ordered on from the Coast for the debate.

"He's due in an hour," said Fergie. "I talked to him last night in L.A. He's coming directly to the studio. Then, if there's time, he'll come to the hotel."

"I'd feel safer if he never left the building," said Forrest.

"Check," said Dale. "Keep him away from the press, too. If he wants to sack out for an hour or so, get him a cot, Fergie. But keep him in the red-badge areas, away from the press. And don't let him leave the building. I'll talk to him when I get there, and it'll be not later than eleven." Dale looked at his watch. "I better get going. . . . And, Fergie, give Ham the dollar tour of the building when you arrive."

Dale found Wilbur Jenkins in his pajamas, hair tousled, sitting on the edge of his bed with the phone growing out of his ear. Jenkins was answering the questions of a wire service man. "I haven't got it yet," he said. "Wait a minute. Charlie Dale just walked in. He might have it. Do you know Conger's route from the hotel to the studio?" he asked, looking up sleepily.

"Yeah. He goes around the Public Square to Superior. He follows Superior . . ."

"You tell him," Jenkins said, handing Dale the phone.

"Hello, who is this?" Dale asked. "Oh, Homer, how are you? Yeah, Conger goes from the Public Square entrance of the lobby around the square to Superior Avenue. They have asked for that routing because they'll have viewing screens in the square, and they want The Man to make the trip around. Then he goes out Superior to Fourteenth Street and turns left. From that point forward, he takes the same route as Green, who, I think, will precede him to the studio. That's right . . . first Green, then Conger. I don't know, Homer. The entrance? No. The car drives right into the building on Waterview Court, a small street between Lakeside and Bethel Court off Fourteenth Street. That's right, we turn right off Fourteenth Street and into Waterview Court. Then right into the building. . . . As of now, we're due there at seven-fifteen. Okay, Homer. 'By."

"Thanks, Charlie," Jenkins said. "How are you?"

"Swamped. And a running target. God, am I glad to see you! The press has given me a horrible time. Here's some stuff. Your invitation to the Press Luncheon NA is throwing, with one hundred extras for your traveling press. Here's your red pass for the studio area tonight. Don't lose it. Each one is numbered. I got twelve, and that's it. No more. It'll get you anywhere. Here's a list of all the NA and local press department guys here in Cleveland. As soon as you know the name of the one still photographer, and the two pool pencils who win the toss for the studio during air, phone their names to me. Use these numbers here on this paper. Those are private lines into our offices at WTSR. I probably won't see you until the press tour. If you need me, Ham Forrest is your best contact. He'll know where I am."

Dale went on to Rufe Little's room, where Little was having breakfast with Abner Shepherd. "Well, if it isn't the impresario of the television channels," said Little expansively. "Ready for the big day Charlie?"

"As ready as I'll ever be, Rufe. I'm glad you got here last night. Maybe Jenkins can slough off the press on you and take the heat off me today. It's been rough with no one here."

"I'll call Wilbur," said Shepherd. "We'll field 'em."

"Good," said Dale. "Here are fifty VIP passes for the WTSR building. They've got two big lounges set up for you upstairs. If you want booze, call Fergie at one of these numbers on this paper. I have ordered no liquor for our staff, although Green has for his. It's up to you. I don't want any in the red area, around where we'll be working."

"We'll get some," said Little, "for after the debate. What are Andy's plans?"

"He'll return to the hotel immediately," said Dale. "As near three as possible this afternoon, call one of those numbers. That's your deadline on pulling Conger. Remember?" Little nodded. "My Fergie will be guarding the phones. If I'm in trouble, you'll hear from me by that time. Please check, though, at three."

"Right," said Little. "Good Luck, Charlie."

"Remember, there's always 'Queen for a Day' when this is all over, Chazz," said Shepherd. "You may be looking for a job at North American. Don't be too hard on the boys."

"Screw, Shepherd," said Dale, leaving the room.

Dale took the elevator to the candidate's floor and checked in at the security barrier in the wing assigned to Conger. The breakfast tray for the plain-clothes men was still on their table, the coffee cups stuffed with cigarette butts. He went over the target departure-times with the officers and passed through to Cliff Harley's room.

The door was ajar. He knocked softly. Harley, showered and dressed and holding a glass of orange juice, opened the door wide. "Come on in, Charlie. Good to see you, champ," he said.

"Welcome to Debate City, Cliff. Got any extra coffee?"

"Sure. Help yourself."

Dale delivered the necessary documents and passes to Harley, who sat on the bed with his coffee balanced on his crossed legs. Harley looked up after going through the material. "Where do we stand on wardrobe?" he asked.

"That's why I'm here," said Dale. "Let's get 'em out. Everything . . . the suits, the shirts, and the ties."

Harley opened Conger's two traveling valpacks on the beds. He took out three suits, each a shade of blue in a different texture. Dale went to the window, raised the shade, and looked carefully at the colors and materials. He knew the suits well. They were Conger's standard traveling "television" suits. Against each different background on a television set, however, a color and texture assumed a specific and special value. Dale made his selection, and Harley called Room Service for pressing.

"Remember, Cliff, no barbers near him today," said Dale. "I don't care what he says."

"Perry Como is off limits, I promise," said Harley.

"Ham Forrest tells me the man's exhausted. Do you agree?"

Harley poured himself another cup of coffee. "His face shows it a little, Charlie. I'm hoping the rest last night and today will help."

"What rest?" asked Dale in disgust. "Try to get him to use a masseur today and maybe take a nap for an hour or so this afternoon. That man has a very rough night ahead of him."

"I know. I'll do what I can."

"How's his voice?"

"Okay. I've been getting him to use the honey and tea every day. I think it's helped."

Harley opened a suitcase which contained only shirts. The two men selected a pale blue one which Dale had purchased for Conger at Tripler's recently. "Do you think he'll prefer French cuffs tonight, Charlie?" asked Cliff.

"He should wear them, Cliff. Besides, they're on the shirt I want. But this is sort of an elegant thing that's going to happen at eight o'clock. I think French cuffs are fine."

"God, I hope I have some cuff links."

"Where's the tie with the little white crosses on it?" asked Dale. "You know, the dark blue one with the four or five tiny white crosses?"

"Haven't seen it for a couple of weeks," said Harley.

"Dammit, I wanted him to wear that one. Look, I'll get someone to go over with me when I leave you—to the store next door. Higbee's. Do you need cuff links?"

"I can't find any, although there should be some here."

"Okay, I'll get a back-up pair over there, too. And two ties. I'll have whoever goes over with me bring them back to you. You keep 'em and give 'em to Conger when he dresses. Let's go over the times now."

"Check."

"I will be at your room, Cliff, no later than six-thirty. That gives us a little water, but not much. I will want a half-hour with The Man. If you can get me in there promptly at six-thirty, we're golden. Then . . . we leave the suite shortly after seven, which puts us at his car around five after. We arrive at the studio easily at seven-fifteen."

"The Secretary still wants you to ride over with him," said Harley, "alone."

"Fine," said Dale. "You'll be along too, won't you?"

"Yes. I'm going to put a security man in the front with me, just in case. So, there will be three of us in the front, you and the Secretary in the rear. Any problems you see on the departure location here?"

"No," said Dale. "It's open, wide stairs. No chance to get mobbed."

"Good. I guess that's it. Where can I reach you during the day if I need you?"

"Take down these numbers."

"Kill eight-seven and two-eleven," said Hans Kleinert into his headset, connected with the North American Lighting Director at the dimmer panel. Kleinert bent to his clipboard again. "Okay, now bring up fifty-nine. Just a trifle. Oops . . . not too much. Back down a bit. That's fine. Thanks, Rudy." Hans turned to Dale, standing next to him in the control room. "That's the best I can do, Charlie. It's the material. It's so hot."

"Frankie," said Dale, turning to the North American set designer, "can you open up the folds—flatten them out?"

"No more than I have," he answered. "It will look skimpy, deprived, cheap, if we go any further."

Dale looked at Conger's hated drapes and curtains once more. He had gone through the motions of trying to make them acceptable to everyone, so that when he said *no*, it would stick. On schedule, and to the best of its ability, NA had lit the backing of the vertical folds. Everyone in the studio knew Dale was going to reject the design, and a tautness crept into the air. Dale and Forrest expertly analyzed the picture on the monitors in the control room. A stand-in was at each podium, two men WTSR had found who looked remarkably like Green and Conger. "See those bars, Ham?" Dale asked softly. Ham nodded. "Sue will say we've put her man behind bars again—made him a convict. I simply can't understand why NA keeps pushing it."

"You know as well as I do, it's not that bad, Charlie," said Forrest. "But, Jesus, after the way he blew sky high last week in Salt Lake when we walked into a local station and saw this stuff, I tell you you're out of your mind if you go with them."

Dale stood silently, legs apart, arms folded across his chest, studying the picture. Suddenly he said, "Okay, guys . . . thanks," and strode briskly out to the studio floor. "Lou Wells . . . Lou Wells . . . Anyone know where he is?"

"He'll be back in a minute," said Smith, seated in a canvas chair at the rear. "What's the verdict?"

"They're dead," said Dale. "I can't buy them. You'll go along with me—right?"

"We're in sync," said Smith. "I suppose we have to wait for Wells to kill these kitchen curtains and get moving on lighting the other set."

"The sooner we start, the better," said Forrest.

Lou Wells walked toward them from around the edge of the flats on the debate platform.

"It's no go," said Dale. "I simply can't buy. I've got five more weeks to get along with my man before this is over, and we can't take enough of the vertical pattern out to make it acceptable. Conger will flip."

"Let's get going on the other set, Lou," said Smith.

Wells stood his ground. "We've got the finest technicians in television out here. There isn't a better lighting man in the business than Rudy Wolff. There isn't a better set designer than Frankie Alton. These men think you're making a terrible mistake killing this set. I think you are. Sandy in the control room thinks you are. . . ."

"Oh, for Christ's sake, come off it, Lou," snapped Dale, cutting him off. "Who the hell are you trying to kid? How naïve can you get? It's overdressed, overtheatrical, overpowering—all those goddam opera folds."

"You're going to overrule the opinion of NA in this?" Wells asked furiously.

"You're goddam right!" said Dale. "Who's controlling this debate? That's all I care about. The drapes are an issue of control. I don't want 'em. You do. My first loyalty is to my man. We will control what's behind Andrew Conger. If those drapes aren't killed by three o'clock, Conger will be a no-show. I have the backing of Rufe Little on this."

"Okay, fellas," said Wells. "You alone are stuck with the consequences. If there's any beef about the background, it's right in your lap, Charlie." He spun around and faced an open boom mike. "Call the stagehands back from their lunch break, Sandy. Strike the drapes. We'll light the other set now. Your man is very stupid, Charlie. And so are you."

"It's going to be a long day, Lou," said Dale. "Mind your manners."

John O'Hanlon, owner-proprietor of the Iriquois Bar and Grill in Bay Village, far out on Cleveland's West Side, arrived at his establishment an hour earlier than usual. He wanted the extra hour to mount a television set above the bar for the debate. It surprised him how much business the bar was doing at noon. Someone off in the dim, beer-smelling coolness at the far end said, "Hey John, got any good numbers today?"

"I'm playing eight, eight, eight, Jim," he answered.

"What's so lucky about that?"

"Who knows? But the big debate's on at eight tonight. I got a hunch. I'm playing eight all the way."

"I'll betcha Green takes him cold," said a counter waitress in a crowded downtown Cleveland restaurant to a steady customer. "Wanna bet?"

"Sure," said the man. "Who's going to be the ref?"

"Hey, you know? I never thought of that. You willin' to take Billy Hank's word on who won? He's gonna do the audience applause thing tonight on his show after the debate. You know . . . with the meter."

"Sure. I'll take his word. It's a deal. A buck?"

"Whaddya mean, a buck? A quarter. And you watch Billy Hank. 'Cause I will."

Cleveland rapidly was taking on the appearance of a carnival city. Candy butchers and souvenir jockeys took their favorite stands here and there. The streets were more crowded than usual. The appearance of police barricades in the Public Square always presaged excitement and an event. The lunch-hour strollers watched in large clusters as the four huge television screens were erected in a hollow square on the turf. A giant canopy was unrolled nearby, to be hoisted above the screens as a protection against rain. "No Parking Today" signs went up along Superior Avenue and Fourteenth Street. A small group of the curious milled around the huge press bus parked at the curb in front of the Sheraton-Cleveland. Well-organized groups of Conger supporters, in a variety of costumes and headgear, came and went as the sun slid into the afternoon sky.

High above these unusual happenings in Cleveland, Andrew Conger worked, paced, and prepared.

Twelve blocks away, at the Statler-Hilton, Governor Joseph Green, after a morning of concentrated reading and research, sat down to a hearty lunch. He was tired. After his meal he would take a nap.

"This will be the final review of all rehearsals, schedules, and procedures between now and air," said Wells to the group assembled in the unused studio down the hall from the cluttered debate Studio Three. "In case you have questions," he continued, looking out over the heads of the seventy or so people gathered for the briefing, "it might be wise to run down who is here." He consulted a list. "We have Weldon Parkhurst, our on-camera moderator for the telecast. For all concerned, we will run through the format once more, so that it will be perfectly clear to everyone connected with the timing and cueing procedures. There are television representatives of the Conger and Green staffs here. Security personnel, the director of physical arrangements, the supervisors of production for NA and WTSR are both here. The NA News and Publicity directors are sitting in the far right corner. Operations, Engineering and Promotion people are here. So if you have a question, ask it now. It's your last chance."

Wells then ran through the format. He covered the different-colored passes for various types of security priority and freedom in the building. He walked the group through the arrival procedure of the candidates. It was decided Green would arrive at seven, Conger at seven-fifteen.

"As far as Studio Three is concerned, it is off limits to everyone —I repeat—*everyone* not directly connected with the telecast. As you know, the building was emptied of all personnel at midnight last night, even those at the switchboard. Then, only those with passes were readmitted. As far as we can tell, there are no unauthorized people in the building at this moment. If you see anyone without a pass of any kind, report it immediately to a security officer. We have full camera and production facilities in Studio Three at this time. And will have through air. Final lighting re-

hearsal will take place between three and five. From now until
three, we will be checking all audio and video circuits with the
Telephone Company and New York. If you try to get into Studio
Three and are not wearing the proper pass, you will be stopped. Press
will be permitted in for a preview at two forty-five—for fifteen
minutes. Then they must leave. If you have reason to leave the
building, be sure and take your pass with you. Without it, you will
not be permitted to return inside."

And so it went, on and on. Each service, each need, facility,
rehearsal period, element of production, traffic control, security, was
checked and rechecked before Wells announced the session was
over. He excused himself to attend the Press Luncheon at the Cleveland Athletic Club.

Dale and Smith returned to Studio Three immediately to
supervise the placement of the two podiums. Their lunch which
consisted of cold hamburgers was eaten off the top of a twenty-
seven-inch Conrac monitor just off the debate set. At that moment,
Lou Wells, surrounded by three wire service reporters at the luncheon, nibbled on a cracker spread with caviar and shredded egg as he
gave them the fine points of preparation for the debate telecast.

The press tour started on schedule. They came through in a
steady stream, buttonholing any member of the crew who could
give them a behind-the-scenes lead for a story. Photographers worked
frantically. Several men broke the rule regarding no interviews.
Wells, however, did his best to prevent any leaks. Smith and Dale
watched the proceedings from the control room, thereby avoiding
any contact with the press. Fergie, however, barged in with a newsman in tow. "Mr. Dale, this is Amos Whiting," she said. "He wants
to talk to you."

Dale's mind locked on the name immediately. This was the
reporter from Green's home town who had talked to Wilbur Jenkins
weeks before. "I've heard of you, Amos. How are you?"

"Lousy," Whiting said. "I just got in town an hour ago. Figured
I might be able to catch you if I took this press swing through the

facilities. This sure is a far cry from our potboiler out in Fairlee."

"Amos, this is Murray Smith, Governor Green's Television Adviser," Dale said quickly to alert Whiting. The two shook hands. "Say, you're an on-camera reporter for NA, aren't you?" asked Dale.

"Just for the campaign, Charlie," said Whiting. "I'm pretty much on the 'in' with Green, so I've been assigned to him. I've got to talk to you . . . right now."

Dale shook his head. "Number One, you're off limits for the working press. Number Two, I'm dead, stuck where the goddam hell I am until probably five. Can it wait?"

"No . . . but I guess it'll have to. Where can I meet you at five?"

"Fergie, leave word at the front desk so he can get back to our offices."

"Oh, the hell with that," said Whiting. "There's a saloon right around the corner," and he pointed, "that way. The Commodore Perry, or something like that. I'll be there at five . . . waiting. If I were you, Dale, I'd keep the date."

"If I can't make it, someone will come and tell you. Right now, we've got a lot of work to do. See you at five, Amos."

Prior to the press tour, the drapes had been killed, and the final debate set was mounted and dressed. Dale's three-o'clock deadline to recommend pulling Conger had passed. Rufe Little called, and was told everything was under control. Dale had the set he wanted. A hundred and one adjustments in camera position, set props, and furniture were made. At one point, Wells ordered the patriotic symbol lowered from the grid. Before the stunned eyes of Dale and Smith, an enormous red-white-and-blue American Shield was dropped slowly into place over the moderator's desk. In the center, standing out in bas relief, was a huge mahogany gavel. The slightly tilted, but almost horizontal handle was the heraldic perch for a hideous screaming eagle. His bared talons curled tenaciously around the wood, and his arched neck supported a fearsome countenance. The curve of the eagle's beak was exaggerated, his jaws were open wide, and a long crimson tongue lashed out at the world. Held in place by the eagle's talons and draped across the top of the gavel, so that it unfurled to either side to form a broad base for the monstrosity, was a wide band of simulated white silk ribbon, antiqued to an ivory color. On it in bold black letters was the legend: FREEDOM OF SPEECH.

"Isn't that just too much!" exclaimed Smith.

"Endsville," said Dale.

"Kill it," said Smith to Wells.

"We spent twenty-five hundred dollars to have that thing made," Wells answered. "It's a contemporary masterpiece of the wood carver's art."

"Kill it," said Dale.

"The Overseas Press Club would give their right arm to get their hands on this," Wells said.

"Oh, well, if you're going to give it away, I'd like it," said Dale. "It'd look terrific hung over the box stalls in my horse barn in Denver. I wouldn't want it in my house, though. That's a cowardly eagle."

"What do you mean?" asked Smith.

"The eagle's looking to the left, back over his shoulder. In heraldry, an eagle who looks backwards—or to the left, for that matter—is cowardly."

"Good Christ," snapped Wells, "since when are you an eagle expert?"

"Lou," said Dale, "don't you understand what's going on here tonight? This is not a daytime quiz show called 'Name Your President.' This is a sober confrontation of two men, one of whom will be the next President of the United States. All day you've been loading up the stage with garbage. We don't want anything between the men and the viewers. We want a direct line—a direct visual line with no detractions—between the viewer at home and these two men. Can't you understand that?"

"We're interested in good television," said Wells.

"We're interested in good statesmanlike television," said Smith.

"We have loads of mail demanding a patriotic symbol on the set," said Wells.

"Okay. So get a flag," said Smith. "Where shall we put it?"

"It goes to the left side of the stage, facing it. To the right of Conger's podium, as per flag etiquette. He's Secretary of State, remember?" asked Dale.

"Which means Conger will appear to be more patriotic than my man. He'll be closer to the flag," said Smith. "No dice. Get two flags."

"Where do we put them?" asked Wells, wearily.

"We'll show you," said Dale. "Just get the flags."

And so it went, item after item. With each tick of the clock bringing the preparation activities frantically closer to air. At one point the pandemonium and noise level in the studio, coming through the control room over the talk-back audio system, rode higher. Wells and Dale could hear the rising swell as they both sat in the dim light, each one thinking his thoughts.

Wells peered through the tinted glass which separated the control room from the studio. "Charlie, who in the hell are all those people out there?" he asked quietly.

"I don't know," said Dale. "We've told them and told them to check every damn person who comes through either that door there or the one at the other end of the studio. And still it fills up just like a sink with ten faucets running full blast."

"I'm going to do something," said Wells. "Right now." He slid his castered chair to the right until it was directly behind the "studio announce" microphone. He paused, collected his thoughts, and then pushed the talk-back button.

"This is Lou Wells. I am the producer of this debate. Some of you know me out there because you're doing your job, and we've been together on this important production for four days. Most of you out there do not know me because we have never met. The reason we haven't met is because you're not in television. You know nothing about television or production. You have never been in a tele-

vision studio before. And you don't belong in this one now. Therefore, I am asking everyone in the studio to leave, everyone except
the security people and the Cleveland police. Everyone is to leave
the studio. That means all the crew, all the supervisors, all the stagehands, all the technical personnel, along with the press, and all you
who shouldn't be in here. I am asking this because I have doubts
as of now that we'll get this telecast on the air. After the studio
is empty, those of you with authorized passes will be readmitted."

One of the light-bell phones blinked. Wells took his finger off the
mike button. "Take it, Charlie." He pushed the button again. "Anyone with an authorized pass will be readmitted. I am asking this be
done immediately and in an orderly fashion. Thank you." He released the button again. "Who's that for?"

Dale was holding his hand over the mouthpiece on the phone.
"It's AP Photo. They say someone said the light values had been
changed since they took their readings this morning, and they
want permission to check and bring in new lenses. I say no."

"Right. Tell 'em the reading's the same, even though the lighting's been changed so many times I can't remember. Tell 'em there's
still one hundred and thirty-five foot-candles at each lectern."

At times, Smith and Dale, standing at the podiums of their respective candidates, asked question after question, each one vital to
the moment, critical to the appearance or well-being of their particular man.

"This podium needs bracing at the floor. When I lean on it, it
rocks. Can we fix it? . . . Where are the pens they will use for
notes? I want to see them. . . . Where's the little lip which was
supposed to be around the top of the podiums to keep the pens
from rolling off? . . . The flags are in the way. . . . I thought we
were going to be given a choice of stools—now you say we only
have one. Let's get some more in here to look at. . . . Do we use
tally lights on the cameras, or not? . . . What kind of water glasses
are you going to use? . . . These note pads are no good. They're

too big. Get some off-white paper. That white will bounce up in their faces. . . . Move Green's flag stage right about three inches. . . . What will the tempeature be in here when we go on the air? . . . That lamp's not on you, it's on Conger. . . . Someone get Conger's stand-in to say a few lines. Okay. 'Blah, blah, blah. When I am President, my first act will be to make clothes illegal, Mother's Day will be banned.' (A cheer rises from the crew.) . . . Tell Green's stand-in to walk from his chair to the podium . . . that's right . . . now look over at Conger. Fine . . . now look down and make a note. Okay. . . . Move Green's flag back where it was. . . . Where's that bad shadow coming from? . . . There's a mike boom in the way. . . . Tell Green's stand-in to talk, looking straight out . . . talk, say something . . . 'I'm tired. I've been standing here three hours.' . . . See, Hans, we get that shadow when I go in with the boom to cover him in that position. Can you see the timing device okay, Murray? Do those floor lights block it, or blind you? I can see it. Push the switches. . . . Yeah, green okay, yellow okay, red okay. . . . Can you see my legs when I stand like this? . . ."

The technical crew watched in fascination as Murray Smith and Charlie Dale assumed the stage positions of their two candidates. More than once the cameramen and technical crew watched, in what bordered on disbelief, as Smith and Dale at the two podiums assumed the positions, attitudes, and speech characteristics of their men, Joseph Green and Andrew Conger. But were these candidates not their trade, their special craft? The two could mimic to perfection every mannerism of their charges. Smith would lean forward on the podium, shaking his finger at the camera. Dale would lean on one arm, making a point with his index finger placed in the upright palm of the other hand. The two television advisers stood like their candidates, moved like them, talked like them. From early in the campaign until Election Day, they *were* their candidates.

"What kind of rug is this? . . . Bring up Green's backlighting, just a whisker. . . . Let's go through how we bring them into the studio again. . . . Will this door be locked? . . . There's that bad shadow again. . . . Is that the air conditioning that's humming? . . . Can we do something about it? . . . What's happened to Conger's key light? Hans! . . . What about those viewing windows on the second floor? Are they blocked out? There's a man standing in one of them with a broom in his hand. Get him out of there. . . . This podium would make a nice bar in my den. . . . My man wants tea . . . no, no food. . . . Where does Conger go to the bathroom? . . . My man wants soup. . . . Someone get Parkhurst. We want him at his desk. . . . Can we tape these cables? Someone's going to trip and fall. . . . Can both you guys see pictures on the monitors? Conger's should be dead now. . . . Engineering, where's engineering? . . . Do we have to have these American flags? . . ."

"Dale, you're wanted on the phone in the control room. Long distance."

Resenting the interruption, Dale made his way to the control room. An engineer handed him a phone.

"Hello, this is Charlie Dale."

"Hi, Charlie, this is George Pinnell," the voice said.

Christ, thought Dale, this is all I need right now. "George, we're awfully busy here. Could I call you back tonight after the debate?"

"Well, I want to talk over a few things before the debate, Charlie. Things involving Conger's personal self."

"Make it fast, George. On this line they may pull the plug on you without warning. Shoot!"

"Well, number one. Does Andy plan to wear garters tonight?"

Good God Almighty! Dale said to himself. "I don't know George. Why, do you want him to wear them?"

"Well, yes. Or else get him some of that knee-length hose I get at Brooks Brothers. When he crosses his legs, his garter snaps show, and he always tugs at his hose. I don't think he should do that on a presidential debate."

"I don't either, George," Dale said, with exasperation. "There's no Brooks Brothers in Cleveland. What's next?"

"What about that tiny bald spot? Are you going to blacken it?

Did you pluck the hairs between his eyebrows, at the top of his nose?"

"No."

"I asked you to do that in a memo to you."

"I never got it. Look, George, we're really awfully busy. I'll switch you to my gal in our office, if I can, and you give all the . . ." It was one device he thanked Little for, cutting yourself off your own phone conversation. In the middle of the sentence, Dale placed his finger on the receiver button. It was the end of George Pinnell for that day.

Slowly but surely, the debate stage assumed its on-the-air form. Lights were in their final positions, each lamp numbered and marked on the master light plot. The dimmer-setting number for each lamp was in a separate column on Kleinert's clipboard. Every shadow, every highlight, every nuance or sophistication of expertise which would combine the requirements of television with that of superb portrait lighting had been employed. All that remained was for the lighting men to see the real articles—the candidates themselves—instead of the stand-ins. After the candidates arrived in the studio, they would work feverishly in the short technical-adjustment period assigned each candidate. The temporary chalk marks on the floor around every movable piece of equipment were retraced in white paint as insurance.

"Well, that's it," said Smith. "No more changes. It's five o'clock."

"My God!" said Dale. "What's happened to the time?" He turned to Wells, sitting nearby in a director's chair. "Okay, Lou, lock it up. I'm satisfied."

"Ditto," said Smith. "It's beautiful. Really lovely. Anyone who can find something wrong with it is a Communist."

"And a spy and fellow traveler," added Dale.

"The drapes should be hanging up there," said Wells.

"No more changes, Lou," said Dale.

"I just hope I can keep everybody in line," said Wells oddly.

"Who's there to keep in line?" asked Dale. "We're all right here."

"What difference does it make?" said Smith. "It's after five o'clock. No more changes by anybody. Not even God."

Smith announced he had long-distance calls to make, and then would go to the hotel to brief his man and bring him over at seven. Dale told Fergie to stand by the phones, and told Wells he'd have his man in the studio on time, at seven-fifteen. "If you need me, call me in my room between six-thirty and six-forty-five. Come on, Ham, let's go."

The group dispersed. Someone began to kill the brilliant but scorching lights to aid in keeping the studio cool. One by one the lamps went out. The shapes of television's hardware stood out in silhouette, each tool facing the empty stage, most of them pointed at the two dark and vacant podiums. The crew departed for their dinner break. Only the protection men stood by the doors.

The studio rested. The pressures faded and died. Without people—and their conflicting desires, deadlines, and fears—tension could not survive. But in less than two hours, Dale and Smith would return with the male leads in this unique drama, the candidates themselves.

But as Dale approached the Commodore Perry Bar, Fred Morgan, still another principal, strode briskly into Studio Three at WTSR-TV.

18

The Showdown

It took Charlie Dale's eyes a moment to become accustomed to the dim light when he and Forrest entered the Commodore Perry Bar. The tavern was depressing, a relic from the days when the area at the foot of Ninth Street was a bustling hub of lake commerce. Cargo and passenger ships had once used regularly the now decaying piers. The lake-front airport and the express highway, however, had all but submerged the marine stores and honky-tonks of the neighborhood. Only the old car barn—now the studios of WTSR—had survived the decline. Television had rescued it. And television had brought the party faithful and the merely curious to Waterview Court. Even at this early hour, people with signs and demonstration banners were lining the police barricades. When again would they have a chance to see two presidential candidates pass by within minutes of each other.

A voice said, "Here I am, Dale. I'm three up on you. What'll it be?" Dale made out Amos Whiting at the far end of the bar, slouched over his drink, cradling it in his right hand. Dale motioned to a secluded table, and Whiting joined him and Forrest.

"We haven't much time, Amos," said Dale. "I'm not a teetotaler, but I've got a long night ahead of me. What's on your mind?"

Whiting studied the two men a moment, and liked what he saw. "I work for NA," he said in a low voice. "Lou Wells is my boss. We get paid five hundred bucks for every exclusive we can deliver between now and November." Whiting paused, then went on: "I've got one—and it's a screamer."

"Does it have something to do with the conversation you had with Wilbur Jenkins a few weeks back?" asked Dale.

"Yes," said Whiting. "So I've got the exclusive of all time—and I can't use it. Because it'll put Lou Wells and NA out of business. Several years ago, when I went to Fairlee from Chicago, I decided I liked to eat regularly and get paid vacations. I like to hunt and fish. I like real people, straight people." Dale was tempted to speed him up, exasperated by his rambling. Maybe it was the drinks, he thought. Whiting resumed. "Has NA been giving you a bad time?"

"Yes, up until now," said Dale.

"Has Lou Wells been putting the knife in you?" he pressed.

"Yes," repeated Dale, "up until now. They've both given me a very bad time. But we passed an important production deadline at five o'clock, and now I'm in the clear. We had a hell of a lot of trouble with a set design that NA wanted, but was totally unacceptable to Conger. We almost came to blows over it."

Whiting gulped his Scotch. "Have they given Green as much trouble?"

"No," said Dale. "From the beginning, they've had it in for Conger. Week after week. Starting way back in the early meetings. But we passed our crisis at five. There's nothing more they can do."

"Except kill us on the air with lousy reaction shots of Conger," said Forrest.

"True," said Dale. "But I don't think they'd dare."

"What if you lost picture four or five times when Conger was talking?" asked Whiting. "When he was making points against Green?"

"What are you trying to say?" Dale asked. Whiting's statement stunned him.

"Do you know how badly NA wants Green to win this campaign?" Whiting leaned forward, his words barely audible.

"I haven't the slightest idea," said Dale. "I've never been really sure they did."

"Before the first convention," Whiting continued, "Lou Wells came out to meet with Joe Green. It's taken me almost three months to dig out the subject of their meeting. But I've got it. And it stinks to high heaven. I don't know the why behind it, but I do know a deal was made between NA and Green to throw everything Green's way. And they did, during Green's convention. They got burned because of it. They played it straight during your convention. I have a lot of friends in Fairlee. My sister works in the State House. I have two cousins who work in the Governor's mansion. They show me memos every now and then. That's how I got onto this thing. I was with Wells when he first came to Fairlee to see Green. But Wells saw to it I wasn't in the meeting. Incidentally, Fred Morgan, President of NA, and Green talked for one hour on the phone a week ago before Morgan left for Italy. Morgan got back from Rome yesterday and called Green here in Cleveland at eight-thirty last night. They talked for fifteen minutes."

"This is all interesting, Amos," said Dale, "and for all I know, NA did have a plan to sandbag Conger. But we've stymied them. They had until five o'clock to pull any goddam thing they could. And I would have pulled Conger if it got too rough. But the deadline has come and gone. I must admit you've given me some ideas. Ham—call the Telephone Company, even though there's nothing as honest in this world as a Telco man. Find out if there have been any unusual requests by NA to place their own people at the switching point on to the cable. Also, make it your business to get the necessary clearances to be in WTSR Master Control during the telecast. Video control is in the control room of Studio Three, so I can keep an eye on the video engineers."

"It wouldn't take much, Charlie," said Forrest, "for him to roll his contrast knob—in the dark. He sits way down at the end of the console."

"Now you're talkin'," said Whiting. "Cover every base you can. Because if Happy Joe Green is in the White House, Mr. Fred Morgan will be the country's first Secretary of Communications. And if Mr. Fred Morgan goes to Washington, who, pray tell, would be the logical choice to become the next president of NA?"

Dale's head snapped up straight. "My God," he said, "Lou Wells. Who else?"

"Now you're thinkin'," said Whiting, smiling. "Sort of makes things clear as crystal, doesn't it?"

"If you're a professional reporter with an exclusive like this, and you work for NA," asked Dale, "why are you telling me?"

"I told you," said Whiting. "I can't use the story. Maybe someday I'll include it in my journalistic memoirs. Secondly, I don't like to see anybody screwed, especially when the cards—and power—are stacked so viciously against him." He downed the dregs of his Scotch, belched, and plunked his glass on the table. "What's more, I'm a Conger man."

"Hey," a voice from the bar said, "any of you guys named Dale?" The bartender was leaning out of a phone booth, the receiver at his ear, the wire stretched taut.

"Yeah, that's me," said Dale.

"Phone. The guy says it's urgent." Dale left his chair.

"The five o'clock deadline has come and gone, eh?" mused Whiting. Forrest said nothing, his eyes on Dale as he lifted the receiver.

"Hello . . . Charles Dale speaking."

"This is Murray. I'm at the studio . . . calling from your office on the private line. If you ever tell anybody I called you, I'll deny it."

"What's up?" The first whisker of pain, of apprehension, flicked through Dale's stomach just below his bottom rib on the left side.

"Fred Morgan is in the studio. He has ordered Lou Wells to hang all the drapes, and that will be the set which will be used on the air. Morgan has killed our set."

"Jesus Christ!" Dale's stomach constricted, pain shooting straight up into his chest.

"It's just by accident I heard about it. I was running past here on my way to the car when Fergie stopped me. She said something fishy was going on, that Morgan was in the building. I walked into the control room, heard parts of their conversation, and saw the stagehands starting to hang the drapes. As you said, we're in this thing together—and I haven't forgotten Boston."

"Thanks, Murray. I'll be right over. Stay where you are, in my office. Don't move. You and I have been played for the patsies of all time. I have a fantastic story to tell you."

Dale slammed down the receiver. "We've had it!" he yelled, as he walked toward Whiting and Forrest. "Amos, you were right." He stood at the table, leaning over to scoop up his cigarettes and lighter. He looked at Forrest. "Morgan's ordered the set up with the drapes. They're making the change now." Whiting looked up with a knowing smile. Dale continued, "Those sons-of-bitches . . . those bastards! They planned it this way . . . this late . . . thinking I'd be back at the hotel."

"What are you going to do?" asked Whiting. "Sing?"

"No," said Dale. "I'm going back to the studio. Ham, call Cliff Harley from here. Clear Whiting to meet me at the security barrier on Conger's floor at six-thirty. If I don't get Wells or Morgan to kill those drapes and give us what we agreed to at five, I want a meeting with Little and Jenkins. I think we should tell NA we're doing the debate under protest. When it's over, we should blast the living shit out of Wells, NA, the whole sick, rotten mess of them. But it's a decision bigger than me." He looked at Whiting. "This is a favor I'm asking, Amos," he said, shaking in his anger at being duped. "Off the record, will you tell Little and Jenkins what you've just told me? I'm going to push to break it—or leak it—the minute the debate's off the air."

Whiting said, "Sure, if it'll help Conger. Why not before?"

Dale said, "No, I think it would kill Conger to break it ahead of air. It would be misinterpreted. That's where Little was correct. And there just isn't time to do it right, or even alert the press. So meet me at Conger's security barrier at six-thirty. Ham will set it up. Get back to the studio as soon as you can, Ham." In almost uncontrollable anger, Dale looked again at the two men. "Those cheating, lying, miserable bastards! This is it. It's either them—or me."

"So that's the story," Dale said to Smith. "NA hasn't phased you in because they probably were afraid you might inadvertently tip it. I kid you not. NA is out to torpedo my man. You've been almost as big a sucker as I."

Smith, face drained white, sat disbelieving as he listened to Dale's description of the Whiting session. "What can I do, Charlie?" he said weakly. "I can't honestly say I object to the drapes. I know they're going to irritate your man—shake him. They won't do anything to my man."

Dale thought a moment. He stood up and faced Smith. "It's too late to pull Conger—you know that. He's going on this debate, and there are not going to be any drapes behind him. Either Lou Wells or Fred Morgan will give the order to kill them. I'll start with Wells. If you're standing in the line of fire, you're going to get hurt, get cut up badly. I'm going to cover this building tonight like cancer. If you're between me and what I have to do, I'll cut you to ribbons. Understand that?" Smith nodded. "Okay, so stay out of my way. Stay anywhere, but stay out of that studio until I get what I want. Give me a wide berth, 'cause, brother, I'm about to do some cuttin'."

When he came up to Wells in the studio, Dale whipped him around by the shoulder so abruptly Wells lost his balance. "Watch what you're doing," Wells snapped. "This isn't my idea," he said, jerking his head toward the set. "I kept my word."

"Don't pull that crap on me. You're in this thing up to your eyeballs," said Dale. "I'll give you five minutes to kill that set. Or I go to Morgan."

"I can't. I'm following Morgan's orders."

"But you gave him the word, didn't you? How Conger and Susan hate drapes. To take yourself off the hook. My tit is in a wringer, Lou. And it hurts. Badly. You're going to get it out."

"I wish I could help you, but it's out of my hands. The boss is running the show."

"Would you like me to tell the two wire service men out in the hall what I know about the deal between you and Green and Morgan, or would you rather have a talk with me in private?"

Wells looked at Dale with no expression in his face. Just flat, dead, inanimate. "Let's find an office," he said levelly.

After locking the door, Dale leaned against it. He offered Wells a cigarette. Dale's mouth was dry with fear. He felt control slipping away. After the months of careful planning, perhaps he wouldn't be able to deliver for his man after all.

"I know everything, Lou. The whole sickening story of what you've been doing to Conger—and me. I'm not big enough. I haven't got enough eyes and legs to fight you and Morgan everywhere in this building tonight. When the deadline came and went with no fireworks, I thought much of what I'd felt was my imagination. For your information, the word on the drapes came from someone who would surprise you. If it hadn't, I'd be back at the hotel now. And it would have been too late."

"I can't control Fred Morgan," said Wells. "This is his baby—all the way."

"You stupid, conniving son-of-a-bitch. How many times do I have to tell you that neither Fred Morgan nor you, nor NA—nor anybody —has a goddam right to screw around with something this big? Do you have any idea how horrible a thing this is that you've done?"

Dale took a step toward Wells. He went on: "Isn't there anyone honest left in this business? Please, please let these men alone tonight. You can kill Conger while we're on the air. Don't think I don't know that. I'm going to breathe down your neck on any reaction shots. But, Jesus, Lou, let these guys alone—to do their best. I'm so tired I'm almost at the point I don't give a damn which one wins. But I give very much of a damn for their right to try—with no interference from you, NA, or anybody." With great weariness Dale looked down at him, aware of the consequences of his attack. "I don't care if I pump gas when this is all over. I may very well do so when you and Morgan get through with me. But, by God, what the viewers see on their TV sets is going to be what Andrew Conger does—not what you bastards do. These guys aren't your slaves. You're not putting on the gladiator games. They're not prisoners—criminals. They're presidential candidates, for Christ's sake. *Their* wishes, not yours, govern this debate. You've conned them—me. We've delivered them. Now you want to display them—on your terms. Blood's what you want, isn't it? You want a helluva show, don't you? You'd like those two podiums to be so close Conger might forget himself, lean over and take a poke at Green. Isn't that what you want, Lou? A little blood, huh? Just like the shoot-'em-ups. Only this time we'll do it with two presidential candidates instead of the guy in the black hat and the guy in the white hat. Is that why you've been fighting all week to get the podiums close together? It's sick . . . disgusting. Where are your ethics . . . your values? What in the hell has happened to you guys? Television doesn't belong to you tonight. It belongs to Conger and Green. And the public. Can't you understand that?"

Wells puffed at his cigarette, looking steadily at Dale. He offered no response.

"These drapes aren't important to anyone but Conger," Dale said. "The whole thing is silly—even to me. I'm so tired of the nit-picking. Pick, pick, pick. But the terrible thing is how serious I am, how sincere I am, when I tell you that anything—anything—Andrew Conger should have tonight is what he's going to get. The important thing is that one of the two guys who's going to walk in here in less than two hours will be the next President of the United States. And what they want is the only thing that's important. Not you, not me—just them."

"The man I work for already is president, President of North

American. And sometimes I think he has the idea he's more powerful than your man."

"I couldn't figure out your involvement in the Green deal until I
realized you probably would become President of NA if Morgan
goes into Green's Cabinet," said Dale, protecting Whiting and at
the same time indicating to Wells the extent of his knowledge of
the deal. "That's a pretty big reason to go along with what someone's boss wants, isn't it? That's plenty of reason to have made my
life a nightmare the last two months. And screw Andrew Conger tonight. Isn't it?"

"My hands are tied, Charlie," Wells said flatly. He sat quietly,
completely at Dale's mercy.

"You planned it well," said Dale. "I've got to hand you that. I've
passed my point of no return. You know it. My man will walk in
here on schedule at seven-fifteen. And when he sees those drapes,
three things are going to happen. One: he's going to blow sky high.
He'll be furious, thrown off his stride minutes before the most important event of his life. Two: he's going to say to me, 'Haven't
you got any control over these people?' Three: Conger's going to
fire me. Not then—he'll be so mad he won't know what he's doing—
but later." Dale paused and pounded his cigarette out. "I don't
want any of those things to happen, Lou. I've gone through a hell of
a lot for this man. So has my marriage, my career, my whole life.
Nothing more is going to happen to it because I won't let it happen. So I've got news for you. Tonight my man gets what he wants.
Not for him—but for me!" Dale leaned forward, his face hovering
over Wells, and close. "For me. . . . Get it? Not for Conger and
his future . . . but for mine. So change those goddam drapes, if
you're any kind of human being. Change 'em! Kill 'em! Right now!"
he shouted.

Wells began to feel the tight knot. He tried to relax the tension
in his neck by tilting his head backwards. The pain subsided slightly.
Wells knew he wouldn't make the change without Morgan's approval. He realized he didn't have the guts to change it on his own

and do what he knew was right. If he did, his future at NA was over. How could this be happening? he thought. How can I do this to another man? Why has it come to this? I'm not really this bad a person. I'm really not. Without any warning, without changing expression, tears welled up in his eyes. He blinked them away as he looked at Dale. He knew he was afraid of this man who could destroy everything he had fought for, this man who could hurt him so. And then Wells heard his own voice saying things he never thought he'd say to anyone, things he himself had never said before.

"I've been wrong," he said, not to Dale in particular. "I've been so very wrong. I can't remember now when it started. Morgan told me I was on the way out unless I came up with something to bring the public and sponsors back to NA because of the mess and scandals. I went to him with the idea of the debates. He wouldn't listen unless I got one man to say yes. I figured Green had the most to gain, so I went to him. I guess you know the rest." Wells paused, lit a cigarette as Dale watched. "What started out as just a way of getting Green to endorse the debates got out of hand," he said. "I never thought it would go on after the convention. Morgan called me in one day and said Green had promised him a spot in his cabinet if he made it. And that if he went to Washington, I'd move in at NA as top man." He looked up at Dale, a weak, rueful smile on his face. "That's when I got lost. I began to have visions of myself sitting at Morgan's desk. They were nice pictures." Wells looked at his hands.

"I can understand that," said Dale.

"It became very important to me for Green to win." He stopped, still looking at Dale, then went on. "What else is there to say? You know the rest."

"If I get Morgan to order you to make the change, can you do it by air time?"

Wells looked at his watch. "Yes. If I get the word in the next half hour."

"You'll get it," Dale spat the words out at him. "And, by Jesus, you be ready. Alert your crew, find Hans Kleinert. God help you if every one of those cameras and lights isn't back where they belong when my man is standing at his podium. Where's Morgan?"

"Ask the operator to get him for you. He's in his suite at the Sheraton." Dale was put through quickly.

"Hello, Fred? This is Charlie Dale. Can I see you in ten minutes? It's urgent. Fine. . . . I'll be right over. Don't leave." He looked at Wells. "And don't you be calling Morgan before I see him. Understand?" Wells nodded.

Dale found Smith waiting for word. "I got the whole story out of Wells—and more," he said. "Morgan's at the Sheraton. He did his work and left, the son-of-a-bitch. I'm going there now. Wells says he'll gamble on relighting our set if he gets the word inside half an hour. Will you cover for me, Murray—with Ham?"

Smith looked at him and smiled. Pleasantly, he said, "Sort of a life-or-death situation, isn't it? Just like one I had last Saturday. I'll cover, Charlie. We'll start by alerting the lighting crews ourselves. Call me the minute you have an answer."

"Wells can advise you." Dale shook his head slowly, from side to side. "Poor bastard. A guy so weak he hasn't got the guts to do this on his own. He knows he's wrong. He admitted it. I think we'll have a clean show now that the air is cleared. If I can get that shit-ass Morgan to give the order."

"Do it, Charlie," said Smith. "Give it to him with both barrels."

Fred Morgan was not alone when Dale arrived at his suite. Morgan was walking toward him, hand outstretched in greeting, and saying, "You know Jim Finnegan, the President of Telenet, and Paul Fenton, President of Global, don't you, Charlie? What'll it be? A Scotch?"

"No, thanks," said Dale. "How are you, Jim . . . Paul?" He said it flatly, now beginning to wonder if all three were in on the plot against Conger. His mouth was dry again as he confronted the three giants of television. "I'll take a little water," he said, picking up a glass on a tray. He drained it in one long swallow.

Huge copper hoods covered simmering chafing dishes of food on a sideboard. An overstocked stainless-steel portable bar stood next to it, canted out into the room. Fenton's fist was stuffed with nuts. He popped them into his mouth one at a time. Finnegan was adjusting the brightness on a twenty-seven-inch television set.

Jesus, I thought he'd be alone, Dale said to himself. What the hell do I do now?

"Uhh . . . Fred . . . we have a technical problem on the debate. It's urgent. Only you can settle it," Dale started. "Could I see you for a moment in the other room?"

Morgan sat down heavily in a corner of the four-cushion couch. "You can talk freely in front of Paul and Jim. After all, they'll be doing the remaining debates. And there will be more. The public will demand them. It might help them to hear what you have on your mind, the type of problem NA's been coping with. Spill it."

A nice dig at the other two networks, Dale thought. He decided to give Morgan a chance. Maybe it wouldn't get down to gut-fighting after all. He spoke, including the other men in his remarks:

"Tonight the real winner is television, Fred. All of us in this room know that. Long after the campaign is over, television will be en-joying the blessings of this incredible event. But to win, television must do a scrupulously honest job of presenting these two candi-dates with the best possible production. Television must be a re-porter tonight, not an editor or an interpreter. It must be as neutral as possible, as technically perfect as possible. Above all, one of TV's major roles in the development of the debate telecast—its format, its staging—has been to make this formidable experience for each candidate as satisfying to both men as we can possibly make it. Any irritation, however small, any distraction to the men, as they work to put across their points of view, must be eliminated." Dale paused, took another sip of water from a fresh glass.

Morgan looked at his watch. "Get to the point, Dale."

"This *is* my point," Dale said. "Sometime after five o'clock, you, Fred, ordered a change in the basic debate set after a hard and fast deadline had been agreed to by all parties. You must have had very good reasons for doing so. We have been here for four days, have met in session on design and production for two-and-a-half months.

The Green man and I rejected this set you just ordered up. We agreed to another one. Our set was up at five. Wells agreed to no more changes after that time. You, however, have seen fit to throw out our choice and put in your own. I cannot accept your decision. Conger cannot accept it. Wells tells me we have time to relight the other set. Can we change back . . . right now?"

Morgan sipped on his Scotch. Then, wiping a trickle off his chin, he said, "Someone has to be responsible for this debate . . . control it. The production, the lighting . . . everything. The only place responsibility can rest is with the network. I have made the final decision. Wells reports to me. I was aware of your feelings, and those of the Green man. NA has decided to go with the set as I have changed it. We will take the consequences. It is our debate responsibility."

Dale leaned forward, elbows on his knees. "The feelings of the candidates must be taken into consideration, Fred," he said. "Conger hates those drapes—can't stand them. We've been through this a hundred times with Wells."

"I wasn't aware Conger *hated* drapes," Morgan lied. "I understood you didn't like them, that the Green man had no feeling one way or the other."

"That's true," said Dale. "So, because we weren't together on the drapes, we switched to the other design which we both liked. Our candidates enthusiastically approved it."

"But which wasn't what we at NA thought was the best design," said Morgan. "I'm sorry if you feel this way, Dale, but North American is presenting the debate, not Andrew Conger." He bit into an ice cube and crushed it noisily. "If there are complaints from viewers, a negative reaction in the press, then Telenet and Global could take them into consideration in the staging of their debates. We think ours is right. We'll take the rap."

Sensing the feeling and emotion beginning to creep into Dale's remarks, Jim Finnegan of Telenet left the room discreetly. Paul Fenton also excused himself, saying he'd left some important papers in his suite he would need later on that evening. Morgan acknowl-

edged their departure with an offhand, self-confident gesture. He
winked at Fenton and, barely moving his head, nodded toward
Dale. Fenton understood: Morgan would tolerate Dale's earnest-
ness. And then Dale and Morgan were alone.

Dale was the first to speak. "I'm not leaving, Fred, until you kill
those drapes."

"Don't be ridiculous," said Morgan.

"I'm not," said Dale. "I gave you a chance in front of Finnegan
and Fenton to see the light, do the right thing. The points I made
were valid. Yours aren't. Why?"

"Stick to politics, Dale. Leave the television to us."

"I've been in television, *not politics*, Fred, for fifteen years. And
I'm not about to leave the television to you tonight."

Morgan rose, mixed himself another drink. He offered to mix
one for Dale, who declined.

Here goes my career, thought Dale. Right down the drain. For
what? Because of my silly, impractical loyalty to a guy named Andrew Conger, I've got to take Fred Morgan on. And I will be bloody
and cut when it's all over. I'll never get another dime's worth of
business out of NA as long as I live. Dale watched as Morgan returned to the couch. Then he rose, and faced the President of NA.

"You know goddam well why those drapes are up there," he said.
"Don't you? Because Lou Wells told you they'd irritate Conger,
blow him sky high. We both know that, don't we?"

"First I've heard of it," said Morgan dispassionately.

"In a pig's ass it is. You're using these two candidates as puppets
. . . marionettes for your dance of decency on television. You've
put your Sunday clothes on for once in your life . . . to bail yourself out of the sick, dishonest way you've been doing business the
last ten years. Oh, it's your debate, all right. Just as you said. It
surer than hell isn't Conger's or Green's. One of those two men tonight is going to lose by what he does up there—in front of a hundred million people. You're the only guy who won't lose, aren't
you? You've got it made. You've got your debate, Morgan. Now let
Conger up off the floor. For Christ's sake, give him an even break

on that set tonight. Don't irritate him. Don't shake him up. Leave him alone, for Christ's sake. Keep your cotton-pickin' hands off this debate. You've got it! Let it alone!"

"You better leave, Dale," said Morgan. "I have dinner plans."

"I'll leave when you change those drapes. I'm not going to pull Conger. You know I can't at this time. He'll be on. You'll have your stinking, bailing-out-the-junkies-of-TV debate. Your future isn't on the block tonight. Andy Conger's is. And so is mine. You've used all of us to bail you out. Okay, so we have. Now leave us alone. Let us put on an honest debate." Dale swallowed hard. "Not a crooked one like the rigged telecast you had planned."

"Get out, Dale."

"You can't see any difference between pulling the strings on the debate or on a quiz show, can you? It's all the same thing to you. The whole goddam American public was up for grabs for years in your stinking rigged shows. Why the hell shouldn't the White House be up for grabs, huh? I know a lot about what you've been doing the past three months, Morgan. Do you want to hear more?"

Morgan reached for the phone. Dale whipped it out of his hand. It crashed to the floor. He leaned down close over Morgan's face. "Answer me!" he screamed. The scar on Morgan's forehead was pulsing, turning purple as the blood rushed to it.

"Get out," Morgan said, "before I throw you out. You'll never work another day in our business."

"I don't give a damn. But you do, don't you? That's important to you, isn't it? A hell of a lot more important than honesty, ethics, morals, fair play. You don't know the meaning of those words, do you, Fred? You're a cheap, crooked, miserable bum. I don't care who you sell your dishonest wares to, Morgan. But you're not going to force 'em down Conger's throat. We aren't buying. Tonight . . . or any night."

"Charlie," said Morgan, leaning back, away from Dale, "you're all worked up. You're tired. Let's forget it. Things have gotten all out of proportion in terms of importance to you. There's a reasonable way to work this out."

"There's no way because I can't offer you a seat in Conger's Cabinet. I can't throw the whole weight of a network behind my man the way you've thrown yours behind Green. I haven't got enough men to cover every employee on the crew you might have bribed tonight. I'm not as big as you are. Your trouble is you don't think *anyone's* as big as you are, do you? Or as powerful?"

"Where'd you hear those lies?" asked Morgan, eyes narrowing.

"They're not lies, Fred Morgan, and you know it. I have a witness standing by Rufe Little's suite right now. I'm not about to throw Conger with this information so close to the telecast. But, unless you change those drapes and put back the original set, we'll deliver our man under protest. And the minute we're off the air, we'll break the whole story. I have a witness to Wells's meetings in Fairlee with Green. I know you talked to Green last night. I know every disgusting point of your deal with Green . . . and Wells."

"You wouldn't dare pull that off. You're a stupid punk. Conger would be the laughing stock of the world. Sour grapes, lousy sport. The press would laugh him off the front pages. Television is on a high plane tonight. We've brought dignity and sober thought to the muck of politics. That's what the press—and the public—think tonight. They won't buy if you try to sell them anything else."

Dale thrust his hand down to Morgan's chest. He grabbed his suit coat, shirt, and tie in a single vicious grasp. Jerking him up out of his seat he thrust Morgan toward a window. With his free hand Dale drew back the curtains.

"Look at that crowd," he said, pointing down to the Public Square, now filled to overflowing with thousands of people. Searchlights chased each other across the darkening sky. A huge bonfire surged and danced at the confluence of four crosswalks. "Look at that. You call that elevating politics? Look at those idiots waiting to cheer their TV Hero! This debate has turned into the biggest political sideshow in history. It's a carnival!" he added, in disgust. "The campaign is nothing but a breather between your goddam two-hour Roman games on television!" Dale, breathing heavily, released him.

Morgan smoothed down his shirt and walked back to a chair.

"What do you want, Dale?" he asked quietly.

"I told you. Pick up that phone now and kill the drapes." Looking at his watch, he added, "We've still got time."

"No . . . I mean, what do you want?" Morgan repeated, with heavy emphasis on the "you."

Dale stared at him, stunned. "What do you take me for?" Dale was seething.

"I never made the offer," Morgan said.

"Oh, yes you did. And I won't forget it. It will be another nice lead for the press release tonight. You never know when to stop. All you're interested in is the big grab!"

"You're through, Dale. Get out! After tonight, you'll—"

Dale cut in. "Nothing is sacred to you, is it? It's all negotiable. Everything's up for grabs, even the Presidency of the United States —isn't that what you think? Well, I have news for you. You're wrong. There are still a hell of a lot of decent, honest people in this world. And they're going to catch up to you lousy infested hyenas who are running television and rip your brains out. Go ahead. Tomorrow . . . next week . . . next month . . . make your millions on the slop you're spoon-feeding the public. But, by Jesus, you're not going to make it at the expense of Andrew Conger. Or Joe Green, for that matter. The mere fact you were willing to do something to even irritate Conger is reprehensible to me. You put your fat, sticky thumb on the scales of simple common decency. If you don't take it off, right now, I am leaving. And we'll let the public decide who's right and wrong after we break the story. You will hear from us before air that Conger appears under protest." His lips were compressed, bloodless. "Now—do I call Rufe Little and set up the meeting on the release? Or do you call Lou Wells and kill those drapes?"

Morgan was beaten. He'd known it for some time. His mind, however, wouldn't accept it. He'd run things his way too long. It was almost a relief to hear someone catalogue his evils for him.

Even so, Morgan wasn't afraid of Dale, or Conger for that matter.

He wasn't afraid of the exposé Conger might release. The NA publicity, public relations, exploitation departments, and network news telecasts would more than offset his efforts. Fred Morgan was afraid of none of these things. He was suddenly struck with consuming fear that his wife Benita was deadly serious when she had said she would leave him if he had made a deal involving NA with Green. Conger's actions would bring it out in the open. Losing Benita was something Morgan could not face, could not even visualize. He knew in that moment that Benita meant more to him than anything else. He must keep her, at all costs. He wondered if Dale had the compassion to listen to one more deal from him which would make it possible to keep the woman he loved.

"If I kill the drapes and give you the set Conger will okay," Morgan said, almost inaudibly, "does your information or our conversation have to go any further than this room?"

"No—if you guarantee to me we will have an absolutely honest, clean debate as far as production is concerned," Dale answered. "I want your okay to put my people anywhere in the building I desire. And I want this to be a straight, flat, fair telecast for Andy Conger and Joe Green."

"You'll have it," Morgan said quickly. "Who else knows what you know?"

"No one important," answered Dale. "The story is dead. I assure you it will not see the light of day from the Conger staff or my source. The one Green man who knows can't afford to say anything." He looked at Morgan and smiled. "Let's be practical. After tonight, Fred, I've got my life to think about. And you've got yours."

Morgan reached slowly for the phone. "Operator, give me television station WTSR. I want the control room in the debate studio. It's Studio Three. I want to talk to Mr. Lou Wells."

19

Ninety Minutes to Air

THE HALL was hushed and still as Charlie Dale walked toward Cliff Harley's room. Here and there a door stood ajar, the wedge of light slanting softly into the darkened corridor. Activity, panic, crisis, had been intentionally removed from the proximity of Andrew Conger's suite for the day of the debate. The candidate was at work.

The rooms of the Appointments Secretary, as always, were adjacent to the candidate's suite. They were the buffer zone, the moat, the Geiger counter of politics. Cliff Harley, however, dealt in pests, phoneys, and time-wasters who, because of political status, could elude the security check farther down the hall. Dale entered without knocking.

"You're late," said Harley. "Did you see the TV press guy who's been waiting for you down at the security desk?"

"Yes," said Dale. "That's part of my being late. I had a real screamer on my hands. It's over now, thank God."

"You look like somebody's been using you for a dart board," Harley added.

"They have. Someday, maybe I can tell you what I've been through in the past hour. Is The Man ready for me?"

"Not quite. He went down for a snooze late. He's in the shower. I'll go in and check in a minute." Harley arranged several stacks of confidential memos on his bed.

"Did Ham Forrest leave a couple of ties with you for the man?" Dale asked.

"He's got 'em. Didn't like either one. Sell him, Charlie . . . sell him."

"How does he feel?" asked Dale.

"Seems fine. Chipper. . . . Talkative."

"How long did he rest?"

"Oh . . . half-hour maybe. No more."

"Who's seen him today? Any idiots get to him?"

"Nope. Little . . . Shepherd once or twice . . . a couple of the speech writers wrang him out on issues. That's about it. Been very quiet. Susan's been in and out a couple of times."

"What has he eaten today?" Dale asked.

"A good breakfast. Soup and a steak sandwich for lunch. Had the tea combination about an hour ago. By the way, are we set with soup at the studio?" Harley asked.

"I think I just ordered tea, but there'll be no problem. No explosions?"

"No explosions," repeated Harley. "Any changes on time of departure?"

"None," said Dale. "We must leave the suite at five after seven. I'm a little worried about the arrival route to the studio. There's a huge mob of people outside the hotel right now. The Public Square is jammed solid. Someone's cranked up a Victory Rally. Wait'll you see it. It may slow us down. There's another crowd gathering outside the studio—mostly Green. So let's not get a late start."

Harley looked at his watch. "What the hell," he said, "come on in with me now." Dale picked up his brief case and followed Harley

into Conger's suite. They walked through the dimly lit drawing
room, down a hall past the dining room, and stopped in front of
Conger's bedroom door. Susan's room was two doors down the
suite's corridor, with an empty room in between serving as a sound-
buffer against Conger's unpredictable all-night conferences and telephone calls. Harley motioned Dale to follow, and they walked in.
"Charlie's here, Mr. Secretary," Harley said, raising his voice over the
tap water running in Conger's bathroom. "You ready for him?"

"Sure," Conger said. "Hi, Charlie, make yourself comfortable. I'll
be finished shaving in a minute." Dale opened his brief case on one
of the beds and leafed through his papers for assurance. "I'll leave,"
Harley said. "I'll be back at seven to check."

"We'll be ready to go by then, Cliff. Let's move at seven sharp,"
said Dale.

"Will do," answered Harley, and left.

Conger's voice, distorted at times as he shaved, came to Dale from
around the corner. "How's it been going?"

"Fine," answered Dale.

"Any last-minute changes I should know about?"

"None, Andy." None, that is, you should know about.

"No problems, huh?"

"Nothing worth mentioning."

"Has Fred Morgan been more co-operative?" asked Conger, walking into the room in his undershirt and shorts, wiping his face. "I
would assume he's kept an eye out for you."

"Yes . . . he has," said Dale. "All the way through." A vulture's
eye.

"Glad to hear that. Any more trouble from that Wells chap?"

"None lately," said Dale. "He's delivering everything I've asked
for."

"Good." Conger threw the towel on the bed, and picked up his
shirt. Dale made a mental note to wire George Pinnell that Conger
was wearing garters, with double snaps. "You can start any time,
Charlie," Conger said. "I'll finish dressing as I listen."

"Can I show you this first?" Dale asked, holding up a large photograph mounted on cardboard. "It's something you should see before we go over."

"What is it?" asked Conger, coming over to the bed.

"This is a picture taken from the podium, from the position you will be in. It shows you, from your point of view on the set, what you will see as you look out into the studio. You will use the Stage Right podium. On television, that's camera left, the left side of the screen. When you look over at Green, we will see more of the right side of your face than the left. That happens to be your best profile. I picked that side, however, because in the theater, Stage Right is the strong side. It's where the important entrances are always made from . . . where your eye goes first, as when you read a book or a page."

"How was that decided?" Conger asked.

"By a coin-toss," Dale said. "That's the way it came up." Dale pointed to a camera directly in front of Conger's podium. "That's your camera, Andy, the one with that glass box on top of it that looks like a Teleprompter. That's the cueing device. It will give you your times, warn you when you're getting down to the wire on allotted times for statements or rebuttal. You always make your statements to that camera for the TV audience. It is yours exclusively."

"Good God, they're using a lot of lights," said Conger. "Can't they get by with fewer than that?"

"Looks pretty rough from the podium, doesn't it? The man standing next to the camera with the headset on is your floor manager. He is dressed in this photograph exactly as he will be tonight. You'll be introduced to him when you get there. He will never take his eyes off you . . . and is available to you at all times during the telecast." Dale then showed Conger photographs of the podiums, the note pads, and the chair he would sit in at the beginning of the program, then put them away. "When you hit the air, you and the other man will be sitting in the chairs, with Weldon Parkhurst, the moderator, sitting between you in the middle. He may decide to welcome you to the telecast. If he does, I suggest you just nod and say 'Good evening,' or something."

"Ummhumm . . ." Conger said.

"Then, Green has the opening statement on the first hour, so you will remain seated as he goes up to his podium. He will sit down when he's finished, and you will have your opening statement. So now we're about twenty-one or -two minutes into the first hour. At that point you remain at your podium . . . you don't return to your chair because Green will now come back to his podium for the rebuttal and rejoinder period. The podiums are solidly braced and bolted to the floor. You can lean heavily on them. You'll see that when we get there."

"What do I do when a freewheeling exchange starts between me and my opponent?"

"You can turn your head toward him when you want to talk to him. Look at him any time you want to in listening to him or talking to him. There is an additional camera placed off the edge of the set beyond you, and beyond the other man, which will shoot you when you do that . . . catch you when you're looking at the other man. Which brings up NA's insistence on reaction shots. I've discussed this with you before. At any time the other man is talking, NA may put a camera on you for your reaction. You should be prepared for this eventuality. Naturally, if you're blowing your nose or blotting perspiration or something, they won't take the picture. Your floor manager will control that."

"What time do we leave here?" Conger asked, looking at his watch.

"At seven," said Dale, "which should put us at the studio no later than seven-fifteen. The other man will arrive ahead of you. Your car takes the same arrival route as his. This was done to facilitate security and crowd control. Your car drives right into the building, where a greeting party will be waiting for you. After the pictures and handshakes, you go into the debate studio with me for a lighting check. No Press. When we're finished, we go to a quiet office assigned to you, where you will remain until ten minutes before air. We'll do makeup there. John Lowell is here from Hollywood. I'll return for you, and we'll go down to the studio for final lighting and makeup checks. You will remain on the set until air time."

Conger listened intently, nodding his head from time to time as Dale made a point. These were the instructions from his electronic second. The duelist filed them away expertly, retaining them for use at their proper time. Conger held up a tie to the light of the standing lamp by his bureau. "Is this the tie you want me to wear, Charlie?" he asked.

Dale stood up and came over to inspect it. Forrest had picked a good pattern. "Yes . . . this is perfect," Dale said. Conger put it on, and Dale pulled the knot slightly tighter. "That looks fine," he said.

"Any more instructions?" Conger asked, pacing the floor in front of the two beds. The pressure was starting. He fussed with his breast-pocket handkerchief, which reminded Dale to tap his own hip pocket and check to be certain he had extras for makeup and perspiration blotting, although this was not a serious problem with Conger.

"Yes," said Dale. "There will be reporters and a photographer in the studio, on a pool basis, during the two hours you're on the air. They will not advance in front of a predetermined section of the studio. The stills will be using long lenses. Neither they, however, nor the pool reporters will be in the studio when you arrive, when we're making technical adjustments, or when you come back down ten minutes before the air for final technical adjustments. It's none of their goddam business what we do during those times. I've banned them over Jenkins's objections."

"I agree," said Conger, slowly nodding his head. Dale felt his man's mind drifting toward the content of the debate, becoming preoccupied with the substance of the issues, his material.

"Andy," Dale said, sliding to the edge of his chair, and leaning toward his man for emphasis, "there are some things I want to tell you now regarding your performance. I don't ordinarily do this so far ahead of air time. Tonight I would feel safer, however, if we could go through it right here."

"Sure," said Conger. "Sure. . . . Go ahead. Do it now."

This is it, thought Dale. Whatever I tell him now might affect what one hundred million people will see on their television sets. Be precise, he thought, and say exactly what you mean. He began.

"I think the most important advice I can give you tonight is to be yourself. Whatever you are, be that tonight. Do not be what you are not. Just be Andrew Conger."

"I always am," Conger said, smiling. Not always, thought Dale. He pressed on, aware of the time. "I'd like you to remember one other thing all through the two hours you're on the air. That man over at the other podium—the other candidate—by winning tonight can take away everything that you've been fighting for for years. He can steal the White House from you in two hours. He can walk away from that studio as the next President of the United States if you let him. So *don't* let him. It's you . . . or him. I'm going to tell you this again just before you go on the air." Dale had decided to get Conger mad, but at the correct time. Dale wanted his man ready to tear Green apart. He felt the physical, visual symbolism of Green at the podium was the sharpest way to make his point.

"I see what you mean," said Conger. "Okay. . . . Anything else?"

"If the other man throws you a hell of a serious question or issue, don't answer immediately. Not too fast. Give the viewers at home— and include them in everything you do—give those people at home a chance to get with you before you slam in with the answer."

"I won't do that," said Conger. "If I know the answer, I'll say it immediately. I can't fake something like that."

"Okay, let's do it your way then," said Dale. "Jump the other man. As he asks the question, start nodding through his question if you know the answer. This will detract from him, detract from his question, and focus attention on you—and your answer."

"Interesting point. Anything else?"

"Nope," said Dale, smiling. "When in doubt . . . relax. That's it. I'll be with you all the way. Good luck, Andy. You look great!"

Conger patted Dale on the shoulder as he rose. Then Cliff Harley opened the door and said, "It's seven, Charlie. We should move, Mr. Secretary."

Conger handed Dale the blue plastic case containing his notes.

"I'm ready," said the candidate. "Let's go."

Susan Conger, dressed and coiffured as beautifully as Dale had ever seen her, was seated at the far end of the drawing room when the men entered it. She looked lovely. "Excuse me, I'll only be a minute," Conger said. Dale and Harley tactfully retreated to the entrance foyer as Conger went to his wife. The two talked in muted, intimate tones, the words indistinguishable to Dale. Conger reappeared with his arm around Susan. "Hi, boys," she said. "Take good care of my man tonight." Susan kissed her husband lightly on the cheek. "Give 'em hell, killer . . . give 'em hell," she said, her eyes filling with tears. Conger smiled. "I love you, Andy," Susan said, and walked quickly back into the drawing room.

"I'm ready," said Conger. "We're late, aren't we Dale?"

"A minute or two, sir," Dale answered. "Nothing serious."

The men were joined in the hotel corridor by a security officer who assumed his usual position several yards ahead of the candidate. Dale walked to Conger's left, with Harley and a second security man to the rear.

The hall was silent except for the soft, muffled sounds of an occasional radio or television set. Conger walked slowly, taking long, deliberate strides. Dale could hear his almost inaudible, random, tuneless hum, a tension-breaking mechanism Conger subconsciously employed. Dale thought of how many great events this sing-song, intermittent, willy-nilly hum reminded him. Ahead of them, a hand and arm emerged from an open door. It belonged to a speech writer. Dale diplomatically dropped back a few paces. This was Conger's hour. The man should walk alone.

"Good luck, Mr. Secretary," the speech writer said.

Conger smiled and shook the hand without looking at him. Several doors down three secretaries stood silently, their faces bathed in compassion and adoration. One girl timidly proffered a flipper-like wave of her hand. Conger caught it and winked. As he walked, his carriage became more erect. At Abner Shepherd's door, a leg and a body emerged. Then a left hand holding a pipe. The staff's underground telegraph was doing its miraculous and inexplicable work. How these people knew the exact moment Andrew Conger would pass their doors was a mystery—but they did. "This is it, man. Clobber him," said Shepherd, his right hand outstretched. Conger grasped it firmly, letting it trail behind him as he passed, never breaking his sure, measured stride. His shoulders were squared, his head up. They passed a closed door on which was posted a hastily made sign. It read "TO THE VICTOR." Underneath was a photograph of the White House. Conger saw it, smiled blandly, and walked on toward the security desk. A final arm darted out, and quickly shook hands with Conger. It belonged to Rufe Little. "Kill him, Andy . . . kill him!" he said. "We'll be watching." Conger's head acknowledged the exchange. That was all—only a slight nod of his head.

Andrew Conger in the long walk down the corridor had become an heroic figure, bigger than life. The fears, hopes, ambitions, and planning of years of public service and dedication to the future welfare of the country could be dashed to nothingness in the next few hours. Or they could rise on a tidal wave of national glory and acceptance that would sweep him along to ultimate victory in November. Which would it be? At that moment, it made little difference to anyone looking at Andrew Conger. He was a man alone who walked erect. Alone with his thoughts. Alone with his personal challenge. Win, lose, or draw, he was a very big man.

They turned the corner and walked toward the elevators. Security had cleared the hall of all guests. Far down the corridor, Dale could see the plain-clothes man at the elevator. The uniformed operator of the commandeered and waiting car occasionally craned his neck around the corner of a post for a preview look at his eminent passenger.

Wordlessly, the party entered the elevator car. The operator said good evening with an accent. Conger asked him what his nationality was. The man said he was from Lebanon. "I have been in your country," Conger replied. "It is a lovely place." The door closed with a soft rumble, and the car dipped for the lobby.

Not another word was uttered during the descent. Conger stood erect in the center of the car, facing the doors, his hands behind his back, looking straight ahead at the closed gate. Only the whir of a tiny fan broke the silence. It was the last moment of privacy and reflection for Andrew Conger before the public storm broke. The indicator lights blinked. The car began its smooth deceleration.

"This it?" asked Conger.

"Yes, sir . . . the lobby level," said Harley.

The car stopped. There was a moment of silence before the elevator doors, the last barrier between the furious tempo of the campaign and Andrew Conger, opened. Then swiftly they slid apart from the center. And a solid wall of hysterical humanity, barely restrained from storming the car, pressed in.

Never in his experience had Conger heard such an ear-splitting roar in such a confined space. His eyes blinked, his head snapped back, and he weaved on his feet. Quickly, Dale gently put his hand in the small of Conger's back to steady him. The party moved out into the screaming, throbbing bedlam.

The lobby was jam-packed from wall to wall as far as Conger could see. Only a narrow lane had been kept open toward the steps to the street. Four bands, in unison, were playing a fight song for the debate. Two hundred Pom-Pom girls lined the route, high-stepping and swaying in perfect unison. The music and words slammed down on Conger as he stepped away from the elevator entrance:

> *Conger will win tonight,*
> *Conger will win!*
> *He wears a grin tonight,*
> *Green's in a spin, ha, ha, ha.*

> *Conger will thrill tonight,*
> *Conger will kill!*
> *With a ring-a-ding-ding*
> *We'll dance and sing . . .*
> CONGER WILL WIN!

A matched troupe of Palominos, the same that had been used at the convention, had been flown in by their owners. They reared and pranced in a roped-off area opposite the front desk. The bands swung into a medley of campaign songs as Conger headed down the open aisle.

The demonstration increased in frenzy and tempo. It pushed rudely into Conger's consciousness. God, he thought, don't break my train of thought, don't break it—please. A well-wisher wormed his way between the costumed girls and thrust out an autograph book and pen. Conger smiled unseeingly, unknowingly, and signed on the pad. As he did so, his mind thought, "Should I hit him with Red China first, or the Berlin situation?" An elderly woman in a wheelchair had been given a place of honor along his route. Conger bent down to shake her hand, thinking, "What about my trip to Russia? Should I mention South Africa in the same context, or let it come from him?" A Pom-Pom girl dropped her tufted wand and clutched his elbow. Conger jumped, whirled around, then smiled. "Wonder what approach he'll take to South America? How can I say what I really would like to say about the Pentagon and the defense effort? There must be a way." A Negro couple waved a banner at him, pushing through the human mass at his side. "There's the red flag . . . civil rights. Probably the hottest issue of the night besides peace."

Through it all, Conger kept the fixed grin on his face, the smile of the appreciative candidate. His supporters in the lobby would probably have been stunned and hurt to learn that his mind was focused solely on the debate—not on them. For Conger refused to let the demonstration destroy his preparation, his stream of answers, positions, attitudes, toward the issues which would comprise the exchange with Green. The order of his mind—the careful foundation for the face-to-face encounter *was* in jeopardy. It was assaulted by the staggering impact of the wild demonstration. His preoccupation with the debate had been shaken, pummeled. Conger walked on. What about NATO? The farm issue, the UN, unemployment, the race for space? I wonder how those will *fall?* He smiled at his supporters.

Near the top of the steps leading down to the street entrance, the band struck up a new song. Every voice in the lobby roared out the campaign words to the tune of "Hot Time in the Old Town Tonight":

> Con-ger wins . . .
> And the votes are pouring in!
> Con-ger wins . . .
> And the votes are pouring in!
> We'll scream and yell,
> As Conger gives him hell!
> There'll be a hot time in Cleveland tonight!

The bedlam continued as Conger waved and disappeared.

Somehow he made the sidewalk. As the sound of the music dwindled and faded, it cross-blended with a boisterous chant that roared from the throats of the thousands outside who filled the Public Square:

> Rock him, Conger . . . Sock him, Conger,
> Go . . . Go . . . Go . . . !
> Take him, Conger . . . Break him, Conger,
> Go . . . Go . . . Go . . . !
> Show him who's rougher!
> Tell him who's tougher!
> Spill him, Conger . . . Kill him, Conger,
> Go . . . Go . . . Go . . . !

This mob was different. They were bold, aggressive, in the safety of the darkness, swept on by hero worship and hysteria rather than contact with or sight of their candidate. Masterfully whipped up, they were strident in their demands to hear from and see their leader, their gladiator. On the enormous four-sided projection screens near the center of the Square appeared a huge campaign photograph of Conger smiling and waving.

"We want Con-ger . . . We want Con-ger . . . We want Con-ger." The chant had started.

Dale saw Billy Dee, the traveling sound man, appear from no-where and hoist a portable speaker and mike to the hood of Con-ger's limousine. This will kill us on our time of arrival, Dale thought, as he and Harley helped the candidate out of the melee and confusion pressing in on the car. Four floodlights picked Conger out as he straightened, waved both hands, and made a victory gesture over his head. Two mobile television crash units tried des-perately to back into position for pictures, their red lights whirling over the heads of those fortunate enough to be caught in the press of bodies near the candidate. A roar went up when the thousands realized their hero would speak to them.

So this is the way the television debates will take the razzle-dazzle out of campaigns, thought Dale. His mind went back to the testimony the network presidents had given in Washington in the early spring. The debates were to bring dignity, new purpose, so-briety to political campaigning. Dale thought how harmless and con-trolled in comparison the crowd in the Public Square had appeared from the window of Fred Morgan's suite. How fearsome, how menacing, how fanatical, it looked at close range.

No campaign, no candidate, no human could withstand the stag-gering effects of such an emotional night again. The deification of Andrew Conger this evening was absolute. It was a frightening thing to behold. Dale felt that the increased penetration of tele-vision into the minds and lives of the public was partially respon-sible. It was true: presidential candidates had become bigger-than-life television heroes, just as popular and dominating as the legendary stars of the shoot-'em-ups! Their hero in the white hat would ride into the White House! This adulation, this unplanned throng of thousands, this chanted hue and cry for the blood of the enemy —how much of it could be laid at television's doorstep? Dale shuddered when he answered the question for himself.

The enormous rally bonfire cast its flickering light over the crowd as Conger quieted it with his famous double arm signal.

"This is the greatest demonstration of support I have ever seen in my life," he started. The whistles and cheers ricocheted off the buildings surrounding the square. Dale hoped the raw night air wouldn't irritate his man's voice. Conger went on: "This demonstration has given me great confidence to meet my opponent in the monumental confrontation which will take place shortly." Another cheer went up. Dale, concerned because of the delay, checked his watch in the powerful lights. "But you should all be at home watching on your televisions." A loud laugh rolled from the darkness. "Take a look out in the Square, Andy," someone shouted. Conger raised his head and looked at the large screens carrying his image. "They won't sell many of those where I come from," he said. "Our houses aren't big enough. But . . . if you have any trouble getting a good view of those screens, I'm sure there are several hundred taverns within walking distance who have their sets on and would welcome your trade!" Another laugh went up, followed by cheers and whistles. Someone yelled, "Give 'em hell, Andy . . . for me!" Conger acknowledged the remark with a wave of his hand in its general direction. "But now you must let me go. We are late leaving here. If we don't arrive at the television studio soon, there will be no debate. And none of us want that . . . do we?" A lusty, hoarse "Nooooo" went up from the crowd. "So . . . thank you again. God bless all of you. And as they say on those big New York shows—*See you on television!*"

The limousine, following the lead car occupied by plain-clothes men and Arthur Baldwin of Conger's staff, left the curb and sped quickly around the square, its route lined with thousands of hand-held torches. The car turned right into Superior for the considerable run up to Fourteenth Street where Conger would join Green's route from the Statler-Hilton. Superior was lined solidly with enthusiastic supporters behind barricades. The width of the street, however, prevented any impediment of the motorcade.

"Are we all right?" Conger asked Dale. "That was something."

"Yes, we'll make it," said Dale. "Your time upstairs in the office will be short. But it was put in there for just such emergencies."

"Do you have that list of the political registrations of the cameramen and the crew?" Conger asked.

"It's at the studio," said Dale. Perhaps he'll forget it later in the pressure of arrival, Dale hoped.

"I'll look at it after the debate—not before," said Conger. The interior of the limousine slipped into silence, broken only infrequently by the electronic crackle of Cliff Harley's portable transceiver, which was in contact with Arthur Baldwin in the lead car. A large confetti streamer slowly slid down the whip antenna Harley had clamped to the gutter rim above the front door on the right where he was sitting. Conger, in the rear with Dale, also sat on the right to facilitate his exit on arrival. He commenced his soft humming again. Dale looked at him, relieved that he had retained his good disposition through the crisis. Psychologically, the thrilling demonstration had given Conger a tremendous lift. Far from being a negative influence, it had infused the candidate with new confidence, new vigor, and an almost physical anticipation of the imminent conflict with Green.

Red flares marked the intersection of Superior and Fourteenth Street. Local police stopped all traffic as the motorcade turned left for the six short blocks to the studio. Only the soft rumble of the tires on the pavement invaded the quiet inside the limousine. Several spectacular Green exhibits were in evidence now. Either by coincidence or design, Andrew Conger would have to pass by the ever-increasing thousands of Green supporters who had selected Fourteenth Street for the location of their massive outdoor demonstration. *Their* hero had passed moments before. Now Conger must run the gauntlet of the hysterical Green enthusiasts. Their spirit, however, changed in tenor and personality as the Green thousands realized their enemy occupied the slow-moving black Cadillac which approached them. A wave of displeasure and hatred swept down the crowd-lined blocks. It preceded Conger's lead car as the word passed. Exuberant manifestations of Green loyalty changed to equally demonstrative examples of dislike for Conger. The crowd pressed on the barriers, shaking their fists when moments before they had shaken Green standards. The motorcade decreased its speed, slowed to a crawl. Conger continued his humming, seemingly unperturbed by the frightening display outside the glass and metal of his vehicle. Now the Green fanatics were closing in ahead of the car, trying to stop the motorcade.

"Keep moving," Harley snapped into his walkie-talkie, to the lead car. "Don't stop . . . keep moving." The Conger limousine halted for an instant when demonstrators ran between the lead car and the candidate's automobile. The momentary halt widened the interval between the two cars. Progress was slowed to a snail's pace.

"Stop the car," said Conger. "I'll talk to them. We've got to get through."

"It'd be suicide, Mr. Secretary," said Harley.

"If we stop now, Andy, we'll never make the telecast," said Dale. "We've got to keep moving . . . no matter what."

"Okay," said Conger. "You fellows run it. Let's just get there . . . fast."

"I'm doing my best, sir," said the paid driver.

"Okay," Conger repeated, his eyes dead ahead, looking neither to the right nor the left. It was surprising how insulated the occupants were to the litany of hate which broke in waves over the exterior of the automobile. It was quiet inside, very quiet. No one spoke. They waited. Then the lead car moved. Conger's vehicle followed it. They were moving forward.

As Andrew Conger's limousine approached the studio building there occurred one of those uncontrollable and seemingly trivial incidents which can determine the outcome of a monumental event. Conger's automobile was less than two hundred yards from the open and guarded drive-in entrance when an egg hit the windshield. It sailed out of the darkness from behind the Green fanatics, who pounded on the car as it went past them. The egg hit the windshield up high, where the glass met the roof. It hit on the right side, in front of Cliff Harley. At the very moment of impact, Harley was wondering when the first hurled object would hit them. Even so, the egg came as a shock—a jolt. Harley's head snapped back when the yolk splattered the glass and started its maddening trickle downward. Within seconds another egg hit, this time dead center of the closed rear-wing window, inches away from Conger's head. Dale wasn't certain Conger heard it or saw it. He gave no sign.

No one said a word. The car continued to crawl forward. The driver leaned down and hit the windshield-washer button. The wipers started their sweep, but no water played on the glass. "Guess it's empty," he said.

"Don't they check those things before you fellows leave the garage?" Conger asked in irritation. The driver remained silent, helpless to do anything about the streaked opaque glaze of egg the wipers were producing that prevented forward visiblity in front of Harley. From where it hit, the egg continued to run slowly and thickly down the glass. The driver turned off the wipers.

"Get it off . . . damn it! Get it off!" Conger yelled. "Can't you do something?" Harley made a hopeless effort to stick his hand around the windshield post.

"Forget it, Andy," Dale said to Conger quietly.

"I'll kill him! I'll kill the bastard that threw that egg. The son-of-a-bitch . . . the bastard!"

"Easy, Andy . . . easy," said Dale, watching the agitation and annoyance building in his man. Please, Andy, Dale thought to himself, don't let this throw you. Think about the debate . . . please.

Conger was silent, working his hands together in his lap. Dale knew the signs of his man's temper, his flashing anger. The egg had seized Conger's attention. He stared at it fixedly, hypnotized by its lazy course down the windshield through the glaze. Dale's heart sank as he watched the meticulous screening, the scrupulous care and feeding of his candidate, the careful efforts to protect and condition Conger for his ordeal, dissolve before him in the form of a small egg laid by a fertile hen whose brain was no larger than a pea. The composure of a presidential candidate had withstood the combined resources of Fred Morgan, Lou Wells, and the North American Broadcasting Company. But the egg had shaken it.

"Common . . . disgusting . . . dirty . . ." mumbled Conger.

With agonizing slow progress, the car inched its way toward the building. Conger continued to watch the egg-spatter with a strange absorption. Finally, the limousine nosed through the open overhead door. The driver picked up speed as he drove toward the marks at the far end of the ramp within feet of the inside door to the debate studio. The terrifying Green mob was left behind them—outside. Dale checked his watch again. Although seriously late, they would make air time safely.

Through the clear glass on the driver's side Dale could see the horde of still photographers, dozens of newsreel cameramen, and the press, positioning themselves for Conger's historic arrival. Dale suddenly realized the importance of the egg to Conger. Every photograph of his arrival, every foot of exposed film, every word written by the press, would feature the damnable egg whose shattered white shell was still stuck to the rubber sealer rim at the top of the windshield. Andrew Conger, alighting from the car to be greeted by the welcoming committee, faced the consuming humiliation of the obscene blemish that had fouled his vehicle.

If he was still angry as he alighted from the car in the exploding clusters of flash bulbs, Conger's outward demeanor belied it. He was a picture of easy friendliness and composure as his hand went out to the person in the receiving line nearest him, a representative of the producing and host network. The hand Andrew Conger clasped belonged to Fred Morgan.

"We got a little worried there for a moment, Mr. Secretary," said Morgan with a smile. "This is a night we in television have looked forward to a long time."

"Sorry we're late," replied Conger. "Those people out there ought to be home watching this on television—eh, Fred?" he added, chuckling.

No one quite knew how it happened. It seemed incredible that again the debate could be placed in peril of not getting on the air —and with but five minutes to go. But it happened, at 7:55. Andrew Conger had one more crisis to survive before he could meet his opponent in face-to-face exchange. This time, however, he shared the experience with Governor Joseph Green.

Some said it was bound to occur because all photographs of the two candidates on the set prior to air had been canceled. It was mandatory because of Conger's late arrival. There would be no time for the still photographers, the newsreels, or the press to witness the historic initial confrontation of the two men as they met on the set. Nor could the various media be privy to their first candid words of exchange as they greeted each other. There simply wasn't time. All such handshake photos and newsreel footage of the men conversing informally on the debate stage would have to wait until after the two-hour telecast was off the air.

The press secretaries of both candidates resented this. Wilbur Jenkins was bitter. His charges were hungry for news, starving for pictures. Television had deprived them of covering the famous meeting. There was resentment at all levels of the working press covering the event.

The cause of the crisis was argued for months at bars in the National Press Club, the Overseas Press Club, and other dreary watering holes of the ink-stained fraternity. An eyewitness claimed he saw one of the two "pool pencils" fortunate enough to be selected for assignment inside the debate studio throw the lock on a door supposedly closed to all traffic, so that he could re-enter the studio quickly after a trip to the men's room. Several claimed that either Wilbur Jenkins or Waldo Duncan tried to slip a favored syndicated political columnist into the studio for an exclusive look at the proceedings. It mattered little why it happened. It was a horrifying moment, however, when it did.

The two candidates were at their respective podiums; Conger Stage Right, Green Stage Left. They were in position for final lighting and camera checks before air. Smith and Dale were in the control room with Lou Wells, standing behind Sandy Jones, the director, who was seated at the console. The cameramen were all business, working at peak efficiency as they crisply responded to directions given them by Jones over their headsets. The NA lighting director and Hans Kleinert worked methodically and quietly on their final refinement of the lighting, consulting their clipboard from time to time, and checking their changes by what they observed in the control room monitors. The floor directors for Conger and Green were quietly conversing with their respective charges, a device Dale suggested to relieve the tension while the two presidential candidates were forced to stand at their positions for the critical inspection and adjustment period.

"All right, sir, Governor Green, sir," said Jones over the talk-back, "could you say a few words for us so that we can get a voice level from you. Please use the normal volume of your speaking voice."

"Yes," said Green. "I am glad to be in Cleveland. This is a beautiful city. The arrangements for this telecast are most impressive. How's that? . . ."

"Fine, sir," said Jones. "Will you please remain at the podium. Murray Smith will be right out." Jones released the talk-back button, and turned to Smith. "Satisfied?" he asked.

"Looks perfect . . . sounds perfect," said Smith. "I'll go out and stand by him. If you need me, holler."

Jones pushed the button again. "All right, Mr. Secretary . . . if you will, sir. We'd like the same voice-level check from you. Any time, sir."

Conger cleared his throat. "Fine . . . I will talk about like this. Naturally, if I am making a strong point, I may emphasize by increasing my volume, but I would assume this is about the way I'll talk." He stopped and continued to look at his camera.

"That's fine, Mr. Secretary. Thank you," said Jones.

"Ask Dale to come out here, will you?" Conger said.

"He'll be right out," Jones replied. "Please remain at your podium, sir."

And that's when it happened. The two press secretaries were near the door. It could have been that they were merely trying to be helpful and admit the pool photographers and reporters. Someone, however slid an enormous floor-to-ceiling sliding door back but a few inches, a slit wide enough to admit a man. Outside in the hall the Press Corps were filing into their viewing studio next door. A man came through the opening. That's all it took. The security dike had cracked, the dam against the press had collapsed. The flood of reporters rushed headlong into the studio.

Fifty still photographers made it through that door, now flung wide open. Twenty newsreel cameramen with hand-held cameras ran through, and started shooting immediately. The stills rushed the debate platform, a twelve-inch riser, and surrounded the candidates. From all sides of their targets, they shot as fast as they could change exposure. Working reporters poured in behind them, forming a solid line where the front of the riser met the studio floor. They bombarded the candidates with questions, none possible to distinguish from the rest.

In their headlong rout toward the debate stage, the press rolled floor lights across the studio, yanked pedestal cameras out of their line of vision, spun dozens of other vital pieces of floor equipment in every direction. Every element was off its precious marks on the floor. The two press secretaries stood at the sidelines, smiling as they watched television in its hour of peril. They were delighted. Finally the working press was having its moment of triumph with the candidates.

"Jesus Christ, Wilbur," Dale shouted at Jenkins, grabbing him by the elbow, "get these bastards out of here! Who the hell let them in? We'll never make it on the air. Look what they're doing to our setup!"

"They'll be out in a minute," Jenkins said calmly. "Duncan and I have it under control."

"That's a lie," Dale shouted. "This is a madhouse. Move them, Wilbur . . . talk to them . . . for Christ's sake . . . do *something!* They're shooting us down!"

Jenkins remained stationary. Then slowly, he halfheartedly admonished a reporter who was screaming at the newsreels to get out of his way so he could ask Conger a question. At that moment another reporter put his foot through a floor lamp. It exploded with a loud "whapp!" Glass flew everywhere, crunched under a hundred shoes. Dale wormed his way to Smith at Green's podium.

"Don't leave your man. No matter what happens stay with him. Keep him here at his podium. I'm going to do something." Grabbing Forrest as he plowed his way through the stills working the stage between the two candidates, Dale said to him, "Stay with Conger. Keep him at the podium. I'm going to the control room." He leaped off the riser and ran for the rear of the sound stage yelling, "Lou Wells . . . Lou Wells . . . I need you . . . I need you . . ."

"What in the hell is NA doing about this?" Dale screamed as he burst into the control room. Wells and Jones were watching the nightmare, partly through the glass of the control room window, but also on the cameras, which were still hot and feeding pictures of the bedlam. "Do something . . . Sandy—for God's sake, do something! If you don't, we'll never make it on the air."

Jones was shaking with shock. He was incoherent with fright. He was in sheer white panic. "Stand by, everybody, three minutes. Stand by . . . three minutes," he repeated over and over, looking at the clock.

Wells, too, was immobilized with fear. He stood glassy-eyed, staring at a monitor which was taking a closeup of a camera carrying-case slung over a still's shoulder. Another camera gave the control room a beautiful shot of the note book and feverish activity of a reporter frantically recording the scene. "My God," screamed Dale, "isn't anybody going to do anything? We're going down in flames!" It suddenly hit Dale. The networks were naïve to this sort of absolute crisis. The panic attendant to the birth of big network television shows was child's play compared to what Dale and his men went through every night of a national political campaign. Crowd control, pushers, the coarse, thick-skinned overrunning by the press, all these were routine to them. Dale was immune to mobs, fear, stampede, because he had lived with them. Roughly, he shoved Jones down the console in his castered chair. "Rudy Wolff!" He yelled for NA's lighting director. "Where are you?" He pushed Wells out of the way.

"He's out on the board," said Hans Kleinert, Dale's lighting man, who was in the control room.

"Kill every light on the set quickly," yelled Dale.

"Now?" asked Kleinert, stunned.

"Right now, and quick. Hurry!" shouted Dale. "We'll never get rid of the stills and reels unless we take their light away. Security . . . where is it?" he shouted. There was no answer. "Fergie, run out to the hall. Get as many cops . . . in uniform . . . in *uniform* . . . in the studio as fast as you can. Hurry! Hurry! . . ."

The lights went out. Shouts and foul language rose from the stills and reels. In the half-darkness Dale noticed Smith and Forrest standing by the candidates, who were quiet and composed in the storm around them. It was almost as if they were too absorbed in the impending duel, too preoccupied with the significance of the next two hours to notice the holocaust roaring all around them. Dale leaned over and hit the talk-back button.

"This is Charles Dale," he said in a calm voice. "I am speaking to you from the control room. This debate may already be destroyed . . . I'm not sure. I am certain of this. If all of you press people are not out of the studio in fifteen seconds, there will be no debate here this evening. The four cameras on the floor have been feeding pictures of your inexusable actions to two video tape-recording machines in the building. If you are not out in fifteen seconds, the debate will be canceled. In its place the networks will telecast, as an explanation to the public for the cancellation, the video tape-recording of your reprehensible and unpardonable invasion of the studio. Get out! Please. Right now! Thank you."

Cleveland's men in blue poured into the studio from four directions. In a flying wedge they swept the studio clean of all reporters, stills, and newsreels. Smith and Forrest indicated to them those in the television crew who should remain. In seconds the studio was clear—and quiet. Startlingly quiet. A deathlike silence gripped the windowless cube. But why not? The stampede had almost killed the debate, hadn't it?

The entire studio seemed to catch its breath, then pick up and go on. It was like the sigh of relief, the exhalation of thankfulness after a close brush with sudden and unexpected human disaster.

Dale slapped Jones on the back. "Take it, Sandy, you've got two minutes. Get cracking!" Jones snapped out of his shock and wheeled toward his station. He calmly gave order after order to his men through their headsets. Moving swiftly and with super-efficiency, the technical crew and cameramen repaired the damage, wheeled the gear onto its marks on the floor.

Dale stood beside Andrew Conger. "That was a close one," he said. "Everything okay up here?"

"Fine," said Conger. "That light on the right side of my face . . . It's too bright. Can you kill it?"

"Which one?"

"That one over there," said Conger.

Dale looked to where his man was pointing. "Oh . . . That's not your light, Andy, that's Green's. That's on him."

"Oh."

The loud-speaker talk-back boomed out. "Thirty seconds . . . Please . . . Thirty seconds . . . Stand by, please." It was Jones.

"I'll be in the control room, Andy. Got to run. Good luck . . . Killer!"

Conger smiled. "Do I stand here?"

"No, the floor manager is asking you to take your chair now. And remember," Dale said, nodding his head toward Green, "that man over there can steal the White House from you tonight. Don't let him do it. Take him!" He slapped Conger lightly on the shoulder and stepped off the debate platform. Once beyond the maze of television hardware, he ran for the control room.

"Okay . . . Stand by everybody!" Jones yelled. "Ten seconds." Dale stood to the left of Wells, who was directly behind Jones. Smith stood to Wells's right, each television adviser assuming the position directly in front of his candidate as they appeared on the monitors.

"Tell Parkhurst to get his chin up. Fine . . . Keep it that way. Stand by for my cue . . ."

Smith leaned over in front of Wells and looked at Dale in the darkened room. His hand was outstretched. "Let's shake on this one. Good luck, Charlie."

"Same to you, Murray," Dale replied, grasping Smith's hand firmly. The two shook, hands clasped in front of Wells's waist.

"No more talking . . . no more distractions," snapped Wells. "Knock it off!"

"My, my," said Smith, in mock surprise.

"Well, well," Dale echoed, softly. "The new Lou Wells!"

"Shut up . . . all of you," yelled Jones. "Okay . . . We're on! Up on 'one'! Cue Parkhurst."

"Good evening," said Weldon Parkhurst in tones known to millions, his voice resonant over the control room loud-speakers. "On behalf of the broadcasting industry of the United States of America, you are about to see and hear the first face-to-face debate ever held in the history of American politics between two presidential candidates. This is an historic occasion. For the next two hours Secretary of State Andrew H. Conger, and Governor Joseph Green, presidential candidates for their respective parties, will engage in an unrehearsed exchange which will deal with the major issues of this presidential campaign. The first hour will confine itself to domestic issues. Then, I will advise the two candidates we have reached the halfway mark. In the second hour the statements of the two presidential candidates will be confined to foreign affairs. . . ."

Parkhurst's voice became lost in the background of Dale's consciousness. It faded from his mind as he hunched forward, staring intently at the monitors. Now the camera was pulling back to include the candidates. Parkhurst was introducing them.

"On my right is our present Secretary of State, The Honorable Andrew H. Conger."

Jones punched up a nice waist shot, medium tight, of Conger, who smiled and said, "Good evening." The camera held on Conger as Parkhurst described his long career of public service. Unconsciously, Conger's hand swept up to his brow in a nervous gesture.

"Oops . . . watch that hand, Andy," Dale said instinctively to the picture of Conger on the tube. "Dammit, keep it down! Ahhh . . . That's nice—nice."

"Goddammit—shut up!" Jones shouted.

"Sorry . . ." said Dale, almost in a whisper. In total concentration, he strained forward to catch every detail of the image on the monitor of his candidate, Andrew H. Conger.

ABOUT THE AUTHOR

Edward A. Rogers served as former Vice-President Richard M. Nixon's Television Advisor during the 1960 Presidential campaign. In that capacity Mr. Rogers was closely associated with the production of the four television debates. Mr. Rogers' association with Mr. Nixon started in Los Angeles in 1950 when he was asked to volunteer his services as a television advisor during Nixon's campaign for the U.S. Senate. This was his first brush with the combination of politics and television, and he didn't hear from Nixon again until the Senator was nominated for Vice-President on the Eisenhower ticket at the 1952 Republican Convention. This time the call came from the Brown Palace Hotel in Denver, where Nixon and Eisenhower had gone immediately after the Convention to hold a series of meetings on campaign strategy. Of this experience Mr. Rogers says: "Nixon asked me to come over for a few days to contribute what I could to the meetings. I got home fourteen weeks later. I remembered Nixon saying he thought the year 1952 would prove once and for all the impact of TV on national politics. I recalled these words two months later when I was involved in the production of the now famous Nixon Fund Telecast."

In 1953 the author came to New York and was associated with the initial development of the United States Hour on TV. In 1955 he went to NBC-TV, where he produced THE HOME SHOW, WIDE, WIDE WORLD and various special programs. Again in 1956 he was called back on the campaign trail. He is now forty-one years old, resides in New York City, and is a free lance television producer.

It is out of this unique knowledge of both television and politics that Mr. Rogers has written this work of fiction.